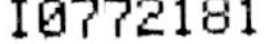

A Novel by Z.M. Celestaire
(but mostly written by Dr. Ackerleigh Sebring)

Expert Consulting by Nico De Falco

Funding Provided in part by Doctor Rose Bennett, Bennett Publishing House

In Cooperation with Ravensbourne University, Laurier, Deubrise

Contents

Warning	1
A Brief Introduction to Deubrise	2
Glossary	3
Map	5
Part I	6
1. Introduction to Family Dynamics	7
2. Fundamentals of Termination	11
3. Introduction to Squatting	26
4. Fundamentals of Gamekeeping	32
5. Fundamentals of Storm Magíq	50
6. Introduction to Small Town Politics	60
7. Fundamentals of Chicken Hunting	71
8. Introduction to Keeping the Peace	79
9. Fundamentals of Attraction	96
10. Fundamentals of Gryphon Captivity	102
11. Introduction to Contagious Boils	109
12. Foundations of Near-Death Experiences	114
13. Introduction to Open-Sea Rescues	120

Part II   125

14. Survey of Pain-Laced Denial   126

15. Intermediate Pining   136

16. Survey of Midnight Conversations   141

17. Intermediate Selfishness   153

18. Survey of a Gentleman   160

19. Intermediate Gryphon Riding   167

20. Survey of a Lover's Embrace   177

21. Intermediate Vulnerability   187

22. Survey of Academic Discipline   203

23. Intermediate Confessions   212

24. Survey of Paradise   227

Part III   238

25. Capstone in Friendship Strain   239

26. Capstone in Hostile Confrontations   250

27. Seminar in Gryphon Maulings   266

28. Capstone in Unforeseen Lineage   276

29. Seminar in Doing As You're Told   287

30. Capstone in Cooperative Healing   294

31. Seminar in the Bennett Publishing House   304

32. Capstone in Laying Future Plans   321

33. Capstone in Criminal Proceedings   328

34. Seminar in the Hazel Mountains   334

Afterword   346

Acknowledgements   347

About Z.M. Celestaire   349

Also by Z.M. Celestaire   350

This book includes scenes which may be disturbing to some. There is an instance of domestic violence which occurs in chapter one, an instance of sexual harassment which occurs in chapter two, and and an instance of gory violence in chapter twenty-six.

If you should come across any other troubling themes not declared on this page, you are welcome to contact me, the author, to discuss your concerns via email at artcoffeecats@gmail.com – Z.M.

B efore you begin this account, please take a moment to study the materials I have included in the introduction. The glossary will serve as a helpful way to navigate the particularities of Deubrisian culture and slang which are used throughout the text.

The map, artfully crafted for my particular use, will help to ground our travels in context. Deubrise's climate varies dramatically from the northern to the southern coast and then again in the mountainous terrain where much of our story takes place.

As with all my publications, please notify myself, Ravensbourne University, or Doctor Rose Bennett should any inaccuracies or errors arise during your reading.

Doctor Ackerleigh Sebring - Professor,
author, and magiqon

Glossary

Andullie (an-dull-ee): Affectionate insult, roughly equivalent to "dumb-dumb". Derived from French.

Chaton (sha-toh, nasal): French for "kitten".

D'ac (dahk): French slang for "okay".

Deubrise (Doo-breeze): A subtropical island country that is the resting place of three slumbering gods that continue to bless us with their magíqal breath.

Enfour (in-fur): Asshole. Derived from French.

Ésprit (a-spree): Term used to describe the breath of the gods that courses through the elements and through the veins of magíqon.

Light-licker: Word used by folks in the country to describe Deubrisian city folk. Not the kindest thing you can call someone. Refers to the preponderance of electricity and modern amenities present only in the cities.

Luneyeux (Loon-yuh): French for moon-eyes.

Magíq (mah-jeek): Considered to be the breath of the gods which imbibes the elements with its power and can be accessed with those who have god-breath in their veins (see: *magíqon*).

Magíqon (mah-jeek-awn): Someone born at the precise moment as an astronomical wonder such as a meteor shower or a lightning strike at the peak of the mountains. Embedded with god-breath which allows them to manipulate the elements, which are also flowing with the power of the slumbering gods.

Ocky (awk-ee): Word used to describe Deubrisian country folk, most often said by someone from the cities. Derived from Australian term. Not quite derogatory, but not kind.

Technocrat (tek-no-crat): Political extremists who ascribe to the belief that magíq is dangerous and wicked. Technocrats seek to punish magíqal sympathizers and implement nationwide policies that criminalize the use of magíq and remove protected status of magíqal beasts.

Tranqui (tron-key): Derived from French, meaning "calm down".

DEUBRISE
Northton
De Falco Farm
Hazberg
Gryphon Eyrie
Hazel Mountains
Sebring Farm
Bed & Breakfast
the mountain god
bed of the mountain god
Bennett Country Estate
Martinsdale
Moundsview
Bennett Estate
bed of the sea god
Leon
Ravensbourne University
Laurier
bed of the sky god
Stoneworth
University of Stoneworth
N
E
S
W

Part I

Fundamentals of Magiq

INTRODUCTION TO FAMILY DYNAMICS

"I didn't mean to hurt you, Mother! I promise, I swear, please don't call me cursed again," my sister sobbed. "Not again, not again." As Stella reached toward Mother, desperate to comfort and be comforted, luminous white flames flickered on her fingertips.

Angry red blisters streaked Mother's neck and chest as she flinched back and bared her teeth with fear in her wide blue eyes. Smoke burned my eyes and coated my tongue: the aftermath of a truly explosive disagreement between mother and daughter.

Pa lashed out at Stella, his eyes fixed on the magíqal flames dancing on her skin. He slapped Stella across the face with the back of his sun-spotted hand, the sharp sound making my heart lurch into my throat. Stella clutched her cheek and cowered back, bumping into the frame of the door.

I wedged myself between Pa and my sister, using the scant two inches I had on Pa to shove him back. Fear and disbelief flashed in his dark gaze, but that only bolstered my resolve.

"Stella, go get our bag and get in my truck," I snapped. When she opened her mouth to protest, I spoke over her, "No, this was their last chance. We're outta here."

As she met my eyes, the fire on her hands extinguished. Silver smoke curled from her fingernails. She sniffed. The diamond-white spark of magíq faded from her eyes and they returned to a dark, stormy blue. She looked once more at our parents, then slammed open the screen door and ran out into the night. Cheese, our golden retriever, scampered after her before the door shut.

My fingers went to the sunburst-shaped scar over my right temple as I spun around to face my parents for one final confrontation. But as I glared at their fearful expressions, the fire in my chest extinguished the same way my sister's fury had turned to silver smoke.

"Eleven years," I told them, slumping against the door and tapping the scar my sister had given me. "You've had eleven years to accept that Stella is a magíqon and love her for that. But instead, you've smothered her, abused her, and taught her to hate herself." I tried to ignore the way my voice broke. Tried to ignore how they looked at me, their eldest, like I was a fool and a stranger for defending my sister. "She's seventeen. She's just a girl."

"She's a monster," Pa spat in my direction, eyes flashing. He knelt beside Mother, tenderly inspecting her burns.

I clenched my fists. "If you'd just nurtured her magíq—"

"It's not up to you!" Mother interrupted.

The fury came roaring back. I turned away, snatching my keys off the nail on the wall and stomping into my boots. "D'ac, so—then what do you want for her? Do you wish she would be locked up in that gods-forsaken estate like Lux? Do you wish the gods' breath had overpowered her as a newborn, so she'd be dead? Would that be easier for you?"

Pa stood up, matching my anger with his own. He jabbed his finger in my direction and snarled, "Magíqon do nothin' but destroy, Nico, and one of these days she'll do more'n leave a scar on your brow! Her kind should go extinct like the rest of the magíqal beasts. You're protectin' a monster!"

"I'm protecting your child!" I screamed, kicking over the wooden table so it clattered across the floor and cracked against Pa's shins. He was smart enough to back off, glaring at me with his chest heaving. To him even more than to Mother, I added scornfully, "And she's gonna thrive without you. I'm all the family she needs."

When neither of them denied it, I shook my head rapidly and clenched my teeth. Turned my back on them. They weren't allowed to see the tears pooling in my eyes. I squeezed my car keys and glared at the veins crossing over the back of my hand. "So be it," I said softly. "Forget this farm. Forget my inheritance. I'm done here."

"Nico," said Mother tearfully, "where are you going to go? You can't just disappear into the mountains—"

I scoffed, watching Stella through the door as she dragged our suitcase across the dirt driveway. We'd had it packed months ago. "Let's face it, Mother. I've been watchin' after her for a long while. You haven't worried where we disappear to before." I sent a sharp glance back at Mother, catching her eye. Quickly, she dropped her gaze to her lap, rubbing her chest. "But we're still gonna take care of Lux since I can't trust you to do that, either. We'll be back to pick up their supplies every week, same as you goin' to Northton." I paused, my voice catching as I added, "As strangers. We aren't family anymore. Stella and I are on our own."

Mother sniffed and murmured my name, but as I leaned my shoulder into the screen door and pushed it open, I didn't look back. A tear broke free from my lashes and tracked a hot line down my cheek. Thrusting my hands into my fuzzy pockets, I left my parents behind in body and in spirit.

When I came out, Stella was heaving our long-packed suitcase into the cargo bed of my truck. Twilight had turned the sky violet with a touch of gold sketching the peaks of the Hazel Mountains to the south. Autumn pheasants croaked from the bush, which smelled of mushrooms and decaying grass. Peach, my chestnut mare, huffed from her stable when she saw me emerge. I couldn't bring myself to look at her and marched resolutely up to Stella instead.

I helped her settle the suitcase in the back next to Cheese, whose tail thumped against the truck bed until I scratched her behind the ears.

Sniffing, Stella went around to the passenger side, pausing to look back at the farmhouse. Sunset-tinted hope lit faintly in her eyes, like maybe our parents would follow us out and beg her not to leave. But the door remained shut on us, and they remained with their backs turned on her. The spark of hope turned to an ember and went out. Stella hiccupped and swallowed a sob before she climbed into the cab and yanked her door shut.

As I started the car, Stella stared at her knobbly knees as tears tracked over the mark that our father had left on her cheek. She folded her hands so tightly that her knuckles turned white, like she usually did after a chaotic display of magíq. It was like she wanted to lock it all inside, only she never could. Whether because she couldn't control it or because she loved it too much, it always came back out. The duality inside her must have been miserable. Life was so much more brilliant because of her gods-blessed blood, and yet there was ruin and pain every step of the way.

"C'mon," I said gently, holding out my index finger. "Spark me."

Stella didn't respond right away. I knocked our elbows together, bringing my finger into her view. Finally she blinked and wiped her tears, smiling shakily. The air in the cab warmed as she called on the ésprit crackling within the wires of the truck. When our fingers touched, a violet spark of electricity zapped between them.

My hand tingled as I switched the truck into drive. "Alright, Stel. Where to?"

FUNDAMENTALS OF TERMINATION

My pen scratched against my paper with enthusiasm as I bowed over my crowded desk. A stack of paper towered precariously near my head to my left, and the books and articles most recently referenced for my lectures sat by my left elbow. As far as Ravensbourne went, this was the happiest and safest place I could be. Composing my thoughts in complete silence was where I was my truest self.

I glanced at the brass face of my watch. I had ten minutes before I had to get to my lecture. More than enough time to finish my analysis of this chapter on gryphon reproduction—which had to be incorrect.

14 September 1964

Though my knowledge of gryphon mating habits is not firsthand as Crier et al. claims theirs is (many of their classmates from the University of Stoneworth—myself included—found the group to be sensationalists and prone to hyperbole), I have compiled a broad list of sources which lend to the theory that Crier et al.'s assumption that gryphons mate identical to birds is misguided. Gryphons, being a magíq-based cross between raptor and lion, are not simply large birds who mate with one other creature for life. Rather, the experiences of several authors (see works cited) who spent time in the Hazel Mountains suggest that gryphons live in pods where a member or two may lay eggs but the whole colony takes turns incubating and then later rearing the young.

I took a slow breath in and smelled the mingling leather of my desk mat and my shoes, and a faint trace of mothballs. I would have to refresh the lavender sachet in my wardrobe.

"Doctor Sebring." A growling baritone voice made my stomach drop into the earth as if attempting to burrow out of sight and escape.

"Yes, President?" I didn't look up, my gaze blurring on my paper. What word was I trying to write? What word? The tip of my pen quivered. What did that word start with again? Every single time President Stephen Brandon came near me, I lost all my faculties.

Heat radiated at my elbow; I froze and glanced sidelong past the golden rims of my glasses. President Brandon loomed over the arm of my desk chair, domineering and too close.

Ten minutes. I had ten minutes to try to finish this thought, and he was invading my space and—

"Haven't you considered what you could gain from my offer?" President Brandon asked, peering down at me with sharp blue eyes, a prominent brow, and a square chin.

"I—I—" I stammered and fell silent. I didn't normally have a powerful voice, but I did benefit from a low register and a serious countenance. Now my throat clamped shut, straining my words like a wrung-out dishrag. "Trust me, you ask so often that I have exhausted all considerations and I... I simply cannot..."

"I'm not proposing you be my boyfriend," President Brandon scoffed.

With a foolish flare of indignation, I swiveled my seat to face him. My knee smacked into his, and the contact made me flinch so violently that my chair slammed back into the wall.

Brandon smirked, leaning his hip onto my desk and making an unread research proposal curl under his weight. The sharp corvid emblem of Ravensbourne University stitched onto the breast of his tailored blazer looked perverse on him. He put this esteemed university to shame every single day. "That would just be in bad taste, you know. Ravensbourne's president and a professor who won't stop writing about magíq."

Indignation erupted into a blaze. "Yes, gods forbid you look like you're in favor of the tenets that the university was founded on," I snapped. My timid quaver was gone, even though it would have been wiser to keep my mouth shut. "Pascale Manon would have happily published my articles—"

Brandon scoffed impatiently. "You really don't know what's good for you, do you?" He sniffed. "What would be so undesirable about a dalliance now and again? You obviously prefer the company of men." He cocked his head, reaching forward with a hand so large it could probably snap my wrist. My heart gave a painful lurch as his hand descended onto my chin. His palm on my body froze me, plunging any coherent thoughts into frigid depths of blank darkness "And you're so delicate," he went on in a purr, "it would almost be like fucking a woman."

A massive sneeze sounded in the hall behind him. Brandon's hand withdrew, but slowly, languidly, like he hadn't a care in the world as he crossed his arms over his chest.

I saw a flash of large amber eyes and a wisp of white hair cross in front of my door beyond Brandon's shoulder.

"I respectfully decline," I managed faintly. "I just—" What was my reason? Aside from the fact that, ever since I was hired at Ravensbourne, each and every time Brandon had touched me was seared into my skin like a grisly brand. Aside from the fact that he held my career in a chokehold, that he was leaning on the very papers he refused to publish. Aside from the fact that I would rather die. "I simply cannot oblige."

Danger roiled in President Brandon's eyes. Predatory, his gaze landed on my throat and I wondered if he was imagining how easily he could rip through my skin with his teeth.

The president grunted. "Hm. Alright then. Interesting choice, Sebring."

My folded hands twitched in my lap. "I—I'm sorry, sir, I..."

He back-stepped into the hall. "Oh, now, don't say that. We're two adults here, aren't we, Sebring?" A false smile slashed between his cheeks. Then, he turned away, heels clopping on the tiles as he slowly returned to his office. The door slammed. Not as hard as students slammed it when they lost an argument with him—but hard enough to express his displeasure.

Turning him down was the most dangerous thing I could have done, I realized grimly.

I pushed my spectacles up my nose; they had slipped down a sheen of sweat clinging to my skin. "I should have done it," I muttered, but the image of his naked body crushing mine made a shudder rip through my ribcage.

My eyes drifted down to my watch. Of course he'd used up all my time before class. I shoved my notebook into my briefcase without closing it, along with several books I may or may not have needed for class.

I got to my feet, stood in place for a moment, swayed, and then collapsed back into my seat. Fingers pressed into my eyes, I bit back a whimper and tried to get up again. Shakily, I wobbled out of my office and toward the double doors facing the university's courtyard.

This morning's coffee had turned into sour bile and was forcing its way up my throat. I swallowed pooling saliva on my tongue as my knees buckled, and I tripped twice before rescuing my footing. My students would not let me live down my tardiness.

"Ackerleigh?" Claire Emérie's familiar voice cut through my foggy head, opulent as black velvet. Her hand pressed hard into the small of my back despite the dampness of my shirt. I felt steadier immediately.

"What's the matter? You're sweating. I don't think I've ever seen you sweat."

I couldn't climb out of my swimming head enough to answer her, even without my asthma choking me. I remained silent as I slipped out of the nightmarish Dell Hall and into the open air.

Ravensbourne was in the seaside town of Laurier. In the late winter months, that meant the constant threat of rain made the air thick and cold. I ruefully gulped humid air and wished for the sharp cold and complete isolation of the Hazel Mountains, even though I hadn't been there for at least a decade. I still dreamed of those mountains, and my grandfather's farm. If I wasn't tied to the rigor of academia... and maybe I wouldn't be for long, if it were up to Brandon.

"Leigh?" Claire repeated, the hibiscus scent of her auburn hair getting stronger as she leaned down to get my attention.

I pushed my glasses up onto my forehead, digging my fingertips into my moist eyes and resolutely gathering my senses. "I'm late," I gasped. "Please walk with me."

"I—what? You don't seem fit to teach, darling, you're..."

I straightened, smoothed down my collar and my flyaway platinum hairs, and lifted my chin to glare at her. "I am."

Recognizing my bullish resolve, Claire rolled her eyes. "Of course. I'm headed there, too, anyway. Come on, then." She fixed my briefcase's fabric strap on my shoulder before hooking our elbows together and turning us toward the quad. My best friend since arriving on campus, Claire had a fashion sense as sharp and feminine as the angular cut of her bob, which perfectly framed her thick tortoiseshell glasses. Today's cool humidity had brought her to campus in a flouncy, cream-colored blouse and a mauve pencil skirt, paired with patent cream pumps. Her sky-high heels made her noticeably taller than me today. She was as curvaceous as a tavern wench and as powerful as a warrior.

I wished she'd been in my office earlier. President Brandon never would have been able to get past her ass; she wielded it like a weapon when she needed to keep people like him away from me.

I swallowed the painful lump in my throat. He'd gotten to me, though, and I had a sinking feeling that my punishment wasn't over yet. How I yearned with burning intensity to exact punishment on my own terms, to stop him from trifling with me once and for all.

But alas. I was small, my leash was short, and my reliance on this position at Ravensbourne was absolute.

Claire marched steadfast through the mingling students. At this early hour, there were many sipping coffee from paper cups, reading textbooks, and eating breakfast at the scattering of tables. All of the seating was made of elegant, moss-dusted stone, and was arranged in neat spokes that radiated to the center point of the quad, which was marked by a large bronze statue of our founder, Pascale Manon.

The moment the first student looked over at me, I dropped my gaze to the leather-capped toes of my floral brogues, letting Claire's pressure on my arm guide me toward the hall. Ravenbourne's student body was mild-mannered, and I had no reason to recoil from them. But shame burned on the back of my neck as President Brandon's words gripped my thoughts. I was afraid they could see it on me. His disdain. His touch on my skin.

My breath hitched. I swung my head up to settle on Mortensen Hall instead. Complete with several turrets and a clock tower, it was four storeys of gray stone contrasted handsomely with thin white outlines. Ivy climbed around the long, arched windowpanes that currently reflected a scattering of fluffy clouds and a blinding splotch of sunlight.

Mortensen felt like a safe haven where I'd spent all three years teaching since completing my doctorate at the University of Stoneworth. This building kept me focused on my purpose. While the politics of Ravensbourne—spearheaded by Brandon—had nearly put me on the streets on multiple occasions, every lecture, every student I'd taught, was worth the discomfort.

Using Claire as a crutch like usual, I dragged myself up the sprawling stairs leading to the three bays of doors into Mortensen. Students sat in clusters on the edges of the stairs and on the wide balustrade.

"Briar, get to class!" Claire snapped at a student with a croissant hanging out of their mouth. They squeaked and clambered up the steps to beat Claire to her chemistry lab. Ducking close to my face, Claire whispered, "Well? What did that ugly pig do to you?"

Shame returned with a wash of prickling heat. I swallowed my panic and the truth. "He wanted a favor."

Claire raised an eyebrow. "A favor." She didn't hide her disdain.

I made a noncommittal noise, and when she refused to look away, my eyes started to sting. "Please don't make me explain." My voice wobbled. "I just need to go teach." I pointed to the corner classroom across the shiny marble floor, the door still open, my students probably listening for my approach. Certainty, predictability, and the comfort of teaching A Critical History of Human Impact on Magíqal Beasts waited for me. No more about Brandon. Just a classroom. Just history.

Claire bit her plump pink lip and nodded sharply. "Okay, Leigh." Her use of my nickname was stabilizing as she gripped my elbow and gave it a fierce squeeze. "Courtyard for afternoon tea?"

"Yes, of course." I gave her a quick hug but didn't let her hug me back before I scurried away.

Last year, after my third asthma attack climbing to one of the higher classrooms, I'd started being scheduled only on the ground floor. Saved my students the trouble of having to twiddle their thumbs while I spent half an hour wheezing before I could teach.

A Critical History of Human Impact on Magíqal Beasts was an elective higher-level course that had garnered eight students eager to think critically and keep up with the dense and lengthy texts I assigned each week. My gait got stronger as I neared the classroom door. Colorful stained glass greeted me with rainbows of light and shadow when I entered the room. The floor of this converted office was particularly creaky, immediately announcing my arrival.

Striding to the professor's desk and opening my briefcase, I let out a sigh of relief and smiled weakly. "I apologize for my tardiness. Blame Doctor Brandon."

"Happily," sniffed the student closest to the door, a senior named Ritika who had an admirably sharp tongue and glossy black hair.

One of the two boys in class turned around in his chair and hissed at Camden Zane, who was snoring softly atop the back table with his notebook tented over his face. Camden remained undisturbed, and I fought down a smirk. Brandon might unsettle me, but Camden Zane, I could deal with.

The teenager in the front row took a sharp breath. Billie Reverdin swept back their too-long fringe, revealing the freckles across their nose and the slight gap between their front teeth. "Did you bring it? Your paper?" They completed their overeager look by nudging their silver aviator glasses up their nose.

"Oh—"

Billie's shoulders slumped. "Doctor Sebring!" they groaned. "Three weeks! Three weeks, you've forgotten it. I need that meta-analysis on mirrored migratory patterns between crows and gryphons."

I hadn't forgotten. Billie was a second year student and the youngest person in my class, hungry for knowledge on Deubrise's rich magíqal history. But I didn't want them to end up like me. I was constantly restraining myself, refusing to indulge their passion wholeheartedly for fear of the consequences.

With a grimace, I shifted my attention off them and back to Camden. David grimaced, knowing from experience what would befall his sleeping friend.

The sadistic pleasure I got from my little ritual to deal with Cam sleeping in class was...well, today, I needed it. Nimbly, I wove between the other tightly arranged tables to reach him. Going to the dark blond hair sticking out above the book he had tented over his face, I secured a single strand between my fingers and yanked.

Cam yelped, the book slid down, and his shoulders jerked as his wide hazel eyes settled on me.

I inspected the hair. "Still blond. Clearly it's only me aging prematurely because of your nonsense, Mister Zane."

His cherubic grin appeared a second later. "You're late, Prof."

"Indeed. Sadly, it couldn't be helped." I returned to my post at the front of the room.

"You were late too," snapped Billie, glaring at him over their shoulder.

Cam sat up, kicking his legs over the edge of the table. He had gotten huskier since turning twenty, but he hadn't settled down in the slightest. "Oh, were you taking attendance for Doctor Sebring again, baby Billie?" Cam tossed his pencil at the back of Billie's head, making them rear up like an affronted cat.

"Settle!" I exclaimed. "Camden, typically success in life demands controlling one's childish impulses."

Cam held his hands up, beaming. "Right, right. Sorry, Doctor Sebring."

Billie scowled as they lowered into their seat.

"I believe you all owe me an essay." Most of the class had their handwritten papers already in front of them, and held them out to me on cue.

Flushing, Billie quickly dug through their leather folio to pull out their typed paper, which was quite a bit thicker than their peers.

When I held seven essays in my hands, I raised an eyebrow at Cam.

Cam got up and slowly went to his knapsack. "I'm ninety percent done," he said softly, "but my eyes got...really tired..." His voice trailed off as he grimaced, making a dimple pop in his cheek. "By the end of the day, Prof. I swear."

"Figures," muttered Billie.

Empathy made my sigh quiet and my nod slight. Camden and I had come a long way since I'd started here during his sophomore year. He could have easily been dismissed as an entitled kid with a bad attitude and no interest in learning.

But I'd seen a spark in him, and halfway through the semester, I'd realized he was dyslexic. Reading came slow and his penmanship was almost illegible. When I asked him about it a few weeks into my first class with him, he had no idea. He clawed his way through primary school and got accepted to Ravensbourne thanks to an amazing interview with the school board. He didn't even realize how much his own neural wiring was conspiring against him.

I noticed the sharp insight in his comments in class, and his passion for arguing with students who voiced ideals aligning more with the local Technocratic logic as opposed to the rich history of magiq. After I adjusted his written requirements in my classes, he started getting top marks and showing up early to class and staying late to ask questions.

He was now in the start of his final year at Ravensbourne. He wanted to be a primary school teacher when he graduated. He kept up his mean kid façade, but I don't even think Billie was falling for it anymore.

"It had better be good," I told him. I slipped the essays into my briefcase and pulled out the slender book we had been working through for the last month. One page was enough to cover the ninety minutes I had with this class.

I glanced at my watch.

Seventy minutes.

"I'm already behind, so let's begin our review of question one. How did the Great Battle of 1812 impact the distribution of magiq-crossed creatures in the Northern region?"

"A bunch of them went extinct," blurted Cam.

Ritika's hand shot up. Before I'd even said her name, she began, "There were three species of aquatic creatures which fought with—"

A throat clear interrupted her. The class collectively turned toward the door.

I blinked. "Crai—Professor Dowell?"

Round, golden spectacles flashed as my colleague nervously pushed them up his nose. He clutched a crumpled paper in his liver-spotted hand, which was stained black with splotches of ink. "A word, Sebring..."

Nodding, I followed Craig into the hall.

"Craig, I'm already behind—"

The wizened gentleman sniffed through his white mustache. His enormous honey-brown eyes blinked several times as his mouth opened and closed. "Ackerleigh."

My stomach seized and plunged toward the sea god's lair. Save me, my blood screamed. I wanted to interrogate Craig, but my lips wouldn't move.

"President Brandon sent me," Craig said softly. "I'm sorry. I tried to talk him down." Lamely, he opened his hand and offered me the crumpled paper.

I unfolded the creases, which crinkled so loud it was deafening, and read the short typed missive aloud.

"Effective immediately, Doctor Ackerleigh Sebring is terminated from Ravensbourne University due to sexual misconduct."

My voice fell into a trembling rasp. The rest of the note mentioned a folder of complaints Brandon had on me, and spoke of the values of this great institution and the responsibility Brandon felt to protect his student body.

"Oh."

"Ackerleigh—"

I lifted a hand, clutching the note against my chest. "No." A dry laugh tumbled out of my lips. A death rattle. "This was inevitable, was it not?"

Craig shook his head quickly. The stooped old man looked as shaken as me, fussing with the lapel of his tweed blazer. He'd been a passive, distracted colleague, but he was one of the few professors in the History department who never spoke a word against magíq, and never questioned my insistence on writing on the subject. And he'd certainly been the colleague sneezing in the hall when Brandon touched me.

"My—" I choked. "I ought to get my things." Stiffly, I went back into my safe haven. My class was silent as I went to my briefcase, which was illuminated by a glow of sunlight as if it were holy. I returned my book to the crowded compartment inside and folded over the flap before I realized how much my hands were trembling.

"Doctor Sebring?" whispered Ritika.

Billie anxiously fussed with their threadbare sweater collar. "What are you doing? What's happening?"

"It looks like class is dismissed." I managed an artificially calm voice, high and airy.

Billie stifled a squeak of horror.

As I swallowed and stared at the desk, a few chairs scraped against the floor and several students fled from the discomfort. Thus, I wasn't expecting Cam's large hand to snatch the missive off my desk.

I lifted my eyes to the tall twenty-year-old and opened my mouth to protest, but the mischief was already draining from Cam's features as his hazel eyes scanned the text.

The space between his heavy eyebrows creased. "Prof?" The single syllable was thin, stunned, and uncertain. The remaining four students crowded behind him, reading over his shoulder.

I let my eyes close as the floor swayed beneath me. The group fell silent, uncomfortably so, until I could only hear the blood slamming in my ears. Hot shame clamped onto my neck once more.

Swallowing hard, I opened my eyes, smiled, and said softly, "Thank you for the honor of being your teacher." I reached for the missive, which Cam slowly set back in my hand.

Billie burst into tears, fat droplets spilling beneath their glasses as misery contorted their features. They shook their head and took a step back while I tucked the incriminating paper into my bag. Swallowing a sob, Billie bolted from the room, the wooden heels of their brogues cracking through the silence.

"I don't believe this," Cam said suddenly. "This is some stinking Brandon garbage if I have ever read a lie in my life." He crossed his arms and bumped into the desk closest to him, scowling.

"And so what?" I shrugged. "What changes?"

Cam's eyes grew wide and misty as he fell silent, staring at me as I made my way to the door. For his sake and my own, I didn't linger.

Craig was gone. An echo of Billie's muffled crying drifted down from an upper balcony, and leaving them alone to their misery felt cruel. But I couldn't dare follow them. Brandon's dismissal was just vague enough that it could describe any sort of misconduct, and I refused to cause further harm to my students.

I clenched the strap of my briefcase, keeping my head down as I hurried for the exit. What a travesty that I'd been inside for no more than ten minutes and—that would be it.

Forever.

My foot hovered over the top step that would lead me away from Mortensen, but I couldn't seem to set it down. A pair of gulls screeched as they fought over a food scrap on Pascale Manon's outstretched arms. Baring my teeth, I raced down the steps and shooed them away, flapping my arms and swinging my briefcase. The birds scattered with angry protests, stubbornly landing at a nearby table.

Chest heaving, I gazed up at the statue of Ravensbourne's magíqon founder. A childish part of me hoped she would come back to rescue me, challenging Brandon and deposing him as an enemy of the institution. But she remained confidently smiling and cast in bronze, holding a gleaming orb of magíq and letting me drown.

Somehow, I was just supposed to... leave Ravensbourne. Gather my belongings, hope my car started, and go home. Home, where I barely had enough savings to cover a few weeks of groceries. Home, where I would be alone with my thoughts and the greasy fingerprints Brandon's touch had left on my soul. My stomach clenched at the thought.

I was supposed to teach three classes today. I was supposed to have office hours. Students from my other classes might be stopping by looking for me before the news traveled that I had been fired.

I knew I should clear out my office, but the thought of crossing paths with the President made sweat rise on the small of my back and nausea ripple through my stomach. I would have to count on Claire to hear about me and pack up my things for me, because there was no way I was waiting around for afternoon tea.

And yet, I couldn't go home.

One of the gulls spread its wings and took off with one powerful downstroke. And so did I, but not to my office, and not to my home.

The waters around Deubrise glittered like stardust at all hours of the day, whether they were the wild and deadly waves outside my hometown of Hazberg or the warm cerulean ripples lapping eagerly at my ankles in Laurier. Ravensbourne University had a hidden drive that led to a private section of beach and, as I'd hoped, it was currently deserted.

Even when the weather was cold and gray like today, the water here was still calm and quite mild. Acolytes of the slumbering gods cited ancient Deubrisian texts which suggested that the god of the sea slept with her lips just below Laurier, accounting for the sweet temperament of the waters, as well as the accessibility and prevalence of water magíq in and around Laurier's tepid bay. The god's breath, her ésprit, would rise into these waves, blessing them more richly than the rest of the country.

Digging my toes into soft sand and bits of sea shells beneath the water eased the tension coiled in my chest. It loosened the wheeze that had been stuck for hours since Brandon's fingers touched my face. I stood with the tide up to my calves, trousers cuffed at my knees, hugging my chest and squeezing my eyes closed.

Enormous and uncertain questions flailed through my thoughts like a flock of panicking birds. I was twenty-seven years old and academia was my only marketable skill. For three years I'd pushed and pushed to make headway in my postdoctoral research just for it to be scoffed at, ignored, and leveraged against me as soon as an excuse to fire me was fabricated.

My throat tightened and so I pushed down the thoughts, down through my spine and past my belly and into the soles of my feet, offering my worries to the slumbering god. Calm filled me, the sort of quiet emptiness that held no answers but invited me to accept this particular unknown as an opportunity.

I snorted, dubious. "I denounce your unknowns," I muttered. A particularly playful gust of wind flipped my platinum fringe forward so it smacked against the arms of my glasses. Frowning, I scraped back my fringe into its preferred winglike shape, but the wind did not relent and cast my fluffy hair skyward once more. Hands on my hips, I couldn't fight back a smirk and shut my eyes instead, hoping that perhaps the salty taste of magíq on my tongue was a good omen.

Introduction to Squatting

"Hello?" I called into the rafters, my baritone voice vibrating a glass vase holding a long-wilted rata flower. Casting my gaze around the open floor plan of this cottage, I took in the dried leaves and grass on the flagstones, the dead mouse by the stairs, and the smell of dust and droppings permeating the still, stuffy air. Spiderwebs trailed from the rafters to the massive brick hearth in the center of the room. "Seems like nobody's been here for ages."

My truck waited beyond the front door of the tiny, two-storey cottage. The Hazel Mountains loomed over us to the west; to the east there was nothing but pastures and a barely-functional dirt road. We were an hour south of the De Falco Farm, and two days out from our violent departure from our family.

"Is that any surprise?" Stella snorted, kicking her boot against the leg of an enormous metal dining table. My sister was a gangly creature whose wardrobe consisted of shirts she'd cropped with her hunting knife; loose, many-pocketed cargo pants; and an olive-green jacket patched with several colorful, crudely-stitched-on squares at the elbows and along the bottom hem. Her sun-bleached brown hair spilled over her shoulders in glossy waves, utterly at odds with her scrappy sense of fashion.

She picked at a lace doily hanging over the back of a couch the same yellow as a lemon meringue, and then poked at a fancy record player under the large bay window. "This looks like some light-licker frippery for being all the way out here in the mountain's armpit." She wouldn't admit it, but I could tell she was excited that we'd found someplace like this. "What is a bed and breakfast, anyway?"

"Like a fancy inn for rich old people," I answered with a shrug, looking up the stairs. I expected there would be a handful of small bedrooms up there, which would be more comfortable than having to sleep in the back of my truck for the foreseeable future. I thought maybe I could steal a mattress or some blankets from up there to keep in the truck for our next destination. "We could probably manage to squat here, but I'd prefer we go talk to Cyrus instead. His farm's not too far from here."

Stella gave me a grimace of disgust. "Closer to Martinsdale, the worst town on the planet."

Most of Stella's classmates lived in or around Martinsdale, so I understood her reluctance. The cruelty they had shown her remained in both our memories like a scar. We would still go to Dolly's Diner in Martinsdale every now and again, but it was usually torture for my jumpy, self-conscious sister to be around that many people. And heaven forbid we be there at the same time as Vivien... once, Stella had thought she'd spotted her former best friend, and she'd nearly hyperventilated and spent the night crying.

Back to exploring, Stella opened various kitchen cupboards to peek inside their abandoned contents. With a hum of delight, she told me, "There's heaps of canned food in here."

I leaned into the one doorway tucked behind the stairs and found an impressively ugly washroom. The tiles on the floor were black and white checkers; the claw-footed tub was bubblegum pink; and the curtains over the circular window were puce-colored lace. It also looked like someone had glued seashells to the vanity mirror over the sink. Shuddering, I retreated and returned to my sister in the kitchen. "All the cities and everyone in them are the worst, Stella... I know. But—we gotta be realistic. If we aren't living with Mother and Pa, there's a lot we have to figure out on our own. I need money for petrol, and we can't really survive on canned vegetables in a house with no electricity."

Brushing me off with a wave, she ran through the kitchen to the back door, sliding back the bolt lock and throwing the door open. A fragrant blast of sweetgrass and fresh, minty air blew through the cottage, stirring up the dust so it glittered in a shaft of early morning sunlight. It silhouetted Stella like a corona. "And look at this garden! There's stuff that's kept growin' on its own. Look at those pumpkins! We're good, Co-Co! We'll be fine here. Nothin' wrong with eatin' vegan."

Since Stella wasn't looking and couldn't be upset with me for it, I started tapping a staccato rhythm on my sunburst scar. She didn't like seeing me touch it; it made her feel guilty for that frightened blast of electricity she'd hit me with when she'd been barely a day over five.

That had been her first display of magíqal power, and everything had gotten worse for her after that. Before then, Pa was able to pretend like perhaps the corresponding meteor shower during her birth had not imbued her with the gods' breath. Ocky folks in the country like me believed that when the gods stirred with dreams, they caused natural wonders like a meteor shower, a forest fire, aurora borealis, or a typhoon. The holy dreams of the gods filled the air with ésprit which would transfer into a brand-new soul and fill their lungs with gods-breath the moment they cried their first cry. Sometimes, this would overwhelm those unlucky little babies and the gods would claim them. But the rare few like Stella who survived were forever changed. The ésprit in their blood would allow them to speak to the ésprit sparkling amidst the elements, giving them control over fire, wind, water, and electricity.

I thought this made Stella blessed. Pa and other old-fashioned folks thought her existence was cursed. As soon as Stella showed she could manipulate the elements—and unfortunately injured me with them—Pa turned his back on her. Mother had followed his lead, albeit more subtly, with passive aggression and biting comments, and by pushing Stella to be "gentle" or "quieter". She thought the safest thing for her to do would be to stifle Stella's gods-blessed nature. Stella had rebelled violently against this notion, turning her into a volatile, bitter girl.

I jumped when I realized Stella was in front of me as she snatched my hand and dragged it down from my temple. "You know what this means, though, right, Nico?"

"No," I sighed. "What does it mean?"

"We're so close to the mountains that the god beneath is extra powerful. I can feel it. It's like tastin' something so sweet it makes your teeth hurt."

I shook my head with a little bit of wonder and more than a little bit of envy. Stella's gift was so beautiful sometimes. I yearned to be that connected to the mountains and the wide-open sky that we both loved so much. To be able to call the wind to your fingertips and spin the waves into a whirlpool with nothing but the beating of your heart.

"That's great, Stella. This is a good place for you, then." She nodded brightly, and something tight in my chest unwound a little bit. "Haven't seen you smile this much in years, kid."

Stella's eyes sparkled as she tipped her chin back and gave me a dimpled grin. "Haven't felt this safe in years, Co-Co. Thanks for gettin' us outta there."

My throat tightened. Combing out a snarl from her hair with my fingers, I managed tightly, "Whatever we do now, I promise I won't let anyone hurt you again."

She cocked her head as if confused by my ardor. "'Course. Never doubted that for a second. But anyway," Stella chirped, "I bet I could keep the generator runnin' all the time with just a little zap." She held her finger out to me, and I cringed but extended my own. She was right: the spark of electricity that jumped between the whorls of our fingertips was so powerful that I yelped and pulled my hand back.

"D'ac, alright!" I exclaimed, shaking out my aching hand. "Point taken. We can try it, alright? We still gotta make deliveries for Lux, don't forget."

"I could never forget." Stella dramatically clutched her chest. "Our baby sibling needs us. Too bad we can never see them."

Lux, originally known as Luneyeux before we shortened the name, was locked up in an awful estate on the eastern coastline. They were some two hours from here and almost three if we had to drive up to the De Falco farm first. We were strictly forbidden from even saying hello to Lux—with good reason, because I often felt if Stella got even a glimpse of them, she'd go feral. Blow up the estate. Free Lux and escape with them into the sunset. And honestly, after being without them for seven years, I was desperate to have Lux back, too.

I grimaced. "I know. It'll give us somethin' to do, anyway. Make sure we don't lose track of the days." There was significantly less to do here than at home, meaning I would be thinking about chores I should have been doing at the farm. Pa had basically handed me the reins at home, happy to slow down and support me running things myself. Stella was in charge of the garden and the grove at home, one of the few things Pa had trusted her to do. We kept six cows, four pigs, a pair of goats, and a massive number of chickens. The chickens were mostly to support Lux's hefty appetite.

It hadn't been the most exciting life, but it had been steady and predictable, with plenty of time for horseback rides by myself and watching for gryphon sightings up the mountains. I could spend entire evenings reading romance books in the barn with nobody to disturb me but the chickens. There, I could trust Stella to be staying out of trouble by roaming in the woods or, more likely, trailing after me and chattering at me 'til my ears were ringing. Any time we were in the house, she kept to her bedroom and avoided talking to Mother and Pa as much as possible.

When she wasn't able to avoid them, things usually ended up like they had two days ago, with Stella and Mother screaming at each other and arguing about her future, or lack thereof. It had gotten much worse since Stella stopped going to Martinsdale primary school when she was fourteen.

"How could we?" Stella scoffed. "This place is practically a paradise."

"How do you know there's not, like, dead bodies upstairs, hm?"

Stella's face lit up. "Oh, right!" She ran for the steps and pounded upstairs. "Wouldn't that be cool? Do you think there was a murder here, and that's why it's abandoned?"

I groaned. "Stella Marie!"

Stella's heavy footfalls clomped over my head as she explored the upper level. "Nothin' up here but a bunch of bedrooms and a workin' phone!" she called.

Wearily, I fell onto the dusty couch and covered my face with my hands, massaging my tired eyes. Maybe this whole thing would work, and Stella and I would be happier not needing to navigate all the tension with my parents. But for how long?

FUNDAMENTALS OF GAMEKEEPING

My studio flat in Laurier had become a depression pit. I was days away from not being able to pay for the electricity bill and thus stayed in the dark most days to try to get used to it. If I was sleeping, it was during the day and fitfully. My meals were dry crackers and reused tea bags, both about as stale as the smell hanging in my flat. I wasn't broke, but what was the point of spending money on luxuries I would soon lose?

I stopped mid-step when someone knocked on my door. The soles of my feet hurt; I'd been pacing for hours. There were track marks worn into my carpet since this was the only way I'd been able to relieve my agitation over the past month.

They knocked again and I lifted my head, staring at my door. I'd paid the rent this week—hadn't I? Truthfully, I might have been thinking of the week before. Or the week before that. Time had blurred during my unemployed days. I'd been doing nothing more than sending out my resumé to institutions and waiting for the inevitable rejection, which arrived every single time without ceremony. Even the University of Stoneworth, my very own alma mater, had turned me down. Hope was fading rapidly.

"Leigh! Open up!"

"Claire?" I asked squeakily.

"Obviously! Come and let me in." She knocked again, hard and fast. "Ackerleigh!"

I looked down at the gauzy nightgown I was wearing, then quickly scooped up a duster-length cardigan and pulled it on, wrapping it around myself. I was self-conscious knowing I hadn't gotten dressed for several days. Also, although Claire knew I loved delicate fabrics like voile, I rarely wore anything so ostentatious to Ravensbourne. Not with Brandon always around, leering at me. I felt if I wore what truly made me feel like my best self, he would see me not as myself—bold, sharp, and sophisticated—but as something pliable to be dominated.

"Coming, coming!" I hurried to the door. Now that I was no longer dissociating, my knees felt wobbly and weak, almost buckling beneath me. As soon as I turned the doorknob, Claire took over and shoved her way inside. Her dark eyes were pinched with worry behind her glasses as she drank in the sight of me, shutting the door behind her.

"Oh, Leigh," sighed Claire, smartly dressed in a tweed suit with her hair pinned back. I'd almost forgotten what a professional looked like. "You look half-dead." She smudged her thumb under my eye and I could tell she was seeing the gray circles I'd noticed were a regular resident on my face now.

"At least I showered yesterday." I paused. "Maybe the day before." I swept back my wispy ashen hair and managed a trembling smile when Claire winced at me.

"Well, your flat looks as immaculate as ever." She glanced at the couch, buried beneath an oversized quilt, several pillows, and my rumpled bed sheets. "But what happened to your bed?" Stepping out of her heels, Claire nudged them against the wall next to my shoe rack and flexed her toes in relief.

I answered dismissively, "It paid last month's electric bill."

"I told you to let me help you! Mathilda offered, too..." Claire's voice trailed off. She looked away uneasily. "She's... not a fan of Brandon, either, and believes there was foul play that happened. We don't think you ever should have been let go. You didn't do anything."

"Yes, well, the five universities that rejected me seem to believe otherwise." I took one of the coffees from her hand. We had always ordered flat whites with honey, so it was easy to know what to get me. The first sip of it made me almost feel normal again.

Claire stomped her foot, making the floor creak. "Brandon ruined your reputation!"

I nodded slowly. "Most definitely."

"But why?"

Shame had kept me silent for the weeks since Brandon had cornered me in my office. If I admitted aloud that I had lost my position at Ravensbourne because I'd turned him down, that would be admitting to myself that I had hardly had a position at Ravensbourne to begin with. I was so disposable to him that the moment I'd wounded his pride, I was gone.

Or perhaps not even that. Perhaps his solicitation was only to set me up, and he had no real desire for me beyond banishing me from his sight. These were the thoughts that had grown dark circles under my eyes, that had robbed my nights of peaceful sleep, and left me to wear tracks into the floor.

"Leigh?" Claire prompted. "What happened with Brandon?" Her voice was an inviting blanket of warmth and safety, ready to hold me while I fell apart.

I swallowed the immediate nausea that followed her question. Claire took a step closer with her lips pressed in a thin line and her eyebrows scrunched together.

"Oh... uh..." Setting down the coffee cup, I closed my cardigan more tightly around myself and kept my arms crossed protectively against my chest. "If you must know—the president wanted to fuck me. Presumably in exchange for my job." I heard myself speak as if outside of myself, a terrible pressure descending upon my head like gravity was crushing me.

Claire's jaw dropped. She said nothing for several moments as she blinked rapidly. "Ackerleigh..."

I laughed bitterly so I wouldn't tear up. That blasted voice was why I'd spoken to Claire minimally over the last month, and I hadn't let her come over. She was too tender. Too soft in her love for me, and I couldn't bear it without getting dragged down into the darkness of the feelings I was trying to avoid.

Obviously restraining herself, Claire said quietly, "That must have been awful to keep to yourself this whole time."

Surrendering, I sank into the dining table chair. "I'm so ashamed." My voice cracked. With my vision turned to wobbly glass, I straightened the pile of papers on the edge of the table. "It was no surprise, was it? Every faculty party, the drunker he got, the closer he'd stand to me. The only reason he never touched me before—"

"He touched you?" Claire snarled, bristling.

"—was because you were there, guarding me. Much as I would like to pretend I am self-sufficient, I cannot protect myself, it seems."

My friend dropped into my other chair and groped for my hand. Angry tears dotted her thick lashes as she shook her head. "I'll quit. I'll quit today. I'll go in and I'll—"

I choked on a bitter laugh. "Why, so you can become destitute, too?"

"Mathilda can—"

"Claire, don't be silly. I would die of guilt if you quit on my behalf. We must all just move on, and accept that the President has always had the power." I sandwiched her hand between mine and dug my fingertips into her wrist. "Just accept this. I have." The lie made my stomach clench.

"Your students haven't." Claire pinned me down with her dark, determined eyes, blinking back her tears. Her cheeks remained flushed and enraged. She opened her folder, turned it toward me, and pushed it across the table. "Camden Zane started a petition to bring you back."

I jolted. "He—"

The list of student signatures was three columns of cramped names in blotchy ink.

"Cam started a petition?" I laughed in disbelief when Claire nodded. "Try-hard." Though Claire blinked in confusion, tears welled in my eyes, and then I fell apart. My face crumpled, my breathing hitched, and I burst into tears. Claire's chair legs scraped across the floorboards and her arm slid around my shoulders and squeezed. Burying my face in my cardigan sleeves, I allowed the power of a good cry to sink my heart down my thighs and through my bare feet into the floorboards. I allowed Claire's woodsy scent to mingle with the whiff of coffee. The smells were a comfort, and Claire's arm was warm and sturdy.

"There are letters." She nudged the petition aside to show a dozen of them; through my swimming vision, I saw Billie, Ritika, and David's names flash on the multicolored papers. Claire rubbed my shoulder until my skin burned from the friction, and held on until my weeping abated.

"I can't go back even if I could." I wiped my face on my sleeve. "I'm humiliated. What must people think I did?" Now that I had begun talking about it, it felt like I couldn't stop. All the ruminations of the last month were uncorked and screaming to get out. "And—and the thought of being around him makes me... Oh, I could vomit at the thought. When he grabbed my face..." It burned like a brand. I furiously rubbed at my jaw with the sleeve of my cardigan. Even now I could feel it. And not just the nerve endings firing, but the violation, the ominous weight of the knowledge he had intentions to do more to me. "I wasn't raped. I wasn't even kissed. Why can't I stop reliving that moment? Why did it paralyze me?"

"Ackerleigh," Claire scolded, wrapping her arm around me again. "Just because it could have been worse doesn't mean it wasn't terrible. It doesn't mean you weren't molested. And we both know he set you up for that. If students knew, they would be pounding at Brandon's door demanding justice."

I shook my head quickly, wiping at the tears that leaked from my eyes and wishing to be numb. "Claire, no. That's never what I've wanted."

She slumped in her chair. "I had a feeling. That's why I brought you your mail." She tugged on an envelope at the bottom of her stack of papers.

I cocked my head, perplexed. "Um... the letters from the kids?" My confusion pushed away my despair. When I wiped my eyes, finally the tears stayed away.

"No. It was on your desk when I was cleaning out your things. I wanted to give it to you sooner... well, sort of. I also wanted to throw it away and never tell you about it. But it's..." Claire trailed off. "And anyway, you've been dodging me."

"I know." I winced. "I'm sorry. I did not want to deal with my feelings, and I can't help but feel them when it comes to you."

"The price of being soulmates," sighed Claire, setting her chin in her hand.

"May I?" I plucked the cream-colored envelope from her fingers. My name was printed on the front in red ink. When I flipped it over, a golden sticker along the wrinkled seam was ripped in half. I gave her a sidelong look.

"Like hell I was going to give you hate mail or some nasty reprimand," Claire snorted. "I had to screen it first."

I smiled faintly before returning my attention to the envelope. The letterhead read BENNETT PUBLISHING HOUSE, their logo a tiny mountain inside a house. My heart leapt in my chest.

I read aloud, "'We would like to extend the opportunity to you to take part in a unique live-in magíq research project with generous stipend included.'" I quirked a brow. "'To confirm your participation, reach out via telephone to the office of Doctor Rose Bennett at your earliest and hastiest convenience.'" I chewed my lip, a cool draft slithering through my flat and picking up the ends of my hair. Goosebumps rose on my skin, making the wool of my cardigan feel rougher.

"I think it sounds suspicious," said Claire.

"Doctor Bennett is highly prestigious as a publisher, but among us scientists she's known for having few, if any, moral scruples."

I reread the letter a few more times. "But Bennett Publishing House is also the most prolific in academic research in the whole country." I pulled over a stack of books from the other edge of the table and thumbed through them. The mountain and house logo shined in gold foil on six of the eleven spines. "To be invited personally to participate in her research might be exactly what I need to climb out of ruin." I swallowed, looking up at Claire. "I don't have anything else, Claire. My intellect is my only skill, and Brandon has made sure nobody wants it."

Claire said nothing, studying my features. "That's not true, you know," she finally said. "You're incredible, Ackerleigh."

I rubbed my cardigan over my lower lip while I thought. Slowly, I got up from the table and reached for the coffee. I drank in silence as I paced behind the couch to the window, peeking out through the lace curtains before turning around and returning to the table.

"This month has been unbearable," I said. "My whole life has been consumed by academia. One would think that being forced to resign would have let me take a break, you know? To rest. But I didn't rest. I just ruminated and cried and... and hoped I wouldn't wake up."

Claire nodded, fussing with her sleeve. "I'd be the same way. No balance for us, hm?"

I smiled faintly. "None."

"Okay." She nodded and stood up, smoothing her blazer down over her plump waist. "I support you. I will always support you. Even though this letter makes my skin crawl." She gestured to the letter. "Just promise me that if they ask for your blood type or anything, you'll hang up."

My smile widened into a grin, and I wished I'd let Claire come over sooner.

"I have to go do some lectures," Claire explained. She tapped the second coffee. "Keep this one, too. I'm done at afternoon tea, and then I'm going to come back and take you out to get groceries. And probably dinner." As I opened my mouth to protest, she held up her hand and cut me a nasty glare. "It's not your choice." Turning with a flourish, she gave me a wave over her shoulder and let herself out of my flat.

The lights dimmed a bit in Claire's absence. I was going to miss working with her every day. She was truly a formidable ally. She always found the gaps in the hyper-independence I wore as armor. And when she finally coaxed me into being vulnerable, she would be gentle with me until I was ready to leap back into the fray.

And she was potentially very wise about my need for groceries, I realized as my eyes skimmed over my barren kitchen cabinets. Their exposed style meant that my destitution was very apparent, which might have prompted Claire's generosity.

Ravensbourne University had barely paid me enough to keep my flat from week to week, and never enough to save money. It was the punishment for not being involved in research they wanted to fund. Brandon would have published my proposals in a heartbeat if I was looking to propose ways to exploit magíqal ley lines for more efficient electricity, or if I was reviewing essays that blamed the extinction of mer on the magíqon involved in the Great Battle.

It was my fault, apparently, for relentlessly submitting proposals on how Deubrise would benefit from creating mindful safety measures to protect the little magíq we had left, such as the gryphon pods living in the Hazel Mountains. It was my fault for believing that more magíq, rather than less, was the key to helping our country flourish.

People like President Brandon were happily crowing that technology made magíq redundant. I did agree that the relationship between the two was adversarial. I believed technology was what crowded the gods-breath out of the air, causing fewer and fewer magíqon to be born. I didn't think most folks noticed their absence, though.

In past eras, magíqon were revered like sages who served as oracles between humanity and the slumbering gods. Magíqal heroes protected whole villages from greedy dragons. Magíq was the key to happiness and harmony. For them, maybe, in a version of Deubrise so distant I couldn't comprehend it.

I couldn't imagine comfortably flaunting my own magíq. My magíq had been a secret I'd been terrified to reveal for twenty-seven years. Privately, I loved the connection it gave me to the history of Deubrise and to the land I lived on. But often it was like a forbidden mark on my soul threatening to expose itself to every hostile Technocrat like Brandon, plunging my life into terrible chaos. The magíqon of the past could call storms, wrangle the sea, and even heal people. Meanwhile, I could barely call a spark without my heart pounding with fear.

As I picked up the letter sitting atop Claire's folder, I tapped my forefinger and thumb together and concentrated on the static charge that rushed gleefully to my fingertips. The violet sparks bounced across my fingernails and swirled through the space between my pinched fingers as I tapped a thoughtful rhythm.

This was the biggest display of magíq I felt safe to do in Laurier. Gods forbid I was caught by a neighbor or a colleague—I would be treated like a danger and turned into a pariah. I wondered constantly what else I was capable of, what I could unleash without fear of consequence.

I brought the paper with me to the chair by my window, using my elbow to edge back the curtain so morning sunlight clawed its way inside. Squinting, I gathered the electricity into my palm as I sat down and kicked my feet onto the velvet ottoman. When I opened my hand, the charge of power jumped out, childlike, eager, dancing across my knuckles into the beam of sunlight that brushed my skin as I picked up the receiver on my phone.

My fingers buzzed and the joints popped as the magíq on my hand raced hungrily down the coiled plastic cord and away into the floor. I punched in the telephone number listed on the letterhead.

"Yes, hello?"

I jolted in surprise at the quick answer. "Yes, I... I have a letter here about a gamekeeper position, and I..."

"Yes, when would you be able to move?" The voice was weary, aged, higher timbre, like a note struck on a hundred-year-old piano. "The station is located in an unused property belonging to the Bennett Estate and will require you to relocate. We hope you will be able to begin straight away."

"I, uh—I have some questions..."

"I'm not at liberty to field questions for the Bennett Family. When is the soonest you can move? We are aware you are no longer employed by Ravensbourne University, so we assume you would be available immediately."

"That's terrifyingly intrusive." Silence. I sighed. "Um, realistically?" I gazed at the room. Everything I owned was in sight. A cheap maple table and a pair of chairs I could sell for a reasonable amount. My couch could get me sixty. I would donate my handful of mismatched cutlery, dinnerware, and cups. My most expensive possession was the leather-and-brass trunk that would fit my papers, books, and wardrobe. It had belonged to my grandfather; I would never sell it. "Two days."

"Please state your position on magíq."

A laugh leapt from my chest before I could catch it. "I am very much in favor."

"Please state your residential address. A courier will hand-deliver a set of keys and your directions to the manor. You will have your stipend available upon your arrival."

I wrinkled my brow. "How do you know that I am right for this?"

"Because you called."

"Wh—What exactly is this job?" I asked with a laugh that was a bit thin and hysterical around the edges. "Why are you as desperate as me? Am I going to die?"

"That depends entirely on you, Doctor Sebring."

Outside of Laurier, the sea became dark and wild. It was a seemingly endless pewter abyss out my windshield, blending into the gray sky beneath a soft drizzling rain. I was out of the soft and luscious southern climate, over halfway to Northton and surrounded by dark bluffs and clusters of wildflowers that looked tougher than me. This region was one strong storm away from being swept into the sea. If the sea god were to grow angry, she would swallow this place first.

Ahead of me was the distinct hook-shaped peninsula I recognized from my packet of instructions, and I knew I was getting close to the mysterious estate. My new station.

I turned off the main road onto an overrun gravel path shining with puddles and divots of mud. My much-abused light-licker car wasn't meant for roads this rough and my stomach lurched as I slid sideways, making slow progress until I reached the gilded gate cutting off my path forward. The package from the Bennett Publishing House had mentioned this. After switching into park, I picked up the letter box from my passenger seat. I dug out the massive, old-fashioned key ring from inside. Cold metal bit into my palm as I climbed out of the car, squinting against the misty rainfall.

The locking mechanism on the massive gates hung under an enormous etched emblem of the house and mountain symbol, with added swirls and floral detailing. My wild mind ran rampant as I gazed at the glinting lines, tracing them with the pad of my pinky, wondering if perhaps I could contribute to the Bennetts' legacy in my own way. Or perhaps go on and create my own unique footprint on the academic world. As long as I was thinking crazy, maybe I could repair man's fractured, abusive relationship with magíq. So that I wouldn't have to hide.

After driving down the remainder of the drive, I reached a cobbled roundabout that circled a stone fountain not currently running. A massive tree grew with knotted roots exposed and coming dangerously close to upturning the cobbled drive. I angled my car around it and killed the engine with the bonnet pointed toward the way out.

I climbed out of my car and opened the boot, wrestling my massive trunk free, grunting at the bulk of the luggage as it dropped onto the stones. With my letter box in hand, I faced the imposing double doors and marched up to them, wielding a key stamped with an ornate B. It slid into the oiled lock with ease, and I pushed my way into the manor hauling my trunk along by its thin leather straps.

A candelabra chandelier hung over my head inside the anteroom. I stared at the wax candles within their iron loops, surprised that they were not electric. How most people would go about lighting candles that high up was beyond me. To mount a ladder with a lighter every time? The only people that wouldn't be inconvenienced by such an old-fashioned chandelier would be someone like me: a magíqon. And I wasn't about to start throwing fireballs around the estate until I'd developed a stronger sense of control.

I tripped. With a gasp, I caught myself on the wall and looked down. There were a pair of shoes under my foot. A man's shoe, quite a bit larger than mine. I bent closer. One of the toes had a dark stain splattered across it. I frowned, a chill tapping against my spine.

The letter and the phone call indicated I would be alone here, tasked to leave a voice message for Doctor Bennett every day. Her liaison had explained they were struggling to retain the groundskeepers and felt hopeful I would be the one to last.

Grimly, I glanced at the stained shoes. I wondered if those belonged to my predecessor, and whether perhaps he'd struggled in a more mortal way than I was led to believe. My throat tightened as I swallowed hard and looked away.

Red velvet carpeted the center of the hallway floor. The walls were unadorned, painted a deep aubergine with icy white accents. A tall, slender table sat straight ahead under a window facing a courtyard. Fresh red roses sat in a vase next to a sheet of paper which read SLEEP IN ANY ROOM ON THE UPPER LEVEL. An envelope rested beside the note, bursting with cash. Greedy delight brought a catlike grin to my lips, although the first things I thought of spending it on were such luxuries as books and fresh coffee.

My fingers trailed over the silky rose petals as I cocked my head over a sudden realization.

Fresh flowers meant someone had recently stopped by. Perhaps they'd dropped off food as well. Eagerly, I went hunting for the kitchen. It was at the end of the hallway, equipped with stainless steel appliances and windows that were almost entirely obscured by leafy rose bushes sprouting red and white blossoms. I poked through the cabinets and found an abundance of shelf-safe canned foods, boxes of dry pasta, and even a bottle of milk in the refrigerator. I gave it an experimental sniff and it smelled delightfully fresh. I was no accomplished cook, but even I could put a good meal together out of these ingredients, and it would be the freshest meal I'd had all month.

Finally, my nose led me to a porcelain tub of coffee beans near the sink, with a coffee press and grinder waiting in pristine condition beside it. I took a long sniff of the beans before promising myself I would return to the kitchen once I'd settled in.

Out in the hall, I found a staircase with an ornate balustrade that took me up to a long and curving hallway of doors, mostly closed. I stood on the upstairs landing with wide eyes, my chest slowly tightening. That was an awful lot of rooms that may or may not have been holding... magíqal beasts, perhaps? Most were thought to be extinct, such as the faun, mer, and dryad. They'd all taken part in the Great Battle and had perished in the process.

I thought about the bloody shoes by the front door. I hoped their owner wasn't decaying in one of these rooms...

Swallowing hard, I lifted my hands, clenching and unclenching my fists. I was afraid to use electric magíq and fire magíq, and I didn't have enough water handy... so I would have to make do with the wind. Hopefully nothing was waiting to pounce on me.

I breathed into my palms and let the puff of air stretch into a wiggling rope, which lengthened and whistled. It whipped my hair into a frenzy as I slowly stepped up to the first door. Keeping the wild snaking wind under my control required all of my effort. I pressed my lips together as I turned the knob, pushed the door in, and jumped back while tugging the wind rope in front of myself. The frenetic energy spun like a pinwheel between my hands.

"Hello?" I squeaked. "I—I'm Ackerleigh, I'm here to care for y..."

Emerald orbs bobbed through the darkness toward me, slitted pupils surveying me from the floor, not more than shin-height. I cocked my head, and forgot to focus on my wind-pinwheel. Promptly, it leapt out of my control and gusted down the hall, moaning dramatically and flipping my fringe over my eyes as a final insult.

"Mow," the shin-height shadow said seriously, squinting as it strode into a dusty sunbeam. Its deep charcoal coat looked slightly matted across its spine.

"Oh."

"Mow." The cat licked its paw and swiped its head clean. I squatted and held my fingers out. A cat I could work with. A cat was welcome. The cat eyed my hand ruefully before deigning to sniff me.

"It's alright, little one. I'm your new roommate." My voice smoothed down the cat's caution; it arched its back and headbutted my knuckles, a deep rattling purr breaking the silence in the house. "Is this your room?" I straightened, allowing the cat to rub my legs as it circled me. We peered into the enormous bedchamber together, and I knew at once that this was the one where I would sleep. It had a four-poster bed with a downy comforter that stood opposite a large fireplace with a marble mantle. As I slipped inside, I asked politely, "May I?"

When the cat shook, a collar jingled around her neck. I bent to inspect it, finding a pink metal circle that said DOVE. Little troublesome Dove. She bent her neck to gnaw on my finger with her molars until I protested and pulled away.

Tapping my foot, I gazed at the empty fireplace. Fresh logs were stacked neatly in the hearth, waiting to burn into a cozy fire. I thought of the candelabra downstairs. Curiosity gnawed at me the same way Dove had chewed on my fingers. Curiosity, and desire.

Despite my obsession with magíq on paper, I had hardly even acknowledged the holiness of my own blood. A few tingles of electricity or a playful breeze by the sea hardly counted—for twenty-seven years, I had all but ignored my potential.

It was difficult enough being at Ravensbourne with a reputation for writing about magíq. Being identified as a magíqon would be terrifying. All the scrutiny and fear... every step I took would be questioned. Every time I sneezed or bumped into someone it would be suspicious.

These days, magíqon were so rare I hadn't even heard of a single living person with gods-blessed blood in the whole country. Several prominent scholars on the subject posited that perhaps as Deubrise embraced modernity, it muffled the potency of the phenomena that usually birthed a magíqon like myself. Made it harder for us to exist.

I had been born near the Hazel Mountains. Privately, I had a theory that it was because of my proximity to such an ésprit-steeped land that I was magíqal at all in a time when we were so scarce. Maybe there were others like me, but it was hard to say. Others might have hidden their gods-blessed nature just as much as I had.

I held out my palm toward the fireplace, cocking my head, drawing my attention to the warmth in my fingers. Fire was equal parts unruly and easy to access, more so than something as slippery as water or as violent as electricity. In Laurier, fire terrified me with visions of accidentally burning down my flat or office. But here... alone in a room with my own fireplace stocked with dry wood? It was perfect.

I held my breath, then snapped my fingers. Between my thumb and forefinger, a golden radiance grew. I bit my lip and stifled a delighted giggle. I allowed the flames to climb over my fingernails, my knuckles, my veins, making my hand glow like magma. Fire tickled, like feathers of chaos and danger.

Dove chirped as she trotted over to me, puffing up with excitement. With a yelp, I held her back with my elbow before she could stick her whole face in my fireball. She rested her chin on my arm, one fang sticking out from her lip.

I grinned. "You're quite cheeky, aren't you, little one?"

I had long suspected that animals were more attuned to magíq than humans, but this was something else. She didn't even seem startled by it. Like she saw magíq even more often than most.

Before my fatigue could make me lose control of the fire, I flicked the warm cluster of flames into the hearth. It jumped hungrily onto the logs, tearing into their bark, snapping and snarling. I cocked my head. That had been in my control. That destruction and fury happened because of me.

And it felt... amazing.

Sharply, with the savagery of a predator's jaws snapping the neck of its prey, my thoughts went to President Stephen Brandon. In the fiery depths of my soul lived a scenario where I was the predator, and he my prey. A burning rage swept through me like a shudder, and for a moment, I was the fire.

I swallowed, tamping it down, forcing myself to calm. I shut my eyes. Willed peace into my bones. Breathed slowly through my nose, savoring the sweet smell of the wood.

A magíqon filled with rage left ruin in their wake. The Great Battle was evidence of that. Angry as I was, I owed it to my holy blood to control myself.

Scratching Dove between the ears, I got to my feet and surveyed the rest of the room by the growing firelight. The western wall was swaddled in dusty peacock-blue curtains, which I pulled aside to uncover long, paned windows that bathed me in afternoon light. Stained glass diamonds ran across the topmost edge of the windows in shades of turquoise and emerald.

The windows afforded me a view of the courtyard, a cramped circular clearing in the center of the manor like a pupil if the rest of the estate was the iris circling around it. With the abundance of softly swaying ferns, colorful berry bushes, fat hydrangeas, and several magnolia trees heavy with blossoms, the courtyard was a vibrant, thriving jungle.

Dove followed on my heels as I padded back into the hall. I left every door open behind me, my knees weakening every time I twisted a doorknob with the uncertainty of what was beyond. The bed in the small room next to mine was stripped, the curtains still open, as if it had belonged to the last person to stay here. Just how many gamekeepers had come before me?

Past a washroom at the end of the hall stood two large glass double doors. They opened onto an elegant balcony with an iron staircase that spiraled down into the courtyard.

Dove darted through the doors the moment I opened them. I gasped and lunged at her, but her tail rose over her back like a cheerful flagpole. She eagerly galloped into the garden, chirping. Almost like she was greeting a friend.

Down beyond the stairwell, I stepped into prickly tussock, forest sedge, and silky red and silver grasses. I tried to pretend like it didn't drive me crazy, feeling them poke up the legs of my trousers. I was going to strip the city off me and acclimate to a wilder lifestyle or so help me.

Sweet smells of greenery and berries and the magnolia blossoms assaulted my sinuses. An edge of manure, or waste of some kind, roamed somewhere beneath the garden fragrance, suggesting something had to defecate out here.

I tilted my head back. Bolted to the roof was an impressive, complex grate of interlocking bars, not more than two square feet each. This courtyard was a cage. This had to be where my charge lived.

As soon as Dove was out of sight, the hairs on the back of my neck all stood on end as my skin prickled. It felt like I was being watched.

I bit my lip before I said softly, "Hello there." I slowly turned my attention toward the shadowed archway that yawned into the earth. Even though it felt silly, I bent at the waist in a shallow bow, touching my hand to my chest. With my luck, even if my charge was down in that stairwell, they were sound asleep and had no idea I was here. But in the event that they were listening, I owed them decorum. "I am your new gamekeeper. My name is Ackerleigh Sebring."

Ducking under magnolia branches, I sat on the edge of a stone bench nestled against the trunk of the tree. Sitting in the middle of this courtyard felt like I was in a glass terrarium bound to wither. Some snatch of something wild and beautiful existed here. Nothing could thrive under such conditions.

The festering, slow death of ésprit stank the strongest within the mouth of a shadowed stairwell ahead of me. Goosebumps jumped onto my arms.

Magíqal creatures swelled in the space they took up, like an air bubble in a sealed bottle. If magíqon were humans who had been brushed by the breath of the gods, magíqal beasts were a breath itself. They were the heartbeat of the gods, bursting with holiness and far more powerful than even the most extraordinary magíqon.

The press of magíq swelled from the darkened stairwell, straining against me as the obscured creature within watched me in wary silence.

A piercing screech made me jump so high I landed back on my feet, heart pounding in my throat as I spun around to locate the source of the terror. It cut off abruptly.

Dove bounded around the trunk of the tree. A white rat hung from her jaw, hind leg still twitching. I recoiled from the feral display. Cheeks fluffed with pride, she trotted swiftly away, toward the stairs, and disappeared into its shadows.

I stared. So she was friends with whatever lived in that... that dungeon. Kindred enough that she'd killed a rat and brought it straight there.

Unnerved, I backed away, blindly groping for the stairs that would let me back into the manor, where I let out a long sigh as I dizzily gathered my bearings. If fire magíq was risky, working with an actual magíqal creature was the equivalent of jumping headfirst into a bonfire.

I understood with painful clarity how desperate these people were to get someone out here. Whatever was down there receiving Dove's rodent offering, their magíqal fingerprints were huge. Huge, and so deadly that the previous gamekeeper had vanished with blood on his shoes.

Fundamentals of Storm Magíq

A crack of thunder shook my bones and rattled the windows, waking me with a gasp. Dove was passed out on her back with her paws in the air, hardly twitching at the noise.

I had a crick in my neck from falling asleep in the middle of the bed. Rain dripped insistently down the chimney and onto the logs. The temperature in the room had plummeted.

Shivering, I put on my glasses then slid off the foot of the bed. At the fireplace, I tried to draw a flame to my fingers. But all the rain and electricity outside made the fire more sluggish, buried beneath the more prominent forces. I kicked open my trunk with a bit of spitefulness to pull on a thick, fuzzy jacket and a pair of wool socks. Dove glared at me through barely slitted eyes, her tail thumping as if to demand me back to bed.

Then I heard someone crying. I froze at once, startled, my eyes flicking toward the windows. It was like a child wailing, fearful, begging for comfort. And it was coming from the caged-in courtyard. I knew at once, instinctually, that it had to be my mysterious charge crying.

"What—how do I know that?" I asked aloud. I peered at the cat, who was sound asleep while the crying persisted. She had to be used to that noise. Like it was her courtyard roommate who would always get upset when it stormed or something.

Swiftly, I slipped on my yellow wellies and jumped into action.

I hurried out of my room and to the glass doors, throwing them open. Thunder rumbled distantly and rain plopped against the cobblestones as I carefully went down the spiral staircase. Lightning flashed, bathing the garden in lurid violet light before darkness descended again. The soaked soil was pungent. Leaves shivered and hissed as rain drizzled upon them.

There was still no sign of my charge, but the crying was so loud it almost overpowered the storm, and it was emanating from the dark stairwell. I edged toward it, cautious, squinting through the droplets on my glasses.

"It's alright," I called over the drumming rain. I wasn't sure where to direct my voice. I first looked at the trees, and then, following an instinct, I turned my body toward the darkened stairwell. "Is it the storm that's frightening you?"

The crying intensified. I had to be hearing things, but I could have sworn I heard some sort of "Yes!" in the wailing.

"It sounds worse than it is! Perhaps I can distract you." Kneeling on the cobblestones, I held my palms up and together, allowing rain to collect in my cupped hands. Rain was essentially water, and I could feel the similarities between it and when I would stand in the waves in Laurier, but the rain was also... different. More feral. There was a pulse to the rain. Like perhaps it was blending with the ésprit of the wind.

It bulged into a gleaming ball of liquid in my hands, roughly half the size of my head, and wobbled as more raindrops rippled into its mass. My fingers tingled pleasantly beneath the weight of it.

Perhaps if I concentrated, a ball like this would stay together even if I weren't touching it. Gently, I rolled it onto the cobblestones and gave the shining orb a push toward the staircase. I held my breath.

For a moment, nothing happened. Deflated, I stood and went to retrieve the rain ball.

Then, a clawed talon reached out like the storm had morphed from weather to beast and gave the rain ball a nudge. It rolled back to my feet.

I wasn't quick enough to stifle a giggle of excitement. "That's it, that's it!" I nudged the ball back toward the stairs with the toe of my boot.

The talon flexed and then dropped like a cage on the ball, three front claws and an opposable thumb, probably big enough to clamp around my head without stretching. Past the scaled foot, moon-silver eyes blinked at me.

I wiped my face and smeared my thumb through the moisture on my glasses, smiling. "Hello there. It's a pleasure to meet you, moon-eyes."

Lightning streaked across the indigo sky followed by a bellowing roll of thunder. The moons vanished, replaced by a wail of terror.

I frowned before a cough started deep in my lungs and tore through my throat with a wet wheeze. "Hang in there, friend. Storms never last." I coughed again. "I'm sorry. I need to get inside or I'll catch pneumonia." I stood up, moving toward the stairs. "Just watch—the sky will be blue by the morning."

Feeling like a coward, I left the miserable creature alone in the rain and hid inside. My footsteps left a sopping wet trail to the washroom, where I stripped out of my soaked nightgown and dried the storm out of my ashen hair. In the green room, I pulled out a house coat and wrapped myself up, nuzzling the fuzzy collar.

I knelt by the fireplace, trying to summon a flame to my fingers. After a few moments, I managed to get enough of a spark to jump onto the logs in the fireplace to raise the temperature in the room to something I could tolerate.

But still, the crying in the courtyard persisted. What could I do for that poor creature from the comfort of my room? Returning to my trunk, I rummaged through my little library. Reading essays on magíq to a holy beast trapped in a courtyard would be in poor taste, but I didn't have much fiction to choose from. I'd brought my favorite romance novel, a title Claire had forced me to read a few years ago called His Scorching Embrace. It was better than nothing, and would let me feel like I was doing something to ease that creature's misery.

Pulling a plush armchair up to the window, I unlatched the glass panes and pushed it open. Rain misted my cheeks as I leaned out and peered into the courtyard. I was, as it happened, positioned directly over the stairwell where the creature hid.

"Moon-eyes, can you hear me down there?" I called.

The cries fell to a whimper and then abated.

"Perfect. How about I read to you?"

21 October 1964

Since the estate has allowed me to develop my magíq more readily, I have been reflecting on the makeup of this gift more often. Everyone in Deubrise, whether gifted with magíq or not, knows that magíq is "the breath of the gods." According to legend and early historical records, there are three primary gods who slumber beneath the bedrock of our island country. A god of the sea, a god of the mountains, and a sky god. Their slow, dormant breath weaves into the earth, the bond of which forms ésprit. It also bonds with the blood of magíqon like myself as well, so that I can interact with the ésprit around me which is present in wind, water, fire, and electricity, as if I were them and they me.

Each bonded element has its own temperament and properties. Wind is playful, easy-going, willing to help lift and carry or sweep away. Water is gentle, flexible, and soothing. Fire is fast and destructive, warm, kinetic. Electricity is the most volatile force of them all, either lighting up the night with beauty or cracking through tree or stone or flesh.

I turn easily toward water as its ésprit is much like my own. Fluid, fitting in wherever it must without ever committing to the shapes that life demands, capable of scalding or freezing or drowning. It's why I love and fear the sea, I believe, because it offers itself to me but could just as easily consume me whole.

Wind is my second most kindred ésprit. I love a refreshing breeze; I love opening two dozen books on the floor of the manor's study and flipping all the pages one at a time with the ésprit of a cheeky wind.

But if I'm being honest, my soul craves heat. My soul craves the power of an inferno. As such, I want to burn. I want to raze the world to the ground.

The doorbell's booming chime was so loud I could hear it in my teeth. My heart was still pounding as I got up from the couch on the first floor where I'd been writing in a thick, tattered notebook.

"Now... which way is the front door again?" I muttered. And was I meant to accept visitors? Of course I knew, in theory, that people would be bringing me and my charge food. But how exactly did that work?

My hair slid through my fingers as I settled the silvery fluff off my forehead and glanced down at my outfit. Heat crept up my neck as I beheld my pale legs beneath the cuffed hems of my plum-colored shorts. I gave them a tug as my anxiety conjured the presence of President Brandon knocking at the door to finish what he'd started. I would never wear something so revealing around him. I would never even wear the fabrics I liked at Ravensbourne, sticking to unobtrusive knits or plain button-downs rather than chiffon or silk, ruffles or florals.

But the tiny white lacebark flowers I'd stitched onto the collar of my pale blue chiffon blouse brought me confidence. Reminded me of who

I was. That this was a fresh start, and I was meant to be my truest self out here.

"Doctor Ackerleigh Sebring, gamekeeper at the Bennett Estate, how may I help you?" I rehearsed a sweet, confident voice as I pushed my glasses up.

The door shook on its hinges beneath an onslaught of angry pounding. Heart thumping, I hurriedly spun the lock and pulled open the big black door. It was heavier than I remembered, and very quickly I realized that was because I was dragging a lanky person along with the doorknob like a fish on a lure.

They let go, flipping long, unruly, sun-kissed hair out of their eyes, which were blazing sterling and furious. As angry as this strange teenager was, it was hard to feel threatened because of their squishy round cheeks complete with smudges of bright red blush against their bronze skin.

"What took ya so long?" the teenager exclaimed, straightening. Her voice twanged with the ocky mark of the countryside. She was taller than me, practically skin and bone but for a slight curve to her hips and a small chest. She wore tied-off cargo pants and a cropped black shirt underneath a green canvas jacket with patches on both elbows and at the wrists.

"Are you a home invader?" I asked calmly.

"No!" the teenager squawked. "Why would ya say that?"

"You were jiggling the door handle."

"Yeah, because—" She stopped, scoffing, the blush consuming her face. She irritably swept her hair back, then jerked when someone standing close behind her kicked her ankle. "Ouch!"

"Sorry about her." The silky baritone voice drew me in like warm sunlight. "This is my sister, Stella, and I'm Nico. We do deliveries for the estate." Nico was tall enough that I had to tip back my chin just to study his narrow features and trace each sun-bleached brunette curl held back from his brow with a folded red bandana. Effortlessly, he held onto an enormous wooden crate with wire wrapped around the bars.

Muscles roped through his tanned forearms among prominent, faintly green veins. "We weren't gonna come in. She's just impatient."

My traitorous gaze wandered down to his muscular thighs beneath his skimpy denim cutoffs. After my initial fears, I was relieved not to be the man with the shortest shorts in this interaction.

"Sir?"

I blinked and hurriedly looked up at the pair of them, but purposely avoided the man's eyes, in case he'd noticed my staring. "Oh. Yes, yes. Apologies. Hello, Nico and Stella. I'm Ackerleigh. Ah, there's lemonade..." I gestured vaguely over my shoulder. "Though you probably know that, if you are the ones who..." So much for sweetly introducing myself, title and all. "Er, that is, how does this normally work? Doctor Bennett's paperwork didn't say anything about you..."

"Of course she didn't," Nico muttered, dropping his gaze.

Stella sneered and said, "We're not gonna share a drink with ya, ya light-licker. You're just a prison guard." Nico shot an alarmed look down at his sister.

My wounded pride cooled my kindness. I pushed back my shoulders. "I didn't realize we are in opposition to one another."

"A'course we are," snapped Stella. "We never wanted any of this. And you..." Her gaze darkened as she tipped back her chin and scowled at me through hooded lids. "You're just another gamekeeper who'll wind up dead."

"Stella!" Nico exclaimed like a mortified parent, kicking her ankle. He wasn't old enough to be her father, so I assumed him to be a sibling trained to act as her caregiver. Tactless, a bit harsh, but accountable to and for her.

Stella grunted in pain, hopping away from her brother. Her shoulders slumped. Like Nico was the water dumped on her blazing anger, Stella cast a final simmering glare in my direction. "Ya better not hurt 'em."

Her words summoned the sound of the creature's frightened cries, provoking an immediate wrench of pity. "Believe it or not," I told her softly, "I actually hope to be able to help them."

The girl warily looked me over. The last of her hostility softened with relief. She huffed, glancing up at her silent brother, and then shrugged emphatically and spun on her heel. She marched over the cobblestone drive and back to the truck. A yellow dog whined excitedly from the open bed.

Nico let out a heavy sigh. "Gods, sir, I'm sorry 'bout her." His fingers reached to tap on his bandana.

"It's alright," I said. "How old is she? Seventeen?"

He met my gaze as his brow creased. "Yes. How did you...?"

"She'll be alright. I have students her age." I grinned. Then my heart fell and took my smile with it. "Had."

Nico gave me a somber smile. "Thanks. Your compassion is... re-freshin'. But we oughta get going."

"Right." I frowned. My compassion was refreshing? What did that mean?

"We deliver supplies for you and your charge every six days. If you need anything before then, you'll have to go into Martinsdale, 'bout forty minutes west of here. We're unreachable when we're not here."

I nodded. My grandfather's farm, where I'd spent the better part of my childhood, had spotty electricity and his landline telephone had rarely worked. I wondered if perhaps his gryphon neighbors disrupted the power. More than likely, though, he just didn't care enough to be accessible. "Understood."

"Um." He scuffed his boot, carefully shifting the box in his arms. "I can bring this to the courtyard..."

"Oh, no." Foolish pride flared in my chest. "I can handle it."

Nico hesitated, dubious.

Embarrassed, I reached for the crate. He relented and set it carefully in my arms.

Easy, I thought, with a smug smile tugging at my lips. And then he fully let go.

My knees buckled; I stifled a squeak of alarm. Nico dove back in, but I stubbornly spun on my heel and set the crate inside the door. Splinters snagged on my forearms, or maybe I was being dramatic.

"Nice." He offered me a breathy laugh, and I gave him a side-eyed glance in return.

The horn on the trunk beeped three times in quick succession. From the bed of the truck, Stella had stuck her front half through the rectangular window in the back of the truck cab to reach the steering wheel. She hollered, "Hurry up!"

I snorted. "Have fun."

A carefully neutral expression slid onto Nico's face. "Yeah. See ya." He turned away and slipped his hands into his rear pockets as he strode to the truck as Stella continued beeping the horn at him.

Quizzical, I watched them until they drove away while I picked at my forearms, which seemed to be splinter-free.

Then something clucked behind me.

My blood went cold. I turned around and squatted, peering through the slats. An inquisitive amber eye blinked back at me. Brown feathers stuck out the other end. Three live chickens were crowded inside.

I swallowed. Dread tangled in my stomach and pinched at my nerves. But I had a job to do. After some hesitation, I picked up the box of live chickens and walked stiffly down the hall toward the downstairs doors to the courtyard. The hens warbled anxiously, shuffling and tipping around unsteadily with my gait.

By the time I reached the courtyard, I was wheezing. My house shoes squelched on the grass—I should have switched to my wellies—and a damp gust of wind whipped my hair into my face.

My arms started to lose feeling. I quickly squatted and dropped the chickens onto the cobblestones near the stairwell. Nico's hesitance had been right—I could barely handle this crate. Perhaps at his next delivery, I'd have to set aside my pride and let him bring the crate out here himself. At least that would give me the opportunity to spark more conversation with him.

Opening the hatch of the crate, I tipped it and forced them out in a flurry of feathers and clucks. The birds pecked at the grass, eyeing me as if I were their main threat.

"Dinner is served, moon-eyes," I called as I went back up the staircase. I wanted to watch their meal and at last test my hypothesis as to what the creature in the stairwell was, but most predators were protective of their food and I wasn't going to start on that footing with my moon-eyed friend.

Back inside, with my heart hammering in anticipation, I peered out at the stairwell.

Dove bumped into my calf. I jumped, swearing.

She blinked, sweet and pure, chirping curiously with her tail crooked over her back. I glared at her, stooped to pet her velvety head, and then returned to watching the courtyard.

The peace remained undisturbed for so long that I started to wander off, back down the hall toward the drawing room where I'd been writing.

Then the first hen screamed.

Heart lurching, I dashed back the way I'd come, slamming myself into the doors in hopes of glimpsing the feast.

But all was still in the courtyard except for a single brown chicken feather floating on a breeze.

Introduction to Small Town Politics

As I stomped on the gas pedal and left the manor behind, Stella's warning to the newest gamekeeper looped in my head with the ever-growing urgency of a siren. I slid my fingertips under the edge of my bandana to rub my scar. My chest felt tight, and I didn't even understand why I was panicking. Fear like this followed a familiar path: straight to Stella.

"What the hell was that?" I snarled through the open window in the back of the cab. "'You're just another gamekeeper who'll wind up dead'?" I repeated, scathing. "Absolutely not, Stella Marie! Learn when to keep your mouth shut, for gods' sake!"

Defiant, Stella glared at the receding manor as she bounced along in the back of the truck with her arms around Cheese's neck. Cheese panted happily, tongue lolling out of her smiling jowls.

"Hey!" I snapped.

Stella's head spun toward me. "What!" she snarled, treating my rebuke like a mere annoyance.

"That person is innocent until we have reason to believe otherwise!" I insisted. With a flash of shame, I realized I was so quick to defend that new gamekeeper for selfish, superficial reasons. He simply looked too sweet to be wicked. Quickly, to push down the feeling and justify my vehemence, I added, "Wishing death on strangers will bring misfortune, to yourself and thus to me."

"I hope he does die!" Stella cried.

I didn't realize I'd pushed my bandana off my brow until it fell off and hit my shoulder. Snatching it up, I crumpled it in my fist and began, "How dare—"

Stella interrupted, loud and monotone and heartbreaking, "Maybe he'll finally be the one they lose that makes them give Lux back."

I fell silent, glaring up at the hemlocks lining the road. "That's never gonna happen," I finally said with a bitter laugh. I'd long since given up such an idealistic hope. I knew Doctor Bennett's clinical nature all too well. "Lux is too valuable to them. Or, what they might be capable of is too valuable to them."

Stella didn't say anything for a bit, massaging the golden retriever's ears with both hands. When I drove slowly through the iron gates, Stella jumped out of the truck to close them behind us. They boomed shut and rattled angrily as Stella swung open the passenger door and climbed onto the bench beside me. Arms crossed, she propped her feet on the dashboard and glowered through the windshield, silent.

With how bad our last month had been, it was no wonder Stella's mood was so sour. She hadn't been the most cheerful kid to begin with, and now... I think it was hard for either of us to relax. Especially since we'd been driving to this miserable estate ever since I was a teenager, out of a stubborn refusal to give up on Lux. Bringing them their chickens was an exquisite type of torture, but it was the only thing we could do for them. Sometimes it felt like we were trying to sneak a glimpse of our sibling after they'd been stolen away to an abusive foster home.

We weren't even allowed at the estate when they were between gamekeepers. They found out when one of them deserted or died because they didn't call, and then one of the men working for the Bennetts—someone paid to be more trustworthy than us, with no conflict of interest—was sent to clean up and tend to their basic needs until the replacement gamekeeper was hired. To them, Lux was a chore.

Treating something as rare and holy as them with such dismissal was abhorrent. I imagined that Doctor Bennett's soul was damned for acting the way she did with Lux. Lux deserved reverence, respect, and kinship. All things they'd had when they'd lived with us. All things that were stolen from us when Lux was taken away.

"I don't like Lux bein' stuck there any better 'n you do," I reminded her.

"It just makes me feel like I should be a prisoner, too," Stella said quietly, her eyes on the sky. "That's what happens to magíq, after all, right? Stuff it out of sight, hope it goes away."

I nodded. "I get that. But that doesn't mean you need to start threatenin' strangers and bein' all nasty to people you don't know. You're only seventeen. You can't have met all the people you're gonna love yet."

Stella dropped her gaze, letting out a soft sigh. "I hope you're right."

I wasn't gonna tell her this, but I got a strange fluttering in my chest meeting that gamekeeper. It had been ages since I'd met someone new, someone without an ocky twang, who seemed to weigh their words with care. And I didn't know if I'd ever felt that enthralled in someone's presence before.

He was so... soft. Delicate and fair, he'd almost snapped in half under the weight of the chicken cage. His voice was light as lace and yet his eyes were a cunning storm cloud gray, full of subtext and calculations despite Stella's verbal assault. As if he was undaunted, if not amused by her hostility. Then his look had changed when he'd met my eyes—warming like stone beneath the sun, becoming gentle and kind. It was breathtaking, strangely intimate, making me feel like every moment before that had been a dream in black and white.

I could chastise myself as much as I wanted for being so sentimental, but it wouldn't do any good. Once my thoughts gathered around something like this, I was helpless to pull them away. Ackerleigh had promptly nestled into my brain and that was that.

While I remained lost in thought, Stella cranked down her window so she could stick her arm out, letting the sun bathe her skin. She got a lot more tan than me; it was one of the few traits she had inherited from Pa. Even if there was snow, she managed to get outside, sunning herself like a leopard seal.

"Alright," Stella said, watching the hills roll by, "now we have another six days with nothin' to do. What're we doin' now?"

I chewed on my lip. "I don't know. Hadn't really thought of anythin'." I leaned my head out my window to check where the sun was.

Stella snickered. I shot her a look with one raised eyebrow. "There's a clock in the truck, andullie." She tapped the center console next to the wheel.

"Stel, that always says it's eight after four."

Bewildered, she stared at the faded gray numbers as if waiting to see if they'd change. "Huh."

I snorted. "Technology can't be trusted. But the sun can." Clearing my throat, I grinned and added, "But it is around four. Which means we should eat."

"Eatin' is for the weak."

"Bet you couldn't turn down one of Dolly's double cheeseburgers."

"Damn!" Stella groaned. "You're right."

"Language!"

Even though Martinsdale was quite small as far as cities went, I was still dreading going there. Cities were overwhelming. The last time I had been in a big city was Stoneworth when I was fifteen, and I'd been close to hyperventilating for the entire trip. All I remembered about that place was cigarette smoke, elbows in my ribs on trolley rides, and too-bright streetlights. When Lux had been taken away when I was seventeen, I'd stopped agreeing to go on any more trips.

We rolled into the little town with the sun creeping down to the horizon, turning everything shades of gold and navy. Martinsdale's mainstreet consisted of a petrol station, the diner, and a convenience store that was only open sporadically. Several blocks of ramshackle houses cowered behind it, interspersed with twenty-foot palms that sounded like a downpour when the wind rustled their spiky fronds.

At dinnertime, the dozen or so parking spots in the dirt lot were all full, so I pulled up along the curb. Before I'd even cut the engine, Stella was out the door and clapping for Cheese to come to her. Gravel crunched under their feet as Cheese bounded around her in an excited circle.

I tugged my rainbow-striped windbreaker free from the small crack between the truck bench and the back of the cab. The temperature would drop significantly as soon as the sun dipped below the nearby peaks of the mountains.

Stella waited for me and pushed her way under my arm when I reached her. She let me drag her along toward the doors. "If any enfour bothers me, I'm gonna light 'em on fire, d'ac?"

I squeezed her skinny shoulders. "No, thank you. We have a right to be here—we're going to mind our business, eat, and then leave."

Stella twitched and shook her head slightly. "Why do I get the feelin' you're bein' naïve?" she asked softly.

Probably because I was. I grimaced as I opened the door to the diner and let us inside with Cheese close behind us.

Heads swung from every table to gawk at us, to decide whether we were friend or foe, local or outsider. A table of teenage girls around Stella's age bent their heads together and whispered urgently about her appearance. Fortunately, Vivien wasn't among them, but Stella probably still knew those girls from Martinsdale Primary.

To my delight, Stella fearlessly lifted her chin and swept her waves of hair over her shoulders. Marching up to the bar, she climbed onto an empty stool next to our friend Cyrus.

Cyrus lifted his eyes, which were set under droopy lids in the wrinkled terrain of his brown skin, and acknowledged Stella and I with a wry smile and a wink. "Sparkler," he said in greeting, using a nickname he'd given Stella years ago. He noted her hunched shoulders and looked past her, finding the table of teenage girls sneaking glances at us. "Now I hope all y'all ain't sendin' those nasty looks our way. Patrice, what would your Nana say?"

The girls frantically shuffled about, stifling giggles and leaning into each other, but they kept their faces turned away and resumed nibbling on their plate of chips. I smiled faintly and squeezed Cyrus's shoulder.

Looking up at me, he patted my hand. "Heard from your Pa that you ain't at home no more."

Stella nodded silently. She and Cyrus both scratched Cheese's head as the dog wedged herself between their hips.

I pulled on my windbreaker, sitting down on the stool next to Stella after I'd fixed the sleeves and straightened the collar. "He put hands on Stella one too many times. I had no choice but to get 'er out of there."

Cyrus nodded grimly. "So what now?"

I started to shake my head, but Stella piped up in an excited whisper, "We found a deserted board and brunch—"

"Bed and breakfast," I corrected.

"Oh!" Cyrus's eyelids rose. "Yeah, I know the one. Some ol' light-lickers tryin' to make a buck in the mountain's armpit. Any wonder they failed, eh?"

"That's what I said!" Stella laughed.

"Well, y'all swing by tomorrow for some food an' supplies, d'ac?" Cyrus went on. "I'm mighty disappointed in Francisco. I remember when your Pa was a kid, y'know? He mighta been a foul-mouthed mountain child, but he honored the land. But as soon as he's blessed with a magíqon in his own family line—he turns into a tyrant 'bout it? It ain't fair. May the gods scorn him."

"Yeah, you're tellin' me," I muttered.

The diner's namesake strolled up to us with a pad of paper in her hand as she plucked a pen from behind her ear. Dolly was a handsome woman shaped like a cinnamon roll, a slash of cinnamon-tinted lipstick on her lips and white shadow on her eyelids that looked like icing.

"Hey, Dolly. You're looking younger than ever," I told her. "I love that houndstooth top on you."

Dolly's dark eyes danced. "You're sweeter than ever, Nicolai." Dolly was an old schoolmate of my mother's—they'd both gone to a private academy in Northton—giving her the rare privilege of using my full name. "What'll it be for you kids?"

"Double cheeseburger and a strawberry milkshake, please, ma'am." Stella kept her voice light and sweet for Dolly. Stella wanted to make sure that she never crossed the diner's owner, especially when her patrons so often caused trouble for Stella.

Dolly winked at her. "Sure, sweetie. Nico?"

"Uh..." I hadn't actually thought about it. "Same as her, I guess."

Cyrus turned to face Cheese, feeding her the rest of his meatloaf and potatoes one by one as she gently took them from his grip. As he sat up and licked his fingers clean, he pushed up his wire aviator glasses and leaned toward us. "So, didn't you say there's a new gamekeeper for Lux again?"

I nodded. "He seems really lovely. Too young. Not the grizzled old farts Doctor Bennett has hired before."

"Oh." Cyrus frowned as he turned back to the bar and took a drink from his amber beer bottle. "That's unusual."

"That's what I thought."

"That's just what Nico thinks," Stella corrected, waving a haughty finger in the air. "I think they're all the same. They just think it's easy money. But Lux sure proves 'em wrong."

A pair of broad shoulders reared back on Cyrus's other side. Hairy arms crossed over a dirty white shirt as our archnemesis, the greatest enfour of all time, Tad gods-damned Neal, jutted out his chin and glowered at Stella beneath a sunburned brow. Stella bit back a startled gasp and shrank into her seat. Her fingers came down to curl under the stool, her knuckles blanching. I lurched out of my seat to step between him and Stella.

Tad acted like I wasn't there, speaking around me. "Ya think it's funny that that cursed creature keeps hurtin' people, don't ya, girl?"

"Hey, hey," Cyrus said quickly. "We weren't talkin' to you, Tad."

"Stay outta this, Cy," Tad growled. He had the dense body and the sharp eyes of a seasoned hunter. He pointed with his disfigured hand; scars slashed across his knuckles up to his wrist, and the tip of his index finger was missing. His hand was a good reminder of the old grudge he held against us, and more specifically, against Lux.

"Nico," Stella whispered uneasily. "Let's just go—"

I stepped closer to Tad, jutting out my chest, wishing the hunter wasn't just as muscular as me. "I'm sorry that happened to you, Tad. But as we've explained before, magiqal beings only attack when provoked."

Tad bared his teeth. "Yeah, so what's yer sister's excuse, son? My daughter didn't do nothin' to deserve bein' terrorized and mocked by that cursed creature." He jerked his chin at Stella. We knew his daughter as Miss Neal—Stella's schoolteacher. The last time I'd seen her was across the field as she allowed Stella's classmates to commit horrible and cruel acts against my sister.

I scoffed and rolled my eyes.

"Thaddeus," snapped Cyrus, standing up with his back to the counter. He raised a hand toward me and a hand toward Tad. "Walk away."

But Tad's glare stayed locked on me as he ignored his friend.

Keeping my voice low, sharp, and articulate, I said, "Stella didn't deserve to have your daughter berate her in front of the class, or encourage her peers to turn on her. What sounds right about a fourteen-year-old being bullied into dropping out by her teacher, Tad?"

Tad looked nonplussed. I glanced away to find that most of Dolly's other diners were blatantly listening to our conversation. Meanwhile, Dolly's back was to us as she worked the ice cream machine, as if hoping she would make us stop by ignoring us.

"No reason for a girl with her condition to get an education anyway," Tad commented. "When the Technocrats are in charge, they'll lock 'er up. Then I'll be the one laughin' as she suffers."

Stella bolted to the doors and threw herself against them, fleeing into the parking lot over a chorus of cruel laughter from the table of teenage girls.

Tad sniffed, a smirk moving his bristly black mustache above his lips.

Snarling, I shoved Tad's chest with both hands so he stumbled back. That wasn't enough to quell the fear pounding in my head as I imagined my terrified sister being cornered. I closed the distance between me and Tad, pinning him to the wall with my forearm crossed over his collarbone and my other hand gripping his grimy shirt. His head knocked into a framed picture and cracked the glass.

I brought my face so close to his that our noses almost touched. His breath smelled like orange soda, so dichotomous with his dangerous words that I had to choke down a hysterical laugh.

"Threaten my sister's wellbeing again, Thaddeus, and I'll feed you to Lux myself. Got it?"

Tad growled at me and struggled under my arm. Then Cyrus's hands clamped around my bicep and pulled me back. As my vision cleared and sense returned, I immediately let the hunter go and staggered away from him.

Cyrus's stance was defensive and pleading. He held his palms up toward me. "Nico, he deserves it, but—"

I nodded, sniffing and swiping the back of my hand against my nose. "I'm good. I'm done. Sorry," I muttered in Dolly's direction. Then I stalked out of the diner without a backward glance.

The cool country air cleared my head. A sunset splashed shades of milkshake-pink across the sky, complete with fluffy whipped cream clouds. My stomach growled, angry I'd left without eating. Eyes on the clouds, I strode briskly through the parking lot, clenching and unclenching my fists.

Stella was curled up like a child in the bed of the truck, hugging her knees with her head down. Cheese, who had thrust her head under Stella's, lifted her big dark eyes and started thumping her tail against the truck. Stella peeked at me from the crook of her elbow before hiding her face again.

"Hey, Stel, don't listen to him." I ruffled her hair.

Stella sniffled, rubbing the scuffed toes of her boots together. "This is why I hate coming into town, Nico." Emotion muffled her voice as she choked the words out.

"Tad's the biggest enfour alive."

"They're all out to get me."

"They're out to get us," I corrected. "You, me. Lux. The De Falcos. We're just cut from a different cloth." I frowned at the sunset before adding more breezily, "But forget 'em. We'll go back to that bed and breakfast. Cheese and crackers by ourselves would be better than greasy burgers with all these stinkin' enfours, don't you think?"

Holding my gaze, Stella managed a slow, trembling smile. "Yeah. Totally."

The doors to the diner squeaked open and we both turned sharply to look. Stella shied away when Cyrus shouldered his way outside. He held up two paper cups and a crumpled-up baggie as a peace offering. "It's alright, Sparkler. I just have food."

With a tight smile, I took the two milkshakes and the bag from him. Based on the weight of the bag, there was more than just a pair of cheeseburgers in there. I reached around to set them inside the cab of the truck before leaning against the passenger door.

A moment of heavy silence hung between all three of us. Head dangling so her hair veiled her face, Stella awkwardly shifted her shoulders and buried her fingers in Cheese's ruff.

Cyrus scuffed his boot against the gravel before hooking his fingers through his belt loops. He cleared his throat. "Thaddeus don't speak for all of us. He might be like a brother t' me, but he's wrong about magíq. You're blessed, Stella. Folks just don't like knowin' a skinny whip like you is so much stronger than 'em."

Stella remained motionless. Then she sniffed softly and lifted her head. Her eyes were glassy. "Thanks, Cyrus. I wish I were your daughter."

Cyrus's wizened face split in a smile. "You're the daughter I chose, Sparkler."

Stella stood up and jumped over the side of the truck, landing next to him. She gave him a quick, tight hug, releasing him before he could hug her back.

Cyrus's dark eyes were radiant as he winked at me. "You two be sure to stop by whenever ya need for whatever ya need, even if ya got this bed and breakfast, ya hear?" He socked my shoulder. "I owe you a drink for scaring the shit out of Thaddeus like that. That was priceless."

I frowned. Shame had my fingers tap-tapping on my scar. "I lost my temper."

"You were protecting your sister. Your temper ain't for nothin'. Your anger's never pointless." He pinned me with his gaze for as long as I could endure it before I looked at my boots. "See you kids soon, d'ac?" I heard his boots crunch over the lot and didn't look up until I heard the diner doors squeak again. When I did, I saw several faces gawking at us through the windows and immediately clenched my jaw.

Stiffly, I said, "Let's get out of here, Stel."

As she opened the passenger door, Stella met my gaze. Her skin looked like gold under the sunset, her eyes like pewter. "Thanks, Co-Co."

"I told you I wasn't gonna let anyone hurt you." I went around to the driver's side as she took her place in the passenger seat. Forcing the discomfort and exhaustion off my features and making sure I kept my hand away from my scar, I held my index finger out to Stella as she started to smile. "Now spark me."

FUNDAMENTALS OF CHICKEN HUNTING

21 October 1964

It was my grandfather who told me about the day I was born. Mother wouldn't; she spoke to me very little in my life. She was severe and distant, and we were both grateful when I left for school at seventeen and didn't look back. She particularly avoided speaking of magíq as readily as her father did, perhaps in reaction to his eager obsession with magíqal beasts.

Grandfather's farm was a whimsical sketch against the wild Hazel Mountains, the only civilized structure for miles in any direction. It was the only thing between Hazberg and the mountains. I believe that with nobody else to bless, the magíq from the land seeped into his bones. Mother thought it made him lose his mind. But I think he was the sanest person I've ever known.

"There was a lightning strike," said Grandfather, sitting in a heavy wooden chair on his wraparound porch. To our left, the mountains reared up with a heavy mist hanging over the deep green conifers. Grandfather's deep-set gray eyes were fixed on the rugged scenery. "In the same hour you were born. Your Ma was giving birth here, assisted by a midwife from Hazberg. The lightning lit up the whole house with the storm raging outside. Then the fire started, high on the mountainside in the brush and forests cloaking the peaks. I thought it would swallow up my farmhouse, bringing you and me and your Ma down with it. But it didn't touch my property. Almost like there was a ward—I think it was your doing. And after a few hours, the rain put out all the flames, while you slept like freshly fallen snow on your Ma's chest."

I was eight or so when he shared this story with me. I'd realized I was a magíqon earlier that year, but I was terrified of it. I hadn't told a soul, nor had I so much as paid attention to the tugging urge to call on the wind or the water and play with its ésprit.

Somehow, Grandfather must have known. I think in telling me about my birth, he wanted me to confess to him. But since I was also struggling with my sexuality at that time, I was so overwhelmed by the lack of control I had over these integral parts of myself. All I could do was assume that he already knew, and would never pressure me to share what I wasn't comfortable sharing. For what it was worth, the thought brought me some comfort.

I have regretted not sharing my lonely secret with him every day since he died when I was seventeen. I have wished and wished to travel back to that moment and tell him how I loved and hated the burden of my magíq. How I didn't dare use it, ever, anywhere, for fear that I would bring ruin upon myself and those I loved.

Now, I think about the talons that closed around my rain ball and rolled it back to me. Now, I wonder if here, in this manor, is where my magíq will truly be born and fostered. Now, I wonder, at long last, if I do not have to be alone.

Another chicken screamed, startling me into pricking my finger with my embroidery needle. I hissed and shook my hand out, setting down my sewing. By my count, only one chicken remained, so I packed my notebook, the romance book, and my sewing pouch inside my brief-case. I slipped on my wellies and moved out to the courtyard with a cup of tea and a heavy cardigan draped over my shorts and blouse.

It was by no means pleasant weather to be sitting outside, but I was determined to allow the beast in the dungeon a chance to see me in daylight. Not just with their food.

Eventually, I discarded the pretense of working on anything and opened the romance book to the page where I'd left off the night before. The third chicken was cowering in a bush, clucking softly, its head twitching to keep its sights on the dungeon stair.

Before I began reading, I glanced toward the stairwell again. "Is it good? Fresh chicken? I imagine it'd be a bit stringy before you cook it. I wonder if you really prefer it, or if you'd like a pot pie better if given the chance."

The moon-eyes, the diet of live game, and the noises they'd made last night had significantly shrunk the list of possible beasts that could be lurking in the dungeon stairwell. But that didn't mean I wanted to venture into their territory for a peek. I was dealing with a creature that hadn't hesitated to attack the gamekeepers before me. Invading their space would be foolish.

"Anyway, where were we?" I flipped to my bookmark, a daisy pressed into wax paper. The hero was trying to settle into his role in a strange and quiet house, and the master of the house was being horrendously rude and stoic. I eased into the rhythm of my own voice, soft as a mourning dove's song. The book transported me as much as it had the first time I'd read it.

I didn't hear the beast emerge... but the air changed. Condensed, grew more humid. The fragrance of the magnolia blossoms intensified. I tried not to stammer as I stole a glance up.

The moon-eyes hung over a beak so sharp it may as well have been cut straight out of an obsidian mine. All the creature's avian features were black as midnight, including their scaled forelegs beneath wispy, trouser-like filoplume. Both front feet were talons with three forward-facing claws and an opposable thumb. Each talon was big enough to crush my head like an apple if that was their desire.

My jaw went slack. "You're a gryphon!"

Alarm fluffed up the gryphon's plumage. Their pupils blew up into dark caverns and they took a few quick, wary steps away from me.

Quickly, I returned my gaze to the book and forced my tongue to form the words in the next paragraph. When I finished, I glanced up again. The gryphon sat delicately on muscular, lion-like hindquarters silver as starlight. Long, and with a black furred tip, their gently swishing tail curled around the sharp, scaled bird claws beneath the breast. Their head, wedge-shaped with slightly feline, tufted ears, twitched and shook slightly.

Swallowing, I lifted the book and tapped the cover. "Do you think Morgan will end up with Mister Rollins or that roguish Victor?"

The gryphon bobbed their large head, clicked their beak, and fluffed their wings again. Jaws still closed, their throat scraped around a sound which copied the intonation of my question. "Victor?" they repeated with a chirp.

Excitement vibrated through my bones and it took all my self-control not to leap to my feet. Gryphons could vocalize! Much like a parrot or corvid, their syrinx was nuanced and gifted in imitation. Already, my thoughts tripped over each other with hypothesis after hypothesis, research paper after research paper. Conclusive evidence on whether or not gryphons vocalized was scarce and much-debated. I never, ever would have dreamed I'd be able to settle that debate myself.

I swallowed a hysterical giggle. This gryphon charge of mine was just trying to discuss His Scorching Embrace with me, not become my research. "Ah. You must like the danger. I've always said I would want Mister Rollins because he's safe and reliable, but now I'm not so sure."

Conversationally, the gryphon twitched their ear tufts and blinked slowly at me, catlike.

"No doubts on your part, hm?" I smiled, and the smile grew into a huge grin, and I couldn't stifle a laugh. "I'm glad you know who you are. Unfortunately, I'm just starting to get to know myself."

I hardly heard their soft cheep, but I saw their sides rise and fall. Then their eyes left me and they relaxed into a prowling slink, sniffing the grass, tail swishing.

Quietly, slowly, I took out my notebook and fat, dull pencil. I wasn't a gifted artist, but the impulse to sketch the beast was overwhelming. I shuffled through to where the unlined pages were in the back, laying down the long, arcing line of their spine to the whip of their tail. Their wings were folded into pillowy Vs, with primary feathers brushing their rear haunches as they bent their head and nosed the dirt, ear tufts quivering as they searched the bush.

The chicken.

Horror welled up inside me like dark water. The gryphon was stalking the chicken. In no way did I desire to see this, having no stomach for gore, but if the gryphon was willing to hunt in front of me—and not hunt me—then this was exactly what I was going to do with my day. And potentially my life.

To settle myself, I rolled my shoulders and blinked hard several times. Then I imagined a future where I could befriend a gryphon and document it firsthand. I could prove to the Technocrats that magíqal beasts were the means to preserving magíq. I could prove that, rather than developing all this technology to push us further and further into our own arrogant creations, we should cherish and protect the beasts made from the feral, unpredictable, whirling breath of the gods.

The panicked squawk of the chicken grounded me with a jolt. The little brown bird bolted from beneath a sweeping tea tree branch and scampered in front of me. The gryphon trotted after it in leisurely pursuit, their plumage spiking with anticipation. Warbling and clucking, the chicken ran for shelter beneath the bottom step of the spiral staircase. Just before it made it, the gryphon lunged and hooked a talon around the chicken's stilted leg and yanked. Feathers erupted every which way as the chicken screamed, falling sideways, and the gryphon's mandibles opened.

I flinched as they clamped onto the hen's neck, snapping it immediately. Bone crunched and blood spattered. The gryphon hunched over their kill, tearing into the breast of the chicken with gleeful abandon. I couldn't look away, even though I wanted to vomit. I could smell the iron tang of the chicken's blood, could hear the ligaments tearing, could see the gullet of the gryphon bulging as they swallowed a whole wing of the bird. I shuddered at the savagery, at the enjoyment evident in the clicking of the gryphon's beak as they relaxed onto their haunches. They held down the carcass of the bird with their claws so they could better tear into gristle and gizzard.

When the gryphon lifted their head with a chicken foot dangling from their beak, I almost bolted. But I kept my thighs glued to the bench. Straining in my discomfort, I forced out a thin, "Bon appétit."

Pleasure rippled the gryphon's mighty form. Maybe raw and bloody was exactly how they liked their meals. The gryphon's wings extended happily as they blinked their moon-eyes at me and sucked the chicken foot into their mouth with a crunch. Offering them a companionable smile, I suppressed a shudder and started to sketch, willing my hand to stop shaking.

"I look like an idiot," I muttered as I sat cross-legged in the courtyard with both index fingers in the air. I kept my eyes resolutely squeezed shut like that would stop me from seeing how ridiculous I looked.

But this was the recommendation written in Doctor Manon's only published guide geared toward other magíqon. I had the small essay memorized, but I'd never gotten to practice magíq along with it while I lived in the more populated cities of Stoneworth and Laurier.

The pages about electricity were spread across my knee, but for as hard as I thought about molecules touching or… something, I could not make a static charge occur on its own.

When I was about to give up, the air stirred and heated, like I was in an oven made of magíq. Startled, I opened one eye.

The massive gryphon had crept out of their stairwell, belly on the grass, their catlike haunches jutting out of their form. Their wings brushed the stalks of lupin as they crept toward me. Their feathery ears were cocked toward me, and their full-moon eyes were fixed on my fingertips.

Static gathered in the layers of their feathery mane; I could feel my hair stand on end. A self-preserving instinct told me to back up and cower, but I gritted my teeth through it and kept my fingers aloft.

Suddenly, the static jumped across the three feet between us onto my fingertips. A slight shock zapped me before the electricity wrapped around my first knuckles like slender silver chains.

I squeaked, straightening up and sucking in my breath. I focused all my energy on the chaotic ésprit, which squirmed on my skin in its eagerness to escape.

I took a deep breath and allowed the strangeness a chance to settle in. This was a new friend, just like the gryphon. It took patience. Curiosity. Uneasiness emptied out of me as I slowly exhaled. The electricity responded eagerly, dancing over my palms and wriggling up my arms.

I looked once more at the gryphon, whose gape was turned up in a silly smile.

I grinned back at them, giggling. As if gathering beach sand into a ball in my hand, I clumped together the electricity and tossed it back toward the gryphon, willing it to keep its shape while it buzzed through the air like a shooting star.

The gryphon opened up their beak and clamped down on the energy like a snack. Sparks raced over their cheeks and down into their talons.

"This is all easy to you, isn't it, my friend?" I asked with a laugh, bouncing onto my knees. Their gaze tracked my every move. "Ah, I can't just call you 'friend' all the time. May I call you Luna? On account of your full-moon eyes."

The slow blink of their silvery eyes was fairly ambiguous. They crossed their leathery talons one over the other, demure and catlike.

"Well, Luna it is unless you tell me otherwise." I patted my knees and shrugged. "I must know—what is your favorite element to play with?" I asked as I called to the ésprit of the wind, bidding it to spiral around me. The bow on my shirt flapped into my chin, and my hair whipped about on the top of my head.

Luna's attention snapped to my gentle cyclone, and it split off from me and whooshed into the gryphon. Fire snarled out of thin air to cling to their feathery ear tufts, and the electricity they'd so recently consumed leapt from the layers of their feathers to crawl and crackle across their skin. Finally, a tendril of water rose from the pond near me. The gryphon effortlessly commanded all four of the elements into a choreography that spiraled, glittered, and danced around their reclining form. Myriad colors flecked through their eyes to complement the sparkles of gold, violet, cyan, and silver that lit the air.

My jaw went slack, lips parting, and my fingers traveled to cup my cheeks. "Well!" I huffed, laughing. "Now you're just showing off."

The gryphon cheeped, pleased with themself, and then released all the ésprit at once into a harmless gust of power that swept through the courtyard. The wildflowers dappling the grass seemed to brighten; the scent of the roses intensified.

Sliding my fingers to steeple them in petition over my lips, I assumed a position of deference and dropped my eyes to the cobblestones under my knees. "L—Luna, would you be willing... to teach me?"

Introduction to Keeping the Peace

The De Falco farm looked eerie in the middle of the night. The weather vane on the spire over the front door creaked incessantly as I stepped lightly over the gravel out front. Windows were dark and reflected only the waning gibbous moon overhead. From the stables, sleepy grunts and soft bleats drifted forth.

The truck was far behind me, past the rickety fence that marked the property line. Carrying a crate of chickens and a crate of food back that far was a pain, but it was worth it to keep Stella out of sight and safe from my parents.

I was right near the back door when I heard footsteps echoing mine, like I was being followed. Jolting, I spun around. Beneath the starlight, Stella's hair and eyes glinted.

"Oh, hey. Fancy meetin' you here, Co-Co."

"Stella! You could have stayed—"

"Ain't no need," she interrupted, flipping her jacket hood up over her head. "You could use a hand, anyhow. I don't wanna be useless."

A wash of light spilled over us. The farmhouse door clicked and swung open toward us. In the oil lamp's moody, saturated glow, Mother held her floral robe closed with one hand and the door with the other. Her short, gray-flecked hair was so tidy it convinced me she hadn't even attempted to sleep yet today, although it was well past two in the morning.

Stella and I stiffened.

"Great gods under the earth," Stella groaned.

I slipped my arm around her and pressed her protectively to my side.

"I was hoping I would see you two," Mother said. Her voice trembled as she beckoned to us. "Come in, won't you?"

I began flatly, "We're only here for the—"

"I have peaches and cream," Mother interrupted. "Your favorite, Stella." She took a step outside, pleading. "It's been six awful weeks and I wished every single day that I hadn't let you leave."

"You didn't let us do anything," I snapped, my ocky twang vanishing as it usually did when talking to Mother. She had always pressed me in particular not to talk like I'd grown up in the mountain's armpit, even though I had. "We left because you let Pa hit Stella again, and it's about time she was allowed to feel safe and accepted somewhere."

Stella reached for my hand and tugged it away from my scar before I'd even noticed I'd been tapping it. I glanced down at her. Her dark eyes were wide and steady as she gave me a faint smile.

"I'll take some food," said Stella, her gaze sliding back to Mother. "I ain't above takin' hand-outs from the folks who sent us on the lam." She turned more suspicious as she peered past Mother's shoulder to scan the kitchen for lurking shadows. "Pa's not around, is he?"

Mother shook her head quickly.

"D'ac, come on then, Nico." Stella pulled confidently on my hand.

Our shoes thumped over familiar creaks in the floorboards. An orange barn cat I'd named Jimmy stood by Mother's feet with his back arched, tail crooked and quivering as he considered us dubiously.

The kitchen was lit by a pair of oil lamps fixed to the wall on either side of the long window taking up the northern wall to my left. An electric light fixture in a glass dome with floral etchings hung over the round family table. Cornbread muffins waited in a basket, fresh enough that their savory fragrance wrapped me up and made my mouth water.

I jerked my chin toward the muffins. "You were expecting us."

Mother paused. "I hoped the timing would work out, yes."

Stella hummed with excitement, snatching up a muffin and taking an enormous bite. She spotted the wooden crate with supplies for Ackerleigh and picked it up, propping it on her hip. "Great, thanks," she said around her muffin. Then she picked up the whole basket of muffins and set it inside the crate. "Gonna take these with me."

"Are you two... able to eat?" she asked carefully. "Where are you staying?"

"Wouldn't you like to know," Stella sang after swallowing. She wiped her mouth with her sleeve, drawing a quick look of annoyed disgust from Mother, who gave me a pleading look.

Panic rose in my chest. Visions from the last time I was around my mother and sister flooded back to me. That devastating argument had started very much like this, with seemingly innocent bickering.

"Both of you, hold on," I snapped.

Stella and Mother turned twin looks of surprise on me. Stella had Pa's slight, lanky frame, but most of her other features came from our mother. The lighter brown hair, naturally wavy, the heart-shaped face, and the dark gray eyes were mirrored in both women. I was happy I had Mother's sturdier build, but otherwise I had Pa's brown eyes and darker, tighter curls. And yet I had neither parent to serve as an example for me, except for what not to do.

"Stella, if you want Mother's food, you will use manners and stuff your attitude." I saw Stella's eyes follow my hand to my temple and I bit back a growl of frustration before making a fist and stuffing it in my pocket.

Deflating, Stella scowled but offered me a slight nod. She picked up the basket of muffins and put it back on the table before slumping into one of the heavy wooden chairs.

"Mother," I said in the same firm tone, "if you want me and Stella to stay, I will not be in charge of keeping your own daughter in check for you."

Mother remained in stunned silence, eyebrows up, lips pursed. She stared at me, her perfect eldest child, her peacekeeper and her good listener—rebelling.

I added in a softer, lower voice, "Six weeks away from you three bickering all the time made me realize that keeping the peace was my entire personality. I can't do that for the rest of my life, Mother." I paused. My breath hitched. "I'm begging you. Everything needs to be different from now on."

Finally, Mother dropped her chin to her chest and sighed. "Yes. Alright."

She remained quiet as she went to the bubblegum-pink refrigerator in the corner of the room, taking out a large glass bowl. I could smell the syrupy sweet fruit the moment the bowl hit the tabletop. Mother had gone so far as to prepare the dessert before we'd even gotten here. The heavy cream sloshing gently in the bowl would have been infused with the sweet fruit juice.

My mouth watered. I glanced at Stella, whose eyes were so round she looked kitten-like as she gazed at the treat. Mother dished up three smaller bowls and pushed one toward Stella, offering her a lingering smile. She then picked up the bowl for me and held it up, fixing me with her dark and wary gaze.

I was still standing near the door, and meeting Mother's eyes made me want to bolt. I felt suddenly claustrophobic, like the collar of my sweater was constricting around my throat.

It was like I was facing down some sort of symbolic turning point. Toward the De Falcos, or away, out the door and into the night in the direction of the unknown. My own fate. Untangling from all of the guilt, frustration, and disappointment that I had felt inside these walls.

But then I slid my gaze away from Mother and onto Stella. She was taking a languid bite of peaches and cream with her eyes closed and her cheeks full. A childlike smile curled on her lips as she held the fruit in her mouth and allowed it to melt on her tongue like she always did.

A sliver of resentment was dislodged by a swell of affection for that soft, feral girl. No matter how desperate I was to leave this farmhouse behind, if Stella needed me to stay put, I would. She was my future, even if everything else was gone.

With a heaviness in my shoulders as I bore the weight of her freedom, I sat down at the table with my mother. "We found somewhere to stay, don't worry." I held out my hand for the bowl of peaches and cream. Mother put it atop the pale pink scar across my palm with a relieved smile. I cut through a peach with the edge of my spoon.

For several minutes, the only sound inside the room was our clinking spoons. Crickets played a noisy symphony outside. Jimmy jumped up onto Stella's lap, making her yelp in surprise as he squeezed between her stomach and the table. Then she took his head in both hands, scratching his ears and kissing his furry brow. His rattling purr joined the comfortable silence, and I relaxed somewhat in my seat.

Mother primly wiped her mouth with a napkin from a tray on the table before clearing her throat and looking between us. "How is the new gamekeeper faring?"

I felt my face heat up at the mention of Ackerleigh. Stella's sly sidelong glance landed on me immediately, and I promptly dropped my gaze and dug into my dessert.

"Nico's sweet on 'im," Stella intoned before stuffing the final bite of peaches in her mouth and licking her fingers.

I stammered with the full force of my twang returning, "I ain't—I mean—I don't even—"

Mother's rich, throaty laughter crowded out my pathetic attempts at denial. "That's certainly something new. Shall I throw in some extra goodies with his supplies? Perhaps one of your baby pictures?"

Stella barked a laugh as I groaned and ducked my head to hide beneath the curtain of my curls. While I was comfortably hidden from sight, I thought of Ackerleigh's dangerous position as gamekeeper to a gryphon who had repeatedly terrorized, maimed, or even killed their former keepers. Ackerleigh was the sixth in seven years of captivity. Lux had begun simply scaring their gamekeepers into leaving. Then, they'd maimed the third gamekeeper and broke his wrist. The fourth was permanently blind in one eye. The fifth was dead within a month. The treatment of the gamekeepers was a warning to Doctor Bennett from Lux, but she simply refused to see it.

And now Ackerleigh. Warm and clever and brand new to the gryphon. If Lux followed their same pattern, Ackerleigh could be dead in a matter of weeks.

"They don't deserve it," I said suddenly, cutting through the easiness of the meal as I set down my spoon and pushed away my mostly untouched dessert.

Mother's expression cooled. She swallowed, wetted her lips with her tongue, and then looked over at me. "Can you please elaborate?"

"Lux doesn't deserve to be locked up, and Ackerleigh doesn't deserve to die because Lux is justifiably angry about being a prisoner."

Stella's mouth dropped open as she stared wide-eyed at me before slowly looking toward Mother.

"I don't think you've tried hard enough to change Doctor Bennett's mind," I went on, speaking into the disapproving silence that had settled over Mother. "If anyone would be able to tell her to end this nonsensical experiment of hers—"

"Nicolai," interrupted Mother in a sharp whisper. "I have absolutely nothing to do with what is happening at that estate. Doctor Bennett..." She spat the name. "... has never listened to anyone." Mother pushed back from the table and stood, picking up the mostly empty dessert bowl and stomping toward the sink. Over her shoulder, she added, "You should know better than to get attached. Just make the deliveries and stay out of it." She slowly turned around, meeting my gaze as I stood up. "It's for your own good. Trust me."

I looked away from her and jerked my chin to Stella, who jumped to her feet.

"I'll get the chickens and head for the truck," she said before turning toward the door. "Um—thanks for the food, Mother." Then she paused, twisted back to the table, and snatched up the bowl of cornbread muffins. She glanced up at me. "Um. Can I take these, Mother? They're—they're really good."

Mother sighed. "Of course, Estelle. I'll see you next week." She made a move to hug her daughter, but Stella squeaked and lunged for the door. She vanished into the night while Mother shook her head and propped her hands on her hips.

Silently, my movements jerky with anger, I crossed behind Mother and went to the refrigerator to retrieve the bottle of milk and wire basket of eggs to bring to the estate in the morning. The calculating part of my brain lurking behind my frustration wondered if perhaps I could skim a few eggs from the basket for Stella and I at the bed and breakfast.

The frustrated part of my brain was in charge as I put the eggs and milk into the crate so roughly that they clanked into each other, making Mother and I both flinch.

"Where did all this anger of yours come from, Nicolai? You're just like your sister," tutted Mother.

"Are you serious?" I laughed. It sounded hollow and scathing even to my own ears before a trickling sound drew my eye. When I lifted the bottle of milk, I discovered it leaking from a crack I'd put in the side of the glass. I slammed the bottle onto the table with a growl of frustration as milk splattered across the wood. "You haven't been paying attention, Mother. You taught me to play pretend with you, that's all."

Mother frowned, tucking a short strand of hair behind her ear adorned with a pearl stud. "So, if you aren't 'playing pretend' anymore, Nico, what do you want?"

My eyes burned. A deep, tender bruise settled into my battered heart. "I don't know." I swallowed the salt-tangy lump in my throat. "Something brand new, I know that."

Back at the bed and breakfast, I didn't undress or shower. I just flopped across the musty mattress in the end room wearing my shorts and sweater and gave up. Sitting with Mother had completely ruined me, filling me with anxiety. Naming my growing dread about Ackerleigh and Lux made it way too real. And seeing Stella's difficulty being around Mother made me feel like nothing could ever be normal with my family again.

I rolled over again, which twisted the sleeve of my sweater on my bicep. Groaning, I pushed up on my elbow, yanking on the fabric to straighten it out.

Had things ever been normal in the De Falco family, though? My childhood had been... unusual, but Stella'd had a few good years. We were both joyful when Lux had been around.

But then when Stella was fourteen, fate struck her down and left her forever changed.

As I threw my arm over my eyes and tried to drift off, my mind began replaying that scene instead of letting me go.

On that grim day in Stella's life, I'd been twenty-one. I had still been very stubborn about living the archetypical ocky lifestyle. I was rebelling against my years in the cities being shaped into the perfect light-licker gentleman.

I climbed onto Peach's saddle outside her stable, while Pa chuckled and jingled the keys to the red truck I now used.

"Ya can use the truck ta pick up your sister, son," Pa admonished. He wiped the sweat off his brow. A piece of straw stuck out from his black curls.

"I'm good." I untied the ends of the bandana I was using as a head-band so I could tighten it and knot it again. "Stel and I like goin' for a ride after she's done with school. Helps her wind down."

"It would also help her wind down if she did her damn chores 'round here," Pa grumbled.

I suppressed an eye roll. "See ya, Pa. We'll be back by supper." As I urged Peach into a gallop, I tried to push Pa's words out of my mind. It couldn't be helped if Pa was the sort of farmer who just had offspring to use for free labor. Sort of served him right, how things all panned out.

It was a dreary-looking day as Peach thundered over the foothills. The mountains were cloaked by a heavy silver mist, and it would only be a matter of time before it descended and turned into a cold rain. It made the air thick and damp with humidity, which soaked through my rainbow windbreaker and sought out every rip in my jeans.

Riding Peach, I got to Martinsdale Primary in twenty minutes. Gorse, lupin, and patches of beech trees kept my eyes occupied until the two-storey brick schoolhouse came into view. Crooked power lines zigged and zagged away from the school in the direction of Martinsdale proper. A small dirt parking lot contained the four or five cars driven by the school's teachers, and a bit further out in the fields, several cars belonging to students were parked in a haphazard row on a patch of dead grass.

In the back field, a number of kids were hanging around. They sat on the merry-go-round or leaned against the backside of the school. I could tell they were uneasy as Peach trotted nearer. They were quiet, shifty, speaking only in whispers.

Peach whickered as I pulled on her reins and slowed her to a trot. I pulled up beside one of the boys who helped me and Pa out around harvest time.

"What's goin' on, Ricky?" I demanded, anxiety sharpening my voice.

The boy lifted his dark brown face toward me. His eyes went round as pebbles. "N–Nico. Er... It's... Just some..." His voice trailed off.

I growled and pressed my heels into Peach's sides, and she jumped forward to canter around the corner of the building. As soon as we did, my ears registered my sister's high, keening cry, and my heart dropped through my stomach. Peach's front hooves jerked up in alarm and I yanked on the reins while throwing one leg over her back. As soon as she steadied, I leapt down, staggering as I ran toward Stella's voice.

Against the side of the school building was a crowd of girls from which the sound of a hollow chorus of laughter rose. A shiver traveled up my spine. There was something uncanny about the noise. Something cruel.

"Vivien," wailed my baby sister's distinctly gravelly voice, "please, why are you doin' this? Please, I'll do better, I promise—"

Through the gaps between the gathered girls, I saw a knobbly pair of skinned knees. Scattered across the knees were chunks of shorn brown hair.

A wordless bellow tore out of my chest. Several of the onlookers ran immediately. I yanked on the arms and shoulders of those not smart enough to flee, flinging a pair of girls across the grass and sending a third stumbling into the wall.

Hazy sunlight flashed on a pair of silver shears gripped in the fist of a girl whose face I'd grown very familiar with this year. Kneeling in front of her, Stella's stocky best friend Vivien ignored my presence as she hacked at Stella's gorgeous waves with her shears. A wicked grin twisted her features, making her look like a stranger possessed.

Beneath her friend's grip, Stella cowered and sobbed, hands up and eyes squeezed shut. Pink and red slashes marked her cheeks, her chin, and her lips. Scrawled across her forehead in black letters was the word CURSED.

Lunging for the shears in Vivien's hand, I bellowed, "Drop those now!"

She jumped, startled, as I blocked the blade from Stella's hair with my palm. Vivien squeezed the sheers closed around my hand, but that just gave me a better grip as I wrenched them up over my sister's head. Vivien didn't let go. I dragged her to her feet, grasping her elbow and bending back her wrist. She hollered in pain and released the shears, which I closed and pocketed in one swift movement.

I shoved Vivien away with both hands. She lost her balance and fell onto her ass, shock mingling with frustration on her pretty features.

"What the hell is goin' on?" I demanded, standing between Stella and the remaining students. All but two or three had fled. Vivien started to stand up, but I barked, "Stay put or I'll make you!"

Vivien's chest heaved as she glared up at me, her eyes hard as stone. "What's the big deal? It's just a makeover."

Rage darkened my vision. I swung back my leg, but hands wrapped around my calf and held me back. I snapped my head down, curling my lip, but my anger dissolved as my sister met my gaze.

Stella choked on tears and snot, gasping for breath. "N–No," she managed. "Don't hurt my friend."

Vivien threw back her head with a hollow laugh. Her glossy blond curls looked spiteful as they tumbled over her shoulders. "Gods, Stella, for the last time—I was never your friend. This was a joke." She leaned forward and added flatly, "I could never love a filthy, cursed magiqon like you."

Stella flinched, but she kept her gaze fixed on me. An echoing, breathless laugh came out of her own mouth, like if she pretended she didn't hate this, her friendship would remain intact. Only a chunk of her hair remained near her temple; everything else was gone. Everything else was shorn to her scalp. Offering me a shaky smile, she used her shoulder to wipe her tears, smearing pink and red across her cheeks. I realized with a jolt of horror that those marks were made from lipstick.

Words failed me. I opened and closed my mouth, then looked away from her and swept my gaze over the schoolyard. Near the front of the school, impassively leaning against an oak tree with arms crossed, was Stella's teacher Miss Neal.

As if I was observing my body from a distance, I crossed beyond anger and into the eye of the hurricane. Unnerving calm settled over me. Maybe part of me died in that moment, I don't know, but the memory of picking Stella up off the ground was hazy to me now. I wished I had said something, cursed at them, or told Vivien off—or Miss Neal, charged to raise good humans but allowing this extraordinary act of cruelty to occur under her supervision. But the horror rendered me mute. I was silent as I hooked my hand behind Stella's knees and swept her into my arms.

"Nico, I can walk," yelped Stella, flopping against my chest and flailing her legs in protest. "I'm fine." She fought to control her ragged breathing, swallowing her hiccuping sobs and frantically wiping her face despite the fresh tears rebelliously leaking from her indigo eyes.

Ignoring her distorted claims, I whistled sharply. From the meadow, Peach reared her head up, ears swiveling to face me. She trotted across the field toward us as I stalked away from the schoolhouse. The handful of spectating students parted around me, wisely giving me a wide berth.

Peach lowered her snout to greet Stella, who sniffled while stroking the mare's velvety skull. I lifted my sister's slight form onto the front of the saddle before pulling up on the stirrup and swinging myself into place behind her.

I shot one final glare in the direction of the school—I couldn't make out the forms of Vivien or Miss Neal all too clearly anymore, and realized I'd started to cry. I shouted, "Shame on all of you!" and then snapped on the reins.

Peach broke into a gallop. She carried us into the wilderness surrounding the foot of the Hazel Mountains. Wind whipped against me and painted my face with hot tears. My palm ached. I slipped it out of Stella's view and opened my hand. A long, shallow cut oozed blood into the crevices of my palm. I grimaced, but it was a clean cut, and I could deal with it later. The less it caught Stella's attention, the better.

That wretched brick building fell into the distance behind us and vanished into the mist. Beyond its influence, the air was redolent with the scent of cedar and fertile soil. I slowed Peach down within the shelter of a heavy copse of trees. Walls of gneiss reared overhead into the greater mass of the mountain, making the forest here seem small and safe by comparison. A symphony of birdsongs filled my ears, offering me a reprieve from the dreamlike state I'd fallen into.

At the feet of my mare, I pulled Stella down with me until we sat cross-legged on a bed of pillowy moss scattered with pine needles. Her puffy eyes were downcast. She lifted her hand as if to push at her hair, then jolted when there was nothing to touch. Her fingers found their way to the stringy tendrils of the one remaining patch.

Grimacing, I withdrew the shears from my rear pocket. "H–Hey, Stel, I'm gonna just clean you up a bit, d'ac?"

When Stella didn't reply, I moved to snip off that last lock. The shears caught her eye; she cried out, scrambling away from me. Peach jumped to the side, stamping nervously and swishing her tail.

Stella trembled in terror, her eyes fixed on the shears, her dirty brow creased.

"Oh!" I threw my hand up to cover my mouth. "Gods, I'm sorry, Stel. You're right. Dumb idea." I twisted around and chucked them as hard as I could toward the forest. They vanished with a swish into a boysenberry bush. "There you go. All gone."

Crouched with her arms wrapped around her knees, Stella lifted her gaze to meet mine. She swiped her hand across her nose with an awkward laugh. "Oh, uh... No, it's... I know. Yeah. I'm fine." She crawled back over to me, sitting so our knees touched.

I dug back into my pockets. Pulling out my handkerchief, I made sure she saw it as I lifted it toward her. She held still, so I went to work removing the cruel writing on her forehead first. It was a stubborn black eyeliner, apparently, and she winced and grumbled while I scrubbed. It seemed like a shadow of the letters was going to remain no matter what. Frustration spiked through my skeleton like I was transforming into a beast made from vengeance.

I chewed on the inside of my cheek for a moment. "Stella, what happened?"

Stella searched my face, her eyes wide like a stunned animal. "Wh–What do you mean?"

I raised an eyebrow. "I thought you and Vivien..."

She blinked several times. "I—" Stella swallowed, looking down. "Y'know what, it's all gonna work out, Co-Co. It was just a fight, and tomorrow we'll talk it out and—"

"What?" I exclaimed. "No! No, absolutely not, Stella Marie. You ain't steppin' foot back in that school ever again, not even if all the gods demanded it!"

Stella recoiled. Her glare fell upon me, so hot it seemed to scald. "Why?"

"What the hell d'you mean, why?" I gestured to what was left of her hair, and held up my colorful handkerchief for her to see all the smudges of pigment.

"This... this... makeover is, it's not that bad." Stella insisted, her voice wobbling. "I c–can rock it." She swallowed, fussing with her single tress and lightly brushing the short remaining length of hair on her scalp. "A'cause I... I need to make up with Viv, Nico."

"No," I snapped. "If you can't see this yourself, I'm gonna—"

"I need her!" Stella screamed.

"No, you don't!" Desperate to be understood, I got in Stella's face and swatted at her lock of hair. "Why'd she do this to you? Why'd she cut off all your hair, Stella?"

"It was a misunder—"

"Why?" I interrupted, grabbing her by the shoulders and giving her a shake. "Say it! Tell me!"

Stella threw her hands over her face and moaned, "No, no, no... I can't, I can't... She t–told me she loved me t–too... She wouldn't have lied, she couldn't have..."

"Stella—"

"Why did she lie?" Stella cried as she began to rock back and forth, digging her fingertips into her cheeks. "Wh–What did I do wrong?"

"You didn't do anything," I whispered. The mist wrapped around the mountains broke free, and a cold rain dribbled down and settled upon Stella's buzzed hair like dewdrops in the grass.

Despair curled through Stella's limbs; she was a wilting rose, fragile and tragic. "What's wrong with me, Nico?"

"Nothing's wrong with you, Stel." My voice caught.

"I want my magíq t' go away," Stella declared, scraping her fingernails down her arms. This kind of scratching had started a year or two ago, and only when she was panicking like this. "Th–That's the problem with me, isn't it? Viv said it's disgusting... A–And Pa, too, and Mother wishes I would hide it... It's my magíq that people hate, it has to be."

"No, Stel. No, little gryphon kit. Your magíq is so special." I grasped her hands to draw them away from her arms.

"I hurt you with it, too," Stella yelped, wrestling herself from my grip as her gaze landed on the scar on my temple. "I don't want it anymore. I don't want it anymore." Her words were a hiccuping, heartbroken cry.

"Hey, you're safe. You don't got a thing to change. I've got you, Stel," I whispered, gathering her up in my arms. She buried her face in my neck while her whole body shook with sobs.

In the following weeks, the public response to this horrific incident against Stella was underwhelming at best. Mother and Pa were, fortunately, quite furious, but talks with the administration at Martinsdale Primary were to no avail. Vivien was suspended for several days. Miss Neal denied any involvement. And that was it.

Quickly, Stella had realized I was right about not going back there, and she never returned. But she refused to transfer to the farther away schools in Hazberg or Northton, forcing me and Mother to tutor her at home. We all limped along this way for about two years, then at sixteen, Stella stopped cooperating with anyone. She'd let me read to her, though. Biographies, cookbooks, science texts, and heaps of fiction. It didn't really matter. It was one of the few quiet, unchallenged spaces we could occupy together.

Stella lived a half-life at best. Despite her magíq, despite being out in the wide open wilderness, Stella's life had just kept shrinking. As the gravity of Vivien's betrayal sank in, Stella's whole personality changed. She became standoffish and quiet. She went from tolerating his grumpy nature to ignoring Pa in all capacities no matter how much it got her yelled at. She would rile Mother up with muttered passive aggression.

Eventually, I got her back to acting like herself. Around me, anyway. But the moment anyone else was in her sight, she would close in on herself like she did when we went to Dolly's. She would sigh and roll her eyes until she was left alone. The older she'd gotten, the smaller her life became. Despite living in the wide open wilderness, despite all the magíq she possessed, Stella seemed to live in a cage, just like Lux.

I sighed and rolled out of bed onto my feet. There was a little bit of light seeping in from the hallway, and I followed it into Stella's doorway. She was laying on her back across her large bed—much bigger than the one in the room she'd assigned to me—and her legs were stretched up against the wall. She wiggled her toes as she bopped to some seemingly silent tune.

I raised an eyebrow. "What're you doin'?"

Stella's stormy gaze found me as her lips quirked in amusement. "What're you doin'?"

"Couldn't sleep," I answered with a shrug.

"Same." She sighed, lifting her neck and pulling out her glorious foot and a half of sandy brown waves to lay over the blankets above her head. "Literally every interaction with Mother makes me miserable." She thought for a moment, then added, "Actually, no, every human interaction, period, makes me miserable. 'Cept you, of course."

"Same." I crossed the ornate floral rug on her floor, climbed onto her blankets, and extended my long legs up the wall next to hers. My hamstrings warmed at once, and all the muscles in my abdomen clenched.

"Don't lie." Stella snorted. "I make you miserable plenty often too."

I laughed. "True." Lacing my fingers behind my head, I gazed thoughtfully at the lit string lights criss-crossing over the rafters. "Why're we doin' this?"

"S'posed to help calm ya down," she answered. "Somethin' about blood flow."

"Ah. That's neat." I counted the bulbs a few times as I thought. There were fifty of them, with seven burnt out. "Stella?"

"Me?"

I scoffed and shot her a glare, which made her giggle. After chewing on the flesh on the inside of my cheek for a moment, I asked her carefully, "Are you happy that you're a magíqon?"

Stella lowered her legs and pushed herself upright. She picked up her brush, pulling it gently through her snarls until they turned into glossy waves, warm as afternoon sunlight. "What're you talkin' about, andullie? A'course I am. Coolest thing about me, contrary to popular belief."

I grinned up at her. "Y'think?"

She nodded and flicked a small whoosh of air toward me so it slapped me in the cheeks and sent my curls flying up. "Duh. Look at that shit."

"Good." My voice caught in my throat and I swallowed quickly, hoping Stella wouldn't notice. "Good. That's good, Stel. I think so too."

FUNDAMENTALS OF ATTRACTION

Standing beneath the heavy rainfall with dripping ringlets veiling his downturned face, Nico mumbled as he held onto a small wooden crate, "Sorry, but there's no milk this week. There was an accident." He looked and sounded like a kicked puppy, the effect accentuated by his soaked homespun sweater.

"Oh, my. This won't do." I grabbed Nico's elbow and pulled him inside. His surprise kept him limp and pliable. He stifled a small yelp as I closed the door to the manor behind him right as I heard his sister yell in protest from the truck parked out front.

Nico lifted his head and blinked at me with red-rimmed eyes. It was like he'd been awake all night and wasn't sure if he was dreaming. There was a thin coat of stubble on his cheeks and trailing down his suntanned throat. The dark brown of his hair contrasted pleasantly with his peach-colored sweater, but he was wearing short denim cutoffs as if he was still dressed for the much fairer weather we'd had yesterday.

"I—uh—will help you bring this to the kitchen?" he offered.

"That would be very helpful. Allow me to thank you with a cup of coffee. Tea. Both, what have you." Then I gestured us out of the anteroom, but Nico paused with the crate on one hip to remove his boots with a litheness that belied his strong form. There was a hole in the toe of one of his stockings, but I quickly looked away, hoping not to make him uneasy.

"I really shouldn't linger," Nico said after a moment. The apple of his throat bobbed as he swallowed. "I want to. I do," he added as he trailed after me down the carpeted hallway toward the kitchen.

I paused to look him over more closely beneath the ghostly hue of the white electric bulbs lining the walls within petal-shaped sconces. I could see the conflict in his pinched features. But the earnest gleam in his eyes refused to dim even in the pallid light. They remained a warm sepia brown like a summer afternoon.

"That's alright." I offered him a gentle smile before continuing slowly into the kitchen. "I won't pressure you to stay, of course." After I switched on the can lights hanging from the kitchen ceiling, I leaned my hip into the island countertop. "It's just a bit strange, is all. You're the only person I've seen in the flesh since I left the city."

Nico blinked as he set the crate on the counter next to me. He tipped his chin down and met my eyes, wiping a droplet of rainwater off the peak of his cheekbone. Then his fingers went up to tap his temple. "Are you getting along alright here? Do you need anything?" His gaze darted to the window behind me, which looked onto the courtyard. Rose petals trembled beneath the rain, the blossoms huddling against the glass.

One could assume that Nico knew about the gryphon outside. His sister's threat suggested the same. But in my position as... keeper, something felt too risky about outright speaking of the gryphon on my own. Instead, I nodded enthusiastically. "It's quite nice, overall. I spend most of my time in the courtyard." Unable to resist teasing myself and my pale complexion, I added as I framed my cheeks with my hands, "I think I'm even getting a tan. Can you tell?"

Nico stared at me for a long and silent moment before he swallowed and managed, "O–Oh. Um." His brow wrinkled. "Yes?"

I stifled a laugh, cocking my head. "You seem so anxious." I moved to the electric kettle sitting by the sink, flicking on the switch to start the water boiling.

"Do I?" Nico frowned slightly. "I think this is how I always am."

"Anxious?"

His frown deepened. "Yeah, I think so." As he rubbed his temple, he glanced at the ceiling and then added hurriedly, "But I am a little... worried. You're sure you're getting along alright here? Especially... in the courtyard?"

Considering his question, I lifted the basket of eggs out of the crate and set them on the counter. Then I picked up a paper bag of muesli. I gasped as a rain of oats, seeds, and nuts came streaming out of a soggy hole in the bottom. I reached to cover the hole, but before I could, Nico swore and snatched it out of my hand. Muesli pelted both of us as he frantically attempted to crumple the bag and close the hole.

"Oh, gods!" Nico cried, flushing brightly from his scalp to his throat. He backed rapidly toward the door. "I'm so sorry! I thought I checked everything—"

"Nico! Nico..." I held out my hands and stepped closer to him. "It's alright, really, don't panic—"

"I–I gotta go." He clutched the bag to his chest, where a trickle of oats continued to escape, clinging to the fuzz of his sweater. "I'm so sorry. Uh... thanks. Thanks, Ackerleigh."

Before I could get another word out, he spun around and rushed out of the room. A moment later as I stood stunned in the middle of the kitchen, I heard the manor door boom closed.

The sound of my name pronounced with his mild ocky twang, with the stretched-out "ay" at the end, remained floating pleasantly in my ears like a bird's song. I put my hands on my hips, snorting and shaking my head.

How deeply awkward. That man was so—anxious. Uneasy. And...
"Handsome," I murmured with a laugh.

For the next six days, I found myself restless with anticipation ahead of the next supply delivery. Maybe this next time, I could coax Nico into staying for a bit. Have some conversation with another human in the flesh. Stare at his pretty face and huge biceps.

Gods, the manor was woefully understimulating. I didn't truly believe that accounted for my daydreaming about Nico, but I could pretend.

Regardless of whether I was infatuated or bored, I decided I could compensate for the latter at least by welcoming back my more obsessive traits. They had been on sabbatical since I had been fired from Ravensbourne; depression had sent my rigidity away. Now, though, I could apply myself once more. I developed a strict daily routine down to the hour. Unfortunately, less of my day was able to be filled with doing magíq than I hoped: it was tiring after a while, and a bit aimless. I was able to pad my schedule with reading aloud to Luna, studying, tidying, and needlepoint and was quite productive at that now.

Perhaps due to the lack of rigor, though, I kept finding my thoughts wandering back to Nico. He was far more graceful than I expected for a man his size, not to mention anxious. I kept picturing his blushing cheeks and the way he kept tapping his temple. It was so cute.

I drummed my pencil against my notebook page. "Luna," I said thoughtfully, "do you know Nico and Stella?"

I received no response. Climbing to my knees, I surveyed the courtyard. "Luna?"

From the other side of the trunk of the magnolia tree, the gryphon's head popped up. A fat white blossom was stuck in their facial feathers, and grass clung to their beak.

I snorted, crawling over to them and gently plucking the flower from their face. "What did you get into?"

The doorbell bonged through the open windows facing the courtyard.

Eagerly, I scrambled to my feet with the blossom still clutched in my hand. "Oh, that's our delivery! Be right back!" I scampered toward the sliding door on the bottom storey. While I rushed toward the front of the manor, I smoothed down my hair and fixed the lace collar of my sleeveless blouse. Yes, perhaps I'd dressed up a bit in hopes that I would get to spend time with Nico... But I'd never admit that to anyone. I was much too dignified.

The sharp plummet of my heart into my stomach was mortifying when I opened the door and saw not a muscular farm boy, but his cranky little sister.

Stella sat on the corner of the chicken crate; the food crate was under her left foot. She rested her chin on her hand while she toyed with the shiny waves of her light brown hair. The expression on her face was one of such immense boredom that I did not believe it for a second.

"Oh." I cleared my throat softly. "Stella."

She slowly swept over me with her dark gaze, her brow wrinkling slightly. Mischief glinted in her eyes as she drawled, "You look disappointed."

I shifted my weight from foot to foot and suppressed a frown. "What do you mean?" It took every bit of my self-control not to glance past her at the red truck to catch a glimpse of Nico. I'd hate to prove this snarky teenager right.

Stella snorted. She stood up and stretched her gangly limbs before hooking her thumbs through the straps of her tattered black shortalls. "Nico's not feelin' well."

"Oh, that's a shame," I said mildly. "I hope he makes a swift recovery."

"'Swift' is a fancy word for 'six days', right?" Stella stifled a giggle at the flash of embarrassment that warmed my cheeks before I cleared my throat once again. She scuffed her boot and turned away, flipping her waves of sandy brown hair over her shoulders. "I assume a tough-lookin' guy like you can get these inside yourself. See ya."

I swallowed a groan as she left me alone. The truck's engine rumbled and rattled, and Stella climbed into the driver's seat moments before it jerked into motion and drove away. Dust plumed into the air, cloaking the truck's departure as the cypress trees swallowed them up. Just like that, I was the only human here again. Just like that, it would be another six days before my next chance to see Nico.

If I thought too hard about it, this would drive me mad very quickly.

I sighed, fixed my spectacles, and began the laborious task of getting the delivery crates inside.

FUNDAMENTALS OF GRYPHON CAPTIVITY

"Sorry that took a bit, Luna." I pushed open the doors to the courtyard with my knee, a ceramic plate in each hand. When I stepped among the ferns, I raised my eyes to the blot against the deep blue afternoon sky.

The gryphon hung upside-down off the grate over the courtyard. Their head thrust through the bars, wings flapping as they reached an arm through their cage and grasped at the sky beyond.

"Oh. Oh, my." I hurriedly set the dinner plates on the stone bench before crashing through the brush to stand beneath the gryphon's dangling form. "Luna, darling—"

"Out," croaked Luna, moon-eyes flicking toward me. "Out. Out. Out."

Tears welled in my eyes. "Oh, chaton... I'm sorry. Trust me, in the five weeks I've been here, I have come to understand that your circumstances—aren't fair."

Luna began a sorrowful wail, biting the metal which clanged beneath their beak, tail lashing with wisps of white flame trailing after the tuft like a comet's tail.

I swallowed hard. "You're a prisoner. That's not just unfair. It's morally reprehensible. You're a gryphon! You're practically a demigod. And you've been locked in here for—what, years?"

The gryphon's mercurial gaze fixed on me. They gave a soft, sad croak and gnawed once more on the bars, not looking away from me.

"You deserve to be free to roam the wilderness," I added. "I... I know I can't say much, as I'm complicit in your captivity now, but if I let you go and they just caught you again, then we would be without each other. Wouldn't we?" It was truly the worst-case scenario, but I'd thought about it often these days. "Perhaps it's selfish, but I've been loving our time together. Won't you come down and see what I've made us for dinner?" I hustled back to our plates, returning and holding them aloft toward the gryphon. "We got some brie this week, so I made us brie and apple sandwiches... And then there were some beets and carrots, so I roasted them—"

Luna's cry faded. They peered upside-down at me, head twitching, beak clicking.

"You aren't free," I added solemnly, "but let me make your prison pleasant, at least."

Luna slowly unhooked their talons from the bars, dropping their lion paws to hang free. Their wings beat furiously, colliding with spiky cabbage tree leaves and lacebark. They crashed into the carpet of moss, and their hindleg dunked into the pond. Luna recoiled with a growl, shaking off their wet foot. I felt the bulge of magíq as they commanded the ésprit of the water, which turned to deep blue glitter as it beaded off the gryphon's leg and back into the pond.

"Ah, you don't like water? Neither do I. In fact, I cannot swim at all."

Luna blinked mournfully at me.

"I can brush you after we eat," I offered. "Perhaps you'll like it as much as Dove does." Once again, I held the plate out toward them.

Flattening their ears, Luna reluctantly plucked one of the sandwiches off the plate with their sharp and dextrous talons. They sniffed it warily before nibbling on the sourdough crust. As they trilled their approval, they tossed the remainder of the sandwich into their maw and finished it off in one gulp. Glancing at me, they purred in satisfaction.

"Ah, excellent," I said happily. "I shall have to ask the siblings for more brie if it's possible. Do you think I ought to say it's for you, too?"

A yellow finch flapped through the slats in the grate. Luna's gaze landed on it at once, and I half expected the finch to be blasted through the grate for trespassing. Instead, they hummed a delicate melody more intricate than that of any songbird, and somehow deeply mournful. Summoned like a honeybee to a flower, the finch swooped down. Luna used two of their claws to pull a chunk of the crust off my sandwich and held it out to the finch. The finch's tiny feet alighted on Luna's knuckle. It picked at the crust while keeping a cautious, beady black eye fixed on me. Luna's expression—for the gryphon truly emoted just as any other intelligent being—was soft and tender as they watched the finch nibble on the crust.

Leaving Luna sunning themself with the finch, I found the telephone in the downstairs drawing room next to the kitchen. I moved the chrome box and receiver to the end of its cord so I could sit on the couch next to the window, still in sight of Luna. The gryphon spotted me and wandered over to scratch a claw noisily down the glass. I knew they were being playful, but I realized as the harsh noise echoed in my ears that the effect could be quite ominous to someone not accustomed to the gryphon's mannerisms.

I smiled at Luna, mirroring their movement and tapping the glass with my fingernail.

Then I dialed my best friend's phone number on the rotary. The call to her home line rang for a minute. "Claire Emérie."

"Hello, it's finally me. Sorry I haven't called all week." I had been busy learning magíq from a gods-blessed beast.

"Oh, at last, I can stop worrying you've become gryphon food," Claire groaned. "Mathilda, it's Ackerleigh. Don't worry, he's alive." I heard the deep voice of Claire's girlfriend in the background and, though I couldn't quite make out her words, I was confident from experience that she was giving me a motherly scolding. Claire added brusquely, "Next time, remember to call when you say you're going to."

I swallowed. "I'm so sorry. Time is so abstract here I often don't know how many days have passed until the siblings show back up with supplies."

"Any luck getting Nico to warm up to you?"

"Unfortunately not. I've only seen him once since the muesli incident, and he was cordial but distant."

Claire laughed. "His poor pride couldn't handle another humiliation."

"It wasn't humiliating." I set my chin in my hand and absently watched the gryphon pounce on a skittering beetle with catlike agility. Once again, my thoughts conjured the imagery from that brief encounter with Nico. By this point, it was so clear that it felt like it was happening right in front of me. The uneasy wrinkle of his brow when he tried to decide how to respond to my proclamations that my skin was tanned. Or the smooth way that he stepped out of his shoes. How his prominent knuckles rippled when he rubbed his temple. "He was adorable."

Claire giggled. "My goodness. Professor Sebring has transformed into a thirsty young man, hasn't he?"

"Oh, hush." It was embarrassing, but she was right. Without the demands of academia, my life had slowed down enough that I was able to imagine myself intimately connected to another individual for the first time. Ever.

Claire said thoughtfully, "Not that you haven't admired people—"

"—Mathilda's head librarian, Sebastian," we declared at the same time.

"—but, at least in Laurier, all I've ever seen you do is reject people," Claire added. "That gentleman at Stonewall... the interim professor who covered for Mama's surgery... the clerk at Tilly's Clothier—"

"Yes, yes," I muttered impatiently.

"You are a lot of people's type," Claire finished brightly.

I rubbed my flushed cheeks. For as much as President Brandon had made me jumpy about being authentically myself, it seemed that my truest self was attractive to many.

"And I'm excited that you have found someone you feel might be yours. Even if he hardly speaks to you."

I whined, "I know. It's infuriating. How do I do this, Claire? Help me!"

She laughed. "I will."

"I haven't even thought about dating for most of my academic life. I was too single-mindedly distracted."

"Truly the embodiment of being 'married to your work,'" she agreed.

"Is that bad?" I asked sheepishly.

Claire gasped, "No, oh, no, of course not!"

"Well, I've got all the time in the world now to figure out how to enchant Nico."

She giggled. "Indeed! You can run any and all ideas by me."

I picked at a stray thread on the embroidery on my trousers. "It's been a lot to get used to, but I've enjoyed having space in my head for anything besides 'Publish or perish.'"

"Yes, I've noticed you seem cheerier." The tone in Claire's voice grew somber. "And I hate to dampen the mood, but... I need to tell you something, Leigh."

"Oh." I straightened, frowning. "D'ac. Go on, I'm listening."

Claire let out a long sigh. "I have been hoping for a few weeks that things would resolve and you'd never have to know. But they keep getting worse."

"What is it?" I twirled the coils of the phone cord around my finger. "Is it you and Mathilda? Are you alright? If you need somewhere to stay..."

"No, not at all. No, it's... it's Ravensbourne. I've been trying to deal with it myself and help out who I can. I've tried going over Brandon's head... Mama Liz has talked to community donors... but Brandon is on a path of destruction, Leigh."

Saliva pooled on my tongue and made me nauseous. "What do you mean? Hasn't he always been destructive?"

"Yes, but... he's targeting your students," Claire said carefully. "It's all a bit intense, I'm afraid. I won't give you a dissertation on it, but after Camden Zane got that petition going..." She hummed, searching for words. "There's a lot of uneasiness on campus, not just among the Magiqal Studies students or the History department."

Groaning, I leaned my head against the window. "It would have been better for them if I'd never taught there at all."

"On the contrary. You've inspired them," Claire said firmly. "Students want Ravensbourne to stay true to Pascale Manon's vision."

"Indeed. It has practically left her behind." Reading everything she'd written these past five weeks had reminded me of what a radical she truly had been.

Out the window, Luna suddenly took off and started racing around the perimeter of the courtyard, thundering through the greenery. They lurched to a halt in front of the window, made eye contact with me with their pewter gaze, and then breathed twin bursts of fire out of their nostrils. I clapped a hand over my mouth to stifle a surprised giggle. It was like watching an unhinged cat who'd been struck by a fit of crazy energy.

"I know there's nothing you can do about it," Claire added after a moment. "But it felt wrong not to tell you."

I leaned back in my chair, flicking my spectacles up to my forehead so I could press my fingers into my eyes. "Thank you. I know my termination caused all this, but I can't help but delight in knowing how difficult the kids are making Brandon's job."

Claire laughed. "Oh, certainly! He looks terrible all the time! Like he hasn't slept in weeks."

"Splendid." I snickered. "Changing broken systems doesn't come peacefully," I added. "I will write Brandon again and ask if I can mark the outstanding work my students were doing, but beyond that..."

"I won't give up on them, either. Craig Dowell, The Owl, has been a surprising ally."

"Good ol' Craig. Thank you, Claire. I miss you terribly."

"It's alright," Claire said vaguely.

"What?"

"It's alright if you're happier there than you were here. With a gryphon. It suits you, you know. Being around all that magíq."

I smiled and tapped the glass. Luna quickly scampered over to the window, bonking their head where my hand rested. "It does," I said softly, "doesn't it?"

INTRODUCTION TO CONTAGIOUS BOILS

I licked the tip of my finger and turned the page of my book. It was all for show, anyway; I hadn't read a word. My ears burned and my eyes twitched with the urge to steal a glance out the window to see if Ackerleigh was looking at me. The afternoon sun beat through the windshield onto my forearms, slowly cooking my skin and making me wish for the cooler days of winter. All I could smell besides my sweat was the grungy scent that clung to my clothes thanks to the largely ineffectual attempts I'd made to wash clothes by hand at the cottage. I was one more sensory nightmare away from being humbled enough to ask Mother to wash our clothes.

Next to me on the bench of the truck was a small wicker basket containing a neatly packed lunch. It even had another one of my books that Stella also liked. Mother had kept up this ritual for over a month now, packing up a different wicker basket filled with goodies—until I'd noticed what she was doing and started returning the previous week's baskets.

At least Mother had stopped attempting to make us sit down with her. Several times, though, she "happened" to be up working on a scarf, making muesli, or canning fruit, and had made me grit my teeth through her pleasantries before she let me leave. Between wanting help with laundry, accepting food donations, and making the trip home every single week, I was feeling the strain. I was living half a life at the cottage, and half a life as a farm boy driving all over the countryside.

For as frustrating as my trips to the De Falco farm were, though, they were nothing compared to coming to the estate every week.

Stella pulled open the passenger door and fell onto the bench as she b lurted urgently, "I tried to tell him you had a contagious boil on your f ace, but I forgot the word contagious—"

"Hello."

When Ackerleigh appeared at my open car window, I practically jumped out of my skin and unsuccessfully stifled a yelp of surprise.

He folded his arms, resting them daintily on the truck as a crease appeared on his brow like a single ripple in otherwise still water. He looked celestial beneath the sunlight as he brushed his feathery fringe back from his steel-gray eyes.

"Oh, uh..." I tucked my curls behind my ear and dropped my gaze. "Hi."

"Ackerleigh Sebring," he said as if somehow I could have forgotten his name. He held out his hand but, when I hesitated and simply stared at him again, he withdrew it and raised an eyebrow. "I thought I would introduce myself since you seem like a stranger."

Stella smothered a snicker behind her hands.

I opened and closed my mouth several times. Between my ears, there was nothing but the buzz of steadily rising panic, humiliation, and frustration.

"The sickness is in his brain," Stella whispered.

Ackerleigh's cool gaze shifted toward Stella with less amusement and more sarcastic acknowledgement in the purse of his lips. Absently, he smoothed down the collar of his flowy sleeveless tunic, which was sprinkled with delicate lilacs. He slowly returned his gray eyes to my face. "Did I offend you, Nico?"

"No! No, not at all." I groped for excuses, but there were none. None except Mother's warning and the looming threat that our gryphon sibling had the tendency to tear apart their gamekeepers at the slightest provocation. The dissonance between pity for the imprisoned gryphon and the persistent worry that they would take it out on a near stranger that I nonetheless fancied a great deal... I couldn't handle it.

Ackerleigh waited in silence, adjusting the golden frames of his glasses. Stella awkwardly cleared her throat.

My stomach clenched with such ferocity that it triggered a wave of nausea. "No, you didn't offend me. We just... aren't allowed to fraternize with you," I finally managed. "We aren't allowed near your charge, either."

"Oh." His expression fell. "How bizarre. Does Doctor Bennett know you've been told that? I'm sure if I spoke with her—"

"No!" Stella and I exclaimed at once.

Ackerleigh flinched, drawing away from the truck. His right arm reached behind his back to clasp his other elbow.

"I'm so sorry." I reached out an apologetic hand, but it was too late.

His eyes darkened beneath his lowered eyebrows. "So am I, it seems." Annoyance flashed in Ackerleigh's features. "I never meant to be involved in such an immoral business as Doctor Bennett's."

"She doesn't usually ask permission," Stella muttered.

I began desperately, "I know you're not the problem—"

Ackerleigh did not attempt to repress a scoffing snort. He looked away, throat bobbing. Briefly, his stony gaze returned to me as he gave me a curt nod. "Feel free to leave next week's delivery on the doorstep. I wouldn't want to make you both complicit." Fists clenched, he strode back to the manor, went inside the massive oak doors, and swung them closed behind him with a boom of finality.

Stunned horror rendered me mute and frozen in place. That was so much worse than the muesli incident. At least then I'd made him laugh.

"Woulda been better if you'd really had a boil," Stella remarked.

Groaning, I threw my head back and hit it against the rear window of the cab. I ignored Stella's alarmed yelp, mashing the heels of my hands into my eyes as I banged against the window several more times. I felt the rattling glass in my teeth, envisioning the pane shattering and feeling the shame that would follow.

"I'm so sick of this!" I cried.

"What, the weather, or...?" Stella asked gently. She sounded like me; it was unsettling.

"This accursed arrangement!" I dropped my fists from my eyes, yanked on the gear shift, and slammed on the gas pedal.

Stella jolted and grabbed her door handle as the truck rumbled like an angry beast beneath us. "Tranqui! Gods!" Gravel pinged into the doors and stirred up a cloud of dust as we roared through the cypress trees.

I snarled, "I hate this gods-forsaken job at this wretched estate and the fact that we've both just allowed our gryphon to be locked up for years!" The hot track of a tear surprised me as it raced down my cheek. Impatiently, I swept it away. "Wouldn't this whole thing fall apart if we stopped participating?"

Stella's eyes were round with uneasiness as her lightweight form bounced on the other end of the seat. At my question, she grimaced. "Naw. She'd find someone else, for sure."

The blaze of my anger began to recede. "You're right." I eased up on the gas. "We'd just be replaced. But... I don't know, maybe I can write to Doctor Bennett... or, hey, it's not that far from Laurier. We could show up—"

"It's not gonna work." There was no hope, no color, no spark in my sister's low, quiet voice. "She always wins."

At the open gates that marked the edge of the property, I slowed us to a stop. I felt a lot like the iron bars of the gate, bent and twisted grotesquely out of shape.

Stella was right, of course. There was no use approaching Doctor Bennett with a sensible argument, because she wasn't sensible. She approached her intellectual pursuits with biting ferocity. When she was chasing a hypothesis, it was marked with her hunter's gaze until she had it in her jaws and it gave her the outcome she wanted. In Lux's case, they had yet to give that to her.

"Fine." The word plunked between us like a dead pheasant shot from the sky. I cast my gaze to the rearview mirror, which gave me a perfectly framed image of the white-trimmed mansion that imprisoned Ackerleigh and Lux. "So she won't listen to reason."

Stella's brow wrinkled. "Um, yep... I know."

I looked at my sister, whose feral magíq was obscured beneath her loose, dark clothes, her wild wavy hair, and her readiness to do whatever I wanted her to do.

"How would you like to do something really stupid and dangerous with me, Stel?"

FOUNDATIONS OF NEAR–DEATH EXPERIENCES

15 December 1964

Tomorrow is the last day of the semester at Ravensbourne. It's been three months since I was terminated. Although I wrote and asked the president, I was not permitted to receive any additional essays from the students in the four classes I was teaching. I find this a grievous offense. My students—all forty-three of them across the four classes

I was teaching—received incompletes through no fault of their own. Brandon's issue should have been with me, not the students he supposedly serves.

I have made Claire's time at Ravensbourne much more miserable, too. Her letters complain of loneliness and her updates over the phone focus on her worry for my students and the general unrest plaguing Ravensbourne.

Guilt overwhelms me. My convictions have brought misery to the people I care about the most. If I were just different, if I did not insist on teaching critical conversations about magíq... if perhaps the gods had not blessed me with their gods-breath at all... perhaps I would be less of a burden.

And yet Luna is different than when I arrived. The gryphon is lively and vivacious in a way that inspires me to breathe and relax, and occasionally even deviate from my own set schedule.

Of all the ésprit, Luna and I love playing with fire the most. The gryphon seems to take the risk out of such a volatile element. It satisfies a craving I hardly knew was there. Luna is happy assisting me when they can sense my uncertainty, and so I find myself as the magíqal apprentice of a gryphon.

Thinking of all I left behind at Ravensbourne as I revel in magíq at the manor leaves me sick to my stomach at times. To have these days filled with glittering magíq and bonding with a blessed beast, and sleepless nights filled with regret and anger about Ravensbourne...

Is my life doomed to be a choice between isolation or secrecy? Must I choose to be alone with my magíq or in the company of others being only half my true self?

My throat tightened. I dropped my stubby pencil and flipped forward to my sketching pages. They were filled with Luna in dozens of poses, and with close-ups of their plumage and their wedge-shaped head, their eyes expressive and their gape curved up in a smile.

Dove sunned herself in the courtyard by my feet, belly up, fangs poking out of her jowls. The magnolia blossoms had faded with the arrival of summer. Lupins bloomed in their stead—a veritable army of them, somehow still thriving within the walls of this hole-in-the-ground. They brushed both my elbows, pink and purple and as sweet-smelling as grape soda.

The courtyard had a roughly circular pattern of stepping stones that dotted the perimeter. Luna was currently hopping between them, spine bending like an inchworm, wings spread out above their shoulders to balance.

I was still annoyed with my interaction with Nico the day before. His manner suggested strongly that he wanted to be near me, yet all these weeks of him staying in the truck, forcing me and his sister to feign civility with one another...

And his comment about being prohibited to *fraternize* with me. Like I was... some sort of prison guard, and they were only indentured servants.

It almost left me feeling like I was being complicit in something cruel and wicked. Perhaps I was even being selfish, relishing in magíqal lessons from a gryphon who had no other choice but to humor me. Was my bond with them so special if they were powerless in our relationship?

I sat under the magnolia tree in shorts and a turquoise high-collared blouse. I'd been unable to resist embroidering feathers onto the collar, using silver thread to make them stand out. Luna had actually noticed them immediately; first they'd stroked them admiringly with a talon, and then they'd tried to eat them.

A breeze stirred my hair, making it tickle the back of my neck unpleasantly. I hissed and swatted at it. It was getting too long for my liking. Claire usually cut it for me. In her stead, I was going to have to start tying it up with a ribbon.

"And that's another question," I mused aloud. "Am I simply meant to live in isolation here indefinitely, or can I have a friend over? Can I visit Laurier—could I even endure that, if it would mean leaving you?"

Luna wandered over as I spoke, scooping a mouthful of pond water into their mouth before calling on its ésprit and spitting glinting blue mist over their head. It looked like a hundred tiny planets orbiting them.

Reaching out with a finger, I beckoned the droplets to twine around my wrist. Luna allowed the rest of the water to settle on their brow like a crown as they came around to prop their chin on my head. Light, billowing feathers tickled the back of my head and brushed against my cheeks like butterfly kisses.

"You are good company, though, chaton. A teacher and a friend."

Splitting open our peaceful solace, chaos arrived. Over our heads, a fireball dropped onto the iron grate and exploded. Luna screamed; Dove fled for the stairs; I dropped onto my hands and knees and threw my hands over my head as chunks of metal rained onto us. The air burned and bubbled, a metal tang filling my mouth and turning my stomach.

I picked up my head, squinting through the smoke. "Luna! Are you alright?"

The gryphon answered with a whistle of anxiety and I located them cowering in their dungeon stairwell. I darted over, dodging melted bolts of iron protruding like arrows from among the lupin.

Luna lifted their head toward the busted grate. Their eyes widened and beak opened as they gasped with delight, "Ella!"

My heart dropped as I looked up. Hanging over the enormous rift in the grate was a familiar brunette teenager, and she was beaming.

"Luneyeux! Come on! You're free!"

Without thinking, as Luna beat their wings with a gust of iron-drenched wind, I threw my arms around their neck. My feet left the ground, my stomach lurched, and the courtyard shrank beneath us.

Stella's wide eyes filled with horror as she saw me dangling from the gryphon. She didn't have time to speak before Luna opened their talons and caught Stella by her biceps, picking her up the same way an eagle would snatch up their prey. She swung towards my head, so when she shrieked in surprise, it was directly into my ear. Her legs scrabbled for security, but we were fighting for the same space, and my knees had barely gotten a grip on the gryphon's rib cage when Stella's boot knocked my legs loose.

"Luneyeux!"

The gryphon's gaze snapped down toward Nico, who was waving both his arms from the peak of the manor rooftop. Luna turned sharply to go back for him.

"Luna, I can't hang on," I yelped as I dug my bare toes into their soft belly.

"Ackerleigh?" Nico called in confusion. "Oh, no, you weren't meant to—"

Luna interrupted him with a piercing cry. "Go, go, go, go." The articulation was frantic and emotional, and I realized suddenly how desperate the gryphon was to escape their prison. As they swooped past Nico, the farm boy fearlessly leapt for their feathered back and landed across them with a grunt.

The moment he was secure, Luna shot into the sky. Their belly rippled and heated with their powerful muscles, wings pumping, legs swimming through the air currents. I caught a glimpse of their silver gaze, and it was filled with determination. Luna's only obvious objective was to flee.

"Oh, my gods," I exclaimed as we rapidly ascended higher and higher over the manor. This was my first time seeing Luna fly, and my first time *riding a gryphon*, but good gods I had not expected to be barely hanging onto their underbelly. Luna's frenzied, noisy wingbeats slapped my face with powerful gusts of wind. The manor was now the size of a child's playhouse, and the sea cut through half of my vision, framed by jagged cliffs.

I grasped Luna's feathery mane as tightly as I could and struggled to keep my knees pressed together, but how long could I manage this?

Nico scrambled up Luna's neck, reaching for Stella as he exclaimed, "Lux, we can get out of here, but first—"

"Help!" shrieked Stella. "Get me up there!" She flailed within her clawed restraints. As she reached for her brother, her knee came up and struck me in the cheek, knocking my glasses loose... as well as my grip on Luna.

My legs swung down; all my weight yanked against my laced-together fingers. Luna pitched forward at the sudden shift of my weight, their nose thrusting toward the earth. I had no strength to save myself, swinging freely from the gryphon's neck and scrabbling to hang on. My clammy hands slipped.

I fell, screaming, lost in a slurry of water and sky and tree as the seconds smudged into an eternity out of control.

A groping juniper branch thrust into my path. It jammed into my armpits, and survival instinct made me grab on for dear life even as blinding pain shot across my chest and stole the breath from my lungs. Blood pounded in my ears. My feet dangled over the snarling sea. I looked up as Luna screamed.

My gryphon dove toward the tree to rescue me... right as the branch that held me snapped.

Introduction to Open-Sea Rescues

Lux's piercing shriek rang in my ears as Ackerleigh's juniper branch lifeline snapped, dropping him like a stone. Stunned, hanging onto his branch, Ackerleigh had his mouth open, but he was now silent as he fell. The juniper tree hung out from a sheer cliff maybe fifty feet above the sea, and—and Ackerleigh was falling so fast, and Lux and I screamed in unison. I tasted metal and rain as magíq exploded from the gryphon and they sent a desperate funnel of wind toward Ackerleigh to stop him from hitting the water. But the magíq came a second too late, and the waves gobbled up the gamekeeper and pulled him under, branch and all.

"Allie! Allie, no! Rescue!" Lux wailed, bucking beneath us. Lightning crawled over Lux's midnight feathers and shocked my hands as I pushed against them.

Lopsided against Lux's mane with one leg slipping off, Stella squawked, "I'm gonna fall!"

Lux gnashed their beak in frustration. They reached back and shoved Stella up into my arms while they banked and straightened out, circling over the water and searching its dark abyss. They were unable to swim, unable to go after their precious gamekeeper, who had yet to surface.

My mind ran rampant with visions of Ackerleigh floating dead on the waves. Broken, blood clouding the turquoise depths, eyes staring and vacant. Every fiber of my being rebelled against the thought of losing him before I'd even had him. Like some twinkling, precious path into my future was being snuffed out.

Resolute, I hoisted my leg over Lux's back and launched off the gryphon and dove for the sea.

Stella screamed as the water rushed to greet me. I pressed my hands together over my head, pointed my toes, and slipped into the waves with my eyes wide open. It flipped my stomach, the sheer power of it. So little separated me from being in control and being swept away by the tide.

The salt burned my eyes, but the weather had graced me with transparent waters. I scanned the gradient of cyan to navy, searching. A limp human form was fading into the shadows, sinking fast. My throat tightened. This reality was overwhelming, terrifying. If I failed and drowned, Stella would be left alone...

Terrible adrenaline urged speed into my muscles. I dolphin-kicked once, twice, the third time bringing me almost deep enough to comb my fingers through a crown of rippling hair turned silver by the depths, like I'd uncovered a mer of old. I lost my coordination, kicking wildly, thrashing till I could grasp the wisp of a sleeve. I kicked my legs under me to face the heavens, and then wrapped both arms around the game-keeper's waist.

I'd never hauled a body out of the water before. The sudden weight sent a shock of fear down my spine, but my feet couldn't touch, and all I could do was keep kicking and pumping us back toward the sun-dappled surface. Silvery fish darted past us with enviable ease as Ackerleigh's dead weight fought against me.

Finally, I erupted at the surface, gasping. I lay back in the water, leaning Ackerleigh into my shoulder to check for a pulse along the blue veins of his nearly translucent skin. Jagged scrapes oozed crimson beneath his left eye. His heart beat sluggishly against my fingers. Too slow, and with the amount of water he'd just swallowed...

I'd known emergency First Aid since I was twelve, having been frightened into becoming an expert after realizing how easily Stella could injure her loved ones—like me—unintentionally.

But knowing First Aid didn't make the realization that Ackerleigh needed my mouth on his and my breath in his lungs any less overwhelming.

Suddenly, I didn't even remember how to tread water. My legs went limp, and the waves splashed my mouth and nose; I coughed, my head bobbing below the surface.

Lux swooped as close as they could with their feet tucked up against their belly. They used a gust of wind to pluck us out of the sea inside a funnel of water and air. Stella reached out and snatched my biceps, so when the wind died down, I fell onto my back across Lux's wings. Ackerleigh flopped on top of me; I heard his teeth snap together and flinched on his behalf. Lux tweeted worriedly as they tried to stabilize me, struggling with my weight on the muscular median of their wings. Stella pulled on my elbow, moving back to sit over Lux's haunches and giving me more room to wedge into their mantle.

"He needs—" I began as I struggled upright, coughing and wiping my eyes. "Air." Frantically, I rested Ackerleigh against Lux's mane, tipped his chin back and plugged his nose, and pressed my mouth to his. I wished for magíq of my own to imbue my breath, which fought against the water in Ackerleigh's lungs and made me feel doomed to failure. I pulled back, feeling Lux's silver eyes on me as I stared at Ackerleigh's bloody, motionless face, waiting for something to happen.

Frantic, I dipped my head in again and sent another deep breath into his mouth, feeling his chest expand under my palm. Still, when I straightened, nothing happened.

Despair and panic were like water clogging my own lungs. "S–Stella, can't you pull the water out of his lungs?"

"I don't—I don't know how," Stella cried, her useless magíqal hands outstretched.

I growled, "Gods, why can't you—"

Ackerleigh choked, coughed, and spluttered as I tilted his torso to the side, seawater gushing from his mouth. He jerked, limbs flailing, and started falling off the gryphon. I wrapped my arms around him and pulled him into my chest so his thighs were slotted over mine and his head fell onto my shoulder. It was—it was a lover's embrace, this, with *everything* touching as Ackerleigh gasped and quivered against me.

"Stay calm, Ackerleigh," I said softly. "You're very injured. And you're coming with us."

"Where—Where?" Ackerleigh began in a thin, pained voice as his fingers dug into my chest. "Ow, ow, ow, my ribs..."

"I know, that must hurt. You had a bad fall." My voice caught. "Listen. It's a safe place we've been staying at. Try to rest—it's a long ride."

Ackerleigh shivered in silence. I glanced down at his long white lashes veiling his pain-clouded eyes. Blood smeared across his cheek and his wet hair stuck to his temples.

"Let's go, Lux," I said, clenching my legs together and patting the gryphon's neck. "To the mountains."

Keening in response, Lux shot into the cloud layer. Goosebumps rose on my salt-caked arms as the wind and the altitude ruthlessly beat the sea out of my skin. Hills colored the deep heather-green of high summer rolled beneath us, dotted with sheep that looked like cotton balls. We left the sea behind, and I wasn't going to miss it.

"Gods, why did I think this would work?" I groaned. Grinding my teeth, I raked my fingers through my hair. It was tacky and gritty from the salt and sand, the curled ends sticky like seaweed. I was so disgusted by it I had to fight my hands away to avoid trying to pull out my hair in a panic.

"I mean—" Stella's voice was small and thoughtful. I felt her fingers graze my ribs above my elbows. "But it *did* work. Nico, look at us. We're... we're with Lux. On their back! Can you believe how *big* they got?"

I remained silent, too overwhelmed to even acknowledge that I had, technically, accomplished my goal. Was it a satisfying victory if Ackerleigh had nearly been killed in the process? I wrapped my arms around his slim shoulders, shutting my eyes and letting the whistling wind whip against me. I carefully measured my breathing. In. Out. Ackerleigh was alive. Lux was free. In. Out.

It would take over an hour for us to get to the bed and breakfast at the eastern foot of the Hazel Mountains. Getting to the Bennett estate had taken us all morning by hitchhiking, but Lux was traveling at least twice as fast as my truck. The countryside blurred by us beneath the cloud layer, an occasional road stitched into the grass like a single brown thread. Lakes glittered, and farmsteads were situated amidst tidy rows of fields ready for tilling. A watercolor wash of pink and lavender lupins blotted out the green meadows.

In. Out. Ackerleigh was alive. Lux was free. In. Out.

Ackerleigh had either fainted or fallen asleep. His head lolled on my shoulder and his body was limp and heavy against my chest. He shivered faintly, and before I realized what I was doing I tightened my grip on him and held him closer. I used the excuse of the temperature. It had gotten cold in the stratosphere, and the wind was brutal as it dried our clothes. Really, though, I was well and truly carried away with the sensation of holding him. The wrong circumstances, by all means, but it was spellbinding. He was so soft and light.

In. Out. Get it together, Nico.

Part II

Formation and
Development of
Magiqal Bonds

SURVEY OF PAIN-LACED DENIAL

Words rumbled against my ear, indecipherable, distant. I was aware of the wind on my brow. A heartbeat, thumping hard and fast against my cheek. A strong grip on my shoulders. These sensations tethered me to my body, kept me from falling apart.

Except for the pain that kept pushing its way back in. Pain so sharp and horrid washed over me in waves, stealing me back into a dark and fitful unconsciousness.

This telltale pain slapped me back into the land of the living when I was laid onto something vaguely soft and lumpy, smelling of dust and mothballs. I groaned, not sure what hurt or, more accurately, what *didn't* hurt. My closed eyes burned and felt heavy with tears, and when I bared my teeth in a grimace, my cheek stung as if it had been whipped raw.

Using a trembling hand, I groped for my chest. How could a body part be so numb and yet *scream* like it had been punched through with a battering ram?

"Ackerleigh..." The voice was the same one I'd felt vibrating against my face. "You're safe. Try to take some slow breaths. Can you breathe with your belly?" I recognized the ocky accent as Nico's but couldn't figure out why he was with me if I was... Gods, if I was *dying*.

"Wh..." My mind ran ahead of my thick tongue, and I didn't know if I was going to ask what had happened or where I was. I swallowed and tasted salt. Helpless and angry, I blinked hard several times and waited for the world to come into focus. But it didn't. I saw Nico's familiar curls framing his tan face, which hung over me with all the detail of a sloppy watercolor sketch. I swiped at my eyes, assuming my glasses needed cleaning, but my fingers jabbed my eyebrow and eyelid instead.

My glasses were missing.

Everything came flooding back to me. The fireball crashing into the courtyard like a meteor. Stella's joyful reunion with Luna. Dangling beneath the gryphon's belly until... I fell, first into greenery, then into the sea, then into darkness.

My heartbeat increased rapidly and my breathing became shallow, beckoning spasms of red-hot agony. I made no attempt to stifle my gasping sobs, even though the pressure in my chest made stars swim through my nearly useless vision.

Near my head rattled an anxious and croaking purr. Feathers whispered against my temple. A wave of relief rushed over me as I reached for the dark form of my gryphon and pulled them close. They roughly nuzzled my face and I planted my lips on their fluffy cheek, breathing in their familiar balsam-scented musk. With the comfort of their presence, I was able to calm myself before I hyperventilated and cracked my chest open.

But what *was* wrong with my chest? I lowered my chin and saw dark stains spotting my turquoise blouse. My stomach immediately rolled in response. I reached a shaky hand to grasp the hem of my blouse, bunching it up at my throat.

The planes of the right side of my torso were hardly recognizable, discolored to shades of burgundy and maroon. Across the outline of my ribcage there were open, oozing scrapes from the branches of the juniper tree that had caught me. Even the shape of my chest was swollen all the way down to my navel.

It couldn't be my body. I had to be back at the estate, dozing in the courtyard and anticipating Nico's next visit. I could never look this bruised and bloody. I was an *academic.*

"I'm so s–sorry," Nico stammered with a wobble in his voice followed by a wet sniff. Shocked into numbness, I blankly looked up at him. I thought I saw tears tracking down his cheeks, glinting in the light from a window behind my head. "You weren't meant to be involved in this at all... I just w–wanted... Lux to be free, and to make sure you didn't... e–end up like the other gamekeepers."

I frowned. "Luna would..." My voice trailed off, faraway and unfamiliar. The creeping anger was strange, too. "Your mission sounds awfully noble, Nico, but I notice some problems with it."

Nico flinched, silent.

"Firstly, Luna and I have been inseparable for weeks, which you'd know if you hadn't scampered off in the middle of our only conversation." This *couldn't* be me using that snarky, irritable tone on the only man I'd wanted to get closer to in years. I wouldn't dare ruin my chances so quickly. "Secondly, and possibly most importantly, if you had offered me the opportunity to assist you in liberating my gryphon charge, I would have happily thrown open the doors."

The man's head dropped between his broad shoulders so all I could see was the circlet of his red bandana and a curtain of frizzy curls.

"Lastly," I went on, voice breaking, "now I can't *see*, I look like *this*, I have no *job*, and your *sister* kicked me into the sea!" I reached a frantic crescendo before a pathetic, childlike sob gripped me by the pit of my stomach, ripping through my chest. Involuntarily, I curled my arms around the terrible, tender bruises that undoubtedly crowded against fractured bones. The harder I cried, the more my vision turned dark around the edges, and then my breath went raspy. Luna chittered worriedly, plucked at my hair. My despair was now edged with shame, but resentment too; I hadn't done anything except accept a strange job out of desperation. Would I never be safe and secure again?

Disregarding my temper tantrum, Nico murmured, "I'm going to touch you now." His warm hands slipped around my shoulder and the nape of my neck. He moved my upper body off the bed while I fought to silence my hysteria. His sudden nurturing gesture helped greatly to ground me, lighting a wary flame in my chest.

Nico stretched over me and piled an extraordinary number of pillows behind my back, propping me up against a luxurious, albeit dusty mountain. He was so close that I could see the shadows shift over his skin as a muscle rolled in his jaw.

Before my body caught up to my addled brain, I threw my left arm around Nico's shoulders and clung tightly to him. He gasped and went motionless. The warmth and solidity of his body was a lifeline extending down into the depths where I had sunk. In my chest, the flame flickered brighter.

"I didn't mean to yell," I whimpered into his neck, which smelled of the muskier salt of sweat as well as the slightly fishy salt of the sea. "I'm just—"

"I know, I know. You're alright. Just breathe." The ends of his hair whisked across my brow. He rubbed a whisper-soft circle on my back. I was beginning to grow used to the immensity of my pain, but unfortunately, the farm boy's touch was deadened, too.

I slowly let him go and leaned back against my pillow mountain, promising myself I would get another chance to feel his warm skin on mine. As I wiped my tears dry, I moved my hand back from my cheek. Blood smeared across my palm, bright and startling. I groaned. I'd felt like my cheek had been cut open because it *had*.

Nico sat on the edge of the bed, tapping his temple and then looking over his shoulder to study my face and soiled blouse with a grimace. Luna moved away from my side to sniff at Nico, plucking at the collar of his cheerful red shirt. I noticed several geode-shaped salt stains near the bottom of the fabric, and started to put together a picture of what had happened back at the estate. But the thought of Nico leaping into the sea to save me overwhelmed me so much that my thoughts turned me away from it.

Burying his hands in the gryphon's feathery mane, Nico murmured to them, "Can't believe how big you've gotten. And I thought you were full-grown before. You're positively massive, Luneyeux." My gryphon shut their eyes with a happy trill, extending their neck to give Nico a better angle to scratch.

An odd feeling settled over me as I watched them. Protective. Possessive, even. I pulled one of the smaller pillows near my elbow onto my lap and hugged it carefully against my chest. Some of the discomfort and sharp, stabbing pain eased off if I pressed it to my ribs while I inhaled.

Nico leaned toward the end of the bed and picked up a metal box painted with a red cross, which he set across his knees. He flipped open the box and rummaged through it, lifting out several paper packets while continuing to explore the rest of the contents. Luna helped him, sort of, hooking their talon through the center of a roll of medical tape and biting it experimentally. As soon as Nico made a noise of protest, Luna dropped it from their beak and let it fall back into the box.

Pulling up his knee and tucking it under himself, Nico turned to face me. With him slightly farther away like this, I could almost see his sepia irises more clearly. A pity it was to have been robbed of my spectacles at such an opportune time. I would have very much benefited from staring at Nico's sumptuous features up close right now.

"You oughta clean those wounds. Seawater isn't as antiseptic as it sounds. It's mostly fish shit."

I quirked an eyebrow. "How do you know all these medical tidbits? Are you a nurse, or...?"

"No, I just got a few certificates as a teenager," Nico answered vaguely. When he saw my other eyebrow go up, he clarified, "First Aid when I was twelve. Certified Nursing Assistant when I was sixteen. I never did anything with that one." He shrugged and added, "Maybe it was just a premonition."

"Well, then, I would like to be professionally nursed." I couldn't blame the shock anymore for how... coquettish my tone had come out. My cheeks heated up and I opened my mouth to apologize before I saw Nico's lips curve upward at the corners. He ripped open a packet, pulled out its contents, and unfolded a thin sheet.

I flinched, expecting the smell of alcohol followed by terrible stinging.

Nico *tsked* as if my expectation offended him. "This is antiseptic, not alcohol." Using his knuckle on my chin, he gently turned my face toward him. "It oughtn't sting overmuch. If it does, let me know and I'll stop straight away." He watched me, motionless, until I nodded my assent. He worked slowly, tenderly, and it hurt less than I'd expected.

The warmth in my heart threatened to incinerate me. I needed a distraction.

"So," I murmured, "do you work for Doctor Bennett? Is that how you—"

A short, hollow laugh escaped Nico. The sound was like when a student dropped a heavy textbook flat onto the hardwood floor. More like a clap of anger than amusement.

"Oh, sorry—" I began.

"No, no. Sorry." He shut his eyes for a moment to collect himself. Then he glanced at the first antiseptic sheet and crumpled it up, setting it aside. It was mostly scarlet. I quickly looked away as he opened a second packet and got back to work.

"My family farm is on the northern end of the Hazel Mountains. When I was fifteen, Stella and I were explorin' when we found a partially-cracked gryphon egg in the foothills. We brought it to the farm and set it up in my room with a heat lamp, just in case the kit was still alive inside. Sure enough, they hatched a week later. The three of us were inseparable for two years, makin' trouble of every kind." When he finished speaking, he blew gently on my cheek, and I couldn't help but squirm at the ticklish, intimate sensation.

"Then what?" I said, too quickly and too loudly. Luna glanced judgmentally at me before they stood up and began exploring the bedroom. They peeked into an open wardrobe, tail swishing between their ankles.

Nico looked awkwardly away. "Then they were taken away by your esteemed benefactor." His bitter sarcasm was obvious.

"Stolen?"

"Oh, no." His eyebrows rose and he rubbed his bandana irritably, as if the fabric were in his way. "They were paid for. Handsomely." In response, Luna twisted to look at Nico, silver eyes narrowing, hackles of feathers rising between their wings as their feelings on the matter became transparent.

I grimaced, then became still as Nico returned to my cheek with a square of gauze, taping it down. It was so close to my eye that I could see fuzzy white along the edge of my vision. That was an alarming realization. I was lucky the juniper hadn't taken my eye out.

"Your chest doesn't have gashes as deep as your face, but you could still afford to clean and dress them, too." Nico glanced down toward my blouse and then quickly back up to my face. "I want to go check downstairs to see if I can find you some Paracetamol at least. If you were gettin' treated in Hazberg or Northton, you'd probably get an opioid—"

"It's alright." I hugged my pillow and took a breath. "I prefer your treatment."

Nico's eyes widened. Color flamed bright across his cheeks before spreading to his ears and down to his throat. He swallowed and managed, "U–Um, thank you. I mean, well, no. It's my fault you're injured, so it's the..." He stood up, took a step back, and tripped on Luna's lion foot. They growled and nipped at his elbow, and he turned and patted their head and ears apologetically. "The least I can... you know."

I bit back a smile. "At the risk of inconveniencing you, I might need your help with getting my shirt off." I didn't think he could blush even more, but alas. "You see, I'm far-sighted, and anyway I'm not sure I can move my arms much..."

"Right, right, right, right." Nico dropped heavily back onto the edge of the bed. "You lost your glasses."

"A scholar's greatest crutch," I lamented. Fortunately, his eyes were downcast so he didn't see me lose my battle with a wide grin. I didn't mean to be cruel, teasing him like this. It was just so easy, and wonderfully distracting.

Nico reached for the loose hem, but I tapped the nape of my neck and told him, "There's a button back here." When he hummed in understanding, he scooted closer and reached around my shoulders. Only a foot or so of open air was between our faces, and it was thick and buzzing with potential.

He paused when he noticed my embroidery. Nico's brow wrinkled as he traced the silver feather with the pad of his pinky. "This is lovely. Did you do it?"

I glanced down. Without my glasses, the feather looked more like a seagull had dropped a blob of poo on my neck. "Ah, yes. Fortunately, it wasn't my best work."

Nico laughed quietly. "My mother would be furious to hear that." He lingered without proceeding for a few more moments, simply studying me, his worry clear without needing a sharp view of his features. "You must be in so much pain. I'm really sorry."

"Nobody made me jump on Luna like that," I commented. "Just... next time, talk to me."

"Right." He looked down before resuming the quest to get my shirt off. Nico's tongue poked out between his lips while he fumbled with the edges of my high collar. He managed to find the button and hook but tugged on them a few times without getting them to separate. To my delight, that meant he had to lean closer, his chest almost touching mine, to peer around my jaw and see what he was doing. I glanced at the nearby shadow standing over me and found Luna's rapt attention on us until I shot them a glare. Luna airplaned their ear tufts and haughtily resumed their bedroom exploration.

As Nico successfully unbuttoned my collar, he leaned back and deftly reached under my shirt, pulling the sleeve away from my armpit and slipping my arm free. Even the graze of his fingers on my bruises brought scalding-hot pain. But he made sure it was over quickly, seemingly having detached himself from his boyish embarrassment and activated more clinical precision.

He had my shirt halfway over my head when the floor creaked outside the door and Stella called, "Lux, are you in here? I found—" The door pushed open. Nico had one hand on my blouse and the other on my waist. Stella's eyes landed on us and the words died in her throat and froze on her face.

Nico jumped like a startled cat, leaping to his feet.

A sly smile spread over the teenager's face as she looked from me to her brother. She was wearing a short black dress and held two large chunks of pumpkin, seedy entrails dangling from them. "Wasting no time, ay, Nurse Co-Co?"

"Andullie!" Nico snapped, his face the same color as his shirt.

Annoyed, I struggled out of my blouse while I drawled, "Oh, look. If it isn't my executioner. I apologize I didn't perish in the sea."

Nico awkwardly rubbed his elbow.

Stella fell into a defensive slouch, jutting out her jaw. Her eyes slid down to survey my mangled chest before she cast her glare toward the ceiling. "Nuh-uh, I didn't—"

Luna interrupted her protests by snapping at the pumpkin in her hands. She yelped and swatted fearlessly at their beak, which brought them down upon her with more fervor. They used their powerful breast to shove her out of the room and into the hallway beyond, ignoring her protests. Her voice got fainter as they retreated elsewhere, the thumping on creaking floorboards suggesting there was a lower level.

Scowling, I used my pillow as a scoop to bring the First Aid kit closer. I could hardly see anything inside it, but Nico had left several more of the antiseptic packets out of place on the lid. I snatched one up, and when Nico began to apologize on Stella's behalf, I said coolly, "No need to cause yourself further humiliation on my account."

I didn't need to look at him to know I'd wounded him. It was all over his puppy-dog whimper. "O–Oh. You're not..."

"Might I have a glass of water?" My fingers shook and my right arm ached as I ripped open the packet and pulled out the cold, wet sheet inside. All of the scrapes on my chest looked like blobs of jam. This was going to be rough. I would have to skip bandaging them if I was doing this myself.

"Er...yeah. Of course. S–Sorry. For that. I wasn't..."

I remained silent, dabbing messily at the nearest scrape. Gods, it hurt.

When Nico realized I wasn't going to speak anymore, he edged toward the door. I heard the hissing start of another apology, but he was smart enough to swallow it without uttering the whole word.

He left me alone, leaving the door mostly open and descending the creaky staircase.

As soon as he was out of the room, I sighed heavily and dropped my head back. Rubbing my temples, I shut my eyes. Nico did *not* deserve more of my temper, and I wasn't even angry with *him*. But Luna had left me so quickly for Stella, and it had made me realize for the first time that a free gryphon meant they weren't just *mine*. Stella had known them since the first day they'd entered the world; I had known them in their prison.

My eyes started to burn. It was possible, now, that not only was my job at the Bennett estate abruptly at an end... I was about to lose my friend.

Intermediate Pining

I stood on a step halfway down the staircase while I tried to pull myself together and fight through the tightness in my throat. I pushed my bandana out of the way so I could furiously rub my sunburst scar until it burned from the friction and grounded me slightly.

Ackerleigh was allowed to act... angry and standoffish; he was injured and scared. But the rejection stung like a slap to the face. I urgently needed him not to be mad at me anymore—no matter what it took. I wouldn't just go get him water; I would find medicine, ice, and even give him food. I would sit there and watch his face until he was pleased again.

He had *hugged* me for gods' sake! Even *I* had been able to tell that he'd been flirting with me. He'd been blushing to high heavens when I was unbuttoning his collar. But something broke when Stella came in, and right now, I was convinced that whatever had been broken would be permanent.

Leaning heavily on the railing, I moved down the rest of the stairs and dragged my feet over the flagstones.

Stella stood by the counter with her back to me, shifting her weight from one foot to the other in an obvious show of anxiety, even though she didn't know I was there. Tap water streamed over a wire basket in the sink overflowing with yields from our garden: lusciously red tomatoes, several avocados, and a bundle of carrots longer than my hand. Outside the door, Lux was laying in the sunshine and gnawing on a zucchini, their wings fanned over their back among the flowers and grasses.

"So, what will your venue be?" Stella asked as she turned off the faucet.

"What?"

"For your wedding to the light-licker." Cackling, she dodged swiftly out of the path of my incoming fist. She went to a second basket, which was filled with cashews still in their apples, fresh peaches, and lemons and oranges. Thoughtfully, she glanced up at me with a hum. "It's kinda weird, isn't it? Every gamekeeper before this guy was a nobody. Selfish and brutish and dumb. And then him." She searched for words. "A... A fancy lad."

"Stella!" I exclaimed.

"What else do I call him?" she demanded. When I scoffed wordlessly, she continued, "He's got that fancy long hair and clothes that are nicer than Mother's, and all those fancy words... Honestly, why did Doctor Bennett suddenly pick him?"

I shrugged, although I'd been wondering the same thing for months. "One can only guess what that woman is thinking. Is there ice in the freezer?" Unable to stop moving, I went to the refrigerator and opened up the door on the top half. But the space inside was warm, and the ice cube tray sitting in the empty box had not so much as a puddle inside.

"Sorry," said Stella, "I just plugged it in when we got back. We weren't bringin' anything partiable with us before now, so..."

"Perishable," I correct in an annoyed grunt. At least I would bring him some water. The glasses were filmy with age but we had thoroughly cleaned them when we'd started staying here. The water from the tap had a yellow tinge of rust; hopefully Ackerleigh could stomach well water. "Paracetamol?"

Stella nodded and led me to the washroom. "I've been tryin' to figure out how I could use magíq for healin' since you asked me about the water in his lungs," she admitted. Guilt snagged in my belly at the reminder of how I'd lashed out at her. "Remember that part in Pascale Manon's autobiography where she said she could do that?"

"I remember." She'd made me read it to her dozens of times in the last decade. I practically had it memorized by now. "I just wish she'd explained *how* she could do it."

"Naw, she was too proud." Stella took an amber bottle out of the medicine cabinet over the sink and handed it to me.

"Just like another magíqon I know." I leaned down to look at her eye-to-eye. My intensity raised a wary wall over her expression, which hardened as a frown grew on her face. I softened the stony look by lightly poking her right check, then her left. "Look, Stel. *I* know you didn't mean to hurt him like that. But Ackerleigh *doesn't*. All he knows about you is that you told him he was going to die like the rest of 'em, and then you knocked him into the sea."

Stella opened her mouth and shut it. Defensiveness washed away into distress as her eyes turned glassy with tears. "Oh, my gods. What if Lux hates me now, too? Did you hear how they screamed for him? They're wild about him, and if they think *I* got him hurt—"

"Tranqui, Stella." I rubbed her shoulders. "Lux just needs to get used to us again. So do we. Y'all were both so young the last time you were together."

"They're *huge* now," she whispered, eyes round.

I laughed. "I know, aren't they? Bigger'n Peach."

She looked past me, her expression softening as she gazed outside. "This would be so awesome if we hadn't gotten that crush of yours hurt."

I straightened, grinding the heels of my hands into my eyes in hopes that it would make them stop burning. "I *know*," I groaned. "And he's—" I wanted to dump all my worries on her about him being mad at me, too, but before the words left my mouth, I suddenly connected the dots. Ackerleigh had called Stella his *executioner.* He was angry at *her.* He might have taken his frustration out on me after she left, but perhaps his rejection had been less about me than I'd thought at first.

"He's what?"

I shook my head slowly. "You know what, Stel? You let me take care of Ackerleigh right now."

She snorted. "Try not to enjoy that too much, Co-Co."

I pinched her bicep, making her yelp as I continued, "You worry about goin' outside and bondin' with our gryphon sibling. You and Lux have a lot of catchin' up to do." As she started off toward the back door, I grabbed her elbow and added, "This does *not* mean you're off the hook from givin' Ackerleigh a proper apology, Stella Marie."

"I *know*," she exclaimed. "But if he yells at me—"

"—Then you'll take it, and you won't give up," I interrupted. "Sometimes people can be angry without You're too young to stop givin' people the benefit of the doubt."

"None of the folks who've treated me like shit seemed to think I was too young to be a monster just a'cause I got magíq," muttered Stella, shaking me off her arm. "But yeah—fine. I'll try, d'ac? Leave me be." Her hands went up to card through her hair and sweep her thick locks back from her brow as she stalked away from me.

"You drive me insane," I called after her.

"Oh, I know!" Waving over her shoulder, she became a silhouette as she went through the open doorway and left the cottage.

With a heavy sigh, I armed myself with the water and pills before I climbed the stairs and went back to the white door in the middle of the hall. I knocked with one knuckle before letting myself inside.

Ackerleigh looked like a body prepared for a funeral, pale and laid out prettily against his pillows. His closed eyes fluttered when I entered but he did not wake. As I approached, I swallowed a groan at the mess he'd made of his chest. He had absolutely needed my help with cleaning those wounds, but he'd banished me anyway. Without me, all it looked like he'd managed to do was smear around his blood, so much so that even his fingers were stained red. All the bloody bruising made it seem like his whole ribcage was caved in. It made it seem like he was practically dead.

I frowned, quickly going to the bedside table and setting down the water and pills. I scooped up the used antiseptic sheets and wrappers, crumpling them and putting them in my pocket to discard downstairs. Then I reopened the First Aid box that sat closed by Ackerleigh's hip.

"Ackerleigh," I whispered, "stay asleep or—rest, whatever, but I'm gonna clean up your chest a bit." To avoid disturbing him, I knelt beside the bed instead of sitting. Grimacing at the smears of blood, I added graciously, "You... you did good." I prayed to the nearby god of the mountain that he'd just stay asleep as I mopped up his chest with swift, light dabs from a gauze pad. Then I used thin strips of medical tape to lightly cover the wounds that were still bleeding, promising myself I could do a more thorough job when he was awake.

Finally, I picked up a folded throw hanging over the headboard. I tested its softness on my cheek and, approving of the velvety fleece, I spread it out over Ackerleigh's bare legs.

Ackerleigh's softly whistling breath remained steady as I worked. It made me worry he was unconscious again until I noticed his hand twitch when I closed the kit again and set it aside on the floor. I lingered briefly, thinking of Mother's warning to avoid getting close to the gamekeeper.

I stifled a rueful laugh as I reached out and brushed Ackerleigh's flaxen fringe back from his bandaged cheek. I said a silent apology to Mother as I admitted to myself that my feelings had ignored her, warming to Ackerleigh and becoming a reckless and blazing attraction.

Survey of Midnight Conversations

Being woken up by the immensity of my own pain was not an enjoyable experience. One moment, I was in a comfortable state of unconsciousness. The next, I was convinced that I was being crushed beneath a boulder. I gasped, which was agonizing, and opened my eyes to near-darkness permeated by the milky glow of moonlight.

I was alone in a bedroom which smelled faintly of lavender, dust, and mold. It wasn't overly unpleasant—no more than the manor had been, anyway—but knowing that I wasn't here of my own volition made me feel uneasy and annoyed. When I shifted my weight from one hip to the other, my body felt stiff and tender. The memories from the day were lost in a dark fog of pain and chaos. I looked bleakly around the room.

My bare legs had been covered by a soft blue blanket, and my chest had been cleaned up and bandaged. I frowned, wishing I remembered Nico's return, but it seemed sleep—or unconsciousness—had claimed me the moment he'd left the room. At least that meant I hadn't done any permanent damage by getting snippy with him.

A cloudy glass and an amber bottle sat on the nightstand next to me; I fumbled awkwardly to spin off the lid while favoring my right hand. I tossed back a few too many pills with a splash of the room-temperature water. Iron coated my tongue. The city had spoiled me; I fought the urge to spit out the well water and forced myself to swallow.

"Toughen up, Sebring," I muttered. "You were used to Grandfather's well water back in the day." I grunted; the slight exhale of my breath was like an earthquake beneath my wounded ribs. My chest felt caved in like a gooseberry shell. Clearly there was no ice here for me... but I did have water. And I *was* a magíqon.

I chewed my lip. Presumably, Nico and his sister were sleeping somewhere nearby. Under typical circumstances, that would mean absolutely no magíq whatsoever. But the pain was unbearable, and thanks to my magíq lessons with Luna, freezing water would not be much of a challenge.

With one eye on the doorway, I dipped my fingers into my water glass. Catlike, I lifted them out and flicked them at my ribs while commanding the water to transform, sending all the tiny molecules crashing together into a dense and tidy pattern. Droplets splattered my skin before freezing to it, prickling me with blessed cold.

This would work. But I needed *way* more water.

I rolled out of bed and onto my feet. My shorts were crusty with salt, and my legs were goose-bumped. To combat the darkness and the cold, I snapped weakly with my left hand until a small, flickering flame grew from my fingertips. The warmth was welcome, and it gave me enough light to navigate.

I leaned my left hip into the wall as I took the stairs down slowly, grateful that they didn't make a sound under my bare feet. It appeared that I was in a quaint little cottage with packed stone walls and tidy flagstones underfoot adorned with a number of threadbare rugs. Herbs and dried flowers dangled from the low, exposed rafters that were decorated with spiderwebs like some macabre bunting.

"Could be cute, under better circumstances," I murmured, tossing my little spark into the hearth in the center of the room. The lick of fire hastily bit into a burned-up log before it extinguished itself, turning into a curl of smoke.

A happy trill preceded Luna as they trotted through the open back door, blinking their moon-eyes at me with their ear tufts eagerly erect. They brought in a cloak of cool night air that tasted like sweetgrass and fertile soil. Excited starbursts of violet electricity gathered in their mane, which puffed up as they rushed toward me.

We all but crashed into each other. I buried my face in their fluffy neck, smelling mountain freshness and sun-warmed skin beneath their feathers. Luna gripped me tightly with their talons, and I could sense their affection within our synchronizing heartbeats. Not letting me go, Luna curled around me and began grooming my dirty hair with such fervor that my neck bent like a palm tree.

"Hey, it's alright. I'll be alright." Laughing softly, I butted my head into their chin. "But who are you, hm? Why didn't I realize you had your own name? The siblings call you... Lux, which is short for Luneyeux?" I said the name with a giggle. Luneyeux translated to Mooneyes, which seemed quite on the nose. Then again, I had named the gryphon Luna for the same reason. "Which do you prefer?"

The gryphon pulled back, their beak almost touching my nose. Their lustrous eyes searched my face before their head cocked slightly. "All," they croaked, bobbing their head.

I frowned, unsatisfied. "I appreciate that, but... I don't know. I think I feel guilty now. To call you by a different name than your family."

The gryphon did not appear to share my concern, simply curling the corners of their gape in a contented smile.

"Alright then. Back to the matter at hand, I suppose. I am going to make some ice to coat my injury."

Luna bobbed their head in agreement. "Ice."

"Shall I put it straight over these bandages? I don't think it matters; my chest is a horrible mess."

"Blood," croaked Luna ominously.

"Yes, thank you." Untangling from the gryphon, I turned on the water faucet. Cool water began to fill my cupped hands. Luna leaned over me, beak poking lightly into my brow as they peered into the sink.

I took the slowest, deepest breath I could manage. One hand remained under the flow from the faucet. My fingers flexed, thumbs touching. My right hand came up against the deepest bruise on my rib, which was so tender it felt like an open wound. When there was a complete connection between the water to my injury, I let a breath out from my lips that willed a change to occur. Liquid turned to mist, and then to the tiniest Milky Way of sleet that glinted like jewels beneath the moonlight spilling in from the window. When the dappling of ice settled on my ribs, I asked it to grow, condense, gather its friends from the stream of glowing water ribboning between my fingers. Unlike playful wind and wildfire, water was kind and attentive, like a cat's tail curling around your ankles.

The swirling rope of water from the faucet gathered on my bruising and turned into an obscure breastplate: thick, solid, opaque in the manner of decorative antique glass.

My body temperature plummeted. A shiver tore through me, goosebumps pinching my battered torso. I allowed the ice to cleave to my skin. Slowly, sensations deadened, wrapping me in a blissfully numb cloak.

"Lunix," I said with chattering teeth. "How about I call you L-L-Lunix? It almost s-s-sounds the same as Luneyeux..."

Something moved on the other side of the gryphon's folded wings. My heart stopped, and an anxious wheeze rasped through my throat.

I stood on my toes, peering over Lunix's curtain of feathers. "Hello?"

The lanky teenage girl froze at the sound of my voice, her right foot on the bottom step.

"Stella?" I whispered.

Hunched over, Stella cleared her throat. "Go back to sleep," she sang, "this is a dre-e-e-am..." As she drew out the final word to sound like she was a specter, she turned around, wiggling her fingers.

Lunix took that as an invitation, slinking over to her and nipping at her fingertips.

Mutely, I strode after them and headed swiftly toward the stairs. If I simply refused to engage with her—

Stella stepped into my path. "Hey, uh, actually—I wanted to say..."

"No!" I made a sharp dismissive gesture. "Nope. I'm not int-t-erested." I realized that she was actually taller than me, meaning I had to glare *up* at her as I snapped, "Please move. You t-tried to kill me mere hours ago, and n-now look at me."

Stella flapped her arms, expression contorting. "That was an accident!" she whined. Her gaze skimmed my form until it came to rest on the icy breastplate I'd made for myself. She went perfectly still, eyes widening.

I'd thought she had seen me doing magíq at the sink. So then why did she look so shocked? Regardless—I could play dumb. I *had* to play dumb. Every survival instinct in my body was screaming at me to escape this interaction. I had not endured twenty-seven years living in secret as a magíqon only to have this... this feral child stumble upon this revelation.

I frowned and said coldly, "Why are you staring at me?"

She pointed a trembling finger at my chest. "That's magíq."

Uneasily, I curled my arm around my ribs. Despite my need to find a way out of this, I was completely at a loss for words.

Stella's chest heaved with quick, shallow breaths as she returned her gaze to my face. "Must... Must've been Lux, right?" She gave an awkward, false laugh.

I made a face. "N—"

As soon as my tongue hit the back of my teeth, Stella's complexion paled.

"Oh," I breathed. She'd known it hadn't been the gryphon who froze my chest. She'd been trying to give me an excuse. She'd realized I was a magíqon but didn't want to out me. But what would motivate that—

The memory of a fireball crashing through the grate over the courtyard returned to my mind as if I were watching it all over again. A little detail, another layer of the image, slotted into place: Stella was behind the explosion of magíq, grinning triumphantly as her own power opened up the gryphon's path to freedom.

I gasped, "Oh!"

Stella was a magíqon.

"Oh, great slumbering gods." A humorless laugh spasmed through me; I squeezed the bridge of my nose. "I... I can't believe this." I clutched my ribs. My heart was pounding so loudly in my ears that I was afraid I was going to pass out.

Stella stared at me, eyes gleaming, her lips moving silently. Finally, she blinked, tapped her own ribcage, and murmured, "That's *your* ice."

"I—" My throat closed up, and my shallow breathing sent shocks of pain through my chest. There was no way I could say the words. There was no way I could admit to *her* that my blood was blessed by the gods as well.

I was jolted out of my panic by Lunix's curved beak tapping my shoulder before the gryphon nuzzled my neck. Their rumbling purr vibrated my teeth. Stella's gaze softened as it settled on Lunix.

I squeezed my eyes closed for a moment, submerging my hand in Lunix's silky plumage. With a careful breath, I opened my eyes, met Stella's hopeful gaze, and admitted quietly, "Yes, Stella, I am a magíqon." My stomach heaved, making me choke on a gag. I absolutely had to pace. "*Gods*," I spat, "that feels *mad* to say aloud." I stalked toward the circular stained glass window in the front door as I intoned, "I can certainly confess that these are not the circumstances under which I ever hoped to meet another magíqon... I hoped it would be another scholar, someone like Pascale Manon—"

"P-Pascale Manon is my hero."

I froze. Stella's voice was laden with emotion. Slowly I looked toward the girl. Her features were contorted, and tears streamed down her cheeks. Despite my deep mistrust and frustration with her, my heart betrayed a twinge of empathy.

"I've always wanted t' meet another magíqon, too," Stella wept, "and I almost killed ya!" She dropped her face into her hands and sank onto the bottom step, pulling her knees into her chest. "I'm s-sorry I'm not wh-what you wanted, not like Pascale, or..." Her fingers were flexed and probed her cheeks like claws. She rocked forward, then back, then forward. For several beats, she sobbed wordlessly. Callous as it made me seem, I glanced at the dark stairwell behind her with an uneasy frown. If she woke Nico up, and he found us and demanded an explanation, that would be it. I would combust, burn up, and cease to exist.

Stella caught her breath, sniffling. She lifted her head, swiping away the hair that had plastered her soaked skin. "You're gonna hate me forever a'cause of how nasty I was to you, just like Nico said, and w-we'll be enemies and start another Great Battle, a-a-and..."

"Oh, Stella... Stella, stop." I caught the girl's arm and lifted her off the stairs, selfishly moving her into the living room so we wouldn't wake Nico. Stella was pliable and limp as I set her on the couch near the hearth. The cushions were hard and unforgiving as I sat beside her.

"Yes, I am angry and very injured," I began, prompting another wet sob from Stella, "and you will have to allow me the right to be bitter and petty, because I am quite good at that..."

"Me too!" Stella choked.

I swallowed a hysterical laugh and rubbed my temple. "But as far as we know, we could be the only living magíqon in all of Deubrise. The gods have brought us crashing into one another and I must believe that's for good reason."

Stella nodded jerkily in agreement, pulling the collar of her dress over her chin and using it to wipe her face. "I'm s-sorry. I'm sorry I'm not a better magíqon—"

"Hush. No." I patted her arm. "No, Stella... I'm sorry. That was unkind of me."

"I'm used to it." She smoothed her hair between her hands, over and over again, restarting at her roots and running her hands down to the tips before starting over again at the roots.

I stifled a groan. This feral child seemed *deeply* wounded. I set my hand on her shoulder, which, tragically, made her flinch. "Look," I said thinly, "I am in desperate need of more sleep. Under ordinary circumstances, I would have many questions for you. Including how you directed *that* much fire today... To be frank, I would be positively terrified of utilizing such a volatile element to such a magnitude, but—"

"I don't understand half the stuff you're sayin'," Stella interrupted. "I stopped goin' to school at fourteen." She swallowed hard and then met my eyes as fresh tears welled along her bottom lashes. "Everyone hated my magíq and thought I was a monster. S... So does my Pa."

Lunix appeared behind us and dropped their chin on the back of the couch, cheeping softly. Their ear tufts tickled my temple. Stella threw her arms around the gryphon's head, burying her face in a bed of downy feathers and provoking a croaking purr from Lunix.

"I wish you'da been there, Lux," murmured Stella. "Bein' all alone as a magíqon, I sorta started thinkin' everyone must be right about me."

I pressed my lips together, stroking the leaf-shaped feathers of Lunix's wing draping over us. "No, Stella. They aren't right about you." A soft pattering began on the large picture window across from us. Raindrops glinted as they trickled down the glass, like starlight against a midnight backdrop.

"Wasn't it the same for you?" Stella asked, looking up with her expression almost hopeful, as if she needed that commiseration. Her eyes followed every stroke of my hand on Lunix's wing.

"No." The word came out as wobbly as a teardrop balanced on an eyelash. "I was too afraid to tell anyone. Nobody knew." I smiled at the gryphon when they turned toward me. I could see myself reflected in their full-moon gaze, which was warm with adoration. "Until Lunix."

Stella cocked her head. "Lunix..."

"You called them Luneyeux, right?" When Stella nodded, I explained, "I'd been calling them Luna. They refuse to have an opinion on the matter, so I combined them…"

Thunder rumbled outside. Stella jumped at Lunix's immediate cry of horror. The gryphon jammed their head into the side of my neck, cowering.

I *tsked* in worry and stood up, coming around the couch to hug them tightly with my left arm. I moved my right only at the elbow so as to not disturb my ribs, and stroked Lunix's ear tufts. "Come now, chaton. You've made it through two thunderstorms with me already. And you're inside for this one!"

Lunix shook their head and hid their eyes in the crook of my shoulder. "Loud, loud, loud," they croaked.

Worry crowded Stella's face as she clambered off the couch, but she didn't approach us. Instead she hung back by the stairwell, wringing her hands.

"How about you come upstairs, Lunix?" I scratched my fingers against the bristly feathers around their cere and managed to get them to purr, though they stopped again when more thunder rumbled faintly around us. "There are heaps of pillows and lots of fuzzy blankets. You can sleep right next to me."

Stella began indignantly, "Lux would never—"

Lunix nudged me toward the stairs, staying so close to my side that their scaly front legs tangled in mine and almost tripped me.

Dumbfounded, Stella stepped aside and watched me pass. Lunix followed me upstairs with their head against my hip. I paused at the top landing to allow myself the chance to catch my breath.

Another roll of thunder rattled the eaves. Lunix crouched and stuck their head between my knees. I haltingly moved toward the bedroom I'd been put in, second from the leftmost end of the hall.

"Wait." Stella's voice was soft and meek. I glanced at her over my shoulder.

The other magiqon was illuminated by a violet cluster of electricity sitting in her hands. It fizzled and pulsed, rootlike tendrils of power reaching toward me and jumping onto the tuft of Lunix's tail. My eyes slowly widened. Over our heads, the bulb in the light fixture flickered on and off several times. Stella's hair was standing on end, and a swipe of my hand over the crown of my head told me that mine was, too.

In the dancing, bouncing light, Stella jerked her chin at the doorway farthest on the right. "That room's bigger." She shrugged, awkwardly looking away. "I... I was being petty, too."

I narrowed my eyes. "You don't say." I was about to turn around and leave her standing alone with her gorgeous ball of electric magíq, but I paused and added more gently, "That electricity is very beautiful. Goodnight, Stella."

Without needing to be invited, Lunix hurried after me into the room at the end of the hall. The rain blotted out the moonlight, and the room was blanketed by inky darkness. I paused to let my eyes adjust while stroking Lunix's head. Stella's violet light faded from the hallway behind me, and I heard a door click softly shut at the other end of the hall.

I tried to imagine how she would go about dispelling such a massive amount of electricity. One would think that, especially during a storm, you could offer it back to the clouds. Maybe this very moment, she was opening the window with her foot and throwing it outside like a rugby ball. I smirked at the mental image. That electric ball was of such a size and under such careful control that her magíq had to have been much more sophisticated and well-developed than my own. Perhaps she used methods of dispersion I didn't even know.

"I'm not proud to be bested by someone ten years my junior," I told Lunix as I shuffled across a fuzzy rug toward an arched window. "But it serves me right, I suppose, since I've been hiding from it all this time and she hasn't." I reached for the dangling cord of a table lamp under the window, but as soon as my fingers got close, a shock leapt forth and snapped against my skin with a bright flash of purple. I yanked my arm back with a scowl, shaking out my hand. "That's not nice."

Glancing at the ceiling, I saw criss-crossing string lights and searched for the end of their cord instead, plugging it into an outlet while touching the wall. Though still fluffed up with fear, Lunix looked at the lights in relief and leaned into my hand when I stroked their cheek.

I turned back to the blankets on the very large, very plush bed. A dozen fluffy pillows piled against the headboard. I climbed into bed, wrapped an extra blanket around my shoulders, and curled up on my side. A shag of dried lavender hung over my head, still lightly fragrant.

The storm was quiet, calm even. Just rain, pattering against the cottage in a way that was quite cozy and soothing. Nevertheless, Lunix gazed anxiously out the window again as rain tapped the glass.

"Now, then, my friend..." I breathed out the ésprit from my lungs so that my words floated through the air between me and Lunix like a butterfly; the fluff on their cheek fluttered as it reached them. Lunix slid their gaze away from the window to look at me. They croaked softly.

"We both need to rest, and this bed has room for you. Come on, then. Come and get cozy with me." Lunix croaked again, dubiously flicking their ear tufts back. "Chaton," I said sternly.

Grumbling, Lunix came closer, giving me a lingering glare that only served to make me smile. They snuffled the slightly musty sheets, stepping onto the bed one foot at a time. They then loomed over me with wings slightly spread, pawing at the blankets piled on me. Turning several times like a dog, they finally laid down, truly swallowing every inch of the mattress I gave them. And still jamming their elbow into my stomach. I grunted, and Lunix shifted and tucked themself in like a cat with all their paws underneath them and tail curled around my hip. One wing draped over me, brushing my bandaged cheek, and the other curtained over the edge of the bed.

"There you go." I patted their beak. "How's that?"

"Cozy," Lunix croaked.

I grinned. "Shall I tell you a bedtime story?" Lunix bobbed their head. "My grandfather always told me stories where I starred as a clever wizard undermining a wicked king. He'd be disappointed to see how things worked out with President Brandon, don't you think?" Lunix's eyes searched my face; they blinked slowly, catlike. It was a soothing reminder that I was as far from that wicked man as I could ever be.

I smiled, tucking the blankets under my chin, burrowing into the pillows. "If you were an adventurer, I'd take you just as you are. You needn't be human. You're a brilliant little hero, who's been trapped in a castle by the wicked Doctor Bennett who thinks her whims are more precious than yours. You dreamt of escape and you dreamt of the companions from your childhood." The gryphon's blinking slowed. "As dreams often do, you beckoned the companions with the strength of your yearning, and finally, finally, finally... one day you were free."

Lunix's eyes slid shut.

"What's in your future, we don't know yet." My voice was as soft as the rain. "What your wild heart will bring you is unknown. What your companions will do with you or me now I can only hope will be compassionate and noble. May they strive for you to be free, as I will. You deserve the wide-open world, Lunix."

Intermediate Selfishness

The shower in the claw-footed tub didn't get as hot as I wanted, but it was cleansing all the same. It stripped the salt from my hair, my mouth, my ears. I felt slippery and scrubbed clean by the time I spun the helm-shaped knobs off. I stood in the dreamy shadows cast by the morning light diffusing through the wraparound shower curtain, circling my scar with my pinky finger.

I was perseverating on contradictory truths. On the one hand, Ackerleigh was here, under my roof! I swore I could feel his presence, like the glow of dawn after the longest night.

On the other hand, the only reason Ackerleigh was here was due to my spectacular failure to protect both him and Lux. That would live in my conscience forever. I was lucky he hadn't died, and I was lucky he hadn't cursed my name and spat in my face after he survived that fall.

Deciding I'd spend forever making it up for him was easy enough. Today, for starters, my one objective was to provide for his comfort however I could. I would be at his beck and call. I would collect every moment with him like sea glass in my pockets.

I was ashamed by the chatter of the silly, sentimental feelings inside me. Nevertheless, a fragile hope kindled in my chest.

I toweled off and dressed in some corduroy trousers, clipped on my suspenders, and pulled them over the shoulders of my striped henley. I slipped on a fluffy cardigan with technicolored sleeves, easy to take off if the sun came out, but cozy for now in the soft light of dawn.

When I left the washroom, I smelled the nutty scent of coffee brewing from the merrily gurgling chrome coffee maker by the back door. Stella was bouncing on her heels as she moved around the kitchen, humming an off-key tune and stopping every minute or two to sip coffee from a hand-thrown mug.

In the living room, a roughly person-shaped mound sat on the couch, thoroughly wrapped up in multiple blankets. Coiled around them was the dozing gryphon, hindquarters on the floor and wings spread elegantly across the couch and coffee table. They rested their head in the lap of the blanket mound, and slitted open one platinum eye to acknowledge my presence.

I smiled faintly and went up to my sister, who spun around when I tugged on a lock of her hair.

"Oh, finally," sighed Stella. "Thought you were gonna use up all our hot water in there. You weren't gettin' weird in there, were ya? We all have to share that—"

"Shut *up!*" I hissed, but she had danced out of my reach before I could hit her.

Stella swept her hair over her shoulders and gave me a cheeky, uncharacteristically happy grin. Her tawny skin and honey-kissed hair seemed to glow in the diffused light of the kitchen. She looked amazing. Renewed.

"What happened to *you?*" I grunted, cocking an eyebrow. Quizzical, Stella tilted her head. I kept a sidelong eye on her as I backed out of the kitchen, returning to the couch. It was probably just being around Lux again, I assured myself. The gryphon and my magiqon sister often seemed to energize each other, as if their gods-blessed blood vibrated together like harmonizing notes on a violin.

When I came into view of the mustard-yellow couch, Lux stretched their neck up with a sleepy trill. I knelt in front of the couch and scratched Lux's fluffy cheeks with both hands. They nibbled on my ear and plucked at my curls as I murmured sweetly to them, forgetting the years that had passed without them. It was like they were a kit again—tender and... incessant!

I groaned, "Lux, c'mon, quit bitin'!" I pulled on their lower mandible, freeing my curl from the point of their beak. "You haven't changed a bit."

Blankets shuffled and drew my attention as Ackerleigh lowered his shroud and gave me a weary, pained smile. A light blue coffee mug emerged from the fold; Ackerleigh raised it to his rosy lips, sipping quietly. Amusement lit in his smoky gray eyes as Lux's jaw clamped down on the strap of my suspender; they began determinedly gnawing on the leather.

"Lux!" I groaned, shoving their forehead. "Get outta here. Go bother Stella."

Immediately compliant, Lux unwound themself from their protective position around Ackerleigh, gracefully rising to their feet. They raised their wings to tuck them against their back and slunk around the side of the couch. Right before they got out of reach, their tail whipped sharply and lashed me squarely in the face.

"Oh, gods!" yelped Ackerleigh, clamping his hand over his mouth to stifle a musical giggle. "Are you alright?"

Sighing heavily, I climbed to my feet before giving Ackerleigh a reassuring smile. "Tragically, I'm used to their harassment." I edged around the coffee table to drop into the armchair across from Ackerleigh. Sharp springs prodded my thighs; I shifted several times in quick succession to try to make the cushion more comfortable, to no avail. "And I'm not the one who's been stolen away and beat up. How are you feeling?"

Ackerleigh gazed thoughtfully at me for a moment, his brow wrinkling. "I feel dazed," he answered finally. "A bit numb. What's not numb is... dreadful."

My index finger flew to my scar, tap-tap-tapping as I swallowed hard. I felt my body disconnect from the heavy rush of guilt, shame, and frustration to hide behind my clinical knowledge. "Honestly, medically speakin', you oughta be restin' in bed and sleepin' for the next couple a days..."

Ackerleigh looked down. He tightened his blanket around himself. "I am having trouble relaxing, it seems. My mind is too busy." His eyes fluttered closed. The edge of a pillow poked out from under his blanket; he hugged it to his chest as he took a measured breath. Uneasily, he used his thumb knuckle to rub his bottom lip.

Stella stalked around the hearth and straight up to Ackerleigh. "Here." She held out a haunch of sourdough smeared with mashed avocado, as well as a bowl of sliced peaches.

Ackerleigh blinked at the offering. For a moment, I half expected him to slap it out of her hand. Instead, he gave her a generous smile. "That looks amazing. But I'm afraid I'm quite nauseous. Perhaps a bit later?"

"Yeah." Stella shrugged. "Lemme know." She took a big bite of the bread and avocado before holding it out to me. When I shook my head, she blew a raspberry at me and stalked back into the kitchen.

Ackerleigh watched her go with quiet amusement. All of the hostility that I had felt between them yesterday was gone, which had me reeling. Stella was happy—and Ackerleigh was being kind to her, even patient. Was that... also because of Lux or something? The gryphon clearly adored them both, but...

I frowned, shaking off the strange sensation that I'd missed something.

Ackerleigh was already watching me when I returned my gaze to him, which almost made me jump right out of my chair. Being noticed was not a common experience for me. I wetted my lips, gathered my courage, and asked calmly, "So, may I ask... what is your mind so busy with?"

Ackerleigh swallowed. He looked away for a moment, and when his gaze returned to me, there was something mournful and apologetic in his face. "I need to go back to the estate."

Something smashed onto the floor in the kitchen, accompanied by my sister's yelp of alarm. Fear jolted down my spine, startled by the noise and also by the terrible sentence that came out of the gamekeeper's mouth.

Stella stomped around the hearth to stand in front of Ackerleigh, planting her fist on her popped-out hip. "I'm sorry, but it *sounds* like you just said you need to go *back* there, andullie."

"Stella!" I snapped, sharp and loud as a tree rent in two by a lightning strike. Both Ackerleigh and Stella jumped.

Lux's head appeared behind Stella, poking around the hearth and giving me a stern look. "Soft," they croaked. Stella's stony glare held similar energy.

My panic had transformed into fury, so I forced myself to pause and squeeze my eyes closed. In all the scenarios my anxious brain had offered up about Ackerleigh's fate since the previous day, this was not one of them. Swallowing hard, I asked without looking, "What is it you need there?"

Ackerleigh's voice trembled when he replied, "Um, well, there's the cat I was watching, Dove. And... I... I was writing. I was documenting every day I had with Luna—I mean, Lunix, and the passages were quite... personal in nature."

"Oh ma-a-a-n," cried Stella. She slapped her forehead. The display *had* to be sarcastic. Afraid to reprimand her again, I finally stole a glance at Ackerleigh.

A scarlet blush had brightened Ackerleigh's fair features. "I do understand the risk—"

I pushed down my panic as hard as I could until all it did was make my voice crack. "Do you?"

Ackerleigh remained silent, watching me.

"You were meant to make daily phone calls to Doctor Bennett's answering machine, correct?" When he nodded, I continued, "I can assure you someone was sent to the estate immediately yesterday when you failed to report. They have quite an efficient system for replacing gamekeepers, you know. What they'll do when they discover that it's their *gryphon* that's missing is bound to be much more serious. In fact—" An edge of hysteria increased my volume— "we probably ain't even safe *here*. If they start looking for us... from—from the farm—then they'll... Well, we're here on borrowed time, and..."

"Nico," Stella interrupted, straightening and fixing me with a look that made her resemblance to Mother increase. She pushed up a slipping strap of her black, patched-up shortalls. "You're spiralin'."

"Aren't *you?*" I exclaimed, rearing to my feet and stalking toward the front door. I raked my hand through my curls before I remembered they were soaking wet. Annoyed, I shook the moisture off my hand and rubbed my scar so hard it ached. "If we try to go back, Doctor Bennett's people are gonna be there, waitin' to drop the shackles on all three of us. Waitin' to drop Lux back into prison."

"Will they?" Stella asked calmly.

I rounded on her. "What has gotten into you? Why are you suddenly on his—" I bit my tongue.

As soon as I paused, Ackerleigh lowered his feet from the couch and stood up, letting the blankets fall away from his shoulders. He padded over to me, clutching his round throw pillow to his chest and wearing nothing but his salt-stained shorts.

Somehow, his vulnerability sobered me abruptly. I turned to face him fully, raising my hands as if petitioning him to change his mind.

Ackerleigh's head twitched to the side. "You don't understand," he said softly, urgently. "I'm a scholar. The subjects I wrote about... and... and everything I own is there. Everything I've ever written is there. I don't want to cause trouble. I just need to go back. Just to get my belongings. And Dove."

Stella clutched her elbow and tilted her head. "And then what?"

Ackerleigh wetted his lips. "I'm staying with Lunix."

I rubbed my scar, my gaze skimming over the man's slim shoulders. I thought of the glasses he should be wearing, sunk to the bottom of the sea. And the bruises on him, which were my fault. If he was so set on going back to the estate, how could I justify allowing him to return here afterward? We didn't know how long we'd have food, or how long we'd last before Doctor Bennett tracked us down—*if* she didn't catch us while getting Ackerleigh's things.

It was entirely wrong to be casting out this man when I finally had the chance to draw him in. But letting him stay here would be motivated primarily by selfishness. My own desires. If I'd learned anything in life, it was that I wasn't allowed to chase my own dreams. And that was all this was: a dream.

I shook my head, resolute. "If we're goin' back to the estate, then I'm leavin' you there and you're goin' home." Ackerleigh flinched but I added forcefully, "I'm not gettin' you six ways of tangled up with us if I can help it. Trust me, you don't want that."

The gravity of our conversation was disrupted by Lux when they stuck their beak into a cobweb-dense corner and erupted into an enormous sneeze. Stella cried out in protest and worry, hurrying to them with murmured chastisement and concern.

"*Home?*" Ackerleigh stared blankly at me. He was silent for a while. I wasn't sure he'd elaborate. When he spoke again, his voice trembled at the edges, as if his bruised ribs had broken his heart. "There's no such place for me to go." He looked past me, toward the gryphon. "Don't you understand? Lunix is my home now."

SURVEY OF A GENTLEMAN

Anxiety turned my empty stomach into knots while I waited for Claire to answer the phone, hunched over the cradle. My foot tapped wildly in time with the ringing. I sat next to a huge window overlooking the rolling hills and candy-colored lupin and tried to allow the scenery to quell my mounting panic.

What was I thinking? Going back to the estate just because of my damned notebook? In it were dozens of confessions speaking of my own magíq, though, and if that notebook wound up right in Doctor Bennett's own hands... No. I simply could not allow that to happen. I hadn't worked this hard for twenty-seven years to hide away my magíq only for it to be revealed to someone as prominent as she, by my own foolish hand.

The most horrible part was that, if Stella hadn't realized what I was trying to protect and hadn't spoken to a frantic Nico on my behalf, I wasn't sure I'd even have convinced him I needed to go back.

And how was I meant to go back, anyway? Simply climb into his noisy red truck and politely sit in the passenger seat while he drove me to what he seemed to think was a suicide mission? Yet my alternative was... my gryphon. Lunix.

"Mathilda Porter speaking."

I jumped, having forgotten I was waiting on the phone. "Mathilda? Hello, I'm so sorry I had to call you at your office, but is Claire with you? I called your house and her office to try to reach her—"

"Ackerleigh? Is that you, baby? It's alright. She's with me. Are you alright? I've never heard you sound so—"

Mathilda's alto voice was cut off abruptly. In its place, Claire demanded hoarsely, "Ackerleigh? What's the matter? What's wrong?"

How quickly hearing her voice unwound my already fraying calm and brought tears bursting from my eyes. I swallowed painfully around the lump in my throat. "Oh, things, um, could be worse, I suppose. Could certainly be better. I'm..." I glanced out the window. "I'm not at the estate anymore, and... Well, I'm afraid I'm quite injured. I think I have a broken rib." I ran my finger over my tender chest and amended through a swelling cry, "Ribs."

"Excuse me?" Claire exclaimed. "What in the heavens? What are you talking about? Ackerleigh, tell me what happened right now or so help me—"

"N-Nico, you know, he had a very noble plan to... free my gryphon, and, well, things got a bit chaotic there and I ended up... Well, I don't remember a lot of it and I was unconscious when we got here..."

"*Unconscious?*"

I pushed onward, my words jumbling together in my haste to get through it. "But yes, I'm going to have to go back to the estate now, you see, because I left my notebook there... I broke my own rules of research, too, and I was sort of using it like a journal, so it's quite, ehm... radical, you could say."

"Oh, no." Claire swore. "It'll make you look like you were involved."

That was less of a concern to me as I'd been halfway through a paragraph when the fireball had struck; it was obvious I hadn't been part of the heist. Still, it was certainly lending itself to the impression that I was not the fastidious and put-together person I thought I was.

"Leigh, you listen here. You need to get yourself back to your car, pack up your stuff, and come back to Laurier. You can live with me and Matty and I don't care if we never see a cent from you. I just need you safe—" She choked. "A broken rib? Good gods, darling. Just come home."

I smeared my face dry with my wrist. "I'm sorry, Claire, but it's not that easy. Not with my gryphon."

"Ackerleigh, I know how much that gryphon means to you, but nothing should be worth your safety."

She was so wrong it wasn't even worth arguing. I said instead, "I need to get my things back. Past that, I don't know what'll happen."

"Wait, are you going back now?" Claire demanded, her tone changing. "Today?"

"Yes, I believe I got Nico to agree to taking me back there. If I come back here, I'll call you tonight, alright?"

Claire paused. I could hear Mathilda protesting in the background. Claire said sternly, "Be careful, alright? Whatever you do."

"I'll do my best," I said, frowning at my ribs, "though I'm not sure I'm as careful as I thought."

Claire hummed with dismay. "I love you, Leigh. Talk later."

Floorboards creaked behind me. I jumped to my feet, dropping the phone onto its cradle and spinning to face the stairwell.

Nico balanced between the top landing and the step below, hands up, shaking his head frantically. "Sorry, I promise I wasn't eavesdropping—" A blotchy blush colored his cheeks. He tapped his index finger several times against a large, starburst-shaped scar over his temple. I'd never gotten to see it before, since he'd generally hid it under a bandana. As soon as I noticed his gesture, he made a fist and shoved his hand into his pocket. The hair surrounding the scar had been shaved down into a neatly manicured section, likely to avoid the appearance of a bald spot where his scar was. It gave him a roguish appearance that every other part of his nature otherwise contradicted.

Nico went on rambling, "And anyway, you were talkin' so softly I couldn't hear a word—and besides, I wouldn'ta wanted to, what with you bein' entitled to your privacy..." He loudly cleared his throat, blushing brighter. "I—I respect that, you know, and you weren't s'posed to be involved in any of this anyway..."

"Thank you," I said seriously, although his charming blush had me fighting down a grin. It was obvious he fancied me, but unlike with past flames, I didn't feel the need to shrink in his presence. His deference was empowering, and his shy and passive demeanor made me more confident.

I'd met a fair number of men with powerful physiques like Nico. They often dressed to emphasize their bodies and remind everyone how mighty they were. People like President Brandon used their size as a threat.

Nico was not like them. He gave the impression that his body was a natural consequence of a hardy and physical lifestyle, and he was otherwise ruled by humility and care. Nico struck me slightly the same way this cottage did. He looked half-formed by the wild mountains, half-formed in the manner of a sophisticated city street made from cobblestones and quaintly matching homes.

I knew I'd only met him a handful of times. I knew very little about him at all, actually. But the few times I had met him, he'd been carefully put together—in an ocky way, but put together nonetheless. Bright colors, slim fits, and cozy fabrics seemed to drive his fashion choices. I'd frequently found myself hoping he'd show up wearing his tiny cut-off shorts that let me admire his muscular, tan thighs and his perfect rear.

I had no complaints about his clothing choices for today, though, either. He'd changed into clingy corduroy trousers with patched knees and cuffed hems. They were hooked to suspenders that strained over a henley striped in yellow and white, unbuttoned past the hollow of his throat. He had his curls tied up on the back of his head in a lively little bun. There was a sprinkle of dark stubble on his cheeks, and I had the unhinged urge to rub my face against it.

Nico added after my distracted silence, "I'm ready to go back to the estate whenever you are. That's why I came lookin' for ya."

I roused myself from my admiration with a slight nod. "I see. Well, I don't mean to be difficult, but I cannot tolerate the discomfort of going out in public looking the way I do." Wearing wrinkled shorts, covered in bruises and bandages... I looked halfway to the grave.

Nico's blush deepened; it made his rugged features so lovely I could cry. He swallowed. "I'm sure I have something you can borrow."

Tapping my chin, I said, "I appreciate your optimism, but I feel your sister's clothes would fit me better than yours."

"Oh." Nico's smile faltered. His slender, dark brows rose. There was a small bald spot on his right eyebrow. "You think?"

"Don't you?" I raised my eyebrows back.

His throat bobbed, as if sensing the trap in my question. "D'ac, we have a suitcase right here." He gestured toward the other end of the hall where a battered black suitcase lay on its side.

Still smirking, I followed him to the luggage, which he flipped open with his foot. Everything inside was neatly folded with a canvas divider down the middle. He squatted and picked up a pair of leggings from the side I presumed belonged to his sister. Her clothes were mostly black, whereas the other half of the suitcase was a rainbow of colors, fuzzy textures, and pale blue jeans.

Clutching my chest, I leaned over his shoulder so my arm brushed his chin. His stubble felt like sandpaper, which sent heat flickering through the pit of my belly.

I forced my attention to return to the task at hand and plucked a purple shirt from his pile of clothes. "This'll do. Much appreciated, Co-Co." I used the nickname his sister had used on him yesterday to delightful effect.

A blush exploded all the way up to Nico's ears. He tipped off his heels, landed heavily on his knees, and buried his face in his hands. "Oh, I'm gonna kill her."

I laughed until it made my ribs burn, stifling myself with a snort. "Alright, excuse me." Nico peeked up at me through his fingers while I retreated. As I closed the door to the room I'd slept in, I caught his umber eye and gave him a wink before the door clicked shut between us.

Switching into Stella's leggings hurt my chest and left me wheezing. I slipped into Nico's shirt, which billowed around me and fell well past my hips. The collar was a deep V loosened with wear, which quickly fell off my shoulder. But I was comfortable, and clothed.

I scraped my fingers through my too-long hair and dreamed of a haircut. Then my eyes went to the shag of lavender hanging on the wall on a long, frayed white ribbon. I lifted it down, untied the ribbon, and used it to pull my hair back into a tiny ponytail at the nape of my neck. At least it would keep it tidier.

I went to push my glasses up on my nose and was startled when they weren't there. I hadn't gone without glasses since I was six years old. Frowning, I rubbed my eyes with the heels of my hands and pushed myself to get moving.

Nico wasn't in the hall anymore when I came out, so I made my way slowly down the stairs with one hand protectively braced against my ribs. The kitchen and sitting room were quiet, too, and the back door, which faced the mountains, stood open. A tiny white moth flapped in a beam of late morning sunlight.

I padded through the doorway and was hit by a wave of vertigo, convinced that the Hazel Mountains were going to swallow me up. The ground reared into a wall of cedars, beech, and other conifers, verdant green and rustling in a cool breeze. I could feel the breath of the slumbering god in my bones, humming beneath my bare feet. Fresh, sharp air smelled like citrus, soil, and detritus. I pressed my fingers to my lips, eyes closed as my magíq threatened to burst forth in a shower of sparks and flames.

"Are those *my* leggings?"

I opened one eye partway to peer sidelong at Stella, who had her arms around Lunix's neck. She looked aghast, but in a superficial way, like she was trying to play the part of the prickly and standoffish teen but was forgetting all her lines.

Lowering my hands, I clasped them behind my back and said kindly, "Yes. Thank you *so* much for allowing me to borrow them. I can't tell you how much more comfortable I am now."

"I—" Stella's mouth fell limply open before she scoffed and turned away in defeat.

Intermediate Gryphon Riding

From my position lounging in the grass with ankles crossed and boots still untied, I marveled over the change that came upon Ackerleigh as soon as he stepped out of the cottage. His complexion warmed, and the wind teased his long, silvery fringe and gave it a life of its own. I'd seen the mountain air have the same effect on Stella before.

What I had *not* seen before was any other human being besides myself able to effectively defuse Stella's temper.

"Well, I'll be damned," I drawled. "Stella, not only have you met your match, you ain't spittin' mad at him for it? You don't know how happy this makes me."

Stella bounded through the grass, wound her leg back, and punted my boot off my foot. Lux appeared over my head and snatched my boot out of midair with their claws. After meeting my gaze with a sparkle in their silver eye, they scampered away to put a gorse bush between me and them. Once shielded, they cheerfully chomped down on my shoelace.

"Hey! Luneyeux, why—" To the sound of Ackerleigh and Stella's joyful laughter, I chased after the gryphon who surrendered my shoe with a squawk and a flurry of wings.

I waded knee-deep into the needle grass around the gorse and fished my boot out of a spurt of yellow roses. My shoelace now ended in a slimy stump, barely long enough to be used to tie. I scowled, turning back to the gryphon, who was hiding behind my riotously laughing sister and a pitying Ackerleigh.

A gust of mountain wind rustled the grasses and filled me with the scent of pine and cedar. The wild fragrance seemed to be acknowledging the strange new feeling of harmony that had descended upon the cottage. Cautious hope once again buzzed in my chest. I glanced up at the peaks of the mountains, wondering what the god beneath had breathed into the air that had thus transformed us. We had the wide-open sky above us, with the fluffy gray clouds drawing back to cornflower blue as the morning progressed. The mountains shielded us from the western horizon, verdant and mighty slopes disappearing into the mist that cloaked the peaks where the gryphons lived.

If the rest of my life could feel like this, I would be a blessed man.

Wading back through the lupin to reach the trio, I met Ackerleigh's gaze and insisted softly, "Seriously, though... I don't know what's changed 'tween you two, but I'm mighty grateful for your kindness toward this wild child."

"Nico!" groaned Stella, flapping her arms heavily against her sides. "You're makin' it weird!"

Ackerleigh's dark gray eyes danced as he offered me a faint nod and a smile so warm I felt its heat in the pit of my belly.

"Alright," Stella said, "we ain't takin' the clunky truck back to the estate, right?"

"Ah, ah." I wagged my finger at her. "You ain't comin.'"

Stella screeched in angry disbelief, throwing herself across the gryphon's neck. "Why not?"

Ackerleigh gave her a beleaguered look. "You simply don't have the temperament for this sort of excursion."

"What?" Stella straightened. Lux's round eyes followed her movement before they snapped at the hook of her suspender. "What's wrong with my temperament? I'm ready to fight to the death for Lunix!"

"Precisely," sighed Ackerleigh.

"Wait." I held up my hands. "What have you two been calling them today?" I shaped the name in my mouth before I tried, "Lunix?"

"It combines Luna and Lux," Stella answered. "Isn't it cute?"

"Huh." I looked at the gryphon, who had turned their head completely sideways to gnaw on Stella's strap. "What do you think?"

Busily chomping, the gryphon tweeted, "Lunix! Pretty. Family." The last word turned into a grunt as Stella threw her arms around their head and squeezed them tightly, all of the gryphon's mussed-up feathers burying her arms and making it look like Stella had wings, too.

I smiled. "Lunix it is."

With maternal fondness in the curve of his smile and his gentle touch, Ackerleigh stroked the ridge of Lunix's eyebrow with the back of his hand. Then he looked back at me and said more seriously, "I did assume that riding Lunix back would be the safest. Driving through the gates seems unwise. We will be sure that Lunix stays in a position where they could flee at any time, of course, if something happens."

"Oh!" Stella exclaimed suddenly as she shoved herself back from the gryphon and onto her feet. She swayed slightly to catch her balance. "Lunix, you oughta eat before you carry these two lugs with ya that far again!" The pair startled a fleet of sparrows into flight as they dashed toward the garden together. Lunix leapt for the nearest bird, but it looked like they missed on purpose.

I studied Ackerleigh for a moment—he was watching the gryphon and the girl—until I spoke. "You're a curious man. Two months ago, you didn't even know you were goin' to be lookin' after a gryphon. Your attitude has changed a lot since then. *If* your story checks out."

Ackerleigh boldly met my gaze, looking like a beat-up storybook hero who just realized that victory belonged to him. "There was no attitude change required."

I frowned. "None?"

Ackerleigh tipped up his chin. "I did my doctoral dissertation on the movement and family structures of the gryphon pods in the Hazel Mountains. I own every book on them."

I regretted opposing this storybook hero; he had the sage wisdom I hadn't expected, and I was scrambling for an explanation. "Are there lots of light-lickers that are interested in gryphons?"

"How do you know I'm from the city?" Ackerleigh's lips curled slightly with a smirk. Heat shot up my neck. But then the sunshine leapt into his eyes, and I realized he was teasing me. "You haven't asked me anything about myself, *Nico*."

My gaze lingered on the shape his mouth made around my name. Not for the first time, I wondered if he remembered when I'd had to give him mouth-to-mouth, or if it was just me being tormented by that memory. I looked away quickly, back to the garden.

Stella strolled over to us, tossing a large red tomato in the air. Lunix slurped a string of pumpkin guts into their mouth as they approached.

"Get on," they chirped, settling their wings slightly away from their sides.

I mounted Lunix past the scapulas of their unfolded wings, humeral feathers burying my knees. They were even wider across the back than my mare, and I'd been surprised the day before that they were so comfortable and easy to ride. Truthfully, I wasn't sad to have another opportunity to ride them again so soon.

Ackerleigh's eyes were round and distant as he watched me climb onto Lunix's back, hugging his injured ribs, silently shifting his weight from one foot to the other.

I held out my hand. "Ready to go?"

Ackerleigh hesitated, his throat bobbing.

My expression fell. "This was your idea, Doctor Sebring."

Chewing his lip, Ackerleigh tossed his head and brushed his hair out of his eyes. Then he said, "I just... I was largely unconscious for the last ride."

"You scared?" Stella taunted, hands on her hips, head bobbing.

"Quite." Ackerleigh nodded and gazed mildly at her. "Any recommendations?"

Stella blinked, then thought for a moment. Ackerleigh waited, silent. Stella's eyes shot skyward and she took a great breath. "Well, I don't really 'member riding them much when I was little. Yesterday, though, it helped when I rocked with their movements. Visualized myself as wind and water, not flesh and bone."

Ackerleigh processed her response with his eyes on the mountains and a slowly widening smile. "I can do that." He nodded gratefully toward her, and she awkwardly rubbed her neck and looked away.

When Ackerleigh turned back to face Lunix, he reached for me with a pleading look. Heart lurching, I quickly grasped his hand. It was slightly clammier than I'd expected. Ackerleigh must have seen my reaction; his ears pinked, and he tried to pull away. I pinched his hand under my thumb and refused to let him escape, instead giving him a swift tug to get him up onto the slope of Lunix's back.

He clumsily swung his leg over, ears still rosy, and settled between my thighs. His spine curved against me, shoulder blades resting softly against my chest.

With his knees nestled against the root of Lunix's forelimbs, Ackerleigh splayed his palms across the gryphon's mantle, gingerly smoothing the small, leaf-shaped tertial feathers which crowded the axials of Lunix's wingspan. Ackerleigh's brow wrinkled as he let out a reverent sigh.

"I know." Too late, I realized the raspy whisper of my voice was quite... intimate. Clearing my throat, I said more loudly, "They're magnificent."

"Play nice, boys," Stella said, exaggerating her drawl as she wiggled her fingers at us and gave me a sly smile. In return, I offered her a rude gesture behind Ackerleigh's back.

"But seriously," Stella added, "don't get caught, or I'm telling Mother."

I nodded. "Head home straight away if we ain't back by nightfall."

Stella's expression sobered. She fidgeted with one of her shoulder straps. "'Kay, but... don't get caught, y'hear?"

"'Course." I winked at her. "Let's go, Lunix." I patted their rump and squeezed my thighs together.

Lunix crouched, lifted their wings, and sprang up on the downturn, launching into the air with a jerk and a piercing cry. Lunix worked with the wind, not against it, allowing an updraft to send us soaring over the cottage and turning Stella into a pinprick next to our neatly plotted garden.

Ackerleigh clapped his hand over his mouth, hunching over, reaching for Lunix's feather mane to hang on. But as soon as he extended his arms, he grunted in pain, elbows folding protectively against his sides, goosebumps rising on the back of his neck. His thighs bucked as he fought to find his center. Ackerleigh's breathing doubled into quick, shallow gasps.

Before I realized what I was doing, I slid my arms around his waist and hooked my fingers together against his stomach. "You're good. We won't let you fall."

Ackerleigh relaxed immediately, gripping his bruised side. His head came back to rest against my shoulder. Silvery-blond hair tickled my nose as the strong airfoil carried us along. I hoped he couldn't feel how fast my heart was pounding against his spine.

With my hands anchoring him as a seatbelt, he peered past Lunix's gliding carpal edge, lips parted, eyes round and awestruck. As Lunix caught an updraft and rose sharply, Ackerleigh lurched with it. His hands shot down and clasped my wrists as he went stiff and squeezed his eyes shut.

"No, no, Doctor Sebring." I tapped my fingers against his navel. "You gotta breathe."

"Breathing hurts," he wheezed.

"D'ac, I mean, pass out if ya want."

Shooting me a fierce glare over his shoulder, Ackerleigh let out a breath through his pursed lips. I grinned, and his brow unfurrowed in response. Slowly, still gripping my wrists, he resumed watching the world pass.

Beneath us, the steppes of the Hazel Mountains wrinkled the ground like a verdant wool blanket spread on the lap of a god. The countryside this close to the mountains was almost inaccessible by car. There were a few haphazard dirt roads that looked like twine beneath us. One heading toward Hazberg beyond the mountains in the west. One heading north, toward the De Falco Farm and then wrapping around the coast to Northton. Other than that, pristine, undisturbed wilderness painted the world. Dark beech forests, rolling hills dappled with pastel lupins, crystal blue glacial lakes surrounded by lush grasses and a rainbow of wildflowers.

We were silent for a while as the wind dried out my eyes and made my nose run. Lunix flapped their wings seldom, using the slots between their feathers to catch thermal columns and climb into the clouds before drifting back down to wait for the next one.

"There's one aspect of Lunix's imprisonment I still feel is unclear," Ackerleigh said after a while. "What exactly was Doctor Bennett getting out of imprisoning a gryphon? She didn't live there, didn't ask for any written reports on their behavior... Just left them to the care of people they obviously despised. Why?"

I remembered the things that Doctor Bennett had said on the farm before she'd driven away with our gryphon sibling... My heart slammed in my ears, and it was like I was experiencing the rage and heartbreak all over again.

"She's been hoping for an egg." I gritted my teeth around the word.

How could she? What could have compelled my parents to think Lunix's life would be anything but torment? My parents let Lunix get dragged away from a family farm in the mountains, where they could have been free and disappeared for days among the crags, mingling with the gryphon pods on the summit. My parents let them go even though they knew Lunix was Stella's whole world. Even though I threatened to reject the farm. Their disregard for us, for Lunix's wellbeing…

"Ouch." Ackerleigh tapped my wrist. "You're squeezing."

"Oh, I'm so sorry." I unhooked my fingers and let them slide to Ackerleigh's hips.

"Are you alright?"

"It—It all makes me so mad."

"They're hoping for an egg?" Ackerleigh mercifully diverted my attention. "What do you mean? How can that be?"

"Lunix is special, biologically." As I focused on the science of the magíq, my ocky accent went into hiding. "Occasionally, a gryphon is born that contains the hormonal imprint for both male and female species. A cloaca with both oviduct and deferens duct. It's the same principle as how twins can develop in the same egg. Does that make sense?"

"Uh-*huh*." Ackerleigh's voice pitched higher.

"What's wrong?"

"I had no idea this was possible." He sounded excited, his words rapid and breathy. He absently stroked Lunix's coverts as the gryphon made an upstroke, their wings briefly caging us in like whistling curtains until they began to glide again. "And you know the *science* for it!"

"Well, of course. It's wise to have a comprehensive understanding of the gryphons for those that live so close to them."

"Do—Do you have contact with the pods in the mountains?"

"Most ocky folks do, Doctor Sebring. Gryphons will come through either hunting or during mating season several times a year. Some of the more devout folks like my friend Cyrus leave offerings for the gryphons. Livestock and whatnot, left in the steppes for the gryphons to take when they come through." I paused, a smirk crawling onto my lips, shifting back into my ocky drawl. "And we can still get books all 'way out 'n the mountain's armpit, y'know."

Ackerleigh's ears pinked. I grinned again, satisfied to be the one who'd flustered him for a change.

When he collected himself, he said, "But gryphons don't mature until they're ten, and Lunix is nine, so..."

"Yeah. Doctor Bennett bought a two-year-old gryphon she anticipated keeping isolated for almost a decade, in the off chance they would end up with a gryphon egg." I caught myself before my grip tightened on him again.

"But is that it? Lunix matures, and then the hormones kick on and they pop out an egg?"

"No. Both hormones only occur if the conditions are right. If enough serotonin is being produced in their brain, then the oxytocin production gets triggered and they start the process of laying an egg. So how they expected an imprisoned gryphon to love their life and feel safe and happy is beyond me."

"Unless they didn't know. The mechanisms of asexual gryphon reproduction aren't written in any books." Ackerleigh twisted to look at me over his shoulder, a little crinkle appearing under one eye, admiring. "The information you possess is completely unique, Nico."

I laughed awkwardly. "Oh. Is it? I see. Uh, well, y'know. Such is the life of an ocky farmer. Knowledge gets passed down, y'know, but not written down."

"Seems that way." Ackerleigh's eyes glittered. He turned to face forward. A stone of yearning dropped in my stomach as I lost sight of his features. I caught myself spreading my palm against his soft stomach before I quickly made a fist.

Ackerleigh didn't seem to notice. "My grandfather lived a life very much like yours. Although he lived at the western foot of the mountains. He told stories of gryphon kits, of the way the creatures nurtured each other, and how protective they were of those that fell under their affections. Those stories embedded themselves in my heart."

"Hence the doctoral research. I get it now. That's lovely." Noticing the ache in my elbows, I briefly let Ackerleigh go to roll my shoulders back and stretch my arms. He tensed between my thighs, quickly leaning back to maintain contact with me, pressing into my chest and grasping my knees. It was such a primal and automatic search for safety that

I stopped mid-flex and returned my hands to his waist. His muscles softened under my touch, but he kept his hands on my knees.

"I am not good at gryphon-riding," Ackerleigh remarked thinly.

"You're doing fine." When he'd scooted into me, my cheek ended up pressed into his hair. "Keep talking—that'll help you relax. Tell me about your grandfather's farm. Was he a Sebring, too?"

"Yes." Ackerleigh's face twitched. "That farm is about a hundred years old, running back four generations. My grandfather, Richard, took that legacy seriously. My grandmother, Louise, died when my mother was quite young. My uncle Andrew ran the farm for a bit, but left my grandfather for Stoneworth, and my mother never visited from Hazberg after I was born. She would send me there during school breaks and sometimes when school was in session, until I got old enough to argue. As far as I know, the farm was abandoned after my grandfather died."

I gave an exasperated sigh. "It's a tale told across the country. How do the cities expect to thrive if nobody is left cultivating the land?"

Ackerleigh nodded, solemn. The ribbon in his hair tickled my throat with a sensation I vowed never to forget. "Yes. I completely agree."

Survey of a Lover's Embrace

Flying low, Lunix spiraled down toward the manor with their silver gaze calculating as an eagle as they assessed their old prison. I was reminded with chilling clarity that the gryphon was a hunter. They might have slept in my bed last night, but they could kill me, or even Nico or Stella, if we crossed them.

The hole in the grate over the courtyard was in grisly contrast to the verdant splendor of the garden within. I found myself recoiling from the sight of this place now, as if glimpsing what was possible for Lunix beyond had made their former prison seem all the more inhumane.

It was all the confirmation I needed: I was not bound to stay here, nor in fact return to Laurier. I was bound to Lunix, if they would have me.

There were no cars except mine in the loop of the drive out front. That was a good sign. I could hardly imagine the sophisticated Doctor Bennett going down that long and dusty driveway on foot. It was possible she'd already come by after I'd failed to call her the night before, had surveyed the damage, and assumed I'd perished in the incident. It was possible they'd already seized my notebook and learned the incriminating truth about my cursed nature.

If only I could stay out in the wild countryside forever, learning and growing alongside another magíqon, with a gryphon as our mentor. And, if I was lucky... I could be with someone who loved me despite my own magíq.

"Only that blue car of yours out front. That's a good sign." Nico's chin bounced against my cheek as he spoke. Out of the corner of my eye, his nose was a gentle slope, rounded at the tip above a florid pair of lips that seemed reluctant to smile. Where his sister had eyes dark and angry as a thunderhead, his were brighter, like sweet tea brewing in a vibrant beam of sunlight.

I was still staring at him when his eyes flicked toward me. Mortified, I snapped my gaze past him to pretend like I had been looking at the scenery instead. It wasn't like me to be mooning over a man I didn't know. Coyness came easily, but this was different. And why was I suddenly getting the sensation that his soft, ruddy lips had already touched my own? Surely I was imagining things, creating a fantasy from the desire I'd just realized was there. I wetted my lips, which were chapped by the wind. "One can hope."

"Are you ready?" Nico's voice vibrated against me. "Lunix is not going further into the manor than here. That way, if we get caught, they don't."

I nodded quickly. "Yes. Absolutely."

Lunix landed delicately on the grate, rocking their wings to balance us on their back. Their talons curled around the bars, with their lion claws scraping into the shingles right behind us. Nico dismounted swiftly and gracefully, and I followed after, pinwheeling my arms until he grasped my elbow and steadied me.

Nico gestured toward the row of bedroom windows which ran along the second storey, underneath us. "Did you have your belongings in one of those?"

I nodded. Pausing to walk myself through the hallway in my mind, I counted windows. "The fourth. Next to that tea tree."

"D'ac." Nico backed off the grate until he was on the shingles, which scraped beneath his sturdy hunting boots. I wished I had shoes on, too, as I eyed the exposed nails that held the sheets of tar in place. He blinked at the look on my face, his eyes skimming my form until he reached my feet. "Shit."

"Don't worry. I'll be fine." To prove it, I climbed onto the shingles. Honestly, they felt horrid under my heels, like sharp, scaly stones. But I had shoes in my room, so as long as my things were still there, I wouldn't need to make a barefooted return trip. I limped after Nico, copying the way his fingers grazed the roof to stay balanced.

When we reached the middle window, Nico lowered to his knees and grasped the gutter, bending to peer into the bedroom. Crouching with his back toward the edge, Nico swung his leg down, checked his hold on the gutter, and dropped off the roof. He kicked the sill, lightly, testing for footholds, finding a lip that let him support himself. The glass rattled as he nudged it with his toe. Fortunately, I'd left my window open the day before, and he gently eased it inward, opening it enough to fit his body. Then he looked up at me with eyes like twin rings of jasper.

"Alright." He straddled the windowsill. "Go ahead and turn around and then let one of your legs come down. I'll take it from there."

"Can't we go in the door?" I asked through gritted teeth.

"Bit late for that," Nico remarked.

Lunix's eyes were on me. "Careful," they whistled. "Careful." Wings rustling, they crouched like a gargoyle on the edge of the roof, tail softly curled around their feet.

I dropped my ass onto the shingles first, scooting toward the gutter, going against every self-preservation instinct in my body to put my foot out into the open air.

I scooted. Scooted, scooted, dangling my leg down up to my knee like I was dipping my toes into cold and uncertain waters. To be helpful, I stretched a bit farther until most of my leg up to the thigh was off the roof.

Nico's warm hand closed around my calf. "Great. Other leg," he instructed softly.

I obeyed, blood slamming loudly in my ears. My throat started to burn, asthma threatening to kick up a wheeze even though I'd barely moved. As my weight transferred from the gutter into Nico's hands, I flailed involuntarily and heard Nico gasp. I plunged into his arms as he snatched me out of the air and pulled me through the window with his arms around my waist.

I stifled a squeak, clinging to his neck, my cheek pressed into the coarse stubble on his cheek. A lover's embrace—absolutely, irrefutably, this was a lover's embrace. Humiliation should have sent me scrabbling away, but the heat from his body melted my ability to move.

His heart hammered against mine as the heaving of his chest lifted me up, down, up.

It gave me a sudden flash to the day before, after I'd fallen, of him carrying me like a bride into the cottage while consciousness had come and gone. He'd truly *rescued* me. So perhaps that sensation of his lips was another snatch of a memory—Mouth-to-mouth?

Heat exploded from every nerve in my body with such intensity I briefly worried I would actually combust. The speculation I'd forced myself to delay yesterday settled in now with blinding clarity. Nico had rescued me from the bottom of the sea, resuscitated me, and had laid me to bed like a swooning damsel.

I froze against Nico, holding my breath, willing my body to not *harden* as it desperately wanted to.

I needed to pull myself together. I was independent and assertive. I had been innocently flirting with a handsome farmer, not fantasizing about living happily ever after in the mountains with my rugged and muscular rescuer.

Now, if I could actually believe myself, that would be great.

As Nico let out a sigh of relief, he slid off the windowsill and set me on my feet. Reluctantly, I loosened my grip on him.

The plush white carpeting was a blessing on the soles of my feet. I safely released Nico's neck to stand on my own. Aggravated by my fall, my wounded chest throbbed with such violence that it made my knees buckle. Nico lunged for me and caught me by the biceps, helping me backwards until my calves brushed the bed skirts. I sank onto the familiar bed and hunched over my wounded ribs, gasping. Stars danced in my vision.

I rasped, "I'm so sorry. I—"

Nico reached for the nearest pillow, which happened to be the main pillow I used. He wedged it under my arms and held his hand there until I pressed it to my ribs to support my breathing.

"You broke bones yesterday. Nothing to apologize for." Nico was still panting, his cheeks blotchy and flushed. He put his hands on his thighs and bent over. "This your trunk?"

I leaned around the curtained post. My grandfather's trunk lay open with my books and clothing as I'd left them the day before. My yellow wellies sat beside them, slightly muddy from the fertile soil of the courtyard garden.

My heart dropped. "Oh. I didn't even think about it—we wouldn't be able to carry that back on Lunix."

Nico's brow crinkled. "Can you empty it? We can wrap the contents in a bedsheet."

"I'm sorry, but I can't leave the trunk. It's an heirloom." I stepped into my wellies, which smarted against the irritation from the shingles. I had to be an embarrassing sight: standing without my glasses, my hair overgrown, in a massively oversized tee, a teenage girl's leggings, and yellow wellies I swore I'd never be witnessed wearing.

The nod he gave me was absent-minded, like he'd already moved onto finding other solutions. He went over and crouched beside the trunk, picking up the corner, cocking his head. "Oh. This'll be fine."

"What?"

Closing the lid on the trunk and flipping the latches, Nico carefully turned it on its side. He slipped his fingers between the seams of the leather as if they'd never been sealed down.

"Um." I hurried over. "Apologies, but can you..."

Using his pinky, Nico prised a slender canvas strap out of the trunk. A soft black shoulder pad was sewn around it. My jaw dropped as he turned the trunk around and did the same thing to the other bottom edge. Gently, he stood the trunk up on its side, allowing my belongings to settle in their new position.

He stood up, slinging the trunk with its newly acquired backpack straps onto his back, looking more giddy than smug. "We have a few of these at the farm."

I brought my hand to my face in dismay. That damn heavy, coffin-like trunk I'd barely gotten upstairs, hanging behind him with all the effort most required to carry a guitar in a case. Nico noticed my dismay and began to issue an apology.

"Hello? Is someone up there?"

We froze, inhaling on the same beat and holding a collective breath between us. The color drained from Nico's face.

"We need to go." Nico's voice was a toneless growl. He pushed me toward the window.

"D'ac, but my notebook in the courtyard—"

"We'll be leaving that."

I planted my feet. "I can't."

"Doctor Sebring, whatever you wrote, you can rewrite." What had been a nudge before was now a shove.

I lost my balance, falling into the windowsill, the marble inlay smacking me beneath the shoulder blades. The impact ricocheted into my ribs, and my vision tunneled and spun with stars. I couldn't breathe, but I could *hear*—footsteps tapping in the hall, making those carpeted floorboards creak and groan.

Discarding the trunk, Nico yanked me down to the floor, rolled under the bed past the sage-green bed skirts, and pulled me in after him. Plumes of dust showered our faces, blinding me and coating my tongue.

The rush of blood in my ears nearly deafened me. Tears streamed out of my eyes—from the impact of the windowsill and the density of the dust all over us. I was sure I smelled a dead mouse somewhere with us, and clumps of cat hair clung to my sweaty neck and bare arms. My lungs and throat immediately seized up, causing a coughing fit I fiercely contained with both my hands pressed over my mouth and nose.

The bedroom door squeaked open, and a pair of red patent pumps appeared in the doorway, just barely visible beneath the edge of the bed skirt. They moved silently across the carpet by our feet and over to the window, where they lingered for a moment. I could imagine the owner of the shoes considering the wide-open window, and hoped, prayed, *begged* that they would determine it was due to my recent presence here.

Dong-dong-dong went the doorbell with merciless volume, shaking more dust loose from the bedsprings. The red pumps jumped and their owner swore before hastily crossing the room and departing. We waited a beat, listening carefully for any indication of their return. I watched the shadowy relief of Nico's profile remain attentive on the doorway as if he didn't believe that the person had actually left the room.

Finally satisfied that we were alone, Nico squirmed toward the foot of the bed and burst out. After securing the trunk on his back, he stuck his hands under the bed and grasped me by the calf and the nape of my neck. He extracted me from the dusty darkness in one swift movement. It was so quick and exacting that it didn't even hurt, though I blinked against the sudden brightness with dust clinging to my lashes. Throwing his arm around my hips, Nico picked me up and bent to put his lips near my ear. "I'm so sorry I pushed you. I didn't mean to hurt you. I—"

"Stop." My voice was more wheeze than word, but I didn't trust that the owner of the red pumps was far enough away to not hear me start coughing. I twitched my head. We were almost nose-to-nose. "Let's go."

I pushed him toward the window with the palm of my hand against his sternum, and he obliged. Hefting himself up and backwards into the windowsill, he clasped his large hands around my waist and lifted me up. My ribs were numb, which didn't feel like a good sign, but it allowed me to painlessly secure my arms around Nico's neck as he stood up on the sill and gripped the gutter.

Hanging onto Nico with my feet dangling by his calves, I glanced down to the courtyard. Under the magnolia tree was the stone bench where I'd been writing yesterday. Shadowed beneath the bench, my notebook was sprawled open, pages flapping in the breeze.

Nico followed my gaze. "Yes, fine, I'll get it," he whispered, setting me on my feet, hanging on until I got my balance as I veritably clung to the window. He looked up and called in a stage whisper, "Lunix, get Ackerleigh! Now!"

"N-No!"

But Nico didn't wait. Still laden with my trunk, he hopped off the windowsill and let gravity yank him down into the courtyard, where he dropped to hands and knees.

A wedge-shaped shadow fell over my head as Lunix poked over the edge of the roof, head cocked, blinking a moon eye at me.

"Someone's here," I whispered.

Lunix bent over the gutter, snapped the back of my collar in their beak, and hauled me into the air like I was their young. The seams of my sleeve popped just as Lunix tossed me unceremoniously onto the shingles so I fell against their hindleg.

Drenched in sticky sweat and tears, I pressed my mouth into my sleeve and let the ragged, barking coughing fit overwhelm me, choking me, turning my stomach until I leaned over on my elbow and vomited onto the roof. It was only bile that burned my throat and splattered on the shingles. Lunix whisked their feathers against my cheek, curling protectively around me, shadows falling as they hid me beneath their wings. I held onto their midsection, my gasping breaths whistling as I clung to the gryphon.

Lunix gently reached back and pushed me up until I was draped across their back, on my belly, unable to make my shaking muscles work. All I could manage was to angle myself onto their fluffy mantle to cushion my ribs, which throbbed in time with my rapid heartbeat. I pushed my left forearm into their bulk to slowly inch upright, feeling horribly vulnerable, alone on the gryphon's back.

Movement within the courtyard showed Nico standing from a crouch beneath the shadow of the magnolia tree. He wore a pained expression as he tucked my blasted notebook into his waistband and snapped it behind his suspenders before adjusting my trunk on his back.

Lunix chirruped in relief as they carefully approached the hole in the grate, toes splayed and claws tightly gripping the iron bars. I tasted the tang of magíq as the air stirred around me. Wind gusted boisterously into the courtyard and whisked all the flora into a fragrant, noisy frenzy. Past the flapping of my dusty fringe, I watched a column of spiraling air—too beautiful and controlled to be a tornado—reach down and pluck Nico out of the courtyard. Curls whipped free of his bun. Mouth open in a surprised circle, Nico kicked his legs like a helpless babe as he was carried up to the gryphon. Lunix's grasping magíq carried him up to me and set him behind me. I felt like we were kids on a pony ride. As soon as Nico's thighs securely hugged my hips, Lunix spread their wings, crouched, and jumped into the air. They glided back to the rooftop where they landed again with a thump.

Nico's chest heaved against my shoulder blades. I felt his wrist press into the small of my back and heard a rustle of paper. He reached his arm around my shoulders and proffered my rumpled notebook in his fist. There were fresh, red scrapes on his knuckles.

Concerned, I lifted a hand to touch the injury. "Nico—"

"Don't worry about me," he interrupted flatly. "You got your precious notebook, didn't you?"

Surprise jolted through my stomach at his cold tone. I thought he'd understood that retrieving this notebook was the whole point. Perhaps he thought I was a selfish fool, cherishing some vain project. Perhaps he was imagining these pages to be filled with self-congratulatory academic drivel—or worse, poetry.

If only I had an excuse to tell him about my magíq. I imagined the relief I would feel entrusting that part of myself to him. I had told his sister my secret mere hours earlier... It was bound to be easier this time.

Besides, any secret would be worth giving up if I could soothe the hurt in his voice.

I stole a glance at Nico and, though he was looking at me with a crease in his brow and his fingers rubbing at his scar, he quickly dropped his gaze so I couldn't catch his eye.

Heart wrenching, I began earnestly, "Nico—"

It was then that I heard a familiar voice drifting up to me on the wind.

"My name is Claire Emérie. I'm a friend of Doctor Ackerleigh Sebring."

Intermediate Vulnerability

Ackerleigh broke off. His head snapped toward the voice from the front door. "That's my friend," he whispered, his voice hoarse from coughing. "Lunix, can you get closer? I want to see." His gryphon acquiesced immediately, lurching forward.

My heart started hammering in time with my throbbing ankle, which I'd twisted when I'd landed in the courtyard. Panicking, I protested, "Please, can't we just get out of here? Lunix, I don't want you—"

"Careful," Lunix tweeted softly. They crawled up the slant of the roof and onto the pinnacle to get a better look at the front of the manor.

Perched like a weathervane atop the roof, Lunix crouched with all four feet delicately meeting underneath, their wings slightly lifted from their sides to keep their balance.

Ackerleigh scooted himself onto Lunix's neck, buried among the small and spiky feathers of their mane like a child hiding in his mother's skirts. With his arms around Lunix's head and slotted between their ear tufts, Ackerleigh leaned forward and peered down to the front door. I couldn't see much from my spot, mostly the roundabout drive and the two tall shrubs that framed the front doors.

On the opposite side of the disused fountain, a long mauve car with a white canvas top sat idling, pointed toward the open gates among the cypress trees.

An unfamiliar voice, deep like the tolling of a grandfather clock, said below us, "He was expecting me today. We were meant to have brunch. Is he around? I thought he stayed here alone."

"Doctor Sebring is... apparently not here."

I recognized *that* voice without needing to see her.

"I beg your pardon, but are you Doctor Rose Bennett? Of Bennett Publishing House?"

"Hm? Oh. Yes. I presume you're from Ravensbourne."

"Yes, Claire Emérie, ma'am. I teach Chemistry. I started the same year as Ackerleigh, but I don't think you were at my interview. But, um—" The woman lifted her eyes and landed her gaze on the gryphon's head. Despite Ackerleigh's enthusiastic wave, she barely reacted before swiftly asking, "You said he's not here? Has... Has something happened?"

For a desperate moment, I considered turning myself in. Jumping off the roof, springing out in front of Doctor Bennett and confessing. It would be so much easier that way. This had been a foolhardy plan from the start. Every day from now on would be spent waiting to be caught, unless I confronted her now. Pled my case.

But that future was certainly bleak. I could not risk Lunix's recently acquired liberation by following that path. Whatever hope they had of remaining free was back in the Hazel Mountains, with me and my sister. And, it seemed, with Ackerleigh.

"I am still sorting out what's happened," said Doctor Bennett.

"Oh, no! Is my friend alright?"

"I have no evidence one way or the other."

Claire's voice hitched with worry, speaking to her impressive acting. She could *see* us. But I had to admit that her fear over Ackerleigh's wellbeing would help keep Doctor Bennett's suspicions off us. "I beg your pardon?"

"Nobody else is here."

"Well, what about his belongings? May I take them home with me to Laurier, just in case?" Claire paused. "I would hate for him to turn up and wonder why I didn't help him out. He can be a bit dramatic, you see."

Ackerleigh scoffed under his breath, making my lips twitch at the absurdity of this entire situation.

Doctor Bennett continued plainly, "You would be welcome to do so, but I didn't see any belongings around."

Claire's eyes flicked up toward us in question. I twisted so she could see the trunk while Ackerleigh nodded and gestured toward me.

"Doctor Bennett, please let me know whatever you learn. Ackerleigh is family, and... oh! A cat."

Ackerleigh breathed a sigh of relief.

"Who's this pretty baby?"

"This is Dove. She was meant to be company for... the gamekeeper. I'm not sure what to do about her right now." Doctor Bennett paused. "I'm allergic to cats."

"Oh, I can take her. I love cats. Come here, Dove. You want to come with me?"

"Good old Claire," murmured Ackerleigh, patting Lunix's cheek.

"Why don't I take Ackerleigh's keys, too? I can drive his car back to Laurier and keep it with me." A pause. "Thank you so much, Doctor Bennett. May I leave you my number in case you learn anything about my friend's whereabouts?"

"That's alright, I can get it from the university."

"Alright. Good day, madame. I'll be off, then." She jingled Ackerleigh's keyring. Claire strode briskly to the mauve car and leaned into the driver's window, holding a very calm gray cat over her shoulder. She bent down and spoke to the person inside the car with several nods in our direction. Her expression and gestures rapidly sharpened until she held up a dismissive hand. She started walking away while she was still arguing.

"Oh, Claire," Ackerleigh groaned as his friend stalked across the drive to his little blue car. She unlocked the driver's door, threw it open, and then craned her neck back to give us a cheerful wave. She pushed up her bold tortoiseshell glasses with a glance at the mauve car as it pulled away. Her hand smacked her lips as she blew a kiss in the other car's direction as it sped away with a rev of its engine suggesting the driver's frustration.

"Go *home*." Ackerleigh gestured southward. But his friend shook her head quickly, pointed toward the road out of the estate, and then climbed inside Ackerleigh's car without another glance at us.

My stomach dropped. "What just—wait. She's not goin' back to Laurier at all, is she? Is she gonna try to follow us?"

"Indubitably," Ackerleigh said drolly.

"But Doctor Sebring, she can't come to the cottage—"

"Let's start by meeting her at the main road to have a chat." Ackerleigh had that flinty tone in his voice again. There was no point in arguing with him.

Lunix dropped like a coiling spring before launching off the pinnacle of the roof, wings snapping in a flurry of feathers as they rose sharply into the sky. Startled, I rocked precariously, slapping my hands onto Lunix's ribcage and clenching my thighs to keep my balance.

Meanwhile, Ackerleigh was securely wrapped around Lunix's neck. He didn't budge as we gained altitude, looking like a gryphon kits clinging to his mother's plumage before his wings had come in.

"Please don't let her come back to the bed and breakfast," I begged.

"Why not?" Ackerleigh pinned me beneath his gaze. His sharp chin rested on the slope of his shoulder. The curled corners of his notebook flapped in the wind where it stuck out from beneath his arm.

Shutting my eyes, I tried to name the heavy stone that weighed down the pit of my belly. "I'm scared of how quickly Doctor Bennett is gonna find us," I admitted. "I'm scared that coming back here has dashed our chances to remain safely hidden away. She's a clever woman; she'll check the courtyard and see the hole Stella made. She'll see enough hints that you vanished unexpectedly and easily conclude that you're with us, and that Claire has spoken with you."

Ackerleigh was silent for some time, brushing one of the slender feathers of Lunix's mane along his lower lip. "Surely you must have thought of these things before you broke out Lunix."

"I thought of it all *three days ago*," I snapped. "You give me too much credit. I didn't think anything through."

He flinched, blinking hard. "That was the day of your last delivery. When I yelled at you." His gaze skimmed over me, taking his time, sizing me up. Then he scooted over his gryphon's mantle; Lunix glanced back at him and banked, leveling out to make his movement safer. Slowly inching his legs up onto Lunix's back, Ackerleigh slipped past the coverts until he was seated between my thighs. The hyper-sensitive muscles of my inner thighs pressed into the curves of his hips. He was a fast learner; unlike on our flight here, his hips rocked smoothly with Lunix's wingbeats. Before my body betrayed me, I forced myself to stop thinking about his hips.

Shoulders against me, he turned his head, wiping sweaty silver hairs off his brow. His eyes were particularly gray against the backdrop of the late morning sky. "I'm on your side, Nico, alright?"

I didn't realize how badly I'd needed the reassurance until I felt a coil of dread loosen behind my sternum.

"We'll keep Lunix safe. I can promise you at least that Claire's assistance will not bring more hardship to either you and your sister or to Lunix."

Vulnerability settled strange and heavy over me, a cool mist I realized I'd felt seldom in my life. I could conjure no words to reply to him, and I fought not to drop my gaze.

"So." His eyes glinted. "You have a temper." It was an observation, not a question.

The strange sweetness of my vulnerability climbed into something hotter and familiar: shame. He wasn't wrong, and I'd proven his point countless times just today.

"I... I do. Yes. When I'm scared." My fingers itched to tap my scar. Instead, I slid my hands around his waist. The impulse to touch my scar immediately receded; its absence startled me. There wasn't a single waking moment in twelve years when I hadn't been fighting to keep my hand off that injury. Until now, when Ackerleigh's soft form beneath my palms brought me peace.

I added more quietly, "I'm sorry that I hurt you."

"You have a lot to lose," Ackerleigh remarked, brushing his fingers against mine. "I'm sorry I didn't take that into account."

The tender touch of our hands made me feel one and the same with the light, fluffy clouds crawling past us. I closed my eyes so that my only sensations were the sound of the whistling wind, the warmth of Ackerleigh against my belly, and Lunix's slow, shifting muscles beneath me.

I recalled hitting Tad at Dolly's, and lashing out at Mother. "Honestly, I haven't been thinking straight about anything since my sister and I left home. I was just in this fog of hopelessness until..." I took a short breath and said quickly, "Until I met you. I didn't want to be a passive observer of my life anymore. I didn't want to keep tolerating Lunix being imprisoned. I didn't want to watch another gamekeeper die. Especially not you."

Ackerleigh turned to rest his chin on his shoulder, giving me a coy sidelong smile. "I *knew* you were sweet on me."

I squirmed under the molten heat of his gaze and blurted, "Yeah, well, I'm sure my behavior today ruined your opinion of me anyway, so..."

Ackerleigh tipped his face down to watch his car putter along beneath us. "I wouldn't be so sure."

Lunix's lazy circles moved northward, slowly edging away from the estate and its winding driveway toward the main road, which split to the right toward Northton and to the left toward Laurier. The shifting spirals must have been helpful, because the blue car followed us with a comet's tail of orange dust. Gradually, the Bennett estate disappeared into the misty blue horizon. Relief washed away my anxiety like the tide erasing footprints.

A few minutes later, Lunix started to descend. Tilting forward, I reached around Ackerleigh to brace my hands on Lunix's scapulas so I wouldn't slide and crush us both against their secondaries. By the time the car was the size of my hand, it had stopped in the middle of the road and the woman had her door open and her mouth agape.

Lunix landed gracelessly, slamming into waist-high, red-tipped needle grass which swallowed us up. The jostling knocked my hands off Lunix's bucking shoulder blades. Ackerleigh grunted as he flattened beneath me with a faceful of feathers. Remiges whisked against my shoulders as I scrambled to sit up. My arm threaded around Ackerleigh's waist to help him upright.

"I'm sorry, are you alright?"

"Yeah, yes," he wheezed unconvincingly.

I lifted my head toward the idling car beside us as Lunix's head twitched and tipped back to sniff the air, mandibles slightly parted. They paid no mind to the woman hiding from them behind the car door, white knuckles gripping the metal as if prepared to lock herself inside.

But then Ackerleigh caught her eye and she exclaimed shakily, "Ackerleigh, *what* an entrance!"

Struggling free from the gryphon's winged embrace, Ackerleigh clambered to his feet, stumbling over to the woman by the car and throwing his arms around her. The slightly taller woman embraced him tightly, and they clung to each other in silent relief.

Lunix wandered into the needle grass, snuffling it and snapping at flax with their beak. I hurriedly dismounted, landed on both feet, and yelped as my ankle rolled.

Lunix's head snapped up at my exclamation. They twisted and snatched my bicep in their talons, helping me get my balance and shift my weight to my left leg. As soon as I was steady, I let Ackerleigh's trunk slide off my shoulders and onto the side of the road.

Lunix plucked at my windblown hair as they let go of my arm. "Careful," they tweeted with a whistle.

Ackerleigh separated from his friend, who promptly began a thorough inspection of his injuries, beginning with his bandaged face. She shamelessly yanked his shirt up to his chin and balked at his bruises. The woman was maternal and curvaceous, with an auburn bob and intense, dark features that slowly filled with horror.

Thunderous eyes fixed on me. The woman raised an accusatory finger as she stalked toward me. "And you! What do you have to say for yourself?"

Before I could so much as think about apologizing, Lunix lunged to my defense. A flurry of flight feathers battered me, disorienting and violent. Lunix reared back onto their hindlegs, screaming at Claire with talons crooked and plumage hackling.

Claire shrieked, as did Ackerleigh, who threw himself in front of her while I dove beneath the gryphon's lion haunches. I stood up against their belly and their breast, pushing into them with all my weight. But with their wings beating, blinded by aggression, Lunix was unstoppable.

Ackerleigh exclaimed, "Chaton, this is my best friend! Please don't hurt her!" He flattened her behind him against the bonnet of the car, arms outstretched, expression stricken. "Please!"

Lunix hissed, a long and pressured sound like an overworking boiler, before they dropped from their hindlegs with their claws landing protectively on my shoulder.

Claire crouched behind Ackerleigh and gripped his shoulders, her complexion drained of color. "I'm s-so sorry—I won't touch your friend. Ackerleigh, tell it I'm sorry—"

Gnashing their beak, Lunix turned sharply. Their tail lashed into my calves. With a final glare at the woman, Lunix charged away, opened their wings, and launched into the air. They screamed again, a piercing hawk's cry as they ascended into the open blue sky, the wind of their downstrokes blasting against me.

I cried in dismay, "Wait—Lunix—take me with you!"

Lunix gave me a cursory glance with their mercurial moon-eyes as they retreated into the safety of the open air. Wingbeats clapped loudly, and their ultraviolet feathers winked with sunlight. I watched them abandon me until they were nothing more than an inkblot against the canvas of the sky.

Sinking against the bonnet of the car, Ackerleigh held his chest with a soft wheeze.

Claire gave a great sigh of relief, one hand on her breast and the other on Ackerleigh's shoulder. "Leigh, I'm gonna be honest, I might have peed myself."

Ackerleigh gave her a dry look as he emerged from his horrified paralysis. "Charging a member of a gryphon's family is usually ill-advised."

Claire pointed emphatically at me. "But he broke your ribs!"

"Not so much him." Ackerleigh coughed into his sleeve with a wince. Clearing his throat, he said softly, "First and foremost, I got my own ribs broken. Secondly, if not me then you can blame his sister's foot, not him. He fished me out." Pewter eyes slid back toward me, the gratitude clear on his softening features. "I'm starting to think he actually resuscitated me, too."

Heat blazed from the crown of my head straight down my spine and directly into my groin. He *did* remember! What an exhilarating thought—and mortifying. Ackerleigh caught my eye and held it with his sparkling gaze before I looked away to avoid imploding.

"By the way, where do you think Lunix is going, Nico?" Ackerleigh asked, squinting heavenward.

"Um—" I had to force myself to carry on the conversation like I hadn't been completely blindsided by the realization that Ackerleigh knew what had happened yesterday. "I–I can't be sure. Probably back to Stella."

He shot me a worried look. "Probably—?"

"I mean, they *are* a wild gryphon, Doctor Sebring."

Ackerleigh conceded with a faint nod, then made a face at me and cocked his head. "Why did you start calling me that today?"

"What?"

"'Doctor.'"

I frowned, thinking it was obvious. When that questioning look remained on his face, I shrugged. "You said you did your doctoral dissertation on gryphon pods. So, you have a Ph.D., don't you?"

"Yes." Ackerleigh blinked at me. "I suppose I do."

"So, Doctor Sebring."

Ackerleigh fanned the curling corners of his notebook paper through his fingers, studying me in silence.

"Figured that since you're as young as you are, you musta worked really hard to get it," I added, awkwardly jamming my hands in my pockets. "Though, I guess, like the light-licker bit, I don't know your age specifically, and a gentleman knows not to guess."

Amusement leapt into Ackerleigh's eyes like tungsten sparks. He stifled a snort and dropped his gaze, his modesty softening his usual coy and flirtatious demeanor. "Twenty-seven," he mumbled.

"Ah, yes." I nodded and gave him a pleasant grin. "That was my guess."

He glanced up, saw my grin, and awkwardly pushed his fringe back from his brow. Then his gaze traveled across the car, settled on his friend, and turned dark and stormy. He snapped at Claire, "You! Put that silly smirk away and get in the car!"

Claire laughed. It was a throaty, deep sound that reminded me strangely of my mother.

To spare him, I offered quickly, "Here, let me get the trunk in the boot. Then I can drive us back, if you'd like."

Hovering near the driver's side, Claire stared at me as her eyebrows rose and fell rapidly, settling behind her glasses in a scowl. She clutched Ackerleigh's keys to her chest. "I never get to drive! Plus, I don't altogether trust you with my friend's safety at this time, you understand."

Ackerleigh rolled his eyes. "Didn't you *listen* to me?"

"Not usually, no," Claire chirped before she ducked and took her place in the driver's seat.

Soon after we broke off from the main thoroughfare running between Northton and Hazberg, the bumps, potholes, and generally unruly nature of the road prompted Claire to switch me into the driver's seat. Ackerleigh was sleeping so soundly that the commotion of flipping forward Claire's seat and my large form squeezing through the gap didn't even disturb him.

My palm crinkled against a piece of paper on the seat as I moved out of the car. I glanced down at it, noticing the Bennett Publishing House's golden seal. Subtly, while Claire grunted and grumbled as she got situated in the backseat, I skimmed the contents of the letter. It was Ackerleigh's invitation to participate in what Doctor Bennett blasphemously called a "research project", and the significant sum of money being offered upfront as a stipend.

I hoped, at least, that Ackerleigh had made it out of that wretched estate that much richer for all his suffering.

I slid the paper under my seat as I switched the car into drive and continued toward the mountains. Sunset painted the sky washes of orange, fuchsia, violet, and navy. Even the fat, fluffy clouds were tie-dyed. The fading sunlight snuck through gaps in the tall evergreens growing on both sides of us, blinding me with intermittent flashes of golden light.

"You're much more amicable than the muesli incident made you sound," Claire remarked suddenly. "And fit. Quite fit."

My eyes bugged as I looked at the rearview mirror, finding Claire's dark gaze watching me in her reflection. "Oh, no! Is that all you know about me?"

"Well, yes, since he said you refused to talk to him after that."

I scoffed, looking back at the road. "Yes, yes." I had no excuse besides—I knew I would get obsessive and carried away... which is exactly what happened anyway. "Well, now I've kidnapped him. Is that better?"

Claire narrowed her eyes. "I can't tell. I can't figure you out. Even your ocky accent comes and goes."

"Oh." I frowned, rubbing my scar. "Yes, I downplay it sometimes. Namely around my mother. Are you from Northton as well?"

She blinked. "Yes, I am. That's… interesting."

"There's a lot of light-lickers who think the ocky accent makes us sound unintelligent. And gods forbid I embarrass my mother."

"Oh." Uncomfortably, Claire fussed with her wispy fringe.

"Plus," I added unnecessarily, "I usually mirror people when we first meet. Makes people happy."

"Ah, that it does," Claire sighed. "Ackerleigh did that too when we first met. He didn't tell me for nine months that he actually hated beer and was only drinking it because I loved it."

I snorted. "Been there."

She welcomed Dove as the cat stood up from Ackerleigh's lap, arched her back, and stepped over the armrest to reach Claire. Her departure roused Ackerleigh, whose first waking instinct was to clutch his ribs with a hiss of pain.

I touched his wrist, intending to comfort him as consciousness returned. Eyes still closed, he immediately threaded our fingers together and squeezed my hand tightly. His skin was cold and damp, giving me the disturbing impression that he was half dead.

"We're almost back at the cottage," I said, "and then it's to bed with ya."

Ackerleigh peered at me sidelong through one slitted eye, gave a start, and looked at our joined hands. "Sorry, I—I thought you were Claire."

My heart responded in a peculiar, painful way. Disappointment and embarrassment had it flopping like a beached fish. I started to pull back, but the movement got stuck on his apology. Perhaps *he* was just embarrassed.

"S'alright," I said softly, hardly believing my own confidence. "Happy to bring comfort, too, if I can."

Ackerleigh relaxed, leaning his head against his seat as the corners of his lips twitched with appreciation. He looked through the windshield and watched the forest roll by. His thumb lightly traced the peaks and valleys of my knuckles. With his other hand, he fanned through the pages of his notebook.

I tried to ignore the lump of discomfort that settled into the pit of my stomach at the sight of his curly script within. It was discordant, wanting to allow for the privacy of a man I'd barely talked to before yesterday, and being desperately hurt by his desire to keep secrets from me. These feelings were all so foreign to me, it was terrible. I was going to have to vent to *Stella* about it before long, and if that didn't make my desperation abundantly clear, nothing would.

Nobody said much before the bed and breakfast began to peek over the foothills in the growing twilight. I wanted to drive behind the cottage and stash Ackerleigh's car near my truck, but the sedan was too low to the ground and would get caught in the grasses. Instead, I took the longer path around to the makeshift gravel drive next to the side of the cottage.

I swung open my door and slowly got to my feet, testing my weight on my stiff left ankle. While rolling it gently, I lifted my gaze to the sierra. A fading outline of deep umber light from the sunset clung to the uppermost peaks, which were misty with the oncoming dark. I had a vain hope that perhaps I would see Lunix up there, circling their prey before returning to us in time for supper.

As Ackerleigh climbed out of the passenger seat, his gaze also lifted to search the mountainous slopes. He grimaced, glancing at me.

"I'm sure they'll come back," I said softly. "Maybe they're already with—"

"Nico!" The front door of the cottage burst open. My sister sprinted out with ecstatic relief on her face. To my surprise, Cheese bolted after her, barking excitedly. I hadn't seen her in several weeks; she was a bit of a wanderer, and had been staying at Cyrus's farm guarding his chicken coop in exchange for brisket castoffs.

Dove, who was in Claire's arms, hissed and puffed up in alarm, forcing Claire to trap her in place with a yelp.

I was just distracted enough for Stella to surprise me as she barreled into me. My injured ankle buckled and I fell into the car with her arms around my neck.

Amidst curses and cries of relief, Stella exclaimed, "That took so long I was about to go tell Mother!"

"Ouch, no, we're alright. Off, please." I unwound Stella's strong grip and set her on her feet, but Cheese promptly took the space she'd left and smothered my arms with slobbery kisses.

"Nico?" Ackerleigh asked, alarmed. "Are you hurt? What happened to your ankle?" He held his notebook curled up under one arm, his other on Claire's bicep as she tried to escape with the angry, growling cat.

Stella caught sight of Dove. "Oh, I recognize her! Hi, baby. Cheese won't hurt you. Just relax, hm? Who's your nerdy-looking friend, Ackerleigh?"

Claire scoffed. "Watch it, little lady!"

"Why, are you his *girlfriend?*" Stella put her hands on her hips, which she swiveled with a sassy bob of her head.

"We're both gay," Claire remarked drolly. "Can I go inside? This cat is shredding my boobs." When Ackerleigh gasped and ushered her toward the open door, Stella swung back to me, flushed from crown to clavicle.

She pointed after Ackerleigh and his friend and hissed, "You've got a shot!"

I grabbed her face with both hands and squished her cheeks together aggressively. "What is wrong with you, Estelle? What is wrong with you?"

Stella laughed wetly and shocked my wrists with a zap of magíq.

"Ow! Gods, you little andullie. Get Ackerleigh's trunk out of the boot, will ya?"

Stella snorted. "Not a chance." Despite her words, she obediently fought with the boot until she popped the hinge and pulled it open. "Gods! We could fit everything we own in one of these."

"Just do it," I grumbled, limping toward the cottage. "I need a shower. And something to eat."

"I made cookies!" Stella grunted as she shouldered the trunk. "They're sorta burnt."

"*Real* food. Wait, how'd you make cookies?"

"Cyrus forced me to take eggs and milk. I swear, I just went there for Cheese."

"We still have cheese."

Stella screeched, "The *dog!* You'll never let me live it down that I named her Cheese, will ya?"

Despite my exhaustion and all the buzzing in my head, I laughed.

I stepped over the threshold into the cabin to the sweet scent of beechwood burning in the hearth. Darkness wrapped the cottage up in shadows, which danced with the flickering firelight. Stella shouldered me out of her way as she came in with the trunk, which she dropped between the stairs and the washroom. She went to the armchair where Dove was furiously bathing herself.

I limped over to where Ackerleigh stood in front of the hearth. He was gazing seriously at his notebook, fingers tracing what looked to be a sketch of Lunix. Then he gripped a chunk of the pages by the edge and savagely tore them out. Like an offering to a god, he extended them toward the hearth fire.

My heart lurched and I tripped to a halt, unable to silence a gasp of surprise. Horrified, I watched the papers float into the flames, where they ignited and turned to cinders almost immediately. Ackerleigh's expression was impassive as he continued destroying all the secrets we'd worked so hard to retrieve, one handful of paper at a time. Embers floated up from the mouth of the hearth. For a moment it seemed like Ackerleigh was one and the same with the fire: destructive and brilliant both, not discriminating between friend or foe, or caring who he hurt. He didn't look up until he had burned every sheet, and all he held was a bouncing metal spiral to which bits of torn paper clung like confetti.

Ackerleigh's eyes were bright with restrained tears as he looked up and met my gaze. "There we are," he breathed, satisfied.

My mouth hung open. Like a spark following a trail of tinder, anger crept up on me. It fed on my injured ankle, on the terrible fear of being found out at the estate, on the contradictions between Ackerleigh's affections and his impervious walls. It ignited when I saw how *pleased* Ackerleigh looked.

"Why—" My voice broke. I shook my head sharply. "No! Why did I take you all the way back to that nightmare for you to just—to just... I–I don't know... shut me out, and then *burn* that godforsaken thing the second we g-got back here?"

Ackerleigh's satisfaction faltered and then fell away. His head tilted slightly; he slowly set the spiral of metal down on the bricks near the fire and then reached for my arm, but I stepped quickly out of reach.

With his hand still extended, Ackerleigh said gently, "I'm afraid there's been a misunderstanding."

"No, shit," I remarked, rubbing at my scar so hard that it stung. I waved my arm, turned away, then turned back again as I demanded, "How can I understand if you don't tell me?"

Ackerleigh's gaze shifted to his friend, who stood awkwardly near my equally uncomfortable sister. He looked back at me, pressing his lips together. "I... I never should have written down what I did. The fact that you got hurt today just makes it all worse. I'm sorry, Nico. I wish I..." He glanced at Stella, and some secret look passed between them. "I want to explain. But I can't—"

The refusal struck like hot coals. My throat constricted. I dropped my head, clenching my fists. I managed a mute nod, brushing past him to reach the back door, which I jerked open. Stella called after me, but I ignored her, barely making it off the back steps before the tears started spilling.

Survey of Academic Discipline

Despite my proximity to the merrily crackling fire, a bone-deep chill descended upon me. Stella met my eyes one more time in a show of solidarity as she hustled past me toward the door Nico had left open. Their dog, apparently called Cheese, barked with excitement and scampered after her, nails clicking against the flagstones. Stella banged the door shut behind them.

I groaned, covering my face with my hands.

Claire's familiar warm arm slid around my shoulders. "Come on, friend," she tutted, carding my hair with her fingers. I sighed into my palms and leaned into her, nuzzling my cheek against her cashmere sweater. I loved when Claire wore soft fabric like this, and she knew it. It was almost like she'd worn it on purpose, like she'd been planning to follow me back here from the outset.

I lowered my hands to sling the accusation.

Claire turned me in a circle and asked before I could speak, "Is there a bath around here? I say this with the utmost affection—but you have never had quite so many interesting smells going on as you do right now, and I'm sure you could use a warm soak."

Affronted, I opened my mouth to defend myself. Yet I couldn't. I was still gritty with salt from yesterday's swim and had added a heavy coating of dust and sweat to the mixture today. "Yes, alright. This way."

"Ah, I also filched some of the pain medication from Mathilda's hysterectomy." She pulled a pill bottle out from the pocket of her trousers, which I gratefully took. Handing her the black lid, I tipped a white tablet into my hand and swallowed it dry. As if the discomfort of the chalky sensation on my tongue was the worst experience of my day.

"With her blessing, of course," Claire added as she took back the bottle and returned it to her trousers. "We know she's more sensible than either of us, but she'll always support our nonsense."

"We need her practicality," I laughed as I used my feet to push my trunk into the washroom. Claire quickly took over and settled it on the tiles opposite the tub. Moving much faster than I could, Claire bustled to the tub and spun the hot water dial as far as it would go, followed by a few taps on the cold. Then she peered at the row of toiletries on a carved wooden shelf against the tiled wall, picking up a jar labeled *epsom and lavender*, and dumping a generous heap into the stream of water.

"Let me stay and wash your hair," she said. The suggestion of undressing in front of her wasn't that outlandish, considering how often we went shopping together. "And if I find a pair of shears in here—so help me, your hair needs me, too."

I knew better than to argue, since she'd been my hairdresser ever since we'd met at Ravensbourne. I undressed with my right arm tucked against my chest. Naturally, when I pulled Nico's oversized shirt over my head, it loosened the ribbon from my hair. Claire caught it on its way down and tied it around her wrist.

"A little memento," she sang playfully.

Although I didn't think I needed the assistance—*she* hadn't seen me climb along the back of a gryphon without killing myself—she held onto my elbow while I got settled in the tub.

Steam rose from the fragrant water. I let it loosen my aggravated lungs and the knot of awful feelings tangled around my heart.

It confused and dismayed me that the only reason I hadn't told Nico about my magíq was because of Claire. Before meeting another magíqon whose family loved and accepted her gift, I never would have known to want the same from my loved ones. My magíq was hardly more than a shameful secret.

But now...

Nico *needed* to know. The look of heartbreak on his face as I'd guarded the secrets in that foolish notebook of mine was not something I could let lie. He deserved to know why I'd hid it before now.

Yet telling a man I hardly knew before yesterday, and *not* my best friend and only companion during my time at Ravensbourne—that felt unfair, too. Claire had supported me in my uphill battle to get my research funded. She had spoken to members of the registrar to make sure all of my classes were on the bottom floor of Mortensen. She had shielded me from President Brandon wherever she could.

But she was still born and bred in the cities, which fueled Technocrat rhetoric in subtle and insidious ways. Children soaked in the belief that magíq was dangerous and magíqon were pariahs. Even if she loved me and understood me in a way even my mother had often struggled to, Claire was a light-licker. Her prejudices could rear up and alienate us without warning, were she to learn about my gods-blessed blood.

I couldn't survive the loss of her, but I'd survived the weight of my secret for *years.*

When I drifted free from my drowsy, dismal thoughts, Claire's fingers were deep in my soaked scalp as she worked a lather into my hair. She leaned over and smiled when I opened my eyes.

"So, where's the nearest grocer?" she asked breezily.

I frowned. "What? Um..."

"How about the nearest hospital that you *definitely* should have visited yesterday?" She paused to rinse my hair before swiftly continuing, "You lost your glasses—what are you going to do to get new ones?"

I sighed heavily, wiping my eyes. "Claire, out with it. What are you on about?"

Claire came around to the side of the tub, sitting on my trunk with her elbows on her knees. "I know your heart is with your gryphon companion," she said pleadingly, "and your mountain man. But you're coming back to Laurier with me, right?"

The water seemed to turn frigid, encasing my body with cold dread. "Well, I—no, I don't think..."

"The Bennett estate was one thing," Claire insisted. "But are you prepared for *this* sort of life?" She gestured to the humid washroom, but metaphorically, I knew she was indicating everything about this remote location. She would be no more equipped than me living out here, in what Nico referred to as the mountain's armpit.

Immediately, staying in the bath repulsed me. I grasped the moth-eaten towel Claire had found, wrapping it around my waist as I rose out of the water, dripping and dappled with lavender buds. Another hour in here would have done me good, but Claire's question had ruffled me. She stood aside and went to rummage in the medicine cabinet while I opened my trunk.

It wasn't that Claire was *wrong*. Nico and Stella had been out here in the mountain's armpit their whole lives. They were physically more capable than me, familiar with the land, skilled at finding spaces to stay and providing for themselves. What did I have? Asthma and bruises.

A sense of resignation and regret felt like ash coating my tongue. With no sign of Lunix, broken ribs, and one car to my name stranding either me or Claire here unless we went to Laurier together, I was running out of reasons why I ought to stay. My throat tightened and my eyes burned. Swallowing hard, I focused on getting into something warm and comforting, and not ill-fitting.

I dressed in the coziest wool trousers I owned beneath a draping tunic and an open, fuzzy cardigan. Claire didn't push me to talk; rather, she extracted my brush from my trunk and gently patted dry and brushed my hair when I had finished changing.

"I see the life this place and these people bring you," Claire said thoughtfully. Her soft words were like a funerary bell; they were kind and observant, but filled with caveats. "I don't discount that, and I want you to feel like this forever. But I need you to be making informed decisions. Which also means I need to tell you about Ravensbourne."

I snapped my gaze to her. My lips parted. "Wh... What do you mean?"

Without responding, Claire ushered me from the washroom straight to the couch facing the picture window. The hearth behind us had pleasantly warmed up the cushions. Dove jumped down from the armchair and trotted over to me, chirping with each step until she was on my lap and kneading my thighs. I noticed a whiff of faintly burnt cookies beneath the smell of the wood burning. I couldn't bear the stark contrast between the perfectly cozy atmosphere and the mounting dread that gripped me.

Claire slowly sat beside me, chewing on her thumbnail. She tucked her auburn locks behind her ear, making the large diamond stud in her lobe flash like starlight.

"*Claire.*" I gripped her knee. "Don't make me suffer. What happened at Ravensbourne?"

"Camden Zane is being expelled," Claire blurted.

Her words slammed into my heart and knocked the air out of my lungs. Breathlessly, I shouted, "What?" I leapt to my feet, dumping Dove onto the floor who hissed in protest. But Claire knew my ways and, with a firm hand on my elbow, she pulled me back into my seat.

Panic, outrage, and the inability to restlessly pace kept my voice raised. "I can't believe that! That is completely and utterly unwarranted." I clenched my fists so hard that my nails dug into my palms. "That... That is a-a gross abuse of power!"

I jerked at the sound of the back door crashing open.

Nico stumbled into view, chest heaving, gripping his frizzy hair with his eyes wide with alarm. "What happened? What's wrong, Ackerleigh?"

My thoughts were clattering with visions of Camden Zane's academic career—which had started in the gutter. Aimless, hostile, and defensive, Cam had come to me on the verge of dropping out. After we'd figured out his accommodations, though, he'd fought tooth and nail to exceed everyone's low expectations for him.

Now, he was ending in the gutter, too.

I winced at the sudden stinging on my cheek and dabbed at my cut, which was when I realized I was crying. "D-Don't tell me it's because..." I choked and looked at Claire, desperate to be wrong. "Don't tell me he got expelled because of that stupid petition."

Claire's pained expression immediately confirmed the worst.

"Brandon is expelling Cam because he dared to *speak up for me?*" I cried, despair and anger warring with one another and making me at once nauseous and violent. I bowed my head and hit the heels of my hands against my temples. "What... What more does he want from me? He got *rid* of me!" A sob wrenched from my chest.

"I hope I wasn't wrong to tell you," Claire whispered.

I couldn't reply, and I knew she wasn't expecting an answer. As I felt the cushion rise and heard her trouser legs rustle together, I lifted my head in confusion. My tear-stained vision made her look like she was underwater as, to my surprise, she swapped places with Nico. He was miming aggressively at Stella and Claire, who exchanged silent grimaces.

Exhausted, I gave up on trying to understand what they were up to and dropped my head into my hands. I was too weary to sob, to gnash my teeth or lament on the injustices.

A large, tentative hand skimmed my shoulders. I peeked from beneath my hands and found the smoldering embers of Nico's gaze worriedly pinned on my face.

Suddenly nothing sounded better than burrowing into the crook of his arm. So I did. It felt like sprawling out in a sunbeam. He closed his arm around my shoulders, brushing his finger against my cardigan sleeve. Listening to his deep, drumming heartbeat, I was finally able to catch my breath and slow my tears.

A cookie appeared under my nose resting on a scrap of paper towel. I jumped, looking up at Stella, who gave me the most awkward grin of all time as she nudged the very dark treat toward me. I took the paper towel from her hands with a choked laugh of thanks and nibbled on the edge of the cookie, which was fairly burnt.

Claire handed Nico a glass of water and nodded to me. I reached for it, but then everyone saw how badly my hand trembled. Nico, on the other hand, was slow and steady as he held the glass to my lips. I wrapped my hands around his, slotting my fingers into the valleys of his knuckles.

After a generous drink, I said with a shake of my head, "Thank you, everyone. I appreciate the attention." I picked up the flat throw pillow I'd used this morning and hugged it to my ribs while I stayed safe in the shelter of Nico's arm. New tears leaked out of my eyes when I pressed my fingers into them. "I just can't fathom using my authority to—to break down and discourage the people who are counting on me."

Claire spoke from the armchair across from me while Dove glared at me in her lap. "The Owl—er, Craig and I, we tried to keep Cam in class for as long as we could. We were talking to the registrar every day, but they couldn't overpower the president's decision."

"Everyone knows Brandon is an enfour," I spat, earning a quick giggle from Stella for my language. "Yet nobody challenges him, and those that do, he banishes from his realm. It's so far from the tenets that Pascale Manon set down for Ravensbourne that I—" I growled and dropped my head back against Nico.

"Here, I made some ice, too." Stella held out a tea towel heaped with ice cubes. I noticed at once how they glowed softly with a glittering sheen of magíq, which prompted an immediate smile. She could have easily left ordinary water in the ice box to freeze, but she'd made me magíqal ones instead.

Carefully, I took the bundle from her. I laid my hand on hers and let the static build up between our skin so the contact hummed with life and a ticklish layer of electricity. She broke into a grin, bits of her sun-kissed hair standing on end.

I gave a start. "Oh, your brother should use some, too, for his ankle."

Nico protested immediately, "I don't need—"

Stella sighed and said over him, "Nico stopped putting ice on a twisted ankle when he was sixteen. I can't change his mind, but maybe you can."

"Perhaps. I'll certainly try," I sighed. The cold seeped into my skin and descended like a gentle snowfall around my ribs, soothing and therapeutic where ordinary ice was harsh and sharp.

Stella nodded before she dropped to the floor, sitting on the threadbare rug next to the coffee table. She made kissing sounds in Cheese's direction. The dog thundered over to her, greeting her with such enthusiasm that Stella almost fell over.

"So," Stella said, eyeing Claire with suspicion. "Who scared Lunix off?"

Claire groaned and covered her face.

"She didn't mean to," I began.

"They stopped by," Stella continued, using both hands to block any further canine face kisses. I sat up straighter, so she directed her explanation at me. "They landed in an absolute huff, like havin' a real temper tantrum, hissin' and growlin', then took a pumpkin and flew into the mountains. To sulk, I think."

"I'm sorry!" exclaimed Claire. "I didn't know—"

"They did this when they were a kit," Nico said thoughtfully, brushing his hand over his stubble. "Any time they got into it with someone, like after they bit off Tad's finger—"

Claire yelped, "They what?"

"I don't r'member that!" Stella exclaimed, looking wounded.

He nodded. "Their emotions are just like the rest of ours. Havin' an outburst like that is exhausting. They gotta isolate for a bit. When they were younger, it wasn't for more than a day." Then he pushed his arm into the back of the couch and gingerly got to his feet. "I'm gonna go make us all some supper."

"No!" Claire exclaimed. "Let… Let Stella and I do that."

Stella whined, "I don't wanna cook! I can't even make cookies! Is it a'cause I'm a girl? 'Cause I'm hardly a girl—"

I pulled the blanket off the back of the couch and wrapped myself up in this, content to listen to the three of them argue with my eyes closed. Eventually, Nico was sent limping to take a shower. Not acting remotely like they'd met a mere hour or two ago, my best friend dragged the teenage magíqon into the kitchen like an auntie would her petulant niece. And Stella let her.

Dove eventually stopped being mad at me and came to curl up on my lap in the folds of my blanket. I was left feeling bittersweet and wrung out. My thoughts went to expelled students and power-hungry tyrants, and yet also to how being in Nico's embrace had felt as hopeful as a sunrise. Warm and gentle, being close to him was a sensation I was desperate to chase. And that meant I had a confession to make.

Intermediate Confessions

Orion. Cassiopeia. Faintly orange Aldebaran. The smudge of Omega Centauri.

Before Stella was born, I'd lived away from home for a total of four years until the homesickness set in. It wasn't for the De Falco farm, although I'd got along with Pa and Mother well enough back then. I was homesick for the stars, and the fields. Dirt under my fingertips and the smell of my sun-baked skin. The soreness in my muscles from simply being *outside*, from climbing hassocks and throwing hay bales and riding Peach for hours simply for the sake of being with her under open skies.

So why, now, did I still feel homesick? What was I craving now, laid out across the bed of my truck with the whole expanse of the heavens swallowing me up? Why were tears burning my eyes and tightening my throat? I had always hoped that I could satisfy my restless heart. When we left the farm a few months ago, that was supposed to have been enough. Wandering the countryside would settle the ache in my bones that had cost me so many nights of sleep. But it was still there. Tonight, I finally realized what it was.

Loneliness.

Betelgeuse. Meissa. Bellatrix. Mintaka, Alnilam, Alnitak. Saiph. Rigel.

My palm spread out toward the warrior constellation, boldly poised with brilliant clarity in the complete darkness.

Sometimes this was how I waited for Lunix to come home. Star-charting hand spread wide, I would watch for their wingspan to cross beneath my thumb and forefinger. Only now, I wasn't just wishing for Lunix. I was wishing for Ackerleigh. Wishing that perhaps the stars would bless me, and bring Ackerleigh into my orbit.

The constellation blurred and went glassy as I hiccuped and swallowed a sob that was toiling with half desire, half shame.

I couldn't afford to be pining after someone. I had to keep my sister safe from folks like Tad. I had to keep us out of Doctor Bennett's grasp. And now, since Pa had turned his back on Stella and we'd been left to our own devices, I was all she had.

Me, and my wretched *loneliness.*

I let my tears fall freely, my ragged breathing harmonizing with the crickets and a solitary Great-Horned Owl calling uncannily in the darkness. Faintly on the mountain breeze, an elk screamed. I wondered if it was facing down Lunix and knew its end was near.

If Ackerleigh were lucky, Lunix would be back by morning. But maybe their resentment for their captivity had changed things. Maybe it would be worth leaving us for the sake of their freedom now that they knew it could be snatched away by any crazed doctor with poor ethics.

Ackerleigh would be heartbroken, but maybe I was wrong to keep worrying about his feelings. It didn't feel like he extended the same courtesy to me. Whatever secrets were in that burned notebook, he cared more about them than me.

My feelings for him were obviously not reciprocated with equal intensity. Despite the affectionate looks he'd given me throughout the day. Despite how he'd nestled into my arm like he'd never felt safe until that moment. I was making it all up, exaggerating the meaning of what we had. I had to be. If it were real, wouldn't he be more honest?

Gods. Was this type of feeling always so maddening?

Swiping my cardigan sleeve over my eyes, I willed myself to stop crying like a baby. I traced Orion's shield into the Seven Sisters as I hiccuped to catch my breath.

Electra. Merope. Maia. Celaeno. Taygeta. Alcyone. I was missing another A.

Ackerleigh.

The back door opened and spilled firelight across the grass.

I sat up. From where I was, the shadows remained deep and impenetrable, but the cottage's light shone through fluffy platinum hair and illuminated silky white skin. Ackerleigh's neck stretched as he tilted back his head to stare at the heavens, hugging his elbows, silent as he stood among whispering grasses.

"Thank you," I whispered to the stars. Then with a fortifying breath, I slapped the side of the truck and called, "Hey-o, Ackerleigh."

The man squinted into the darkness. "Nico?" He cautiously picked his way through the tall grass and the garden, muttering uneasily until he made it to the open hatch. "So this is where you got off to. I doze off for two seconds, and you vanish into thin air."

I laughed. "I think it was a few hours." I scrambled over to the end of the truck, making the hydraulics squeak as I shifted my weight. Before he could try getting up into the truck alone and end up hurting himself, I wound my arm around his waist. He sucked in a small breath, hands landing around my neck. I lifted his slight weight easily and set him on his knees on the bed of the truck. This was *not* the time to be thinking of this space as a bed, however, and I felt my ears heat up as I let him go.

Ackerleigh's hands remained on my neck as he got his bearings. "This is quite the cozy space," he observed, nodding to the thick duvet and flannel blanket spread out under us. He slowly unwound his grip from me and crawled further across the bed to where I'd made myself a rumpled little nest.

"I like t' be prepared to hit the road at any moment," I explained, returning to my spot and trying not to crowd him. "And plus, I like t-to stargaze." Nerves jangled through my body, provoking a stutter. I felt like a little boy trying desperately to contain a scream of excitement. *Ackerleigh* was in my *truck!*

Partly to busy my hands, I unlatched the utility box wedged into the corner against the cab. "H-Here. I have a light." I pulled out an electrical lantern, switching it on.

Glowing like the Milky Way, Ackerleigh offered me a faint smile. He'd taken off the cardigan he'd been wearing earlier, and the tunic underneath had short sleeves. Goosebumps rose along his bare arms as he hugged his knees to his chest. He looked unbothered, but I wasn't buying it.

"Doctor—Ackerleigh."

"Doctor Ackerleigh, eh?" He chuckled softly, giving me a wry look and sending my heart into a frenzy. Was I too young to have a heart attack?

I ignored his teasing. "It gets below freezin' in the mountain's armpit at night."

"Good. Perhaps my ribs will feel better then." Shivers vibrated his limbs.

I peeled my cardigan off and swept it over Ackerleigh's shoulders.

Ackerleigh was paralyzed for a moment until he blinked hard. He tenderly stroked the fuzzy collar. Mother had lined this cardigan with fleece to give it extra warmth, and I promised myself I'd remember to thank her.

I frantically groped for something to say, but my absolute panic about these circumstances was making it hard to think. I had just been comforting him on the couch mere hours ago, but...

This was different, and so much more intimate than when Stella and Claire had bullied me into sitting with him then. As pleasant as that was, it was a setup, and I'd had an audience. Now... I had him all to myself.

The cacophonous sounds of the night filled the silence between us. Which was good, considering any and all conversational skills I possessed had fled from me the moment Ackerleigh sat down in my truck.

I tap-tap-tapped my scar. "Ackerleigh?"

Ackerleigh bundled himself up in my cardigan. He slipped his arm into one of the pastel sleeves so he could rub it against his mouth before his twilit gaze shifted toward me. "Nico?"

"I don't understand." My fingers found their way to my scar again. "About the notebook. And I'm tryin' not to be bitter about it, but... one minute, it seems like I'm closer to you than I've ever been t'anybody, and then the next moment you're blockin' me out and makin' me feel like a fool." The last words that left my mouth wobbled unsteadily, betraying my childish dejection.

Ackerleigh didn't react right away. A slow, thin sigh left his nostrils. "Nico, I'm so sorry. You're completely right. I feel terrible." He lifted his gaze to the sky, eyes darting back and forth as he searched for words. He wetted his soft, pink lips with the tip of his glistening tongue. "Let me... I suppose I'll just pick a place to start."

"Alright, I just—"

"I talked to your sister last night after you were asleep," he said hurriedly. "It ended up being... quite enlightening."

"Oh," I gasped. Suddenly, their interactions today made so much more sense. "Oh-h-h! I was wonderin' why y'all were gettin' on so well. But, uh... all due respect, what's that got to do with..."

"Ah, I'm sorry." He laughed nervously. "I'm not accustomed to talking about any of this yet. I—I, you see... I have been keeping a secret, Nico—but until last night, it hadn't even occurred to me that life could be any other way."

Noticing his obvious struggle, I kept quiet and occupied my hands by flipping the handle of the lantern back and forth. I stole a sidelong glance at him. The expression visible on his profile was somber, and the inflamed, scabbed gouges under his eye brought back his storybook hero appearance.

"Ackerleigh, I don't want to force you…"

Ackerleigh's next words tumbled out from him in a rush. "I'm a magíqon, you see, and meeting someone else—" He laughed breathlessly. "—Someone like me, and realizing how *unlike* her life mine has been…" He trailed off, eyes downcast. After a few beats where we both remained perfectly still, he glanced up at me. Tears swam in his eyes and shined like crystals in the lantern light. "Nobody ever knew. I'd never dreamed of anyone knowing. Until yesterday." A single tear raced down his cheek.

"Oh." My brain was somewhere far off in the distance, trying to shout the meaning of Ackerleigh's words across the void, but I refused to understand him. "You're… wait." Finally, his words linked together in my head and blinked on like a seldom-used light bulb. I exclaimed, "You're a magíqon?"

"I'm a magíqon. Yeah." Ackerleigh's lips spread, neither in a smile nor a grimace but some bittersweet marriage of the two. "I was using that notebook as a journal," he rasped.

I felt like I'd been punched in the stomach. I gasped, "Of course." I'd been such a fool! I'd harped and whined about not knowing his secrets, but… this was literally *huge*, that there was another magíqon and he'd found his way into my sister's life and—and Lunix's life! This was all eons larger than me or my feelings, and I'd been a selfish, stupid… "Fool."

Looking stung as his cheeks flushed, Ackerleigh began, "I beg your—"

"Not you!" I exclaimed, slapping my hand into his knee so hard that he flinched. I softened my grip apologetically. "Not you, I'm sorry. *I'm* the fool. I thought… I don't know, you'd written… sonnets, or—"

He laughed loudly and hard, covering his face with a hand. "Good gods. I was afraid of that."

"You *were?*" I cocked my head. "This is a very specific shared fear."

Ackerleigh laughed harder, hugging his arms around his ribs and wincing as he stifled himself. "No, it wasn't anything… sweet, or silly.

Much worse." He sobered. A wheeze came with his next inhale. "I was careless. For the last two months, Lunix has taught me a considerable amount of magíq. Granted, I knew how to do nothing with the gods-breath in my body before them, so they have officially taught me everything I know."

"*Wow*," I breathed. "Lunix helped Stella, too. The two of them were doing magíq together all the time. They were wonderful. And highly, highly dangerous." My finger tapped at my scar.

"Yes, but that furthers my point... If I had any desire to teach again, my chances would be completely annihilated if Doctor Bennett had found that notebook where I confessed to my own magíq. I couldn't even keep my job because I taught *about* magíq." He curled his lip, derisive. "Nobody in this country wants to deal with magíqon anymore. Most people would rather we didn't exist."

I grimaced, but couldn't deny it. "Yeah. Stella's had nothin' but trouble with folks out here knowin' what she is."

Ackerleigh looked at my hand where it absently rubbed my scar. With a gentle finger on my chin, he angled my head so my sunburst scar was on full display. As I uneasily lowered my hand, he traced the shape of the impact on my head. The touch was overwhelming. Intimate. I'd never let anyone else come near it, not even to dress it when I first got it. But his gentle fingertip drew out the electricity that at times still seemed to fizzle within it. Like an antivenom bringing immediate relief.

Ackerleigh's gaze was inquisitive, but his voice was soft as feathers. "This is from magíq, isn't it?"

"Yes," I whispered. Catlike, I tilted my head into his hand. He tenderly stroked the buzzed section of my hair before trailing his fingers along my jawline. I shut my eyes, unraveled completely by this man's attention.

I didn't realize it, but I'd never actually shared about the accident with Stella. My parents had been there when it had happened, and Stella barely remembered it, so I sat in the residual fear and pain in isolation.

Safe within Ackerleigh's concern, I sighed and began, "For my twelfth birthday, my parents got me my own mare. Peach. *Gods*, I miss her," I muttered before continuing, "Stella was five. She was silly and happy and she'd never used any magíq before." Strange parts of the memory returned to me as if I was still there. The taste of pennies on my tongue, and the smell of my singed hair. Warmth in my lap from having wet myself, my entire body having been convinced that, in that moment, I was about to die.

"Stella wanted to ride with me and got underfoot, and I almost trampled her. I... I was so mad, and scared, that I just *screamed* at her. Between the tramplin', and me yelling, she got so scared that electricity just sorta..." I searched for words. "...jumped out of her, like an arrow." My arm rose automatically to shield my face before I coaxed it back down and took a breath. "Food tasted like metal for *years* after that, and I shocked everything I touched."

Ackerleigh quietly clicked his tongue, twining my individual curls around his fingers, tickling my scalp. "I was petrified of hurting people like that when I was a boy. I didn't realize until I was seven that I had my own magíq, and I cried for days." He paused, looking again at my scar. "You touch that a lot. Does it still hurt?"

Shame heated my face up. I ducked my head. "N–No, not really, I just..."

"It's alright," Ackerleigh interrupted, easing my rambling unease. "It seems like it comforts you to do that."

I slowly lifted my gaze to him. His expression was painfully gentle, and his eyes were silver as stardust. A chilly mountain breeze teased his platinum fringe. He glanced up at it, eyes narrowing as if to have his hair mussed in such a way was a familiar bother.

As soon as his focus fixed on the wind, the draft spiraled away from him and into me. The glittering ribbons whipped my hair into a frenzy. Curls went everywhere; I flapped my hands, spitting as they snaked into my mouth.

Ackerleigh stifled a giggle, and I realized with a start that he was manipulating the wind. Indignantly, I opened my mouth to protest. His eyes promptly flicked away from me, and with it went the wind. My vision was obscured by misplaced hair, which he helped to rearrange and smooth down.

"Sorry," he laughed.

I rolled my eyes, but couldn't fight my own grin. "Oh, well, it's better than Stella's constant need to shock me."

"Oh! Isn't that in poor taste?"

"She don't know any better, hardly. It's just her favorite element. Maybe someday it'll stop making me anxious every time." I shrugged dismissively. "But what a life I lead, being the only man in the country to be harassed by not one, but *two* magíqon."

Coquettish, he brought cheek to shoulder in half a shrug. "It's only out of love."

I hummed dubiously and opened the utility box again, rummaging around inside. Within a pile of greasy rags—meant to hide it from Stella—was a mostly full bottle of brandy, which looked like liquid gold in the lantern light. I cradled it between my knees while I used the edge of a hunting knife to pry out the cork.

Ackerleigh watched me, inquisitive, as I tipped the bottle and took a long swig of the heady liquor. It had been so long since I'd last drunk alcohol that I gave an involuntary shudder.

Eyes sparkling, Ackerleigh plucked the bottle out of my hand. For being so soft-spoken, he had no shortage of assertiveness. After taking a drink, he tilted the label toward the lantern light and gave it a quizzical look. He glanced up at me. "Is this what you do after a stressful day when a stranger makes you fly all about the country while repeatedly hurting your feelings?"

I chuckled quietly. "Stop that. There's no bad blood here." I paused for a beat while holding his gaze to ensure he took me seriously. "And no. Unlike my Pa, I only drink on special occasions."

Ackerleigh brightened. "What's the occasion?"

"I have company over." I held out my hand for the bottle.

He laughed, the sound soft and tinkling like tumbling sea glass. He extended the bottle to me, but didn't release it when I tugged on it. "I'll only give this to you if you answer a question," Ackerleigh said, mischief in the curl of his lips and the crinkles of his eyes.

I feigned a frown of displeasure at his imposition, reclining on my elbow and propping my chin on my hand. "If you insist, Doctor Acker-leigh."

He snorted. His gunmetal gaze skimmed over my thin turtleneck, which I realized beneath his scrutiny was quite snug around my chest.

Wetting his lips, he seemed distracted for a moment before he blinked hard and looked up to meet my gaze. "We know I'm gay, thanks to Claire and Stella."

It suddenly became much more difficult to appear nonchalant. Ack-erleigh had to be manipulating my body temperature the same way that he had the wind, as I was about to burst into flames. "U-Um. Yes. Is... ah... is... that somethin'... you've known for—some time?"

"Excuse me, have I asked my question yet?" Ackerleigh demanded, taking another swig from the bottle and then shuddering.

My lips twitched. "Well, *now* you asked a question, so..."

"Drat!" he exclaimed. "I blame the drink. It's mixing quite strongly with my pain pill. Here, take it away from me."

As I accepted the outstretched bottle, I couldn't tamp down a grow-ing smirk. "Now I have the bottle, *and* you lost your question. What do you think—shall I give you a freebie?"

Ackerleigh's jaw dropped and a crease appeared between his eye-brows. "You ought to, unless you're cruel!" I almost felt guilty, but then his open mouth turned up at the corners, offense changing to amusement. He scooted closer to me and lay back to rest his head on my thighs. "But you're not cruel, so anyway... Yes, most people know I'm gay without needing to ask. I knew I was destined for lace, chiffon, and attraction to men by the time I was... I don't know, nine?" He glanced at me. "But what about you? What's your experience been?"

My fingers skimmed straight over my scar and found their way to Ackerleigh's hair. It was like touching delicate threads glinting with drops of starlight, and silky against my skin.

"I don't think I've ever put a name to it all," I admitted. "But for me, attraction doesn't seem to be based on gender." Or even their lack of gender—that ambiguous space between masculine and feminine, which

Ackerleigh seemed to occupy with the finesse of a flower petal dancing on a breeze. "It's more about a feelin' I get from bein' around someone." I allowed my gaze to remain on him. "I'm drawn to folks who make my heart beat fast. I'm attracted to folks who make me feel safe, since that doesn't happen too often. Honestly, I don't know if it's... ever happened before now." I paused as he lifted his full-moon eyes to me. "So far, aesthetically, all I know is that I'm wildly attracted to gray eyes and hair that's practically silver."

Ackerleigh gazed back at me, bundled up in my cardigan, cheeks flushed. Ethereal beneath the night sky. He brushed his fringe out of his eyes, not needing to smile with his lips in order for his sheer delight to be obvious.

I thought of my sister's powerful, gods-blessed blood, and now his. A pang of envy gripped me. "I just wish I had more of my own to offer," I admitted softly.

His delight fled and was replaced by indignation. "What in the heavens do you mean, Nico? How could you possibly think that about yourself?"

The urge to rub my scar subsided as I resumed combing through his hair with my fingers. I chewed on the inside of my cheek, considering. "All I do in life is *react*. I do my duty. To my parents, to Stella. That's my life. I bring nothing of my own into the world. Not like you do."

Ackerleigh pushed himself up with his elbows, and when he winced, I helped him the rest of the way with light pressure between his shoulder blades.

He promptly scooted closer to my face, leaning down until he was hovering over me. "You are showing your magiqon sister unconditional love and support, Nico. And I'm sure it hasn't been easy. And that's just the gifts I've seen you give in—" He thought. "—I don't know, thirty-six hours. Which means there's most certainly more." He frowned slightly, as if prepared to argue in the event I disagreed. Silently, he searched my features and held perfectly still.

I almost kissed him.

It would have been easy. Our faces were inches apart. The look he was giving me—reproachful, self-assured, and deeply affectionate—had my limbs tingling so strongly that I was fighting the urge to shake them out. My gaze found its way to his slightly parted lips.

Yet a sliver of doubt remained, just enough to paralyze me. I couldn't bear kissing someone who didn't want to kiss me just as badly. And I just didn't know. *I do, I do know!* my body screamed, not sharing my heart's fear of rejection. My body, and truthfully a big part of my heart, was desperate to hold him against me. Chest to chest. Lips on lips.

If not his feelings, at least I trusted his patience. I wanted to *want* him—body and mind, without a doubt. And he would wait for me until the icy sliver of fear had melted away. I just knew it.

Oblivious to my internal conflict, Ackerleigh glanced away with a sigh. "To be honest, I envy Stella."

I frowned. "How come?"

"Because she has you." He smiled bitterly. "I can't even... Claire, I mean, I almost told her earlier—but, it's such a gamble, you know? For all her love for me, this part of myself... Well, I fear the scenario where she throws it back in my face. Or it makes her love for me die."

My chest hurt at the heaviness in his tone.

"I'm sure my mother knew, given the circumstances of my birth, but... I never even told her outright. I lacked enough warmth and love from her as it was. Or my grandfather, who, of anyone throughout my life, I believe would have loved me as a magíqon the most." Eyes downcast, he smoothed his fingers over the hem of the cardigan sleeve.

I cupped his knee in my hand. "I'm sorry. You should never have to worry about being loved less for your truest self," I murmured.

He remained motionless, fingering his sleeve. I heard him release a shuddering breath.

Fearing I'd upset him too much, I shifted slightly, removing my hand to scratch at my stubble. "And anyway," I added hotly, "how in the heavens do all these folks who pray to the slumbering gods justify hating the *literal gods-breath* that flows around us? Like since magíq refuses to be harnessed by the everyday person, now it's cursed? The dichotomy makes me livid."

Ackerleigh scoffed, "*Ugh*, exactly." He lifted his hand, which trembled slightly as he brought his fingers together and snapped. A small spark leapt forth, growing into a flickering flame that warmed Ackerleigh's twilit features and danced in his eyes. "This is precisely what motivates my studies," he said as he turned his pinched fingertips this way and that. "I want to illuminate the beauty that magíq brings into the world. I want to show how much it's blessed humans over the centuries, and how dangerous it is for us to turn our backs on it."

"*Yes*," I agreed. My heart hammered with excitement.

"The government is not going to change the presence of magíq in the world. It's just going to make us more dangerous." He flicked the fire into the air and blew on it, the sudden burst of ésprit-infused air extinguishing it. "It's just going to make us throw fireballs at the bars that hold us in."

Something inside me split open, crystallizing into a blade of sharp and glittering determination. "How can I help?"

He found my gaze. "What?"

"Look, it's not just a… theoretical problem for me that this country is trending increasingly hostile toward magíq." I gestured to the cottage. "I care very deeply about two people who are possibly the only living magíqon in the country. I can't be ambivalent. What can I do?"

Ackerleigh helplessly threw up his hands. "What do you think I've been doing for my entire academic career? At most, I'm inspiring some folks from the younger generation. But beyond that, look at me. Fired and slandered for my efforts."

"How could Ravensbourne fire you for teaching magíq? Pascale Manon literally wrote the original tenets for Ravensbourne around integrating magíq into a modern world…"

Quizzical, Ackerleigh stared at me for a moment. "Yes… she did."

I snorted and explained, "Stella loves *The Philosophy and Teaching of Magíq*. I've read it to her like…" I thought. "Five times."

Ackerleigh grinned. "Of course."

"Please. Continue. Tell me how Ravensbourne has gone so far astray that somehow you, a magíqon teaching about magíq, were somehow problematic enough to be fired."

Heat and fury chased the affection from Ackerleigh's features. "Brandon," he spat.

The enfour he'd mentioned inside. I nodded, but remained in expectant silence.

"President Stephen Brandon has been in charge of Ravensbourne for six horrid years. He's a... a pig." Every word made his anger burn hotter; his eyes were bright and wild. "He's a wretched, tyrannical, abusive bureaucrat. He's a... a despicable, perverted villain."

I frowned. "... Perverted?"

Ackerleigh twitched. He rubbed the collar of my cardigan against his jaw several times. The movement was jerky and frantic. "Ever since I was a teenager, I began to draw the attention of certain kinds of men. Men who wanted everyone to believe they were straight, but yet I caught their eye, and they thought they were... entitled to me." He dropped his hands and wrung them together. "That they could make me fit some... fetish of theirs. That I was not a man enough to mean that fucking me would make them gay."

My heart sank. "Oh. Oh, Ackerleigh. And he—"

"The day he terminated me, President Brandon proposed an—arrangement." Ackerleigh started rubbing his jaw again, his skin turning pink and raw beneath. "And anyway, I turned him down, and then... Well, that was it. In his notice to faculty and students, he accused me of sexual misconduct." He spat the words and shuddered involuntarily.

My mouth fell open. "But you're—you're brilliant. And he—Gods!" I punched my thigh, wishing it were that terrible man's face. "How *could* he! How could he end your career like that?"

Ackerleigh jerked his chin, a muscle rolling in his jaw as he glared into the dark grove. "How? Because, especially in the cities, Technocratic rhetoric breeds like cockroaches among folks that are falling in love with modern amenities and, before you know it, there's this vile dichotomy pitting magíq against technology as if the spiritual breath of the gods is a threat to human innovation... and now I'm twenty-seven and no university in the country will hire me, because Brandon told all of them just enough vague half-truths about me to make me sound like too much of a risk." Tears raced down Ackerleigh's furious face. He smeared them away with the heel of his hand with a mutter of, "I'm sorry. Sorry." His efforts to clean up his tears reopened the gash on his face and smudged blood across his cheek.

Slowly, I turned my hand so my palm faced the stars and slid it toward him over my thigh, letting my fingernails brush his wrist in invitation. He startled, looking down at my hand; I had the immediate urge to pull away and apologize. But then he used his elbow to push up my hand and he slipped under my arm in one smooth movement, nestling into my side. A brittle chill came with him as if his torso were wrapped in ice.

I lowered my arm around him, my hand coming to rest on the soft curve of his shoulder beneath the folds of my cardigan. It took every muscle in my body not to spasm with delight and make a fool of myself. Every time I touched him felt like the first time. I stammered, "N-No wonder you're so ready to dedicate your life to a gryphon."

"It's been a rough year," he whispered, voice wobbling. "But now what?" He tucked his knees up to his chest. He was so small against me, and all of his feelings were making him vibrate violently. "The gryphon's free."

Before Ackerleigh became gamekeeper, I wouldn't have cared about putting someone out of their job at the Bennett estate. The losers before him deserved their fate, whether Lunix scared them off or mauled them. But Ackerleigh was entirely different. Thinking about him being as lost and aimless as me...

"Stay with us." I held my breath for a moment. "Stay with me."

SURVEY OF PARADISE

Night was a heavy, frozen blanket when a fluttering of feathers roused me. Not enough—I was still paralyzed by sleep, deeply lost in the fold of a dream. I felt Nico's body heat rolling over me; his ribcage gently rose and fell beneath my head.

Feathers shuffled again, making my sleep-addled heart leap. A beak tapped my ribs. The ice armor I'd frozen over my injury had long since melted and dried into my clothes, but the beak caressed my skin with soothing cold. All the moisture gathered beneath the point as if summoned from nothing. Sweet relief rushed through my bruised body, and the struggle to breathe abated. Immediately, I drifted back to sleep.

Lunix is back Lunix is back LuNIX IS BACK my brain screamed, promptly ripping me from sleep with a gasp. Periwinkle light chased away the dark, and I realized hours had passed since their beak had touched my ribs. I gripped my chest, disbelieving, panting so hard I started to wheeze.

"Ackerleigh?" Nico's voice rumbled pleasantly through my skull. "Are you alright?"

I rolled off my back to nestle into his side. "I dreamed that Lunix came back," I whispered hoarsely, sliding my arm around Nico, clinging to him.

"Look," he whispered.

His directive plucked me out of my paralyzed half-sleep and I woke properly. My eyes flew open. Dawn had not been an illusion; the sky was a pretty pastel—but it warred with the darkness that draped directly overhead.

A canopy of feathers insulated us from the chill of the morning. Lunix was wedged into Nico's other side, their large body almost too long for the truck bed. Their head was curled down and tucked into the plume of their breast. Blood splattered their hindquarters, and some viscera hung from their facial disc like they were a toddler who had been playing with their food. The violent decorations had attracted several sparrows, who were hopping across the ridges of Lunix's wings and picking chunks out of their fur.

I gagged. "Oh, that's revolting."

"I know," giggled Nico. "But at least it means they ate well."

"I understand. I eat my feelings, too."

Nico's giggle escalated into a full, rolling laugh. "Me, too."

Waking with a chortle, Lunix opened their full-moon eyes, pupils contracting to block out the blooming light of the morning. They cocked their head and peered down at us, their gape turning up in a smile among fluffy facial feathers. One after the other, they bent and plucked at our hair. Their attention flipped my fringe over my eyes, and Nico's curls landed across my mouth. "Missed you," they croaked. "Missed you."

I unburied myself from hair and started to sit up, eager to embrace my messy gryphon. As soon as I pushed back on my elbows, I remembered I was injured. A hiss of fear rushed through my gritted teeth. But

I felt none of the tremors of pain I'd expected. There was pressure and tightness, true, but yesterday I'd almost passed out the first time I'd tried sitting up on my own.

Nico gripped me lightly by my shoulders, helping me up the rest of the way and following suit so he remained closely pressed to my back.

Stunned, I traced my fingers along my ribcage. "That—That hardly hurt." The swelling had gone down significantly. Yesterday's peaks and valleys that I'd felt along my bones were nothing more than bumps and potholes today. Curiosity overwhelmed me. I pulled up my tunic, peering down at my chest.

Bruising still mottled my skin, but it wasn't as dark, having faded mostly to shades of yellow and green. I ran my fingers over my ribs and, although tender, touching them didn't bring stars to my vision.

"Whoa," Nico breathed, so close that I felt the steam from his breath on my temple. "That looks way better than yesterday. How can that be?"

"Nico—have you ever heard of gryphons having healing capabilities?"

Lunix touched their beak to my ribs the way they had in my dreamscape overnight.

"Lunix..." My jaw went slack as I met my gryphon's full-moon eyes.

They croaked softly before deftly turning in place, tail tuft and feathers whisking over us as they moved to the far end of the truck bed. There, they sat back and began aggressively grooming their hindquarters.

Picking up the lantern to switch it off, Nico frowned thoughtfully. He pulled in his legs to sit criss-crossed, which made his stomach muscles tighten into a washboard beneath his clingy turtleneck.

"Stella said just this week that she thinks Pascale Manon was able to use her magíq for healing. It makes sense, honestly." Nico propped his chin on his fist while his other hand tapped his scar. He watched Lunix groom themself with a bemused smile. "Why couldn't the different elements cooperate to knit damaged cells back together? Hydrate with water, promote nerve response with electricity, and use heat and wind to stimulate muscle repair."

My hand itched for a new notebook to start jotting down theories. Now, because both Nico and his sister knew I was a magíqon, I could freely take notes of any kind around them. What an absolute relief, a freedom I never thought I'd feel, like the ésprit in my veins was singing. And yet...

And yet.

I sighed. Lunix's silver eyes shifted up to look at me as I frowned and rubbed my cheek on Nico's soft cardigan collar. It even smelled like him: sweetgrass, musk, coffee... a little bit of floral, from me and my epsom and lavender bath. Parting with this article of clothing was going to be miserable.

"I've woken up with an unfortunate resolution." Both the gryphon and their mountain man looked at me. "I have to go back to Laurier."

Lunix's ear tufts flattened against their head. "Go?"

I winced, nodding. "Yes. I have to leave. I have some unfinished business."

Nico's smile faded. "Excuse me?"

"I can't let my student get expelled. I can't let Brandon do that."

"Didn't Ravensbourne fire you?" His eyes darkened. "Didn't Brandon sexually harass you?"

I nodded.

"Then don't be an idiot," Nico snapped.

Patiently, I explained, "I cannot be responsible for four years of a student's work going to waste because of the pig that's running that school."

Nico looked away, a muscle rolling in his jaw as he ground his teeth together. He pushed his hair behind his ear and tap-tap-tapped his scar. Finally, he said, "You're not an idiot."

I laid my hand on his knee, tracing a small circle with my thumb. "With regard to Ravensbourne, I might be."

"Doctor Sebring—" Nico's expression contorted, cheeks flushing with emotion. His throat bobbed. "I really don't want you to go."

My hand on his knee stilled. "Nico, I..." I trailed off. I—what? I wasn't brave enough to stay? To veer away from academia and into the unknown? To turn away from that scholarly lifestyle I thought I'd always been made for?

Nico's curls fell over his features. "Please. D... Don't go."

That *heartbreak.* Reaching for his face, I scrambled from a sitting position so I could kneel in front of him. He instinctively uncrossed his legs, letting them stretch out on either side of me. One hand clasped his neck and with the other I gently touched my finger to his chin, lifting his face so he simply had to look at me. Because I'd moved, our faces were at the same height. I was quite literally in his face.

"Do not consider it a departure. Think of it like..." I searched his tragic eyes, which were amber and mahogany swirls like the oncoming sunrise and kept flicking down as if he couldn't bear to look me in the eyes. It was my sovereign quest to soothe his wounds enough so that he could, so that meeting my gaze was a balm and not a bruise. "Think of it like a business trip I must take, where I leave home but for a short while. I must attend to my duties, but my heart—" My breath hitched. Like the sound was a pebble dropping into a still pond, Nico's eyes filled with tears. "My heart is here, in the mountain's armpit, with *you.*"

Before he could do anything more than keep his hopeful gaze on mine, I leaned in and kissed him. His perfectly soft, full lips were paralyzed by surprise. Then he melted against me, his mouth yielding to my urgency. Nico slipped his powerful arms around my waist, hanging on as if afraid that I was no more substantial than the wind.

I didn't move away until I'd run out of air, and when I did, I brushed our lips together one final time before lowering myself to my knees. Nico's lashes fluttered open. He studied me in silence, eyes darting as he drank in every pore and line on my face. Something about his expression seemed... relieved, like he'd had questions that only my kiss could have answered.

Rising back up, I threw my arms around his neck and held him tightly, carding his curls with my fingers as if hoping he'd tangle me up and trap me here. He buried his face in the curve of my neck; his fingers dug into the small of my back and into my shoulder blade. Even his legs closed around me, so I was practically sitting on his lap. I was no longer simply clinging to him; he was wrapping me up in all his limbs like I was an air bubble suspended in amber. I happily let his embrace devour me.

Our gryphon cooed, and a blast of raw meat breath puffed into my mouth and nose and made me gag. I turned and found Lunix inches away from my face, their pupils so large I could see me and Nico reflected in their curious eyes.

"Kiss?" they cheeped.

Nico used his shoulder to push the gryphon back. "Lunix! Don't make it weird." Lunix chirped and snapped at his ear, missing substantially.

Nico paid them no mind and instead turned his attention back to me, his brow furrowing. "You aren't leaving now, are you? You can't..."

"Let's see." I gave him a crooked smirk as I reluctantly slipped his cardigan off and handed it back to him. "Perhaps I can beg Claire to stay an extra day."

Carving a path through diamond-bright dewdrops and candy-hued lupin, we left the intimate haven we'd created in the truck, making our way past the garden and through the back door into the cottage. Lunix bounded after us, chasing a yellow butterfly with childlike glee.

The rich aroma of coffee greeted me when I got inside. It splattered noisily into a glass pot inside the cottage door to my left. I was about to pounce on it when Cheese came racing toward me, leaping onto my legs and knocking me back into Nico as I yelped in alarm.

"Cheese! Down!" Nico exclaimed, his arms slipping past my hips to push the dog to the ground. She smothered his hands with kisses before turning to mine, though I discreetly lifted them out of her reach.

"*Finally*," drawled Stella. "I thought you two lovebirds had flown the coop." She sat cross-legged at the large table with a coffee mug cupped in her hands, wearing a black dress with a mesh panel over her shoulders. Her hair was in an elegant plait with Claire's signature four strands telling me that my friend had done it for her.

Next to Stella, Claire wore a smirk brimming with mischief as she hooded her gaze and sipped her coffee. A second later, though, her skin blanched and her eyes went wide.

I glanced back as Lunix arrived in the cottage, burying Nico's frame in the fluff of their breast until he stepped aside.

"Lunix!" Stella cheered.

Claire swallowed. "Is it... still mad at me?"

"Oh, yeah," said Stella. "Ya never mentioned what ya did to our gryphon friend."

Claire took a moment to unpin her terrified gaze from the gryphon. "I... uh... yelled at your brother, about Ackerleigh," she squeaked.

Stella snorted. "Nice one, andullie. You found the quickest way to agonize them."

"*Ant*-agonize," whispered Nico.

"That's what I said," growled Stella with a glare. She sauntered over to Lunix, clambering onto their neck like a gryphon kit. Resting her elbow on the crown of their head, she said to Claire, "They understand you. You can always apologize."

"Oh! Really?" Claire straightened, setting down her coffee mug. She tucked her auburn hair behind her ears and assumed a serious expression. "I swear," Claire pressed her hand to her breast, "I will never cross you again, blessed beast. Forgive me." There was no obvious irony in her demonstration, and a strange feeling settled in my stomach. Perhaps if she honored the beasts of the gods in this sort of way, she would be open to... me. A magíqon.

Sitting by the sink with their claws in the basket of vegetables, Lunix sternly appraised Claire. Then Dove jumped on the tuft of their tail, making them flinch and ruining the effect of their severity. After gently extricating their tail from the cat and curling it safely around their hindquarters, they bobbed their head once. "D'ac."

Claire slumped with relief. "Oh, thank you."

Stella said to Nico, "I forget how light-lickers act around gryphons."

Nico grunted wordlessly, leaning against the counter with his arms crossed. He watched me pick up a pair of hand-thrown coffee mugs and fill them at the coffee maker. I picked up the milk and raised my eyebrows, and he shook his head. Sniffing indignantly, I poured a generous helping of milk into my cup while Nico raised one judgmental eyebrow at me. I asked the same nonverbal questions about the sugar, and he allowed me to add two lumps to his cup.

As I passed in front of Lunix and Stella, the girl groaned, "You two are disgusting." But she failed to hide the twitch of a smile when I winked at her.

I handed Nico his mug and relaxed against his side, cheek on his chest and chest on his waist while I sipped my coffee. It tasted so much sweeter with my body against Nico's and his fingers trailing whisper-soft over my back.

Something brushed my ankles. I looked down to find Dove curling around me. She lifted her head to give me a fangy smile and a soft *brrp*.

My throat tightened. This place was a paradise... an eden. Warm, cozy, fragrant, and full of love. Stepping resolutely toward Claire, I said thickly, "Claire, please stay another day."

A quizzical furrow appeared between Claire's eyebrows. "What? Leigh..." She searched for her words, setting her coffee mug down. "No, I—I've already stayed longer than I should have."

"What difference would one more day make?"

Stella slid off Lunix in a flurry of feathers. She sauntered over to Nico and dragged his cardigan off his shoulders, stealing it for herself. As she shrugged into it, she screwed up her face and sniffed the collar. "This smells like flowers," she said as she shot me a critical look.

I responded with an eye roll before returning my attention to Claire, answering the next question from my best friend before she could ask it. "I'm coming back to Laurier with you. But I really can't bear leaving this place yet. Please, Claire."

Claire blinked hard. "You're coming with me?"

"Temporarily," I said quickly. "But I don't know how long it's going to take for me to sort everything out in Laurier. So, please. Stay another day."

Her brow wrinkled sympathetically as she clasped my hand. "Acker-leigh, I can't. It's finals week. I already missed administering one yesterday, and I have two more this afternoon. And you know Mattie—she worries. I... I can't."

I swallowed the lump in my throat. "Right. Of course. I was being foolish." I stood sharply from the table. "Let me get dressed." Avoiding her gaze, I went swiftly to my trunk by the back door, unclasping it and throwing it open. I selected a pair of shorts and a blouse without much thought, then dug out *His Scorching Embrace* and tucked that under my arm. Everything in my vision seemed obscured by a dense fog, and my chest was tight and hollow. I moved automatically in the washroom as I dressed before splashing my face with water.

Tucking my sailor shirt into my high-waisted shorts, I forced myself to accept that this dream was ending. At least for now. When I opened the door, I was greeted by a wall of gryphon feathers, mournful moon-eyes, and Nico looking equally mournful while leaning into the gryphon's neck.

"Don't go," my gryphon croaked.

"Oh, my loves," I sighed as I threw my arms around both of them. Nico melted into my grip and wrapped his arms around my shoulders, resting his chin on the crown of my head. Lunix's feathers absorbed me until it felt like I was floating.

"What if we can't stay here 'til you can come back?" Nico asked, his chin bumping me with each word. "How will you find us?"

"I was thinking about that last night," I said, leaning back to look up at him. "If the cottage is no longer safe, you can go stay at my grandfather's farm. It's only ten miles north of the Hazberg pass." With his head down, Nico's dark and sun-kissed curls veiled his eyes. I reached up and tucked them back behind his ear, then cupped his face in my hand. "I'll be back with you before you know it, alright? I promise."

Lunix twittered sadly, nuzzling my cheek.

"Here." I held up the book and pressed it into Nico's hands. "Lunix and I have been reading this together. What do you think, chaton? Can Nico start it over so he knows what's going on?"

Lunix cheeped and bobbed their head. "Victor."

Nico's ears flushed bright red before the rest of his face caught up. He scrutinized the saucy, muscular chest of Lunix's preferred love interest, and the delicate male half his height cradled against him. "Y...You were reading a gay romance book to Lunix?"

"It was either romance or history essays," I said with a laugh. "Give it a chance. I think you'll enjoy it."

Nico swallowed. "If you say so." He moved back to let me out of the washroom.

Lunix stayed pressed to my side as we went to my trunk, where I threw in yesterday's outfit and pulled out a pair of embroidered wool mules. I slipped them on and gave my gryphon another tight hug, pressing my cheek to theirs.

"You're safe, and you're free," I whispered into their downy ear. "We'll be reunited before we know it. And you must help bring me back to Nico, alright? You know better than I that he's something special." Stroking their mane and their bristly shoulders, I held my gryphon as they trembled against me.

With Dove clutched to her shoulder, Claire and I left the cottage bound for my blue car, the others filing out after me in strangely reverent silence. Claire craned her neck to take in the colorful field of lupins, deeply inhaling their candy fragrance drifting on the breeze.

"Keys?" I glanced at Claire, who tossed them to me. Lunix lunged for them and snapped the ring out of the air; it jingled as they trapped it in their beak. We all froze, wide-eyed and open-mouthed, staring as my gryphon held our fate in their jaws.

"Lunix—come on then," I said soothingly.

With a devious glint in their eyes, Lunix lowered the keys over my outstretched hand and dropped them. They plopped wetly into my hand, covered in gleaming saliva.

Curling my lip, I mumbled, "Yes, thank you, I suppose."

Nico sighed audibly with disappointment and glowered at Lunix. Stella snickered mockingly, making him yell and smack her shoulder. The pair fell to squabbling. I shook my head, smiling as I went to the driver's side of the car.

The metal of the door handle bit into my fist as if trying to ward me off. Every instinct in me told me to let go, toss Claire the keys, and remain at the cottage with Lunix and their human family. Every instinct told me that Laurier would bring trouble and strife and failure.

Yet the injustice of what was happening to Camden Zane simmered behind my ribs and threatened to sear a hole straight through my heart. It was more than just the fate of a single student. It was the insult to magíq, and to Pascale Manon's institution which had been founded in order to preserve the history of magíq and those who yearned for it. Like Camden and Billie, and the other students who kept enrolling in my classes.

I couldn't let it be. I was fortunate to have found out about the punishment Brandon was doling out on my supporters. I felt fortunate that, even though Lunix's liberation had thrown my life into chaos, I could now go back to Ravensbourne to right wrongs.

Somber and determined, I opened the car door and bent to get inside.

Nico leapt around the boot of the car and rushed over to me, and the cloak of his fuzzy cardigan fell across my shoulders, quickly followed by the warm brush of his lips on my cheekbone. "Don't forget about me."

Electricity surged in my veins and threatened to jump delightedly onto my skin at the tender gesture and heart-wrenching words. I began to turn, but the ache inside me intensified, and I could not meet his eyes for fear of all my resolve crumbling.

Stella jumped onto Nico's back, hollering about the cardigan, but her words were simply a buzzing in my ears against the absolute overflowing of affection in my heart.

Part III

Unification and
Amplification of
Magical Forces

CAPSTONE IN FRIENDSHIP STRAIN

I was drenched in sweat within ten minutes of our drive wearing Nico's cardigan, but it was going to take more than overheating to make me take it off. Claire's stare was drilling a hole in the side of my head as she waited for me to confess my feelings about him. I chose to focus on getting us back to the main road and heading southeast toward Laurier. My car bounced and creaked dramatically over the pocked and dusty gravel.

Claire finally broke the silence. "I've been waiting to see that look on your face for three years, Leigh. I will admit, I'm surprised it's someone like Nico. A nervous, juggernaut farmer made of muscle?" She hummed, cocking her head. "Interesting."

I snickered at the description. "You know, I'm a bit surprised too. But he's so…" I sighed wistfully. "I'm glad I kissed him."

"You—" Claire screeched, an ear-splitting, glass-rattling, Dove-terrifying full-on scream. I flinched away from her and knocked my temple into the window.

She exclaimed, "You kissed him?"

"Gracious!" I rubbed my head. "So loud! Why?"

"Because you kissed someone!" Beaming, laughing, bouncing her legs, she shook my arm, then shoved her glasses up the bridge of her nose. "*You* kissed *him?*"

I shot her a glare. "Am I not allowed to do the kissing?"

A grimace spasmed over Claire's features before she waved her hand dismissively. "Oh—no, no, but I assumed you were more likely to be *the kissed*. You're just so cute—"

I scoffed, "Good heavens! You'd hate it if I called you 'cute,' Claire."

Claire opened her mouth, eyes widening with aggravation. "It's a compliment—"

"For a *child* with a frilly dress and sticky cheeks," I snapped. "Just because I'm small doesn't mean I'm cute, or demure, or—" I shuddered. "—passive."

"Of course, Ackerleigh." Claire squeezed my arm. "Of course."

I pulled away, curling my lip and feeling my cheeks heat. "I'm much more dominant and assertive than Nico. He's quite meek. Plus, I'm older."

"Ackerleigh, I believe you. I'm sorry. You are not demure in the slightest."

Perhaps the version of myself I'd curated for Ravensbourne had been misleading. Regardless—I would not be indulging that image anymore. "I feel like you're just saying that to placate me, but yes, if you've had thoughts that I'm some sort of… soft, passive man, that is not how I want to be seen."

"Alright." Claire nodded firmly. "Understood."

"President Brandon—brought out a fearful side of me," I added. "I always had to watch myself around him." Urgency tightened my throat, pitching my voice higher as I gesticulated sharply. "I-I-I changed how I dressed. I was made to teach in an actual storage closet, and told that my passions were wrong for the university. I had to make myself smaller around him. I couldn't... I couldn't *be* myself." I hugged my arms across my chest.

Claire remained silent, pain and grief in her expression as if this were dawning on her for the first time.

"Consequently," I continued, "that means that often I wasn't able to be myself around you, either." The secret of my magíq threatened to burst from me then and there. It had been comfortable to keep Claire in the dark about it before now. But confessing to Nico last night caused a shift. Keeping this part of my identity a secret from my best friend didn't fit as well anymore, like a wool sweater that shrunk in the wash. It felt like we were strangers.

"Great," Claire whispered flatly.

"I want... I want things to be different now," I said more gently, wringing my hands. "I want something brand new."

Claire gave me a trembling smile, touching my arm. "Absolutely, my friend."

The trees that grew around the Hazel Mountains were primarily coniferous, but as we followed the swells of the steppes, clusters of beech and palm started to crop up.

Eventually I nudged the pack on her lap and Claire unwrapped the tea towel. She popped the lid off a sturdy glass container. Inside was a rainbow of cut fruit, a pile of cashews, and a neat stack of crackers that was protected from the fruit by a wall of sliced cheese. Claire cooed with delight and, between the two of us, we devoured the whole container until nothing was left except sloshing fruit juices and a few crumbs. That modest meal would stay in my thoughts for quite some time. It felt like a token of affection. A parting gift.

Outside the steppes, the road to Laurier took us through a mossy forest where the canopy was so dense that we were cast into rich green shadows. We drove with the windows all the way down, naming all the species of birds roosting in the trees and sweeping us up in their chorus.

Dove made two attempts to escape by climbing over Claire until she had to roll up her window. The third hour brought us into the outskirts of the town—

"Moundsview." Claire squinted at the map. We were a little over halfway to Laurier from where we'd left the Hazel Mountains. "Let's stop for petrol and snacks. I'm hungry again."

Moundsview was an underwhelming bastion of suburbia, somewhere between the grubby seaside town of Laurier and the grandeur of Stoneworth. Teenagers and dog walkers mingled near the large petrol station. It was almost jarring: I'd felt such a sense of timelessness staying at the Bennett estate and then the cottage, I'd almost forgotten what modern life looked like. It was so... ugly. Colorless and monotonous.

After locking Dove in the car, Claire stretched her arms over her head, flexing her back and squeezing her eyes shut, groaning as she flexed. Then she fished her leather wallet out of her trouser pockets. "Someday you have to pay me back."

"No—I'll pay." Popping open the boot, I hurriedly dug through my trunk until I had fished out the envelope of money.

"Oh, goodness!" Claire exclaimed at the sight of it. "That's so much money. Is that all from Doctor Bennett? Isn't she going to—demand it back?"

"Doctor Bennett said she's started paying gamekeepers upfront since the work has been so high-risk," I explained. "And indeed it was." Smiling, I gave my bruised ribs a tap. Claire frowned at me but didn't argue as I slipped some bills out of the envelope and strode into the station.

It smelled like stale popcorn, sweat, and cleaning fluids as I moved through the aisle of snacks. I selected a few of my favorites and a few of Claire's favorites before assembling several bottles of water and cans of soda.

"Spectacles!" My exclamation drew the eye of the bored teenage boy slumped at the register. Being far-sighted allowed me the accessibility of reading glasses meant for aging eyes which, while not perfectly my prescription, could more than tide me over. My glasses lost in the sea had been gold rectangles, but I selected a pair of chunky oval tortoise-shells to mix things up. The teenager remained silent and sleepy-looking as he rang me up for the petrol and snacks, then deposited the paper bag of goods into my hands.

Feeling like myself again, I strode with confidence out to my car. Claire was hanging up the petrol pump and opening the driver's door when I returned. We took our places and buckled up in silence, then I settled Dove on my knees and set the bag of snacks by my feet.

"We're almost there." She studied me with a little rosy smile. "Tortoise-shell. Bold. Fits the new you."

"The new me?"

"Yeah. Gryphon-taming, scraped-up, boy-kissing, secret-keeping Ackerleigh." Claire started the car and focused on getting out of the blessedly cobbled parking lot. Bitterness was unmistakable in her voice.

"Claire, you shouldn't have to bear it."

"Your secret?"

"Yes. It could compromise a lot. Our friendship, for starters."

"How come? Are you in love with me?" Her smirk was coy.

"What? No, thank you."

"Excuse you. My boobs look great in this outfit." She squished her shoulders together to deepen the line of her cleavage.

"Objectively true."

"Thank you."

"Always."

Claire frowned as the neighborhood of Moundsview vanished behind us and thinned back into urban farms and power plants. "What could you possibly think would be able to alter our relationship, Leigh?" She paused before adding more quietly, "I'm just really hurt. You've never kept secrets."

I swallowed. "This one's different. I've kept it a secret forever."

Frustration creased her brow and drew down her lips. She said nothing.

"Fine. I want you to remember how desperate you were to know this. You might regret it." My fingers curled into fists until I forced them open to pet Dove. It was time. "I am a magíqon, Claire."

Very little changed on her face at first. The crease left her brow. On the steering wheel, her knuckles blanched. Abruptly, a tear broke out of her eye and raced down her cheek. She hurriedly wiped it away. Her throat struggled with a swallow. "Oh."

I pressed on. She at least got to know *why,* in those conscious moments when I'd thought about it, I'd still concealed this about myself. "I care about your career. I care about your position at Ravensbourne. I care about the trust in our friendship. It's for that reason I never even entertained the notion of telling you. To be frank, I never before entertained the notion of telling *anyone*. It could be dangerous for me. But I simply do not have the option to be silent when it's my life and my safety that Deubrise would like to see criminalized."

"C—" She shut her mouth.

"What?"

"Can't you just not do it? Magíq."

My lips separated, hanging open as I tried to wrap my head around her question. "No," I exclaimed harshly. "No. That's not an option. I want to do it. I would have it no other way. When I can't do it, I feel half-alive. Why do you think I seem like a new me? *That's why.* I have been able to do magíq without fear for the first time in my life. When I have to hide it or fit myself into the confines of a world hostile to what I am and what I can do, I walk around with a gaping wound that never stops weeping. Claire, why would you want that for me?"

She managed a twitching nod. "Sorry."

Silence stretched between us. That really must have been her only question. And it just seemed like... the wrong one. "That's all you wanted to know? If I can make this go away?"

Her sigh answered for her. "Ackerleigh..."

"Alright." I scoffed. "Well, even if I could, I wouldn't. Sorry if that disappoints you."

"It's not like that—"

"But you're dismayed. You asked if I can just not do it. And I know that look on your face. It's the face you made when you found out I stole President Brandon's best pen because he insulted my blouse at that faculty meeting."

She bared her teeth as she shot me a fleeting glare. "You're right. I am dismayed! It's a dismay you didn't tell me for all these years. It feels like I was missing this big piece of who you are, and without it, you've been an enigma. It makes so much more sense why you're so brilliant and yet you risk all your prospects with these extreme and opinionated research proposals which are all but actual treason."

My jaw dropped.

"You're not just radical in writing, you're living that life." Her expression softened, but only slightly. "It doesn't *have* to be like that for you. If you just reach back out to another university—like Stoneworth, or Leon, and let them know that you're willing to take a more conservative approach—"

Mouth still open, I held up my hand so sharply that Dove flinched.

Claire stiffened, glaring through the windshield.

"I am not changing my position. Ever." My heart slammed in my chest so hard that it hurt my healing ribs. Blood drummed in my ears, deafening. "Why in the heavens would you think that? If my connection to magíq has motivated me this whole time, why would I? Do you want me to stuff it down and ignore it?"

"Yes! I mean—" Tears swam in her eyes. "I want you *safe*."

If she got to cry, then so did I. "I wanted to tell you because it came up when I was talking to Nico and I felt guilty he knew my secret and you didn't. I wanted to tell you because I... I thought you would be proud of me for—I don't know, standing up for myself."

Claire opened and closed her mouth. "Yes. I mean—yes." She wiped her wrist across her cheek. "Yes. You are the bravest, most reckless person I know."

"That's an insult," I snapped.

"No. And yes." She sniffled. Her hair stuck to her chin and she sharply swept it back, using her moistened hand to push her locks off her forehead. "I'm sorry, I'm saying all the wrong things."

"Correct." I pulled Nico's cardigan around myself, hands trembling, fighting down the hysterical sob that wanted to bring me into despair. The fuzzy texture on my cheeks, on my salty, tear-dampened lips, helped me keep my thoughts from falling apart. I wiped at the gash under my eye, but it didn't feel as raw as yesterday. "Unless your intention was to break my heart; if so, you're doing a wonderful job."

"Ackerleigh." Her voice was thick and clotted by tears.

"Shut up."

She reached for my arm. I smacked down her hand. Impatiently, she shook her head and said forcefully, "You've known this whole time I agree with you on everything, but—"

"Bullshit."

"What?" Incredulity darkened her countenance. She hunched in the driver's seat, the foot not on the gas pedal shuffling restlessly as if she'd rather be pacing.

"You can't say you agree with me and wish for me to be different." I sounded frustratingly petulant, frustratingly like a wounded child. "You can't say your beliefs are the same as mine and then in the same breath tell me to stuff mine down just so I'm—I don't know, more palatable."

"That's not why!"

"Alright, then I don't care the reason, because that's the message I'm receiving from you right now." I was almost screaming. I'd have loved to. To make the windows rattle with my fury. Call the wind to press down on the car like a bellows until we were wiped off the face of the planet. Ask the electricity and heat in the engine to explode us. *I could, I could, I could do that, and why shouldn't I?* My fists heated until my blood was molten lava, ready to leap out of my skin and burn Claire to ashes.

Claire remained silent, sniffling, hiccuping, snot on her lip and daylight shining on her tear-soaked cheeks. She nodded, swallowing, licking her lip clean and picking out more of her hair plastered to her face. With another hiccup, she nodded again.

"What?" I snarled.

"You're right. You're right." Her face crumpled. "I completely spoke out of my ass."

"Completely." I glared out the window and visualized myself bursting into flames. Nothing could stop me then. Everyone would have to yield to me, fragile and adorable Ackerleigh Sebring, a human torch that could burn the whole country to the ground. "I regret telling you." I used my collar to dry my face as anger boiled away my grief.

"I—" Fresh tears fell off her chin as she clamped her mouth shut. Focusing on the drive, we fell into a tense and wounded quietude. Dove, frozen in terror until now, finally crawled off my lap and jumped to the bench in the backseat. When Claire sniffled again, I wanted to reach over and pinch her slimy nose closed so I didn't have to hear that awful noise anymore. Eventually she stopped, and eventually my face dried up, although I felt no closer to speaking to her.

Different versions of this conversation played out in my head with none of them as terrible as the real thing. Whatever place she'd spoken from didn't matter when her hope for me was to hide myself for the sake of a prosperous future. But damn the future: I had never tried to fit into the constraints necessary to get the grants or accolades or promotions before, and I wasn't about to. Not now, especially. Not after I'd spent these days away from the city being *honest* for the first time in my life. She should have known that.

Claire's lips turned down with a new wave of weeping. "I love you, Leigh. I panicked because I just don't know how to keep you and your magíq safe."

I swallowed. "I'm not concerned with safety."

"Clearly!" she exclaimed. "Try to tell me you're not just coming back to Laurier ready to fight."

My silence spoke for me.

"So I—I guess I have no choice," she said softly.

Terror struck me like lightning. "Wh—wait, what? Claire, you can't tell anyone... Please, for the sake of our fr—"

"No!" Horrified, she looked over at me and gripped my hand. At first I started to pull away. But her palm was as clammy as mine and sealed our skin together, and the years of our friendship was its own glue. "No, Ackerleigh. I mean that I'm all in. Your conviction was nearly enough on its own, but now I know that all this Technocrat rhetoric Brandon spearheads, all the hostility in Deubrise, is going to hurt *you*." She looked at our hands and sighed. "I can't pretend like I'd rather not deal with it."

I scoffed and jerked my arm, but she squeezed hard enough that I groaned a complaint.

She let her attention leave the road to fix me with a determined scowl, a glint in her eyes. "But I am not going to abandon you!"

Now *I* was crying again.

Lacing her fingers through mine, she squeezed me tightly enough that my fingers blanched. "I never could. You should know that."

"I hoped. But you... you just want me to stuff it down, and pretend like..."

"Yes, because *I* would do that. Hell, when I realized I wasn't attracted to men, I wanted to hide from that, too." She laughed, humorless. "That's what I would do, in your position. I know you better than that, though, and I know you're better than me."

"I'm not *better* than you."

"I think this conversation proved it, Leigh." She sighed, adjusting in the driver's seat, forced to slow as the road grew more crowded with city traffic. Our words lapsed again, but the tension had dissipated. I was exhausted, rent open. The cottage was years in my past, distant. Recalling it was like trying to spot a pearl buried at the bottom of the ocean. Eyes closed, I dug my fingers into my sockets as the age-old crying migraine started drilling.

Plastic rustled as Claire picked through my petrol station snacks. "Hungry." More packaging rustled. Claire muttered something. Rustling intensified. Uncovering my eyes, I snatched the bag of crisps out of her hand and tore it open. I took out one of the water bottles and downed half of it before I held the other out to Claire, who took it with a too-sweet smile.

"Just to reiterate—" She swigged from the water bottle and balanced it between her seat and the armrest between us. "—I would never, ever tell your secret for you, Ackerleigh. And I'm honored you decided to tell me."

I rolled my eyes.

"Please believe me."

"Maybe if you hadn't led with all that bullshit about taking a more conservative path—"

Sighing through her nostrils, she pressed her lips together and didn't speak.

I dug into her bag of crisps and crunched angrily on them. I knew she wanted me to let her off, but my heart was shredded, and I couldn't force myself to soften. Instead, I unwrapped the jerky and held it out to Dove, whose nose pointed skyward as she crawled across the seat and toward me. Awkwardly, I picked her up and pulled her back into my lap to feed her. Her hind claws swiped across my wrist as she seized up.

"I'm surprised you can do that with your ribs." Claire's eyes were wide.

"Oh, that? I think Lunix boosted my healing." I didn't want to give her that information, technically, but I also wanted to shock her for the sake of making her emotionally suffer. Because yes, with Claire, at least, I was extremely petty. "I'm feeling alright today."

Her eyes bulged. "Come again?"

My focus returned to Dove gnawing on her jerky. I offered no more explanation.

"A gryphon healed you? You've never mentioned they have healing abilities."

"I didn't know they did."

"Ackerleigh, that's so amazing!"

"Oh, magíq's amazing now all of a sudden?"

She gave a cry of frustration and looked back out the windshield, glowering.

I snorted.

"Is it funny, torturing me?"

"Quite."

CAPSTONE IN HOSTILE CONFRONTATIONS

My skin seemed to itch beneath the surface, like an allergic reaction to the city. I resented the power lines scratching across the deep powder blue of the afternoon sky. I was furious that over the last hundred years, the bush had shrunk by half to allow ugly bungalows and factories and shopping districts to puff out their proud chests. Such enterprises encouraged folks to build lives that only took and never gave back.

I felt worse and worse the closer we got to Laurier. I puzzled over this new reality that Claire knew my secret, something I'd kept deeply buried within myself, deeply hidden. Deeply protected.

"Please don't tell Mathilda." I glanced at Claire as she flinched, and then she nodded, somber.

"I wasn't going to."

"I hate to breed secrecy between you two." Reaching over, I tucked Claire's warm brown locks behind the shell of her ear. Her diamond earring sparkled as it emerged.

"I know. But this secret is for your safety."

Fretfully shaking my head, I dug my fingers into my forearms, dimpling my flesh. "This is why I said I didn't want to burden you with this."

"That's what friendship is, Ackerleigh. We'll be alright. Nothing's different, right? You've always been a magíqal little man."

"Rude." But I laughed, and we let Laurier welcome us home. Narrow cobblestone streets between short brick storefronts and globular streetlights, flower boxes under open windows with lace curtains stirred by the salty breeze. Seabirds screaming, people chattering at cafes under white umbrellas at dainty iron tables.

Whereas Laurier felt oppressive to me, Claire was like a parched flower being watered. Sitting straighter in her seat, shoulders rounding from their slump, bouncing her leg. Humming a tune I heard her sing often with Mathilda. That had to be nice, returning to a lover. Maybe thinking about Nico like that was going too far, but regardless, the only pair of lips I could think about were leagues behind us with the potential to vanish into the wilderness at any given moment.

"What's your plan?" Claire looked over at me, the pillow of her lip jutting out with her anxiety. "Do you need to stay with me? Do you have... business to attend to at Ravensbourne?"

I had a rough outline of what needed to be done at Ravensbourne. All of it could ruin my life. More. But I had a car and I knew how to get back to the mountains, so the little I had to lose would only be temporary. "Ravensbourne first. I won't stay with you. I've imposed enough on your relationship."

She nodded, not arguing. We both knew how worried Claire's absence would have made Mathilda.

Sitting on the thick envelope of money gave me an idea. "I think I'll start by checking into an inn. The one by Ravensbourne, with the blue siding. And go from there."

She slumped. "You aren't going to rent a flat? Even week by week?"

Shuddering, I shook my head. "Unless things take a very unexpected turn today, I do not intend to lay down any sort of roots here."

Claire clenched her jaw to bite back an argument. I let her stew and looked out my window at the familiar dirt road leading to the faculty parking. Students reclined on picnic blankets under the sunshine. Couples walked hand in hand with the easy gait of those in no hurry to reach their destination. Atop evenly posted flagpoles, Ravensbourne's gray banner flapped in the tangy sea breeze, the black raven sigil mocking me with its keen gaze.

The back corner of the lot was empty and the isolation was equal parts reassuring and intimidating. I left Dove on the seat as I climbed out onto the rust-colored gravel. Perplexed, she peered up at me and blinked her loamy green eyes.

"Don't worry, little one." As I cupped her delicate skull in my hand and rubbed her velvety fur, her purring climbed into my bones and vibrated my whole arm. "I'll be back out in a heartbeat, alright? I'll treat you to a fish filet for dinner, fresh from the sea. How's that sound?" Dove's purring mingled with the smallest trill. Cranking the window down two fingers, I closed her inside and then rushed to the boot of the car before I lost my nerve. I tucked the money back into its place among my books.

Over my sailor top, I pulled on a black sweater with the Ravensbourne badge on the left breast. I thought that would annoy Brandon in particular, and I couldn't pass up the opportunity to have my appearance alone antagonize him.

After everything was tucked in, smoothed down, and combed out, I turned to Claire, who watched me with a worried frown. "Well, I'm off to confront Brandon."

She grimaced. "As expected. I have to call Mathilda."

"Sure. You can eavesdrop, but stay out of sight. It's important that you don't look like you had anything to do with my return."

Claire hesitated, surely worried that it would look like she wasn't supporting me. But it was important that she appeared distant in order to avoid Brandon's wrath turning to her. She nodded before twining her arm through mine and starting us off toward the faculty building. Dell Hall lurked beyond the majesty of Mortensen, which meant we had to pass through the popular quad. While not everyone might have heard I'd been fired, the petition Cam started which resulted in his expulsion was sure to have attracted a lot of interest. Which meant everyone was going to be staring at me. My favorite.

I nodded to a sophomore who'd written an extraordinary essay exploring the parallels between power lines and ley lines. His head turned to track me as I passed the bench where he sat holding hands with a freshman he'd sat beside in my Introduction to Magíq in a Modern World course. At least it seems like my departure brought the two of them together.

The circular stone tables dotting the bullseye shape of the quad were mostly occupied. A cluster of students even sat around the statue of Ravensbourne's founder Pascale Manon, her hands clutching an orb of magíq. I met her gleaming eyes for courage as we passed her. A glance at the clock tower on Mortensen told me it was nearly five in the afternoon, which explained the crowd. Classes were over, and dinnertime approached. That explained my growling stomach.

When a pair of knee-high socks beneath a plaid mini skirt came tearing toward me between the tables, I lifted my eyes to behold Billie's round face already contorted with feeling. Their backpack dwarfed their body, bouncing so hard it hit them in the back of their head. Not so much as hesitating, they crashed into me with their arms squeezing my waist and their chin directly on the worst of my bruising. I sucked in a breath and counted on the general shock of our encounter to excuse my pained moan.

"Billie—"

"I knew you'd come back, Professor!" They stood back and surveyed me joyfully, their lips splitting to show the gap in their front teeth. Hope danced in the springwater pools of their eyes. They shoved their glasses up their nose with a familiar gesture, which made me oddly emotional.

"I... yes, but not honorably." I glanced over at Claire, who smirked and shrugged.

"Good." Straightening, Billie assumed a scowling demonstration of fury. "We need you, Professor. Everything's fallen apart since you left, at least for us in the Magíqal Studies program." They swallowed, smoothing their hand through their mousy brown hair, which they'd buzzed off. Billie's wild eyebrows lowered as they narrowed their eyes. "Which Brandon is *cutting* at the end of the year, if you haven't heard."

"What?" A harmony of rage erupted from Claire and I.

"He can't do that!" Claire stomped her foot.

"He wouldn't *dare*." Fury sparked in my chest as I thought again about letting flames lick over my skin and pool in my hands. "You've a right to learn Deubrise's history!"

"That's what I told him." Tears sprang into Billie's eyes. "Doctor Sebring, that was my whole dream. It's dying right before my eyes."

I clutched Claire's arm instead tightly enough that she hissed at me. "No, no." I crouched and waited for Billie's gaze to lock onto mine. "Whatever you do, Billie, don't despair. Nothing is hopeless yet. Alright?"

They wiped away the teardrop on their cheek and nodded resolutely. "I like your new look, Professor. That shorts and mules combo? *So* cute."

I laughed. "Thanks. So is your hair. Say, have you seen Camden around?"

They pointed with a small hand at the space between Mortensen and Northrop Hall, at the rows of oak trees which lined a long walkway with their shadowy canopy. "I think he's packing up."

I had to hurry then. "Thank you. If you see him try to leave, don't let him. Not yet."

Billie beamed. "Great." They hugged me again, quickly, with just one arm, and then they scampered off toward the oaken walkway en route to the dorms.

"They could be your own kid," Claire remarked.

"All the more reason to do everything I can for them." Linking our arms back together, Claire and I took off toward Dell at a brisk clip. Our shoes thumped against the cobblestones. It felt like the noise made everyone stop and stare, but I squared my jaw and kept my eyes on Dell.

"Come through the side door." Claire towed me along around the side of Dell, avoiding the handful of professors clustered in discussion near the front doors. A direct outlet to Claire's hallway with the other three chemistry teachers, this let us sneak through a silent and empty passage and took us to her shadowy closet of an office. Her philodendron hanging over her desk didn't seem to do well when the sun slanted at this angle in the height of summertime. Not that her window was large enough to let a whole lot of light in. I slipped into the office behind her and shut the door so nobody saw me before I wanted them to, leaning against the paneling while Claire picked up the white rotary phone atop her tidy desk. She chewed her lip and flipped her hair back from her brow while she spun the dial.

"Mathilda, hey, babe. It's me. I'm—" She pressed her fingers into her eyes. "I know. I know, I feel awful. It's been... yeah. I'm alright, not that kind of awful. But I...yeah. I should have two more exams, but I don't think I've got it in me, and I'm not dressed for class. I'm going to see if Elizabeth can step in for me. Can you come pick me up? An hour? Yeah. That's fine. No, he won't. Yeah. Just for now." She dropped her voice and shielded her mouth. "Things are tenuous, Mathilda, and—"

I slipped out of Claire's office despite her protest and closed the door on her. The small chemistry corridor fed into the longer hallway housing the history department across from *that* office.

Unfortunately for him, Brandon left his door open. He looked up sharply when I appeared under his lintel with spite in my eyes.

Behind his grandiose desk, he looked surprised at first like a child caught stealing cookies. Then he started laughing, unkind, cruel and cold as a winter gale. "What the hell are you doing back in my face, *Sebring?*"

Visualizing Lunix's moonlight eyes, I called forth their savage courage and declared, "What the hell are you doing to this school, *Steve?*" He made it known he hated when people called him that, which made the way he flinched absolutely delicious. "This has got to stop. Camden Zane deserves to graduate, and these students deserve access to a magíq education. Pascale Manon did not open this university just to have you spit on its foundations."

Brandon rolled his eyes, pushing away from his desk to get to his feet. I forgot how much taller he was than me. He'd even make Nico look... well, regular. "Ackerleigh, this ridiculous agenda of yours has to stop. Your time at Ravensbourne is over." He strode across his plush carpeting to flick the badge on my sweater, and it was my turn to flinch. "Camden Zane has been a poor student for four years—he can barely *read—*"

Incredulous, I scoffed and started to defend his dyslexia, but Brandon pressed on.

"—and then he decided to incite unrest and disobedience among the students? Come now, Sebring. You can't really think he was going to graduate." Brandon shrugged, gazing down at me through heavily hooded lids, a smirk playing on his lips behind his graying beard. "I just took the guesswork out of it."

It was so hard to keep my voice level with how close he stood. I was reminded of the Yule gathering last year, when vodka clung to his breath and turned his hand on my shoulder and my back into hot coals. "You only lashed out at him because he stood up for me. How does it feel that nobody believed your claims of sexual misconduct?" I put the term in air quotes with my fingers and watched his eyes dart to my hands.

"Do you think that's the only claim I can make against you?" Brandon bent at his waist, making the buttons gape on his black suit jacket. "Do you think anyone will cry for a lost magíq program when they learn that you only championed it because you, yourself, are a magíqon?"

I recoiled. I shouldn't have—I shouldn't have—I shouldn't have. It happened automatically, with horror, with the way my whole body went hot and then cold and then... numb. So, so numb. Did he—did he know? But the look on his face when I pulled away provided just enough clarity to make me realize my mistake. He'd made something up. He'd guessed. But my reaction gave me away. Why did I always misstep around him? Why did he always crowd out any rational thought from my head?

"So all you can do as a leader is lie your way through it, isn't it?"

Brandon chuckled. He knew he had complete control of this conversation and could surely see me losing my composure.

I thought again of Lunix's clear gaze, of their midnight plumage shot with moonlight. I held onto the vision of the gryphon as a reminder that Brandon was nothing, nobody, against the backdrop of such majesty.

"As a *leader*," he repeated cooly, "I will do whatever necessary to protect this institution from abominations like you. I will say whatever must be said in order to uphold the integrity of Ravensbourne University." He stepped closer, the edges of his jacket brushing my stomach. I could feel his phantom touch on my face. All my muscles clenched, and my vision turned black around the edges. "And I will do my part to eradicate magíq from this whole damn country."

Fear took over. I turned on my heel while lurching toward his door, nearly tripping into the hallway beyond his office. Slamming into Claire, I caught myself with one hand on the wall and my other arm around her waist as we both fought to stifle our cries of surprise and pain. Her nose banged into my temple and her shoulder rammed into my bruises. We clung to each other as we hurriedly shuffled through the alcove and to the front doors.

We burst out into the warm sunshine. Angry tears threatened to burst from my eyes, but I fought them down, chin trembling.

"You sounded amazing, Leigh." Claire nudged our hips together. Her head flicked to the left, eyes widening. She fixed her glasses as she blinked hard in the direction of the oak corridor that led to the dormitories. Neon-green leaves rustled, an archway bursting with life. A pair of students, as opposite as a sprout and a sycamore, tore down the cobblestones in our direction. Surely it wasn't Billie with Cam—

"Prof! Professor Sebring!" Huffing, red-cheeked, and looking like he'd stress eaten the whole semester, Cam ran up waving both hands. "I can't believe you're here!" Tragically, he too wore Ravensbourne gear. His tee was stamped with the school's name under an undone plaid shirt, his jean shorts noisy as he ran up in sandals.

"Cam." Relief and guilt sighed his name with me. "Billie found you."

"They almost broke my window chucking a rock at it, and I'm already *barely* getting my deposit back." He laughed and reached to muss up Billie's hair, but they hissed and dodged his hand.

"Camden—" I pressed my hand to my chest, the words clambering out of my heart. "I am *so* sorry for what's happened to you this semester. You were doing so well. You'd almost made it. When I started here, you were angry, barely going to class, and just scraping by."

Cam's gaze dropped. "Yeah." He barely made a sound. "Well, you're the reason I got this far. It's kind of poetic, going out this way."

"If my idea works, you don't have to go out this way at all."

Billie gasped, and Cam's hazel eyes widened and rose to stare at me.

"What do you mean?" Cam tried very hard not to look hopeful. Sparks lit in his eyes and gave him away.

"If I recall, you need three classes after this semester. Two bestiary and one history of magíq. Correct?" I was nearly hopping, my voice pressured with my anticipation. When Cam nodded, I continued, "You can get those credits with me. Off-campus. You can work on your thesis based on a field study. When everything's done, I'll bring all your work to the rest of the school board and make it impossible for them to withhold your degree."

Both of my students stared at me with slack jaws and marbles for eyes. Billie unfroze first, clapping and hopping in a circle. Cam shook his head in disbelief.

With a crooked grin, Cam asked, "What kind of field study?"

Claire yelped, and Billie gasped. Fury erupted in Cam's face and terror in Billie's.

With a good guess as to who upset them so much, I spun around.

As soon as I faced him, Brandon snatched a handful of my sweater collar and dragged me closer to him.

"You're a pestilence!" Brandon cried, shaking me.

Buzzing blood in my ears turned into a roaring inferno. He shook out the last shred of my self-control and it tumbled through the soles of my feet. In their stead, fire. Wind. *Desperation.*

He would take his hands *off* me.

Wind came first. Blazing down the oak corridor near us and climbing up my legs, spiraling around my torso like a sparkling silver tornado before whipping into Brandon, blasting him away from me. Releasing my sweater, he staggered back and fell to one knee—as if he was bowing to me.

Emboldened, I called to the ésprit of the fire that was flickering beneath my skin all day and willed it to explode. My hands erupted into flame, the heat welcome in my clammy palms, tracks of fire following the veins in my arms. All eyes were on me, but I called on the pair of moonlight eyes that lived in my heart and I did not back down.

"Your lies can do nothing to me now." I stepped toward Brandon, who was too shocked to get up, true fear on his face which already gleamed with sweat from the heat rolling off me. Remembering how Lunix could calm a feral spark, I took a risk on this volatile element. Rage had fed it for the last three months since Brandon crushed my career here. Rage would ensure it was only the President who got burned. As I stretched out a fiery hand toward him, skin almost lost beneath flickering orange and silver tongues, I imagined the scream he'd make as I melted the skin of his neck down to bone.

And I stopped.

I let my hands fall. Let the fire extinguish. Let my arms smoke, large coiling ribbons of gray drifting into the sunset. For a moment, I simply inhaled the scent of smoke as a paralyzed silence stretched longer. Brandon's eyes were squeezed closed, as if he hadn't yet realized I'd stayed my hand and spared him.

"Aw, man!"

I glanced back at Cam, raising an eyebrow.

"Couldn't you have lit his beard on fire or something?"

Next to him, Billie silently flapped their arms, their face an image of absolutely feral delight.

From the quad, someone screamed, "Down with Brandon!" A chorus of boos and cheers erupted. An apple came flying between me and Claire and thwacked off Brandon's shin as he climbed back to his feet. A beastly snarl consumed his features.

Claire crossed her arms, smirking. Only I could tell how she trembled. "I'd get out of here if I were you, Brandon."

Snapping his blazer and smoothing his hair, the President stalked past me. He tried to shove my shoulder with his, so I called the static clinging to my sweater to the surface. A great lilac spark crackled when he made contact with me, making him jump back with a yell.

Billie and Cam erupted into raucous cackles of delight. Several of the closest students whooped and jeered.

Brandon hurriedly backed away before retreating, making swiftly for the faculty parking lot. He had a long walk through a gauntlet of shame, past the statue of our founding magíqon, to get back to his fancy car at the closest spot in the faculty parking lot.

When he was a dozen paces away, he turned back and jabbed a finger toward me. "This is not over for us, Sebring."

Cam booed him out.

High as I was with the thrill of showing my hand at long last, and with Brandon forced by the opposition from his student body to slink away with his mangy tail between his legs, fear remained. As loud as the support of Claire, Cam, and Billie was to my ears, I could tell with one quick pass of my eyes over the quad that opinions were mixed on what I'd just been forced to do in public. It was emptier than when we'd passed through earlier. I imagined students running when I called the wind. I imagined watchers in the windows of Mortensen, whispering of the disgraced professor using magíq. Most students would have never seen magíq used before their eyes... and it was coming from me, someone who had put everything on the line for this, whose reputation was never pristine to begin with.

My hands curled into fists as tension coiled like a snake inside me. My chest tightened; I coughed into my sleeve. "I need to get out of here, too."

"No!" Cam whined. "Hang out with us, Prof."

"I told everyone I could that you were here," Billie said with an unapologetic smirk. "If you want to share a bit more about this *field research*—are you only gonna let Cam do it, or...?"

I coughed again. "Oh. Uh." The Hazel Mountains summoned me back and with them many magíqal learning opportunities, but I'd only concocted the plan to save Cam his credits. But... I pushed my glasses up my nose. "You'd be interested also?"

"*Ob*-viously." Cam scoffed beside them, crossing his arms and elbowing Billie in the shoulder. Billie put their hands on their hips and turned to him. The pair took to bickering heatedly. If I were a more sentimental man, I'd be quick to point out how they seemed almost like friends now, but I let them enjoy their superficial rivalry and made my exit without either of them noticing. Claire trailed after me, distracted and blank-faced.

Mathilda's maroon station wagon idled on the curb in the faculty lot. Fortunately, Brandon's spot was vacant; he hadn't lingered. The woman was leaning against the car, full pink lips curled down in a frown. Her neatly manicured hand went unconsciously to her small, tidy afro in a gesture I'd come to identify as one of anxiety. I made her anxious, and returning Claire to her in this kind of state wasn't likely to help that.

Claire threw herself into Mathilda's waiting arms. As one of the highest officials at the Laurier Public Library, Mathilda was a vision of professionalism in a ruby pantsuit that made her dark brown skin look lit from within. She clutched Claire fiercely, kissing the slightly shorter woman's brow and murmuring to her.

"Doctor Sebring. You came back, too." Mathilda fixed me with serious eyes that frustratingly reminded me of Nico.

"Against my better judgment," I said with an awkward laugh. I stole a glance over my shoulder and the students who had been staring at me from the quad mostly had the tact to pretend they hadn't been. I was desperately ready to flee to my car and go sleep at an inn for the rest of the day, curtains drawn, cuddling Dove, but it would be remiss of me to flee a conversation with Mathilda when she actually wanted to talk to me.

"For the best," said Mathilda. "I came across some information today that you should probably hear too."

Claire stood back, frowning, clutching the hem of Mathilda's blazer. "What do you mean?"

Rather than answering, Mathilda's eyes roved the quad behind us as she shook her head slightly. "Not here. We should go home and talk about this."

"I was going to stay at an inn," I began.

"No, you're not," Mathilda said frankly.

Claire and I exchanged looks of confusion.

"You're going to stay with us. There's no need to spend money on a room when we know you won't be staying in Laurier permanently. We have a guest room and an abundance of cat food." Obviously not willing to accept no for an answer, Mathilda crossed around the bonnet of her car and got into the driver's seat without another word. Claire grinned and shrugged happily.

I opened the passenger door and bent down to meet Mathilda's eyes. "D'ac, but since most of the school just found out, you should know too that I'm a magíqon." Grabbing my elbow, Claire sucked in a sharp gasp.

Mathilda eyed me in silence for a moment, one glossy black eyebrow raising. "Oh, wow, I'm *so* surprised."

Perhaps I had needed to end up grievously wounded and at the center of public scandal and extensive discourse, because I sort of enjoyed being doted on by my loved ones. Warm and dry, I sat in a deep velvet armchair with Dove on my lap, tea and biscuit in hand, while Mathilda and Claire conversed privately in their room down the hall from the sitting room where they'd put me up. I was beside a large-paned window on the top storey of their brownstone that overlooked the beach, which, due to the pleasant weather, was dotted with striped umbrellas and folks bobbing in the sacred cerulean waves.

Mathilda emerged into the drawing room, having replaced her blazer with a chenille cardigan, her hair securely tucked into a silk bonnet. She was holding a stack of brown folders that she deposited on the marble coffee table in front of my chair. Dove chirped at her. Claire followed Mathilda with a braid in her hair, wearing silk pajamas. Their orange cat, Decimal, trailed on her heels and stopped dead when he saw Dove, whose chirp turned to more of a strangled yowl. I kept her on my lap while Decimal slunk over, tail lashing, stretching out his fluffy neck to give her hind leg a sniff. Dove bent to sniff his ear, swatting his cheek with her tail.

Dropping dramatically into the studded loveseat across from me, Mathilda pointed to the stack of folders. "So. I have a friend, Thèrese, who works in Accounting at City Hall. We got talking about President Brandon a few days ago, and so I started pulling records on him after hours at the library.

"The funds he's been moving indicate he's conspiring with Technocrat extremists who are moving to criminalize the use of magìq. There are money wires, receipts, and missives we've found with confirmed and outspoken extremists that come from someone who only identifies himself as "S," corresponding with withdrawals from the Ravensbourne accounts. He shouldn't be able to operate Ravensbourne while also hoping to become a City Council Technocrat member and acting in a manner which endangers the education of the student body of Ravensbourne. There are clauses that make what he's doing illegal. That's the bottom *three* folders."

My mouth fell open. I shoved my spectacles up my nose and blinked hard. "M...Mathilda, I don't know... I don't even know what to say."

She nodded faintly, but was unable to keep the warm affection out of her eyes. "At their core, these findings are pragmatically problematic for the most prominent university in the region. But I'm also happy that it makes his treatment of you all the more corrupt, and effectively clears your name, since it's clear your research interfered with his goals and he would have wanted you out of his way." Mathilda looked up and grasped Claire's hand as my friend took a seat beside her. Then Mathilda's gaze returned to me. "I know how important you are to Claire, and from what I've heard you're very important to many students at Ravensbourne, too. None of that changes just because you're a magiqon. You deserve to be treated fairly, and Brandon can't use the school to elevate his political agenda like he has been. Oh, babies, you can't *both* be crying or else—!" Her voice cracked as she joined Claire and I as we openly wept. Claire threw her arms around her, and after a moment, I got up with Dove under my arm and rushed over to hug them both, too.

20 December 1964

For the past two months, I lived with a gryphon. I called them Luna until I learned their family of origin called them Luneyeux, so with the gryphon's blessing we came to calling them Lunix.

In my time with them, two significantly groundbreaking hypotheses have emerged, with collaboration from the gryphon's family of origin. These hypotheses are so staggering that they demand years of further research and refinement.

The first is that gryphons have the magiqal capacity to heal. Though the evidence of this phenomenon is currently scarce, it is indeed quite compelling, with several witnesses able to give testimony, including chemist Claire Emérie, Ph.D. It is believed that it is through the use of the ésprit of the water that this skill is executed, but it is significantly possible that the process actually accesses electricity, fire, and wind as well. It will be some time before an experimental design can be developed as it is ill-advised and unethical to manipulate variables to test this ability with either a magíqon or a creature like a gryphon.

The second hypothesis is that some gryphon specimens are in fact asexual, possessing both male and female sex characteristics, and are able to generate the necessary hormonal formula to produce a fertilized egg independently. This would serve to grow and populate gryphon pods and put less stress on mating between specimens, thus improving pod relations and community rearing of kits.

An expert witness proposes that the gryphon Lunix is asexual and that this was part of why the esteemed Doctor Rose Bennett wanted to keep Lunix in captivity. She may have meant to manipulate this aspect of their biology, but no such event occurred nor would have been likely to occur based on the general emotional health of the gryphon in their forced captivity.

As I have lost my standing with the universities in Deubrise, it is unclear when I will be able to resume the publication of research on gryphons. However, even if only for my own improvement or for a better understanding of Lunix, my studies will persist.

Seminar in Gryphon Maulings

The blisters on the bottoms of my feet squelched and threatened to burst while I ran. Mountain bush rose ominously on my left side, practically vertical, towering over me. Dawn had barely arrived. Roots and bucking stone invited me to trip and twist my ankle—again—but I wasn't worried about that. Not with Lunix circling over my head, high above the treeline, hunting for game and keeping an eye on me. Cheese crashed through the underbrush nearby as well, kicking up the scent of fertile soil and rich vegetation. Birds protested at her graceless romp.

I ran furiously, teeth bared, fists clenched, heedless of the treachery in my path. I would happily go down broken. Nothing else was happening in my life. A broken ankle wouldn't do a damn thing one way or the other.

One, two, three weeks had passed since Ackerleigh's departure. Lunix was mopey without him and had been sleeping in the bed they'd shared with him, much to Stella's dismay. To be honest, I was moping, too. Ackerleigh seemed to take all the colors in the world with him when he left. I wanted to sleep constantly, to just hibernate until he came back—if he came back—but I just tossed and turned every night.

Stella was wearing on my nerves, something that only happened now and again. Being alone in hiding with her, though, left me feeling intensely claustrophobic. We could only listen to the same three records so many times before I started fantasizing about snapping them in half. I could only improvise so many meals before getting sick of mixing spices wrong and ending up with inedible sludge. We had long since run out of Cyrus's eggs and milk.

Our days were truly free, but with liberation and safety came... emptiness.

Everyone probably knew by now that the gryphon was missing from the estate. Showing up at Cyrus's, or even the De Falco farm, would risk the tentative grasp on freedom that we had. Doctor Bennett excelled at placing immense pressure on people in order to get what she wanted, and what she wanted was Lunix. I wasn't sure even my parents would be able to let us come and go freely, knowing Doctor Bennett would have her sights on the farm.

So, we were here, subsisting on a diet of fruits and vegetables. Happy with our gryphon, but watching our world shrink along with our block of cheese. As terrible as I felt about it, I was beginning to wonder if this had been worth it.

Stella strongly disagreed. She was cheerful and lazy and playful with both me and Lunix. She slept easily, and had been snoring when I left her in the cottage.

Meanwhile, I slept fitfully, staring at the dusty flower shags in the rafters for most of the night while I imagined a posh light-licker life with Ackerleigh.

Still heartsick, still embarrassed, I gulped in air like it would save me from my humiliation and let me go back to pretending like I didn't resent my sister for how my life was slowly shrinking to match hers.

Overhead, Lunix shrieked. I flinched and stumbled, throwing my head back.

Something was wrong.

Their call reverberated against the sheer mountain face and rattled my blood and my bones. I slowed my pace, following the arrow of their majestic eagle half as they pointed in the direction of the cottage.

I shifted my route to take me out of the bush while whistling for Cheese, who bounded out of the underbrush and into line behind me. Through the grove of fruit trees I dropped to a jog, squinting to try to figure out what Lunix was doing. I thought they were spiraling down to land, but it looked like they were still hunting. Cheese barked at me and then ran on ahead, her tongue flapping out of her jaws. When she tore around the curve of the cottage, she barked again—and again, and again, rapidly becoming more aggressive. Her hackles flared between her shoulder blades.

Sprinting after the dog, I was about to call for Stella but clamped down on my tongue the split second before I did. Cheese and Lunix both thought something was wrong. It was best to contain it, to deal with it myself, to keep it from Stella.

A pickup truck was parked right outside the front door. Mottled with rust and red with caked-on mud, it looked slightly familiar. Cheese's howls were aimed at the front door, where someone peered into the stained glass windowpanes. A black fleck reflected in the glass; Lunix was watching, gliding over our heads, waiting.

Heart lurching against my ribs, I tapped Cheese's back. She silenced immediately as I stalked toward the overgrown flower beds framing the front entrance. "If it isn't Tad Neal. What a disappointing visitor."

Flinching, Tad spun around. His dark eyes seemed to gobble me up. "I knew you kids were hidin' out here!"

"Tad," I groaned, "don't tell me you came all the way out here just to pick a fight." I held my hands out, easy-going. Determined not to allow him to make me defensive. *He* showed up here. *He* was invading.

"I heard you kids are thieves now." Tad crossed his arms. He was so hairy it gave the illusion that he was a large man, but he looked like he *used* to be and was rapidly losing his edge as he aged. "In fact, I saw that wild sister a' yours pokin' around in Cyrus's barn with mine own eyes."

My eyes slid heavenward. Of *course*. "Maybe you did. Maybe that's not your concern."

Tad shook his head sharply. "No, what ya don't get—because y'all have never asked—is that Cyrus can't *afford* y'alls moochin' off him. His hip's bad—he can't keep up with his farm like he usedta."

I frowned, my stomach aching with guilt. I offered him a slight nod. "D'ac, you're right. I didn't know that."

"Why ain't you takin' food from y'alls' own farm?" Tad demanded. His gaze sharpened. "It don't happen to be that y'all are out here hidin' with a stolen gryphon, is ya?"

I tried very hard not to glance skyward. I couldn't see them while keeping my eyes on Tad's overly red nose, but I could feel the sphere of Lunix's magíq all the way down here. Hairs on the back of my neck stood on end at the thought of their keen moon-eyes staying trained on Tad as they silently circled.

I swallowed. "I don't know what you mean. We're due at the estate in four days," I said, hoping he didn't notice the tremble in my voice. Since tapping my scar was an obvious tell, I fought against my anxiety by digging my fingernails into my palms. I had underestimated Tad's observational skills but, doing the work he did as a hunter, he had to be sharper than he seemed.

"You kids don't need to live like this," Tad said, hands out as if he was petitioning me to understand that suffocation wasn't a bad way to die. "Ain't the De Falco farm yours for the takin'? And your grandparents—"

"Tad," I interrupted impatiently, "just stay out of our business. Then we'll all be happy."

Tail wagging between her hindquarters, Cheese sniffed her way between us to investigate Tad's boots.

"You kids don't have the privilege of livin' under the radar." Tad waved at the cottage. "Y'all are squattin' when you ain't gotta be. We all let y'all get away with it because—"

"Tad, you *know* how my parents treat my sister. What's so bad about letting her—"

"She needs to be under *control!*" Fury lit into Tad's eyes. I'd always known he hated her. He tolerated me, as... as an unremarkable, unmagíqal farmer, I supposed. Someone like him. But not Stella. "The things she did even when she was a kid, terrorizin' my daughter n' all those other poor kids... Gods, she's only gonna get worse, ain't she?"

"She can control herself." I crossed my arms.

"Then how'd she break a window twelve feet off the ground at Cyrus's?" Tad snapped. "A window *I* helped him fix a'cause all y'all do is *take*. Ya don't give back, do ya?"

Stella hadn't told me that. Swallowing, I stayed silent, trying to get my bearings.

Tad snorted. "Do *you* even fully know what she's capable of, Nico? You know, I've started goin' to these meetings over in Hazberg... There's a lotta people who think kids like Stella should be locked up with the likes of your gryphon."

The front door burst open, striking Tad in the hip. I leapt back; Cheese yelped in alarm; Tad howled and clutched his side.

Stella stumbled out into the hyacinth bush, dropping to a crouch with her hands hooked into claws. "You enfour! I'll give you a reason to lock me up!"

"Stel—"

White-hot streaks of lightning jumped into her palms. Glowing violet, it lit her veins up fuschia. Her hair stuck up with electricity, making her look like a snarling, spitting cat. The tang of metal coated my tongue, and I instinctively threw my hand up over my face as my body returned to the moment she'd injured me as children. Static buzzed around us, shocking my eyelashes. Cheese yelped and fled.

Tad backed up, reaching for his door handle. It shocked him viciously, loudly and blindingly, like a firecracker. He snarled, clutching his blackened fingers.

With an unfamiliar voice as if the wild gods within the earth had crawled inside her and taken over, Stella giggled. She was a nymph, a feral creature, scarcely human. I'd never seen her this far swallowed by her magíq. The lightning sparked into the thicket of flowers under her feet and splattered onto leaves and petals. Fire jumped forth and shot tendrils of black smoke toward the heavens before the flames climbed up Stella's legs, harmless to her as feathers.

Tad stretched his arm inside his truck. Electricity leapt from the metal frame and ate at his body with loud, bright shocks, making him groan in agony. He withdrew a rifle and cocked it.

As suddenly as having switched off a light, midnight fell. Lunix had arrived. Wings of darkness kicked up a gale, and the roar from Lunix's throat was thunder, summoning dark clouds that streaked across the early navy of the sky and banished the morning. Lunix's eyes were no longer moons, but the hottest stars smoldering in the sky. The fiery flowers extinguished. Stella greeted Lunix with a whoop of delight. She tossed a frothy string of lightning toward the gryphon, who caught it in their beak and shook it like it was a rope.

Eyes bulging, Tad stumbled back and fell on his ass. His firearm went off with an ear-splitting *crack*. Stella yelped in terror, covering her eyes as the lightning exploded, clinging to her skin as if to become a shield. I saw the bullet streak toward the rooftop and knock loose a clay tile.

Outrage made the gryphon rear back on their lion haunches, talons grasping at the sky, their wings knocking both me and Stella down onto the grass. The wind whooshed out of my lungs, so I couldn't scream as Lunix lunged.

Tad did.

He hollered, pointed his rifle, and pulled the trigger again just as the gryphon pounced on him. All I could see from my angle was silver haunches, muscles rippling in their rump, and tendons stretching around their dewclaws. Lightning clung to their tail, which lashed back and forth with an electrical buzz. Talons swiped. A scream.

Red, red, red. Viscera flung over Lunix's fluffed up mane and stuck to the arc of their wing, bright and terrible against ebony feathers. Soon the screaming stopped. Lightning died, sparks wormed into the dirt and vanished. Lunix wasn't done, didn't call it good enough until bone snapped and flesh and fabric tore.

"L-Lunix!" Horrified desperation made the cry of my voice almost childlike, and Lunix's head shot upright and swiveled around to face me. Intestines pierced by the tip of their beak whipped about in a macabre dance. My stomach cramped and promptly emptied, hardly giving me enough warning to lean over so I didn't vomit all over myself. Tears followed shortly after and forced my chest to heave in hyperventilating gasps.

Next to me, Stella stared at Tad between Lunix's limbs and started to laugh. High-pitched, hysterical cackling, her trembling hands steepling over the mad cavern of her mouth.

Lunix's wing's flipped as their attention slowly returned to Tad. From the body rose a soft, gurgling groan.

"Holy shit, he's alive?" I climbed quickly to my hands and knees. "Stella, go in and call for the ambulance!"

"What?" Sharp eyes, still violet, shot toward me. "Hell, no! I'm not—"

"Stella, if you don't do it, so help me I will never speak to you again!" *Bellow* was the only acceptable word for what had exploded from my chest. Spittle flew off my lips and my vision turned spotty. I dug my fingers into the dirt and tore up a handful of grass and soil, pitching it at her.

The madness snapped out of her features. Stella scrambled to her feet and stumbled past Lunix, disappearing into the cottage.

Trembling, I climbed upright and, with both hands outstretched, edged my way around Lunix. Every fiber of my being wanted to look away from the body on the ground, to spare myself from future nightmares. But Tad hadn't gotten to spare himself from being gored by a gryphon. The least I could do was honor that by...

I promptly gagged and vomited again, only bile. The smell—gods, the smell... Ten times worse than the awful stench of gralloching a prize buck. Red so profound it was nearly black, offensive patches of pale flesh. Tad's face was slashed through with deep gouges that had popped an eye from its socket. The other blinked sluggishly at me, almost unseeing.

Squatting over him, I said breathlessly, "It's... It's gonna be alright—"

Tad's remaining eye went still, clouding over. A final wet breath departed from what remained of his shredded lungs.

The only reason I stayed on my feet was to avoid stopping so close to his mutilated corpse. I stumbled away from the now-cursed front door. Cold sweat clung to my skin.

Lunix turned to follow me. They lowered their foreleg, screamed, and collapsed. I froze with a gasp, reaching instinctively for the gryphon as they went down.

"Lunix?" Heedless of the human gore splattered across feather and fur, I fell to my knees in front of them.

Lunix dropped their head to rest their chin on my shoulder. They smelled like sour, cooked flesh, which made my stomach cramp again. "Pain," they croaked.

"Alright, Lunix," I whispered unsteadily, "I'm going to feel for the wound. Hold still. Don't... don't hurt me."

"Never." They clicked twice. "Never."

My hands roamed the gryphon's flesh near the leg that had buckled. Quickly, blood smeared over my skin, but I didn't feel anything pumping. It was so hard to see...

"Stella!"

My sister reappeared in the doorway. She edged around Tad's lifeless body, the press of her lips suggesting that her delight had worn off. As soon as she saw the tableau of Lunix on the ground with me kneeling at their head, she gasped and rushed over.

I cleared bile from my throat and commanded, "I need you to wash all this off Lunix. They're hurt and I can't tell where." I'd barely finished speaking before Stella swept her arms toward the nearby washroom in the front corner of the cottage. Water thick as a tree trunk spurted toward us, lit up with the luminous turquoise glow of magíq. Lunix flinched as the liquid slammed into them and drenched them and me. I shut my eyes, shielding myself with my shoulder. At first the water washing over us was filthy, chunky and pink, but Stella kept the flow going until we ran clean, and she cycled the grisly, stained water away from us and dumped it in the bushes.

Wiping my eyes dry, I went back to inspecting Lunix's dripping mane. Blood oozed from above their left foreleg, feathers bent at wrong angles all radiating from an unmistakable bullet hole in Lunix's silver, pockmarked flesh.

"Wh-What do we do?" Stella rocked on her heels, covering her mouth. "Their heart is near there. Their air sac is near there. They—Th-they—"

Panic spiked through my chest. "Stella, shut *up*. Go bring my truck 'round to us." When she opened her mouth, I snarled, "Go!"

As she sprinted away from me through the tall grass, I turned my attention back to Lunix, who was blinking water out of their frightened eyes and mewling softly. With gentle fingers I wiped their eyes, stroking their slick cheek. "We've got you, Lunix. I know it hurts. We're gonna take good care of you."

The truck roared up to us. Stella leapt out and opened the back hatch, letting it fall with a heavy clang. To get the gryphon into the truck, I... was clueless. Two men my size might not have been enough to lift a gryphon-worth of dead weight. Determined to try, I shuffled to Lunix's midsection and started to wedge myself under their belly. Carefully, Lunix helped. They used their other leg and got their hindquarters under their body, but I felt clumsy and bound for failure.

Wind whipped into my face, hard enough to draw tears into my eyes. Understanding what Stella was doing, Lunix laboriously lifted their wings to allow the wind to flick between their rachis. The load of them lightened, and with the help of our gryphon and the wind, I eventually hauled them into the cargo bed and on top of the blankets.

"What can you do?" I asked.

Stella tore her eyes from Lunix, clutching her elbows. "What?"

"You have to be able to do somethin' for them." I moved up to the driver's door and climbed behind the wheel. "Get back there and try something. This is your fault."

The rearview mirror showed me Stella's jaw dropping. She gaped at me, frozen.

"Get in the fucking truck!" I roared.

Flinching, Stella obeyed. She clambered up by Lunix's head and slotted herself in against the wheel bulge and the gryphon's shoulder. She whistled, and Cheese jumped up and scrambled into a safe pocket behind Lunix's wing, licking her lips nervously.

I switched the truck into drive and slammed my foot on the gas, knocking Stella over so Lunix had to use their uninjured arm to pick her back upright.

"Where are we going?" Stella had to shout to be heard over my speed.

"We're taking Lunix to Ackerleigh."

Capstone in Unforeseen Lineage

I wished that the Ravensbourne School Board had chosen some-where less ostentatious for this meeting than a second-floor lecture hall in Mortensen. I attracted more than a little bit of attention as I strode with false confidence through the main floor atrium. Classes weren't in session between terms, but students were allowed to stay on campus, and many hung out in Mortensen—apparently.

At least my new light-licker clothes infused me with confidence. Pointed-toe boots with a chunky, loud heel, and new trousers black as Lunix's mane made me feel sleek and sophisticated. And, because Brandon wasn't here to prey on me anymore, a soft and delicate blouse had beckoned me: silk, salmon-pink, with lantern sleeves that had lace cuffs, and a high lace collar fixed with a moonstone brooch at my throat.

I was finally outfitted once again with prescription glasses. After enjoying the tortoiseshell frames I'd gotten in Moundsview, I'd ordered a similar pair, only in smoky shades of silver and black, and round as full moons.

I wheezed up the stairs and took a left at the top, clenching and unclenching my fists repeatedly. My palms were sticky and cold, which recalled the look Nico had given me when he'd helped me onto Lunix. Sometimes I thought people expected my skin to be as dry as the books I pored over. But I had no such luck, cursed with nervous flesh.

"Psst!"

I jerked toward the sound. Cam waved from a bench in the corner of an alcove. When I met his eyes, he jumped up and rushed over to me, hooking his arm around my neck. He was dressed like he was prepared for an interview, in a button-down shirt with a tie striped black, gray, purple and white, with slacks and velvet brogues.

Sweetly smiling, he asked, "Sure I can't come in?"

I wheezed out a laugh. "Quite sure, but thank you for the solidarity, Mister Zane."

"Oh, look!" Cam held out his thumb and forefinger pinched together.

I blinked, squinting at the white hair between their fingers. It was a fluffy, bendable strand like Dove would leave on my lap after a cuddle. Frowning, I looked up at Cam and shook my head, not understanding.

"A gray hair. You're stressing me out, Doctor Sebring." Cam gave me a big, crooked grin as he recalled my comment when I'd woken him up that fateful morning when I'd been fired.

"Gods," I groaned, grinning back. "You're a rascal, Camden Zane."

I left him beaming at me as I hurried off to the double doors of the auditorium that was holding my review meeting. I was several minutes early and only half the seats in the front row were occupied by council members. Most of them were some of the older professors who had been at Ravensbourne for decades: the Chemistry professor Claire called "Mama", Elizabeth Mooney; my colleague in the History department, Craig Dowell; and the Provost, Professor Davidson. In addition, several parents of current and past students served on the Board, as did some wealthy alumni from before my time. I refused to analyze anyone's expressions for fear of what opinions I would find there.

Claire wasn't able to attend this, and I wanted to kill her for it. She was working with the registrar to sort out spring registration, which we all knew Brandon had failed to handle appropriately, including Cam's eligibility for enrollment.

"Doctor Sebring, dear." Elizabeth tutted worriedly at me, hurrying over to me and giving me a tight hug. "You look well! You've gotten a bit of sun, haven't you?"

Laughing, I tipped my chin. "Thank you for noticing." The involuntary memory of Nico made my stomach hurt as my body tried to determine whether to be comforted or wounded by the thought of him.

Elizabeth motioned to the professor's desk sitting opposite the auditorium seating. "You can sit there, alright, dear?"

I pulled out the rolling chair at the desk and sat carefully. Under the table, my knee immediately started bouncing. My breath whistled through my throat and I wished for a spot of water. I wondered if I could use magíq to purify my sweat to drink...

"I think there's just one more person on their way. Several council members opted not to be here," said Craig Dowell. He was barely dressed for the occasion, wearing a short-sleeved collared shirt with the top buttons open to show the edge of his undershirt.

"Ah, yes." I smiled humorlessly. "I caused quite a scandal."

"Essentially." Craig nodded. "Your..."

"Magíq."

"... *interesting* display was very off-putting to a number of us. Some say you lost control," remarked Craig.

Brandon was alive, wasn't he? I kept the thought to myself and shrugged. "People are welcome to speculate. I'm happy to field questions for those comfortable with speaking to me directly. Admittedly, I am in the infancy of the cultivation of my own skills, but it has been an enlightening period of learning."

"Are we beginning?" chirped Elizabeth. "Is this the meeting?" She glanced down at the row of faculty members and then back at the other board members.

"I'm transcribing," mumbled The Owl. He hunched over his own folio and began scratching pen to paper.

Provost Davidson met my gaze. "The purpose of this meeting is to review the claims made by Doctor Stephen Brandon concerning your conduct, and to determine whether or not to reinstate you as a Professor of History. Most of us are personally and professionally unsure whether or not your magíq makes you a liability." Aging gracefully into a sprinkle of gray hairs, Davidson was tall with dark eyes and a dark complexion, wearing a tweed three-piece suit and swiveling back and forth in his chair. I had always got on with Davidson, thanks to our similarly practical natures, not to mention a shared wry sense of humor.

"I understand that." I wetted my lips, choosing my words carefully. "But my magíq is nothing new. I have never displayed magíq around students or other faculty, Claire included, in my personal time or otherwise. Much like we may never know that someone enjoys collecting vintage spoons as a hobby, not because they do it any less but simply because they keep it to themselves."

Elizabeth giggled. "I see you've heard about my spoons."

Even I couldn't withhold a laugh, the tension in the hall promptly diffusing. Elizabeth had that effect on any room she was in.

I rubbed my moonstone brooch. "Point being, I am no more or less a liability than I was before anyone knew."

"Ackerleigh," said Craig softly, "Regrettably, I do think it's important you state in your own words what transpired between you and Stephen Brandon that day."

Leaning back in my seat, I sighed heavily and rubbed my face. An inevitable part of my council meeting, but by far the part I was dreading the most. I was still angry at myself for how often the scene looped in my head. Even now, I could hear the crinkle of papers as he'd leaned his hip into my pile of rejected proposals. I could smell the leather of my desk mat.

Elizabeth huffed. "Must he? We already know—"

"I know, Liz," sighed Craig. "I mean, good grief, I saw it myself. But we are conducting a formal review, and—"

"It's fine," I interrupted. "I expected this." Embarrassed, I whisked my fingertips through the hair on the back of my head and added, "I practiced."

Covering her mouth, Elizabeth groaned and shook her head. "Alright, dear. Go on."

I swallowed and said evenly, "The day he dismissed me, the only interaction we'd had was when he solicited me for sexual liaisons." My nails scraped against the emotional brand his touch had left on my chin. "I turned him down. He... he said that, uh, I believe, I 'didn't know what was good for me.' And..." I swallowed. "I left, went to class, and didn't even have time to start my lecture before he sent Craig to deliver his note. He didn't even have the spine to fire me himself."

Shuffling in her seat, Elizabeth began, "He ought to—"

Provost Davidson loudly cleared his throat and she fell silent, scowling. Then The Owl resumed his transcribing, and I stewed in the heavy quiet of the room. Allowing myself a quick glance at the other board members, I was surprised to observe... sympathy.

Perhaps I'd internalized more guilt than I ought to have. Some long-frightened part of my soul uncoiled and relaxed.

More casually, I added, "I suspect Camden Zane's right outside, if you need corroboration from students who were in that class."

The Owl glanced up. He nudged his glasses back into place on his wide nose and looked at the Provost.

Provost Davidson dismissively waved his hand. "We've spoken with your students."

"Oh." I blinked hard.

"Yours is the last testimonial we needed," said Elizabeth, smiling. "I don't mind telling you that there is a *heap* of evidence condemning Brandon's conduct here at our esteemed university." To my relief, Davidson nodded in agreement.

"However," the Provost added, "we continue to struggle with the notion that Brandon only dismissed you because his unwanted advances were rejected. He did not bother to do much more than note that your research proposals over the last three years were too sympathetic toward magíq to remain impartial. And, unfortunately for you, the discovery that you are in fact a magíqon makes this seem more accurate."

I grimly squeezed my eyes closed. "But this university—"

"I know," interrupted Provost Davidson. "Pascale Manon was also a magíqon. But your kind are rare now, and we must consider that the general hostility toward magíq might bring dangerous and unwanted attention to our student body as a whole, were it to be common knowledge that one of our own faculty members is a magíqon."

"Ron—" began Elizabeth.

"No, he's right," I said quickly, lifting a pacifying hand to Elizabeth. "Student safety is the top priority."

A parent from the second row lifted her hand and said gently, "I struggle with the notion of you returning in your former capacity to this institution. Even if you are as generally well-liked, as my daughter Ritika says you are, aren't you worried that your... notoriety will cause distractions?"

I nodded. "Yes, Madame Chakraborty, I've considered that and share your concern. There is important history that must be preserved in our future generations. I don't want to turn into some sort of curio."

The woman cocked her head. "So, then what..."

"I honestly have no inclination to return to teaching full-time." I rubbed my moonstone.

The Owl dropped his stylus and lifted his head, practically hooting with surprise. "You don't? But, Ackerleigh—"

The provost was the only person who remained silent. I'd voiced my intentions to him earlier that morning. He regarded me sagely, fingers steepled under his chin.

I smiled kindly at Craig. "You can't think I expect things to be as they were, either. I would like to be able to have access to the institution when I'm here, but I'm planning to move to the Hazel Mou—"

The double doors opened. Doctor Rose Bennett stepped through, looking flustered, shaking her head with an apology.

The final syllable of *mountain* squeaked out of my mouth a full two octaves above my usual voice. I clapped a hand over my mouth, lucky I hadn't eaten anything that might have come back up at the sight of my benefactor. Why was she *here?*

Oh. Gods.

She was on the school board.

Quite tall and imposing in stature, Doctor Bennett was slightly heavier than I remembered. She was dressed handsomely in a pantsuit the same red as the ripe skin of a Honeycrisp apple. It offset the poppy-red cat-eye glasses perched on the end of her severe nose. Her face was slender, a bit heart-shaped, with something familiar about it that I couldn't place.

Elizabeth waved a hand. "We know you got here when you could, Doctor Bennett. I hope you don't mind that we got started without you."

"Of course not." Doctor Bennett tapped her way over to the first row of seats in her red patent pumps. Feeling phantom dust on my skin, I flinched at the sight of her shoes. It was particularly tragic realizing the risky return trip to the estate had been all for naught, considering I'd literally outed myself as a magíqon the very next day.

Doctor Bennett sat on Elizabeth's other side and adjusted her blazer over the black lace blouse she wore underneath. She lifted her wintry blue eyes and met my gaze. "Doctor Sebring. Glad to see you're alive."

Craig muttered something, tapping his stylus against his paper and looking at the provost, but Davidson was watching Doctor Bennett with a queasy look on his face.

Her words hit me like a slap to the face. I shuddered. "Um—yes. I… I returned not long after the—um—incident in the courtyard." I was *so* not prepared to be taking accountability for everything that had transpired at the estate. Especially not the *kissing* of the person who'd *stolen* her gryphon prisoner. My body temperature rose so rapidly I worried I'd combust. If I burned down Mortensen Hall out of embarrassment, they'd *definitely* ban me from teaching.

"You two will have to catch up at a later time," Craig finally said with a huff. "This meeting is regarding Doctor Sebring's post at the school."

Doctor Bennett raised her eyebrows. "I don't see the problem with—"

For the second time, the heavy doors beside me opened. Irritation surged in my belly, and when, good gods, Cam's sly face appeared in the godforsaken gap between them, I almost screamed.

"Prof!" he whispered harshly. He glanced at the row of people, gave them an awkward laugh-wave, and crooked his finger at me. "Come here."

"Camden, shoo!" I clenched my fists. "I wasn't joking—"

"No, for real, Doctor Sebring, get out here." No mischief lit Cam's hazel eyes. His expression was pinched, brow drawn, lips turned down toward the slight acne on his chin.

Unable to look at the Board as I sighed and got to my feet, I stormed over to the doors. I burst through them with such fervor that I almost crashed into Cam.

"Don't you understand?" I hissed at him. "This isn't just to get me back here, it's to let me take *you*—"

Cam pressed his lips together and pointed to the left. I whipped my head in that direction, ready to berate my student more. But then I saw someone halfway down the hall, shadowed in the diffuse light from the stained glass windows. My heart stopped. A wheezing breath lodged itself in my throat.

Leaning against the wall, hugging his arms across his wide chest, Nico De Falco stared at his mud-caked trainers. His sun-kissed curls were sloppily bound and spilling out of his bun. Rust-red water stains streaked his tight shirt and set my stomach on fire in a nauseating marriage of desire and horror.

"Nico?" Forgetting Cam was on my heels, I rushed forward. I hardly believed Nico was here—in Laurier! I thought for certain I'd lapsed into some delusional fantasy meant to take me away from the Board proceedings. "What are you doing here?"

He twitched when he heard my voice, but otherwise remained paralyzed. I leaned into him, hands on his hips, cocking my head to try to force him to meet my gaze. But it was no luck. His eyes were distant, darker by far than I remembered them being, as if the weeks apart had stolen the light from him.

"Nico, what happened to you?" I tipped his chin up with my finger. He yielded easily, and as soon as our eyes met, his expression crumbled.

"Ackerleigh." The sound of my name on his lips was a tragedy. A whimper from someone who was irrevocably wounded. My heart dropped into my stomach as I wondered what horrors had broken Nico De Falco in such a way.

"Talk to me," I whispered.

"I need your—" Suddenly his gaze sharpened and hardened, his attention stolen by the squeak of a shoe. His eyes slid toward Cam. "Can ya give us some—"

"Oh, no." Cam planted his feet like a tree. "You're not getting rid of me."

"Camden Zane!" I snapped, protectively gripping Nico's arm. "You have two seconds to get your ass to the end of the hall or I will make that happen for you." I sent a whip of wind right over Cam's head. Nico jerked in surprise, his brow furrowing at my display.

Cam's hair went wild, his hazel eyes went round, and he straightened immediately. "Yessir." He stifled a hysterical giggle before scampering away.

Scowling, I returned my attention to Nico, touching his forearm. His prominent veins seemed to be throbbing with his panic. "Don't worry about him. What happened?"

Eyes wet and glassy, Nico leaned down to speak in a whisper that trembled like the tiniest pool of water cupped by a leaf. "Lunix killed someone. And Stella would have, if they hadn't."

Cold flooded my veins and brought every coherent thought in my head crashing to a halt. "Oh, gods. What? How? That's... Where are they now?"

"Lunix—they're wounded. They got shot." A single teardrop escaped Nico's lashes, and when he spoke again, his deep voice warbled. "Stella's been keepin' ice on the wound, but... they went unresponsive 'bout a half hour ago while I was tryin' to find my way here."

"No! No, they can't d—" My voice was much louder than I intended, pushed to a frantic volume by the sheer disbelief and horror of the idea of Lunix having been *shot.* "Where—" My throat seized, making my voice crack. I swallowed hard. "Where are they?"

"By the—"

Those godforsaken doors opened again. It could have been The Owl. It could have been Elizabeth.

But it was Doctor Bennett, with the curiosity of a cat suspecting a mouse was scratching at the floor near her bowl full of food.

She silently assessed the scene before her. Camden, awkwardly at a distance. Me, stiffening under her scrutiny, so very tempted to set her on fire if it would spare Nico from her.

But something shifted when her gaze found Nico. Her jaw dropped. Her eyes widened into icy blue marbles. Softened, inexplicably. She slumped her shoulders.

Nico stared back at her, frozen, lips slightly parted. A hissing sigh left him, no different than a death rattle, as his shoulders sank and his eyes slid shut. He dropped his head against the wall and covered his face with both his hands.

"Nicolai Diamante De Falco, I *knew* you were involved in this." Doctor Bennett stalked toward him, reaching out as Nico dropped his hands to look at her as her fingers pinched together. I realized she was going to grab his ear. Without thinking, I wedged my shoulder between them so she wasn't able to make contact with him, and when her startled gaze found me, I resolutely glared back at her.

Nico squeezed my fingers, cutting a narrow-eyed glare at Doctor Bennett. "Of course you did, Grandmother." His words came out sharp and enunciated. It was the most pronounced and sudden shift I'd heard him make away from his easy-going ocky drawl.

"I—?!" I gasped. Incoherent gibberish tripped along my tongue before I snapped my mouth shut. I managed to squeak, "Grandmother?" Woozy, I tipped off balance and fell into Nico's chest. He gripped my shoulders to stabilize me. Stars dancing in my vision, I wheezed, "For the love of all that is holy, you could've warned me…"

Doctor Bennett wagged a finger at Nico. "What did you do with my ward? You let your sister explode my estate, and then vanished into that blasted countryside with even your poor mother none the wiser—"

"Grandmother," groaned Nico, "I don't have time for this. Tad Neal showed up where we're squatting and—"

She scoffed. "That meddlesome simpleton. Curse that Neal family."

"I know!" Nico exclaimed. "Stella tried to—"

"She didn't." Doctor Bennett's eyes widened. "Did she kill him?"

Nico shook his head. "No, but Lunix did."

Doctor Bennett straightened. "Nico, this is *why* the gryphon was safest at my estate! Why you two took it upon yourselves—"

"Grandmother, stop, *please!*" Nico spoke through gritted teeth, tears springing into his eyes. "Scold me later or Lunix *dies.*"

Blessedly, Doctor Bennett gasped and fell silent.

"Tad shot Lunix. I need to get Ackerleigh over there as quickly as possible. Stella can't do enough for them on her own." As Doctor Bennett opened her slender painted lips, Nico raised a hand. "I know you'll want to come with, but please don't. Stella will explode. She can't handle seeing you until after we know Lunix is stable."

Doctor Bennett glared at the vaulted ceiling. "I see your point."

Nico rallied himself, pushing a curl behind his ear and reaching a pacifying hand toward his grandmother. His grandmother—Doctor Bennett. I could *not* get that through my head. "We'll come back here, I promise on my honor as your grandson. Just wait here." He pushed away from the wall and held my elbow gently in his hand. "Let's go."

I nodded. "Lead on."

Seminar in Doing As You're Told

Being back with Ackerleigh was the first moment of sanity I'd had all day. No, it was the first moment of sanity I'd had since... since he left.

But I had so many questions. What was he doing in front of a School Board? Was he trying to get his job back? And had I really seen him use magíq right in front of one of his students?

He let me pull him along at a clipped pace, out of the dim and echoing hall and down its austere staircase under a gray sky. The heels of his shoes clacked against the cobblestones. Confused students watched my trajectory as I cut through the quad scattered with stone tables, tea trees, and clusters of flowering bushes in shades of magenta and ivory. Large silver banners flapped over my head of a raven on a book with spiky waves beneath it. I allowed the statue of Pascale Manon to encourage me like a magíqal boon.

Ackerleigh garbled something incoherent behind me. I skidded immediately to a halt. He crashed into my back, and I quickly spun and grasped his elbows apologetically.

Rubbing his nose, Ackerleigh wheezed, "Sorry—asthma. Can't—run."

"D'ac, I'm so sorry. Put your arms up." I didn't wait for him to obey; I lifted his arms myself, holding them above his head. "I gather my grandmother is still on the School Board? What truly unfortunate timing."

Ackerleigh nodded. "How did you find me?" he asked, his voice so thin I could barely hear him. He barked several dry coughs into his shoulder.

"Crudely. I went into Mortensen and started calling your name. That obnoxious kid practically jumped over the balustrade to come find me."

Ackerleigh choked on a snort of amusement, triggering more coughs. I rubbed clockwise circles on his back until he could take some less-labored breaths.

"Where did you park?" he rasped.

"The beach."

"That's a mile from here!" Hysterical, Ackerleigh wagged his finger in my face. "No way in hells are we walking, Co-Co." He gripped my bicep. "Now come along. We're driving."

"A mile's not that—" I squeaked as his fingernails dug into my muscle. He glared daggers at me. I quickly said, "No. Absolutely. You're right—Lead on."

As he led us around the cobblestone quad and toward a small parking lot, he slipped his hand through the crook of my elbow and said grimly, "This is not how I hoped to reunite."

"But you look amazing," I blurted. The soft, dreamy fabric of his shirt and how it billowed around his wrists—the rainbow-flashing stone at his throat—and the *color*... not to undersell how good he looked in those new glasses...

Ackerleigh turned crimson, lightly bumping his head against my shoulder as we hustled toward his car. "You don't mind shirts like this?" He indicated the billowing sleeve.

"Of course not! You're just like moonlight and flower petals." I flushed. "Er—I mean—"

Stepping in front of me and turning to face me, Ackerleigh grasped my hips and said tearfully, "Thank you. That means more to me than you know." He held my gaze, searching my features as a slow and tender smile spread on his lips.

I shifted my weight, lifting a tentative hand and touching his cheek. I grazed my thumb under the rim of his glasses over the almost-healed gash on his cheek. The scar made him look distinguished; it was a glimpse of his tough constitution which was otherwise obscured by his delicate appearance. "I missed you so much," I whispered.

"I missed you, too," Ackerleigh replied immediately, nuzzling my hand.

The gods gave us the grace of a few more tender seconds before Ackerleigh pulled his keys out of his pocket, pressing his lips together. I nodded and went to the passenger door. We got in the car with a grim sense of purpose.

Rumbling over cobblestones, the car followed a winding road between Ravensbourne banners before taking a right onto a quaint main street lined with curated trees, tall brownstones, and restaurants with busy patios caged with iron fences. Laurier was so *different* from the rugged north where I'd grown up, beautiful like a carefully composed painting.

"So," said Ackerleigh in a tone both light and cautious, "Doctor Rose Bennett is your grandmother. Interesting you chose to omit that information before now."

My fingers flew to my scar and tap-tap-tapped. "I'm sorry, Doctor Sebring," I said quickly. "Are you angry with me?"

Brow creasing, Ackerleigh glanced from the road. "Nico, no—"

I hurried on, "I wasn't intending to be deceitful. Truthfully, when you were staying at the cottage, I didn't make the connection between you and her both being at Ravensbourne." Gods, this sounded so *lame!* "Y-You see, I avoid associating with her as much as possible. I know that sounds flimsy and lame but it's because I... I have a lot of practice avoiding painful thoughts. For me, Grandmother Rose is a broken bone that was never properly set, and if I focus on the pain then I will lose all hope, and if I lose all hope then Stella..." I forced my mouth closed. "I'm sorry, though. I didn't tell you the whole truth."

Frowning in discomfort, Ackerleigh returned his eyes to the road. "Right."

"Doctor Sebring, I'm begging you, you need to understand—"

"No, I do." He nodded faintly. "I'm just processing. I'm processing *so* much."

"I know, and all while you were trying—er, what were you trying to do at Ravensbourne? It—er, y'know what, it doesn't matter."

"Take a breath, Nico." Ackerleigh managed a faint smile. "May I ask some questions?"

I nodded rapidly, sitting on my hands.

Ackerleigh's fingers drummed against the wheel. "So, if Doctor Bennett is your grandmother—that's how she learned about Lunix, isn't it? Because they were yours."

"Yes. She saw something she wanted, and as usual, she decided that meant she could take it for herself." Ackerleigh's gaze snapped sharply toward me when my voice cracked. "I'm sorry. I'm just so sick of all of this." Tears burned my eyes, and through my glassy vision I saw Ackerleigh's pale hand lay across my thigh. His palm was reassuring, warm. Safe.

"I'm here for you," he told me softly.

My traitorous chest heaved as I began to cry in earnest. "My family is a curse." Still rocking, I gripped Ackerleigh's small hand and shut my eyes. "I—I love them, I suppose, but... I simply don't fit, I can't relate. And yet I am never left alone. I am dragged into it all and I drag myself back in because—because they're all I have, and yet they simply lash out at me, again and again... and what did I do to deserve that?"

Every wound I'd prayed for the stars to take from me came back to me now. "All my life, I've done as I'm told. I learned etiquette and listened to my tutor and traveled everywhere for Grandmother, and I baled the hay and fed the chickens for Pa, and I listened without complaint when Mother cursed her lineage and her offspring—and yet... and yet... it was never enough to earn me *peace*." I smeared my hands through the tears soaking my face, sniffling.

When I finally shut up, I realized I couldn't hear the engine or the gravel crunching under the wheels anymore. I blinked through wobbling vision. A vast turquoise horizon greeted me.

Ackerleigh had unbuckled his seatbelt. He had one hand on my back and the other on my thigh, but I was torturously numb to both until I met his eyes.

"I'm here for you," he repeated, dabbing at my tearstained face with a dainty handkerchief. The lace of the cloth was coarse, and I realized with relief that I could also feel his hand on my leg again. Slowly I ceased rocking. He let me take the handkerchief and clean myself up, remaining silent in the sort of way that was filled with reassuring words that didn't need to be said aloud.

"There it is," I groaned.

"There what is?" Ackerleigh asked patiently.

"My biggest secret." I leaned forward and into his shoulder. "I'm a people-pleasing doormat with no dreams of my own except to be left the fuck alone."

Ackerleigh's gentle fingers carded my grimy curls. "You're more than that," he murmured. "You're kind and brave and brilliant."

"Ah—" I choked as another wave of feelings washed over me, threatening to dump me under and drown me. "I c... I can't keep—anyway." I straightened, sniffled, and pointed through the windshield. "There's the truck. Let's get going." My voice was thin and pressured, and a migraine was settling behind my eye. I was in no state to help two magiqon save a gryphon's life.

As if reading my thoughts, Ackerleigh squeezed my thigh. "You're going to stay in the car."

I blinked, pushing my dirty curls off my cheeks. "Stella needs—"

"Stella needs to help me, and I need to help her." Ackerleigh pulled down my tattered, fuzzy cardigan from the back of his seat and drew it around my shoulders. "I brought this with me today as a comfort. Don't get any ideas that it belongs to you again." He gave me a coy little smirk so sure and playful that I melted into an exhausted little giggle. "But the sea breeze is cold."

Slipping my cardigan on and buttoning it over the bloodstains on my shirt, I relaxed into the seat and breathed in the familiar perfume that hung inside Ackerleigh's car. Glue from the spines of old books. A soft whiff of floral.

I glanced at the pickup truck, knowing Stella was watching us. "Stella won't like that I stayed back."

"Nico." Ackerleigh grinned. "I am not frightened of your petulant teenage sister. She and I are the same. It's alright."

"You two are *not*—"

"It's something you wouldn't understand, Nico."

I blinked. The words were so blunt and almost mean, yet *he* wasn't. He was just naming a fact. He didn't bury his meaning beneath decorum and pleasantries like other light-lickers. I appreciated not having to wade through conversations with him to get to the point.

"When I came back here three weeks ago, I fought back with magíq too," Ackerleigh added. "Against President Brandon. I didn't plan it. I could have killed him. Maybe I stayed my hand because I'm ten years Stella's senior. Maybe because I've got a lot less hurt than her. But a part of me still wishes I had made him suffer." He shrugged. "I suppose Stella and I need each other. Is that alright?"

I cried wetly, "It's—It's more than alright. I'm... so grateful. For you."

Ackerleigh leaned in and pressed a cool kiss to my filthy cheekbone. Then he got out of the car, unpinned his brooch, and slipped out of his sunset-colored blouse so he was only wearing a thin lace camisole. *He* should have been the one in my cardigan. But there was not a drop of unease when he leaned into view, winked at me, and closed the door.

Ackerleigh left me, jogging across the sandy lot. The terror and the fury that had carried me this far abandoned me. Exhaustion struck hard and fast. Visions of Tad Neal's mangled body returned the moment Ackerleigh was out of sight. I hit the heels of my hands against my temples, trying to banish the images or, even better, trick myself into believing it never happened.

Tears raced down my cheeks once more, carrying with them a heavy grief and a frantic sense of uncertainty. Before I knew it, I was crying so hard that my stomach heaved with each sob. I buried my head in my arms while I rocked and rocked, snot and tears soaking into my forearms.

I... needed this reprieve. I needed to let someone else help Stella for once.

Capstone in Cooperative Healing

I let adrenaline finish off the last reserves of my miniscule physical strength in order to reach Nico's truck. The edges of Lunix's wings fluttered in the sea breeze like a midnight banner on a battlefield.

Cheese jumped out of the truck to greet me. Her long golden fur was caked with blood and mud, and her tail wagged low between her legs as she anxiously licked my extended hand.

I gave her head a scratch before I pointed at my car. "Go get Nico, Cheese. Go." Fortunately, the dog seemed to understand and took off, kicking up chunks of wet sand. I saw the passenger door open and heard Nico's distant voice call to her.

"Wh-Where's Nico?" Dirty tear tracks streaked Stella's face, which looked washed out and pale against the backdrop of the silver sea. Her frantic gaze swept past me, searching the expanse of the beach for her lifeline and security.

"We don't need him for this, so he's resting. I've got you, alright, Stella?" I climbed into the bed of the truck, my thoughts involuntarily going to the last time I'd been back here, under the stars with Nico.

Lunix's hindquarters quivered slightly as I lifted my leg over their hips. I got caught in their feathers, losing my balance and slamming my elbow into the side of the truck. Stella grunted with worry, pulling me upright.

She was crouching in the only space where I'd be able to get a good look at Lunix, so I fitted myself in thigh-to-thigh with her. I could feel her trembling. I reached out to touch Lunix's left forelimb where Stella had grown a chunk of rapidly melting ice, silver-blue and luminous but shot through with swirls of crimson like spilled ink in water.

"This hasn't been stopping their blood loss; the bullet's still in there—you can see it—and I think they went into shock." Stella swallowed. "I didn't know what else I could do." She stroked Lunix's forehead between their closed eyes; they responded with a weak gurgle.

My stomach clenched painfully at that noise, far worse even than their awful keening when they were afraid. This was the sound of a dying creature.

I slid my arms around her shoulder. "You did great, Stella. You kept them stable for hours on your way here. Lunix was lucky to have you."

Stella whimpered, "N-Nico says this is my fault."

This poor disturbed and fearful girl. I tried to imagine what they'd both seen today, being present when Lunix killed a human being. Lunix was used to it—they'd killed before, and for less reason than... well, whatever the circumstances around this Tad Neal character were. I hugged her tightly to my side, getting a heavy whiff of gore mingling with her sweat that had me fighting down a gag. "His fear spoke for him. We can yell at him together later, alright?"

She managed a choked giggle and nodded. "Wh... What can we do?"

"Don't worry. I think I have a plan." I stood up. "Let's get Lunix into the water."

"Wait, what?" Stella gazed up at me as she wiped her face, sort of drying her tears but mostly just smearing dirt around.

"Come on, then. I'll explain when we're there. Call the wind with me?"

She nodded, using the truck to stand. Her legs wobbled and I caught her with my hand on her elbow. Grateful, she leaned on me while she steadied herself.

Calling out to the ésprit of the wind next to Stella, our magíq mingled and rose to meet one another's. With staggering clarity, I felt the depths of Stella's fear and despair and… self-hatred. My throat clenched as the girl's misery threatened to overwhelm me. But as our magíq formed a new shape that was neither mine nor hers but ours, the intensity of her feelings receded. Excitement swallowed us up. I laughed first—a surprised, quick bark, quickly joined by a delighted giggle from Stella.

The gale we raised howled and whipped around us like a hurricane, twirling our hair and splattering waves and sand into us. We slid the excitable magíq underneath Lunix's prone body like a stretcher, wedging it beneath our gryphon and slowly creating an updraft that lifted them out of the truck. Wind that glittered like mica slapped our faces, frigid and salty.

Carefully, carefully, carefully we moved the limp gryphon toward the waves. I made sure to balance Stella's inclination to lift the gryphon far above our heads; instead, I barely wanted them to leave the ground, allowing the breeze to catch in their wings and stop them from dragging in the dense and soaking sand.

"The shallows," I instructed. Speaking to Stella while we performed magíq transformed my voice into something greater than it was, into wind itself, softly whispering and yet heard with the perfect clarity of ringing bells.

We lowered Lunix into the tide, which greeted them with lapping tongues of delight. Bubbles pooled around their shape with the ebb and flow of the waves. The water sparkled around the gryphon's body, coming to life with a salty-sweet tang coating my tongue.

Consciousness abruptly returned to our gryphon. Lunix tucked their head into their breast with a hiss, lifting their wings out of the water as they squeezed their eyes shut. I dropped off the hatch of the truck, tearing off my shoes and socks and jumping barefoot into the sand, dashing over to the gryphon. Splashing into the shallows, I fell to my knees before Lunix as if returning to my god.

Lunix blinked open their moon-eyes, squinting at me with a glaze of pain on their features. They croaked softly, and then recognition arrived. Pupils blowing out, they thrust their neck forward and curled their head around my shoulder, leaning heavily on me as their breast heaved with labored breathing. "Lonely," they croaked deep in their throat, vibrating my chest all the way down to my heart. I hugged their ruffled neck. Warmth spread slowly across my lap. With horror, I looked down and realized that Lunix was bleeding more than before. Heavy, dark rivulets flowed from their leg.

"Stella." The girl was at my side in a heartbeat. The sea breeze teased her hair and pushed it over her shoulders, toying with her, picking up strands and tossing it into her lashes. She swiped it away, irritated, looking down at me.

"Lunix can perform healing. I think we can, too. Together."

Stella's eyes grew wide, reflecting the sea in their steely, blue-black depths. "No way! Just like Pascale?"

"Yes, exactly. I doubt that it's much effort to stitch flesh back together for a being of magíq like Lunix, and for us, I believe using the ésprit of the water will make it possible. Especially here, in Laurier. Do you feel how close the god of the sea is beneath us?"

Stella nodded rapidly, speechless.

"So, do you think we can do this together?" I gripped her hand. "Will you follow my lead?"

Holding my gaze, Stella took a quick breath. "Yeah."

I smiled at her. "D'ac. We need to get the bullet out. I wonder if you have more precision than me and you can make us two ice picks."

In answer, Stella dipped her hand into the water and, as it dripped off her fingers in rivulets, they became solid threads of ice, diamond-bright beneath a sudden shaft of cool white sunlight cutting through the clouds.

"Splendid," I whispered beneath the crash of the waves, and she grinned at me.

She broke them into equal halves and crouched low, peering at Lunix's feathered arm. I flattened the branches so we could see their silver skin around the oozing red crater of the bullet hole.

Stella's breath hitched as she moved in with the ice picks, fingers trembling. I let the picks lay across my hand, steadying the points until they slipped into the wound. Lunix whimpered, squeezing my thigh with their talon. Beckoning to the salty moisture hanging in the air, I froze a little cloud of mist over the bullet hole to numb the area, and subsequently felt Lunix's grip on me relax.

"Tell the picks to shape around the bullet," I offered. "Tell them to freeze to it."

Stella's tongue poked out through her lips. Slowly, she moved her hands back as Lunix began to moan, almost human in their agony. A moment later, the bullet popped out of the gryphon's flesh. I caught it before it hit the waves rocking beneath us, pocketing it. Like we'd pulled a stopper on a tipped-over barrel of wine, blood gushed forth from Lunix and stained our hands, soaked their feathers, and splashed into the sea where it swirled around our legs.

Instinctively, Stella pressed the heel of her hand onto the wound as Lunix screamed, wings flailing. Stella shushed them again and again as tears raced down her cheeks.

"Don't panic, or we won't be able to do this." I rubbed her back; I could feel goosebumps on her skin beneath her cropped shirt.

I dipped my hands in the water and washed them clean before placing them atop Stella's as she put pressure on the wound. The seawater bubbled around our hands, glistening and effervescent, responding to my intentions to take a shape I'd never seen my magíq make before.

"Help me make this bigger, and send it into Lunix with me, straight in like a—a sunbeam through a window." I kept the wind-like quality of my voice—soothing to her and to Lunix, and tricking me into feeling as confident as I sounded. Stella lifted her other hand and touched her finger to the bubble, flinching at the chromatic ripple which radiated out from her fingertip. This was working.

Bolstered, I slipped one hand down to collect more seawater, feeding the bubble. Stella copied me until it was bigger than our heads. Gently, trying not to pop it, I gave it a push. It resisted, bulging against Lunix's haunch.

I knew this was going to be the hardest part. To convince Lunix's body and the healing bubble that they were compatible, cell tissues and their white blood cells wanting to intercept their injury. But Lunix was made of magic, birthed from the elder god of the mountains eons ago.

"Please, please, please." Stella's plea was thick with tears and hiccupping desperation.

I joined her, whispering a petition to the slumbering god of the sea, begging her to stir enough to aid us. I couldn't lose Lunix. Stella couldn't lose Lunix.

Iridescent bubbles rose around our orb like a barrier reef and slowly, slowly, slowly it sank into Lunix as I gave it another nudge. I didn't stop begging, and Stella's crying redoubled, this time laced with a wonderful, delicate hope.

Lunix trilled, their facial disc fluffing up, eyes which had been closed slitting open to peer down at us with the slight arc of smiling relief. Their claw moved up to the small of my back, pulling me closer against them. Electricity tingled between us, warming my damp clothes. Stella and I didn't stop until the bubble had disappeared inside Lunix's muscles. A misty silver breeze rustled their foreleg feathers, tickling my nose, Stella's hair swirling over to brush my cheek. Lunix shook their head. Their ear tufts perked up; their beak rose as they sniffed the fishy, salt-tangy wind.

Tenderly, they whistled, "Thank you." And I don't think they were thanking only us.

Stella collapsed into the foam and let out a ragged, sobbing sigh of relief. I joined her, wrapping my arms around this other brilliant little magíqon.

Lunix rose shakily to their feet, using their wings for balance. They carefully tested their weight on their bloodstained leg, wincing slightly as if the healing were not complete. Anything less than imminent death was... I mean, not great, but better. We could nurse them back to full health.

I gazed up at the magnificent creature standing over us in the waves, flicking water out of the tuft of their tail. Lunix spread their great wings to their full span; from underneath, I was able to admire the muscular plane of their axillaries, fluttering secondaries, and the reaching hand of their primaries, like a full moon at midnight with sunlight glinting through the slats between each feather. They were a holy thing, and they were alive.

Stella grasped my hand. "Ackerleigh."

"Stella?"

"Thanks for trustin' me. I didn't deserve it."

I smiled, watching Lunix preen the crushed feathers circling their wound. "Most seventeen-year-olds don't."

Halfheartedly rolling her eyes, she returned my smile. "You're a good teacher."

Nico strode stiffly up to the shoreline, standing over us with his arms crossed. Cheese cowered behind his legs, whining softly.

"Looks like Ackerleigh was right," said Nico, crouching down to run his hand over Stella's wild hair. "Y'all didn't need me in the slightest."

Stella smiled with relief, leaning into his hand like a cat.

Lunix stretched over me to nip at Nico's earlobe; Nico barely flinched, brushing his fingertips over Lunix's ear tufts. Stella and I both sat up, drenched and sandy, but Lunix's body blocked the wind as they waded out of the shallows to crowd the three of us beneath the shelter of their wings.

"Stella, I'm sorry." Nico's eyes were downcast as he hugged his knees. "I-I lost my temper today, and said some shit that was unkind and harsh when y-you needed my patience."

Stella cocked her head, wrinkling her brow. "Are you kiddin' me, Co-Co? You're fine." She whacked his knee before looking out at the waves, frowning as she added in a soft and serious tone, "Lunix tore a guy open like a bag a' flour. I dunno about you, but that made me real... psycho... real fast."

Nico flinched, shutting his eyes. "Me, too."

My stomach rolled; Stella's wording brought involuntary visions of gore to my thoughts. And that was just my imagination. How horrid the memories in their heads must have been! I clutched Nico's arm and hugged Stella to my side again. "Oh, you three, I'm just dreadfully sorry for the day you've had."

"Yeah, you know what?" Stella shook off the glazed look in her eyes. "We're gonna process that later."

I grimaced, hoping that were true as I reached for Lunix as the gryphon preened the mussed feathers on its foreleg.

Stella tapped Nico's chest. "Nico, did you see? W-We did healing. Ackerleigh and me."

Nico smiled. His eyes were the solar eclipse to Stella's lunar glow, warm amber ringing his pupils instead of steely gray. His gaze shifted from her to me, and I was suddenly conscious of the way my hair stuck to the back of my neck and my soaked chemise clung to my pebbled nipples.

Dropping his already deep voice a level lower, he offered me a soft and lopsided smile. "You're spectacular."

My cheeks exploded with heat.

Stella awkwardly looked away from us. "Gods. Instant regret." Then the color drained from her face. "Is... Is th-that Grandmother?" Rage shot through her fear. "What the stinkin' pig piss is she doin' here?"

Scoffing, Nico twisted around. "Not listening!" The wind caught his shout and threw it to where Doctor Bennett leaned on the fence between us and the parking lot. Such was the mischief of the ésprit of the wind, which wanted to play games even with those who lacked magíq.

Beside Doctor Bennett, Claire and Elizabeth waved cheerfully. Craig Dowell stood behind the fence with Provost Davidson. And Cam and Billie, who were beginning to feel like my chaotic feral children.

"W-We had an audience?" Stella shrank down, all but burrowing beneath Lunix's fluffy breast to hide.

"Tranqui, Stella," I assured her calmly, my voice blending with the roar of the waves. "They all found out I'm a magíqon three weeks ago. We surprised nobody. If they showed up here, it was to admire our work."

She twitched. "I thought your magíq was a secret."

I nodded. At first, admitting to what happened caused me horrid shame. But as I'd settled into this new truth, I felt proud. And amused. I smirked. "Until the day I came back here and lost my shit."

Stella stared at me, considering. She looked like Lunix's offspring, half-consumed by their plumage, not even reacting as they curled their neck to pluck at her hair. "How does it feel? With everybody knowin'?"

"Terrifying," I laughed. Then I sobered, clutching my hand to my chest. "And... liberating."

Stella smiled faintly. "Well I'll be." Then her expression hardened. She glared back at the spectators. "Well, anyway, I ain't talkin' to her!" Stella let the wind amplify and funnel her voice toward Doctor Bennett, who gestured in frustration before crossing her arms.

"That's fine." Indifferent, Nico shrugged. "She offered to let us stay at her Laurier house, and I accepted." Nico's eyes softened, and his high, finely sculpted cheekbones flushed as he looked at me. "You're invited, too."

As lovely as Claire and Mathilda had been for the past three weeks, I knew I'd been overstaying my welcome. I nodded. "I won't refuse." Beyond that, I wanted to stay in the same place as Nico again as soon as humanly possible.

"She talked to Claire and is sending someone to retrieve your things." Nico had obviously been conversing with her while we worked. "I don't know if you have a choice."

My thoughts snagged on the idea of Nico catching up and making plans with the woman who had been imprisoning Lunix for seven years. I rubbed my knuckle along my lower lip.

Stella groaned. "Classic Grandmother."

"So, let me clarify." I used Lunix's shoulder to climb to my feet, seawater trailing down my legs and sending a rattling shiver through my bones. Glancing between the siblings, I said, "You've been on the lam from your grandmother for three weeks, and then you run into her by chance today, and now... everything's fine?"

"Everything is not fine." Stella scowled up at me, not getting out of the water and looking quite like a toddler refusing to get out of the bath. "She's going to try to convince us all that Lunix is better off going back to her cursed estate."

Lunix whistled and buried their face in my neck. "No. No."

I brushed my palm over their prickly ear tufts. "That won't do, will it? Let's go have a chat." Slapping sand off my rear and the backs of my thighs, I marched toward our spectators with a vengeance.

Seminar in the Bennett Publishing House

I dodged out of the way as Lunix erupted out of the sea, dumping Stella into the merrily spraying tide. Lunix half-flew, half-hopped after Ackerleigh, croaking his name. Coughing on a mouthful of seawater, Stella came up and scrambled to her feet, dashing after the gryphon, tripping over herself. When she neared Ackerleigh, he grabbed her forearm and pulled her into an embrace against his side while he threw his other arm around Lunix's neck. Cheese splashed after them through the dark, waterlogged sand, tail flapping and nose busily investigating.

My throat tightened as I followed them all with a smile spreading on my face. The realization hit me all at once, and it changed me irrevocably.

Ackerleigh was the missing piece. Me, Stella, Lunix—we'd all been stumbling through life waiting for Ackerleigh to find us. Finally, finally, finally, we were no longer alone.

The sand suctioned to my trainers, but hope made me light-footed.

Everyone waiting along the fence looked so... intense. My fingers inched toward my scar. But then Ackerleigh looked over his shoulders, eyes bright and determined as he met my gaze. The ache to tap my scar faded as Ackerleigh slowed to let me catch up.

Since I'd left my grandmother waiting here, two more people had joined the group. One of them was Cam, that student who took me to Ackerleigh. With him was a shorter person with a buzzed head and large silver glasses, who was staring awestruck at Stella with their lips slightly parted. I blinked, wondering at first if they were actually staring at Lunix. But no—definitely Stella.

Ackerleigh marched directly up to my grandmother, still holding my sister and the gryphon in what looked like a fiercely protective gesture. He opened his mouth to speak, but Grandmother beat him to it.

"An impressive display, Doctor Sebring. I do hope you'll submit a write-up of the mechanics you just used."

Ackerleigh froze, his brow crinkling. "I—suppose I could... wait—"

Grandmother got that look on her face akin to a satisfied cat lapping from a bowl of cream. "I have some more items I'd like to discuss, if you'll join me at my estate. It's several miles inland from Ravensbourne."

Straightening, Ackerleigh puffed up his chest—to surprisingly good effect, considering he was only in his thin camisole. Maybe it was the faint blue misting of magíq that clung to his skin transforming his usual confidence into absolute prowess. He declared, "I want your word that everyone's participation in dialogue with you is *optional*. And I want your word that you have no intention of doling out punishment on your grandchildren." Then he stroked Lunix's chin; the gryphon hummed happily and nuzzled his palm. "Finally, the gryphon is to remain free *forever*. That is not a request: that is a fact."

Behind my grandmother's back, Ackerleigh's two students silently cheered. I snorted and elbowed Stella, who snickered when she saw them. Then she locked eyes with the student with the buzz-cut. Stella's smile shifted, becoming more self-conscious. As she tucked a honey-brown tress of hair behind her ear, both she and the student turned bright red.

Contemplating Ackerleigh's vow, Grandmother blinked slowly. As usual, she remained infuriatingly neutral. "Right. Of course, Doctor Sebring." She pushed up her cherry-red glasses. "These results indicate in no uncertain terms my methods were flawed if not at times dangerous."

I jolted. Did she—just take accountability? I glanced up at Lunix, whose silver moon-eyes warily scrutinized Doctor Bennett.

"You don't say," Stella growled, but gave herself away by shifting her weight uncertainly.

"I will obviously be redesigning my study going forward," Grandmother added. "I would prefer to collaborate in doing so, by the way." A slight shiver vibrated her frame. The wind felt like it was getting colder by the minute.

"No more blind studies," Ackerleigh said swiftly. "*Ever*. Else I am prepared to take our gryphon's ethically dubious imprisonment to court, Doctor Bennett."

"Yeah!" Stella sneered. "Then *you'll* get locked up, Grandmother!"

Rather than admonishing her granddaughter, Grandmother grinned, eyes closed, shaking her head. She held up both hands toward us, and to Lunix. "Tonight, I invite you to my Laurier estate as dinner guests," she said gently. "As *family*."

After a long pause, Stella made an agonized sound. I glanced down at her in alarm to see her eyes swimming with tears.

Confusion flared quickly in my chest before fading just as fast. Of course Grandmother's words hit her hard. When was the last time anyone besides me had called Stella family? It wasn't just since we left the farm last year—it has been even longer. Stella was treated... well, like our gryphon. Volatile and unpredictable, resented by our community. An outsider. Mother had compensated somewhat for her part in driving Stella away earlier this year, but even when we had peaches and cream with her the other night, Mother was tense and distant. Treating her own daughter like a stranger.

Grandmother was hated by my mother for good reason... or so I'd thought, for as much as I listened to Mother complain about her over the years. But now I was beginning to wonder if perhaps the biggest barrier between the two women was a fundamental disagreement about what was best for Stella as a young magíqon. Whether Grandmother wanted to shield Stella beneath her wing or lock her up like Lunix, I wasn't sure, but regardless... if she wanted to work with Ackerleigh, and if she now understood Lunix needed to be free—then maybe she understood that the same was true for Stella, too.

"I c–can't forgive you so easily, Grandmother," Stella choked, tears tracking pure, clean lines through the blood, dust, and salt caking her face. "You stole my gryphon and then you—you never came around again... did you even love me?"

Grandmother's expression softened. "Oh, my silly girl. Come here." When she lifted her arms toward Stella, I could see all the conflicting emotions battling on Stella's face and in her hunched shoulders.

Using my elbow, I gave Stella's back an encouraging nudge. That was all it took. Stella stumbled into our grandmother's waiting embrace, clinging tightly to the tall woman.

A satisfied sense of closure rippled through the small group who had witnessed today's unprecedented miracle. The two older men walked together back toward the handful of cars. Ackerleigh's students started speaking excitedly to Claire.

Ackerleigh's arm slipped around my waist. He rested his chin against my chest, despite my grungy appearance and my embarrassing melt-down in his car. Over the rims of his lovely new glasses, he gazed up at me and smiled warmly.

My grandmother's house in Laurier was a place of extraordinary nostalgia. Warm and brightly colored, dozens of crystal lamps made everything glow happily. I smelled nutmeg and freshly cut roses, just like I always used to. A stained glass window fixed to at least one wall in every room. Plush patterned rugs and deeply saturated wallpapers gave life to the space in a way that betrayed my grandmother's apparent stoicism. She had a soft and cozy side, even if it was rarely seen.

As soon as I walked in, I felt like a child again. I remembered running down the hallway and pretending that my paper bird could fly. I remembered savoring honeycomb treats with my grandparents with all the windows open so I could smell the sea. Though I hated to admit it, being in this house again was deeply comforting.

Grandpa Gene's tall, stocky body filled the foyer when the front door opened. His booming voice greeted us with jocularity. "My grandchildren! Why, I wasn't sure anymore whether or not you were real." He swooped in on Stella with speed belying his large frame, crushing her in an embrace. She squeaked in surprise, but let him hold her for much longer than I expected.

Grandmother gave him a peck on his cheek. "We will be entertaining half the School Board, two magíqon, a murderous gryphon, and the rapscallions who freed said gryphon from their captivity, my dear. An enviable soiree if I may say so myself."

"Oh–ho–ho," Grandpa shook his long finger at us. "You two are awfully naughty, aren't you? Just like your mother."

Stella scoffed. "Yeah, right."

While unbuttoning her blazer, Grandmother put her head together with Grandpa's and murmured in his ear.

Grandpa frowned beneath his white moustache. His droopy eyelids lifted as he looked up and met my gaze, his small oval glasses flashing beneath the chandelier. It had been... I don't know, six years since I'd last seen him. And I knew without needing to ask that Grandmother had just told him about the violent day we'd had.

"Oh, son," Grandpa breathed. Reaching out, he pulled me into his chest and held me tightly against his shoulder. He was one of the few people I knew who was taller than me. Retired from the Royal Navy, Grandpa was a boulder smoothed and polished by time into something tender and overflowing with compassion. He had all the warmth and affection as well as proud masculinity that Pa lacked, and right now, his embrace was like that of a father's.

I sobbed, "How—do I have—more—tears—left?"

"It's alright, son. You're safe to cry."

He might be feeling that now, but less so when he realized how much snot and tears I was getting on the collar of his sweater.

When my stomach hurt and my sinuses felt dehydrated, I pulled back and let Grandpa pat his heavy hands on my shoulders. Wiping my face off with the inside edge of my shirt, I croaked, "What—What're we gonna do a… about Tad? A—And his body, and…"

Grandpa shushed me, like a mother would her mewling infant. "Nicolai, my boy…" He put his arm around me and led me out of the foyer and into the ground floor library on our left. In addition to a pair of work desks, the room had a plush couch and Grandpa's favorite overstuffed armchair. Grandpa flicked on the electric lamp next to the couch and plopped me onto it. He proffered me his monogrammed handkerchief, but I shook my head and pulled out the lace one Ackerleigh had left with me. I was a bit worried about abandoning Ackerleigh in my grandparents' house, but I couldn't fight Grandpa enough to do anything about it.

Grandpa sat beside me and put his arm around me again. "Look, Nico… your gryphon friend has killed a handful of folks since your grandma had them moved to the country estate."

"You mean when she *stole* them," I muttered bitterly.

Grandpa patiently shook his head. "Your grandmother might have seemed cruel back then, but she was trying to protect you kids. Not from the gryphon, of course… but those deranged ocky folk who already hated Stella enough before the gryphon came along. Folk like Tad Neal and his nasty daughter."

I wrung Ackerleigh's handkerchief between my hands. "It's n–not fair. How can I not feel bad for that man's fate and still b–be so wrecked by what I saw?"

"Because he was attacked by a wild animal," Grandpa snorted. "That could not have been pretty."

My face crumpled; I dropped it into the handkerchief spread in my hands. As soon as I covered my eyes, I was once again leaning over a torn open face and hearing Tad's gurgling final gasps. Floral notes from Ackerleigh's handkerchief accompanied each of my shuddering breaths, and with the help of Ackerleigh's calming scent I was able to slow my breathing once more.

"Now, we have a whole procedure for when your gryphon does this," Grandpa continued gently. "I'll be on the phone tomorrow and traveling out to Martinsdale the day after. We have it sorted. We always do. Your gryphon's worth protecting, and we've got the influence to make sure they're safe."

"—But they need to be *free*," I snarled, leaping to my feet. "Do you understand that?"

Unruffled, Grandpa gave me a kind smile. He grunted as he stood up. "Yes, my boy. You keep your gryphon. I'll take care of that ocky fellow."

"C–Can you make Stella talk about it, too? I... I don't know if I can be the one to help her process this."

"Nor should you be," said Grandpa. "Leave it to me."

I looked past him, skimming my gaze over the rows of leather-bound books and golden name plates. There was a whole section near the front window that was dedicated to Pascale Manon. I'd have to show Ackerleigh later, see if there were any titles on her that he hadn't seen. Grandpa and Grandmother had many first editions and one-of-a-kind tomes in their private collection.

"Did you know how often I went on hunting trips with Pa, Will, and Tad?" I asked with a tremble in my voice. "Now he's dead. Because of a creature I love with my whole heart."

"I know, my boy." Grandpa hugged me again. "Life and death coexist in chaotic dissonance." He spread his huge hand on the back of my head and scratched my scalp in the way he used to when I was a boy, and I melted against him. "Set it down for tonight, how about? You need a bath, a hot meal, and a stiff drink. What do you say?"

"D'ac," I murmured. "I feel disgusting."

"You *look* disgusting." Grandpa roared with laughter, softening the blow of his admission. "So." He clapped me on the back and led me out into the hall. We followed the din of conversation and the savory smells of food being prepared. "Who's the handsome man with you? Is he a professor? Don't tell me—that's the gamekeeper my wife chose."

I flushed. "Y–Yeah."

Francis, Grandmother's assistant, bustled by toward the front door looking anxious. She was clutching a notepad and muttering about blouses and trousers and *gryphons*.

Past the kitchen and the dining room, Grandmother had brought everyone to the largest drawing room with plenty of floral settees, argyle armchairs, and velvet loveseats.

Despite the day's grim happenings, Grandmother was evidently boasting of Stella's prowess as a magíqon. She held Stella around her skinny waist as they spoke to the loose semicircle of people, all who had been at the beach with us. Stella was blushing as Grandmother prompted her to recount what she'd done with Ackerleigh. Claire was beside her, enthusiastically responding to Stella and letting my sister cling to her arm for support.

"Nico." Ackerleigh rushed over to me as soon as I appeared in the doorway. Lunix, looking anxious, trotted after him with their ears pinned down and their pupils blown out. "Are you alright?" Ackerleigh noticed Grandpa. "Oh. Sorry, hello. I'm Doctor Ackerleigh Sebring…"

"Hello, son." Grandpa shook Ackerleigh's extended hand with such vigor that Ackerleigh's small body was like a blade of grass in a gale. "Your reputation precedes you! Enjoy yourself tonight, hm? I'll leave you two."

"Is your arm alright?" I laughed.

"Of course." Ackerleigh grinned, turning back to me as his expression slowly sobered. He stepped into my space so our chests brushed together ever so slightly as he loosely draped his hands on my hips. "You were crying again. How can I help?"

"It's alright," I murmured hoarsely. "I mean, no, it's not alright, but... I'm gonna set it down for tonight." I felt a swell of emotion as the words left my mouth, but this time, there was a generous helping of relief mixed in. "I'm just so happy to see ya."

Gentle as a breeze, Ackerleigh slipped his arms around my waist, hugging me tenderly and nuzzling his face into my soiled shirt. He murmured, "I missed you so much."

I almost fell apart again as I leaned my cheek into the crown of his head, smelling hibiscus and sea salt as I wrapped him up and squeezed my eyes shut.

I straightened after a while, sniffing wetly. "Wh–Why don't we sit?" I gestured to the settee against the nearest wall, close to the crackling fireplace.

"I'm afraid to sit down." Ackerleigh brushed at the grime on his trousers, which looked expensive—or they had been before the sea ruined them.

I shrugged, picking up a silk throw pillow and tossing it up like I was flipping a coin. "Hey, she invited you here. If you ruin her settee, so be it."

When I said 'settee,' Ackerleigh gave me an odd look. He fought down a grin, lost, and snorted with amusement.

"What?"

"You've shown your hand, Nicolai Diamante." His merry eyes sparkled with a hundred flames from kerosene lamps flickering on the walls and side tables. "Gone is the wild mountain man." Laughter turned his voice into flower petals. "You're a little rich boy."

I scoffed and looked away, lest his teasing overwhelm all my sensibilities until I kissed him right in front of everyone.

"So, what's your name?"

The person with the buzz cut stood in front of me. They had to be at least a foot shorter than me. They rocked on their chunky heels and sucked their lip into their teeth, showing off the gap between their top front teeth.

"Uh... I'm Nico."

"Lovely," the person said, voice pitching higher as they fussed with the collar of their sweater. They glanced at Cam, who nudged the small of their back. Unease grew in the pit of my stomach until the person blurted, "And, uh, that—magíqon, with the long hair, is your...?"

"Ah." Understanding dawned on me. The blushing at the beach—their eyes fixed on my sister rather than the gryphon. I smiled down at them. "She's my sister. Stella."

"Stella," they breathed.

"Billie," Ackerleigh said reprovingly as he appeared at my elbow. "What're you after? And, also, more importantly, why are you two *here*?" He tapped his foot and frowned at both students. "Cam I expect, but Billie—have you lost your mind?"

Billie cringed, pushing their glasses higher on their nose. "D'ac—But, but, Doctor Bennett said we could!"

"Oh, Doctor Bennett said you could?" Ackerleigh crossed his arms. "Is she your mother now?"

I hid a snort behind my hand.

"No," Cam retorted with just as much attitude as Ackerleigh, "but she *is* interim President."

"Oh," I groaned, casting my gaze toward the copper ceiling tiles. Grandmother was running Ravensbourne now. If I thought she was meddling before this, now it was a guarantee. "Well ain't that... sweet."

Grandmother's butler entered pushing a multi-tiered tray with a variety of drinks on top. Ackerleigh glanced toward the tray, his gaze landing on a bottle of brandy on display. "Ah." He gave me a bemused look. "That explains the expensive bottle in your truck."

I blushed and dropped my gaze. "Ah, you noticed."

"Yes, Nico and Stella enjoy filching things when they come to stay." Grandmother strolled over to me, her irritated tone offset by the beleaguered smile on her painted lips. "But if I call anything a gift, they hiss and spit like cornered cats."

Ackerleigh laughed. The sound was kind and soft, and I felt it was more for me than her. "Doctor Bennett, what prompted you to bring these two along?" He gestured to Cam and Billie, who were fixing themselves tea from the butler's tray.

"It was a good introduction for your field study," Doctor Bennett answered.

Ackerleigh's eyes grew wide. "My..."

"The class should be capped at two students, last the normal twelve weeks, and in addition to parental permission and involvement, should have extensive safeguards and liability waivers signed."

"We agree to not hold you responsible if we get torn apart by gryphons." Billie grinned wickedly.

"Wait, what's happenin'?" Stella and Lunix trotted over from the curtained wall of floor to ceiling windows. Both Cam and Billie stiffened upon the gryphon's arrival. Billie unfroze first, lifting their hands to cup their face as a quick squeak of excitement left them.

"It was Doctor Sebring's idea for getting me my last credits," answered Cam. "He wants to go *to* the Hazel Mountains! Can you believe it?"

My jaw dropped at the same time as Stella's. My fingers crept toward my scar as the visions I had of running off alone with Ackerleigh started to dissolve.

"I can still do it?" Ackerleigh squeaked. His hand shot out and grasped mine, surprising me out of my dismay.

Surprise flashed across my grandmother's face as well, and all her calculated coolness abandoned her as she beheld our joined hands. Her eyebrows shot up and a pleased smile touched her lips. My cheeks flamed, first with the embarrassment of a boy caught with his crush, but then with pride. Ackerleigh... wanted me. I was part of his excitement.

"Oh," Cam gasped, pointing at our hands. "Oh? Oh-h-h!"

"*Hush,*" growled Ackerleigh.

"Do what?" Stella demanded.

Billie gave Stella a gap-toothed grin and exclaimed, "A field study! With me and Cam!"

Grandmother looked harried, speaking to Ackerleigh over the excitement with her hand in the air. "With precautions—"

Ackerleigh sniffed and nudged his glasses up his nose. "My syllabus is thirty pages, ten of which are safety and liability clauses."

Bewildered, Stella asked, "Syllabus? What even—"

"*Stella*," groaned Grandmother. "Go chat with your friends by the fire, please."

"Can I pet the gryphon?" Cam immediately asked.

"Oh," said Stella, waving her hand toward the fire and guiding Ackerleigh's students in that direction. "It's really up to them, but they're very sweet as long as you're polite an' ask permission—"

"The gryphon is a *them* like me?" Billie cried.

As their ruckus faded, Ackerleigh held tight to my hand and asked Grandmother, "And the rest of the school board is agreeable to the field study? It's a magíqal history and bestiary course—we don't have to shut down the Magíqal Studies program, do we?"

"Of course not." Grandmother turned to the drink tray, picked up the bottle of brandy, and poured a finger each into three crystal balloons. She handed Ackerleigh and I each a glass before continuing, "I intend Ravensbourne University to share a vision like yours, Doctor Sebring. You and Pascale Manon are of one mind. Your expertise and unique skills are a scholarly asset. Your vision for a future where we cherish and foster magíq is one I share. I want my granddaughter's life to be better for her gifts, not worse."

"I'd been wondering..." Ackerleigh rubbed his knuckle along his lower lip. "How much of this informed your decision to offer me the gamekeeper post?" His expression was vulnerable, his brow knit together with anxiety. I instinctively laid my hand on the small of his back.

"Quite a bit," Grandmother answered swiftly.

Ackerleigh opened and closed his mouth. "You didn't know I was a magíqon... did you?"

"I rather hoped you were." She shrugged one shoulder. "I had long been curious if magíqon would get along more easily with a gryphon than ordinary humans, on account of the shared ésprit."

"Grandmother!" I snapped. "You mean to tell me that you *purposely* endangered Doctor Sebring's life on the *possibility* that he might be a magíqon himself?"

Grandmother gave me a bemused smile. "My darling, have *you* read every single one of Doctor Sebring's essays and research proposals over the past five years?"

I blushed. "Um—"

Ackerleigh blushed too. "It shouldn't just be magíqon who care about the preservation of magíq and magíqal beasts!" he exclaimed.

Exasperated, Grandmother rolled her eyes. "Yes, Doctor Sebring. What do you think I'm doing here? Why do you think I want you to continue your work with your students?"

Ackerleigh fell silent, his tungsten eyes round.

Just like that, her attention blinked away from us like a spotlight. "Ah, Francis. That was fast." Grandmother turned to her assistant, who was buried beneath loudly crinkling shopping bags.

But my attention remained on Ackerleigh, who was paralyzed, eyes brimming with tears as he fought to take a shaky breath. He dragged his gaze off my Grandmother to look up at me. Wonderstruck, he beamed.

I grinned back at him, clinking the rims of our glasses together. "Cheers to you, Doctor Ackerleigh."

"Please," said Grandmother, "you lot should freshen up and then join us in the dining room. You remember the way, Nicolai?"

"I'm not wearing your stupid light-licker clothes!" Stella announced, before sticking out her tongue. But then Lunix stood up, plucked the back of her shirt with their beak, and dragged her toward Francis like she was a very oversized pup carried by her mother. She squawked in protest but couldn't get her arms bent right to free herself from Lunix, who approached Francis with confidence.

"Clothes," Lunix croaked.

Looking pale, the assistant rushed to deliver two of the five bags to Stella. But dangling beneath Lunix's jaws, she kept her arms resolutely crossed, refusing them. Lunix dropped her, took the twisted paper handles of the bags in their beak, and then headbutted Stella in the rear. They ushered her firmly from the room.

Holding aloft the remaining bags, Francis stood with mouth agape, staring at the retreating gryphon and girl.

"*I* wanna be mothered by a gryphon!" whined Billie, while Cam laughed beside them with tea and saucer in hand.

I collected what was left of the bags, nodded quietly in thanks, and led Ackerleigh out of the drawing room into the shadowy hall beyond. Around the corner, the noise of Grandmother's guests faded and silence picked up in their place, and Ackerleigh responded with a sigh of relief. I led him down the hall to the stairwell beyond another small sitting room, currently only lit by a sconce on the wall.

"My old room's up two storeys by Stella's. I think there's an empty guest room next to me." The carpeted stairwell creaked quietly under us and doubled back on itself. Over my shoulder, Ackerleigh was trying very hard to stifle his wheezing. "So, you're asthmatic?"

"Ignore me," Ackerleigh puffed. "Please, for the *love* of *gods*, ignore me."

Instead I stopped on the last landing short of the third floor and blocked the stairway so he had to pause. "Nothin' to be ashamed of."

"Easy—" *Huff. Huff.* "—For you to say." Ackerleigh glared at me—no, he glared at my chest, arms, and thighs, and I understood his point.

With a dismissive smile, I leaned against the baluster, absently picking at a cuticle. Ackerleigh's breathing switched to his more measured, slower setting and after he stifled a cough with his shoulder, his wheezing abated. In the quiet we were able to hear Stella chattering away with Lunix, who cheeped back with a single well-informed word every now and then. Evening twilight colored everything in the landing violet, and a bird sang the last melody of the day in the tree outside the window.

I grinned. Ackerleigh's gaze rose and fixed intently on my face as if enthralled by my expression alone. I forced myself to look back through the window. "One time, when I was eight, I climbed that tree and threw a rock through the window because Grandmother tried to make me go to school here in Laurier." I put my hands on my hips, more than a little bit smug about that.

"Ah, so Stella learned from you, the original spitfire." Ackerleigh grinned. Twilight was his time of day. His hair glowed like threads of silver and his skin was milky white. He was a relief carved from marble with the softest brushes of indigo and blush paint.

His smile softened faintly as I stared at him, as I'd no doubt let my ogling go on too long. Ackerleigh looked like a flower bud on the precipice of blooming, asking for a brush of sunlight for its petals to unfold. I knew I was the sunshine but I was much too hot, desperate to cool down before I melted into a puddle.

Panicking, I cleared my throat and gestured up the stairs. "Should we—"

"Of course." Ackerleigh gave me a bemused smile and followed me up the remainder of the steps.

I should have kissed him, I realized abruptly. Every fall of my muddy trainers repeated my own regret. I reached for my scar and gave it a fierce rub until the taut skin burned.

Letting myself into the grand old room at the far end of the hall made my throat tighten. I'd done *so* much work on this room, even in the few visits I'd made here throughout my teens after losing Lunix.

One entire wall was crowded with three bookshelves. I had a vast collection of fiction, several dozen reference books and maps, and also a shelf filled with natural oddities. Mouse skulls, a molted feather from Lunix's ear tufts, several geodes, and some pressed flowers I put between glass. I forgot I even had a large collection of Bennett Publishing House titles.

A second wall was an entire picture window I kept uncovered and now gave us a stunning view of the sunset, and the third wall had the doorway connected to the private washroom.

Though Grandmother hated it, I'd thrown an additional rug over the plush carpeting, lemon-yellow with white rosettes. I'd refused a four-poster bed and had a simple sleigh frame bearing a large mattress. Clearly the room was cleaned regularly; there was not a speck of dust, and though the bed was still covered with the same patchwork quilt my mother had made, it was tidy and smelled like lavender. I pitied the housekeeper having to clean an entire room this size in the off-chance that the wayward grandson would return for a visit.

I switched on the light fixture overhead, a planetary mobile casting calico shadows over us as Ackerleigh clasped his hands behind his back and strode confidently to the bookshelves.

"You want the washroom first?" I asked.

"Oh, no." Ackerleigh didn't turn around. His bare shoulder blades were the most graceful snowy mountains dipping toward his spine. "I have some investigating to do here."

"Oh, right. My mistake," I laughed before shutting myself in the washroom.

In the handsome tiled shower, I let the water run so hot it steamed before getting under it and letting it scald away the nightmares from today. The sweat that was stale on my skin from my mountain run. A man's lifeblood. Salt and sand from the beach.

My own cowardice, which barred me from closing the distance between me and Ackerleigh.

A bar of soap still in its wrapper sat on the ledge opposite the shower curtain and it created a frothy amber-scented foam I used all over. The shampoo smelled like eucalyptus, a much finer fragrance than we could obtain in the country, and soothing on my sun-beaten scalp.

In the interest of dinner waiting, I didn't linger as long as I'd like, scrubbing dry with a fluffy white towel that, unlike at the cottage, wasn't caked in mildew and abandonment. Then I investigated the contents of the bag, sighing but unsurprised as I found dress clothes rather than jean shorts and a henley.

Resigned, I slid into a pair of slacks that were suspiciously exactly my size and tucked in the dress shirt. It was sunny yellow silk with a busy floral pattern, honestly incredibly handsome and like water on my skin. Grandmother even remembered my preference for suspenders, and I admired the fine embroidery stitched into the elastic as I snapped them in place over my shoulders. Grandmother wasn't going to be able to stop me from rolling the sleeves up to my elbows, though.

With the mirror over the pewter sink, I tried my best to towel dry and tame my curls, using the hair pick on the shelves in the corner that was seemingly untouched since I'd last been here. I hooked a black hair elastic onto my pinky and tied half of my curls back from my brow into a little bun just beneath the crown of my head.

When I let myself out of the washroom, I paused to admire the sight of a beautiful man sitting on my childhood bed. He was paging through a leatherbound copy of Deubrisian Folktales and seemingly unaware I was standing there. His legs were delicately crossed and his bare foot bounced gently.

"Your turn."

He jumped, slamming the book shut and looking up at me with a sheepish grin. When his eyes skimmed over me, doubling back to my exposed forearms, something transformed in his countenance that had him as flustered as I had been on the stairs, jolting to his feet and mumbling something vaguely like a thank you and an excuse me.

Capstone in Laying Future Plans

The dining table of Rose and Gene Bennett was enormous, but while Nico and I were upstairs, everyone but the couple themselves had been dismissed. The six of us—for Lunix had their own plate over a portion of the table not set with a chair—took up a miniscule portion of the expanse. I tried to imagine this high-ceiling dining room filled with important people from across Deubrise, falling over each other to have an audience with the Bennetts in hopes of benefitting from their esteem. Indeed, when I was in graduate school and every book I needed for my studies seemed to be stamped with a Bennett Publishing House emblem, I'd had similar aspirations.

Yet now we were an intimate party, and I was the only person not part of the esteemed family itself. It was a twist of fate that I never could have anticipated. The braised lamb, boiled potatoes, fresh dinner rolls, and red wine were as grand as if the Prime Minister herself was among us. I was admittedly ravenous, having been unable to stomach any food before my meeting with the School Board. I forced myself to eat slowly, like a civilized academic.

As if in older times, Nico was placed opposite me, and Mister Bennett at my elbow. Doctor Rose Bennett sat at the head of the table, with Stella between her and Nico.

Properly groomed, Stella looked uneasy. Yet I noticed Doctor Bennett's choice for her clothing was still somewhat *Stella*. She'd been dressed in a black velvet camisole under a chunky, olive-green cardigan and pleated wide-legged slacks, and her black brogues had the heaviest heel I'd ever seen. At least she hadn't been put in a frilly pinafore.

Similarly, I was *euphoric* in the outfit chosen for me. As if emulating my clothes from my meeting, Doctor Bennett had chosen for me a lacy blouse in powder blue with a high collar and flounced sleeves, cinched tightly at my waist with shank buttons. The garment had come from a tailor around the corner I'd passed before but had dismissed as well above anything I could ever afford on my strangled professor salary. And Doctor Bennett had gifted me with it. Knowing I was a magiqon. Somehow, both my love for delicate finery and my volatile gods-blessed blood were accepted here.

That was not to speak of the slim white linen pants that came with it, and the white leather boots with heels I would be salivating over for days.

Nico's grandmother was unscrupulous—but she *saw* me.

I washed down a tender, flavorful bite of lamb with the richest, most full-bodied wine I'd ever tasted. "There's one adjustment I wanted to make to the stipulations for the field experience." I offered Mister Bennett a kind smile before my eyes settled on his spouse.

"Go on, then." Doctor Bennett didn't look up from the carving of her lamb, spearing a golden potato and popping it into her mouth.

"I'd like a third student added."

She gave me a hum of curiosity, listening.

"I'd like it to be Stella."

Stella looked up sharply, candlelight flaming in her eyes like she burned from within. Doctor Bennett's pale gaze slid to her granddaughter, silent.

Wine glass in hand, Nico chuckled. "Stel's not gonna wanna—"

"I'd like that." Stella stared at me, unblinking, serious.

Nico's jaw went slack.

"I'd take any class you teach," Stella added, still not blinking, intense as an acolyte.

Nico's shock turned to delight. He leaned over and punched her shoulder, and she promptly punched him back hard enough to make him flinch.

"Bravo, my girl." Mister Bennett raised his nearly emptied glass of wine before taking the final swig.

Stella's expression softened as she gave her grandfather a faint smile that turned her large cheeks cherubic. Lunix started to wander away from the table to sniff around until Doctor Bennett summoned them back with a matronly clear of her throat. Lunix shot her a silver-eyed glare that had me snorting into my wine glass.

"What about you, Nico?" asked Mister Bennett. "Doctor Sebring, here, shaping young minds and the future of magíq; your sister: a university student..."

"Not *exactly*," said Stella quickly as she fought down an enormous grin.

"Oh." Nico poked his fork into the lamb, peeling off a chunk and letting it plop onto his juice-soaked plate. "I hadn't thought about it. I guess I'm not sure."

"You know, I've always wanted you as my assistant in the publishing office," Mister Bennett said hopefully.

I blinked rapidly, trying to reconcile the Nico who'd slept with me under the stars with the man who had just been offered to work in the most esteemed publishing company in Deubrise.

Nico sighed, shaking his head. "All due respect, Grandpa, but that's not for me."

Mister Bennett looked mournful as he received a full pour of wine from the butler standing over his shoulder. "Yes, yes. I know."

"What are you meant for?" My voice was soft, curious.

His finger traced the rim of his wine glass. A crease appeared in his brow beneath the shadow of an escaped curl as he considered my question. When his tongue darted out to wet his lips, I nearly melted into my seat. "I got my heart set on this man, actually." He glanced at me.

Stella made a face like she'd bitten into a lemon. The Bennetts exchanged knowing looks as I blushed with delight. What I wouldn't have given to leap into Nico's arms and catch his lips with mine. I hoped it was clear on my face as Nico's umber eyes found me again. A timid smile warmed his features.

"Well, my boy," chuckled Mister Bennett, "you have my full support no matter what." He clapped his grandson on the back, and Nico grinned.

"That's wonderfully sentimental," Doctor Bennett remarked with a sigh. "But might we determine some specifics?"

"Ah, yes." I set down my fork and took a sip of wine. "I had imagined utilizing the cottage where Nico and Stella had been staying, but after what transpired there today..." I squared my shoulders. "I would like to reclaim my grandfather's farm. It's on the western side of the Hazel Mountains near the pass. And it's about forty minutes out of Hazberg."

"Ah, a legacy of your own, is it?" Mister Bennett nodded approvingly.

I nodded. "It's been abandoned for a decade. It would need to be restored."

"I'll send a contractor out to make an appraisal tomorrow, and they can start repairs next week." Doctor Bennett picked her lamb shank clean.

I stared at her. "Oh—all due respect, but I'd like to see it first. I want to see what I can do myself. Once it's up and running again, I expect to live there."

"How delightfully working-class of you, Doctor Sebring." Doctor Bennett smirked.

I cocked my head, unable to place the tone of her comment.

Nico dropped his wine glass heavily onto the tabletop. "I'm sure we can manage to restore it without a veritable army of your people, Grandmother." Nico's tone, on the other hand, was easy to read. Dry. Scathing. Protective.

Doctor Bennett rolled her eyes. "Allow me to finance your needs, then. Don't cut corners on materials."

Nico narrowed his eyes, but cast his gaze to me, yielding.

I nodded slightly. "Money I can accept, given I was never able to save while at Ravensbourne."

"That's because Brandon had a chokehold on your research, it seems. Expect that to change. Expect to be busy in your free time, Doctor Sebring."

I smiled, my fingers tingling with electricity as I curled them in my lap. "I look forward to it."

Floating with the effects of all the wine from dinner, I peeked into the large drawing room. Lunix was dozing in front of the fireplace, their wings draped open across the rug, tail softly twitching. On the couch facing the fire, Doctor Bennett sat with her back to me, her arms working in a soft rhythm. I silently padded a few steps into the room to peer over her shoulder. Stella sat between her knees, eyes closed as her grandmother brushed her hair in long, gentle strokes, the buttery brown locks glossy in the firelight as they draped across Doctor Bennett's palm.

Tears stung my eyes as I backed into the hall. That girl had been so wild and deadly but, really, all she'd needed all along was folks who believed in her. Who saw her potential, not her destruction.

I might have been more addled by wine than I thought, because the hallway disoriented me. It felt like I was back in the manor trying to navigate my way to the peacock room in the dark. I knew I should have left the dining room with Nico, but Mister Bennett had kept catching me in inane conversation about the gossip at Ravensbourne, which I knew much of thanks to Claire's nose for drama. The butler—Lewis, I'd learned was his name—seemed to have realized I was trapped and had gently coaxed Mister Bennett off to bed.

Now I was alone in the halls of Doctor and Mister Bennett's home, and quite lost. I thought the dining room had been on the *right* side of the drawing room doors, so I spun myself toward the left and marched with false confidence in the direction I hoped was the stairs. Oil lamps lined the walls, taking on a strobing effect in my confusion.

I finally caught sight of the stairwell washed in moonlight and, proud of myself, I quickened my pace. My eyes fell off target as I passed a large bay window looking down on the sleepy main street. The only people out at this time of night were the lovers not wanting their evening to end.

Glowing beneath still-lit street lights, Nico sat with his knees tucked up to his chest, gazing outside in perfect stillness.

This was even better. I'd thought I was going to have to wheeze all the way up to the third storey to find him. I came and sank onto the cushioned seat beside him. He flinched, surprised, tearing his gaze from outside to offer me a weary smile.

"You look troubled." I leaned my back against the glass, which was cold through my thin shirt.

Eyes returning to the view of the street, Nico hummed. "I'm just thinkin' of what comes next for me."

The streetlights made him look like he was dipped in gold, his shirt bursting with floral light and his eyes gleaming warm as hearthfire. "Do share."

"I'm a simple man." Nico tapped his scar before lacing his fingers together. "I don't want very much. I'm content with simple things. And today is the first day in months—" He closed his eyes. "—Years, maybe, that I'm somewhere warm and dry and there's no *catch*. There's no fear that it's all going to fall apart." He fell silent, his chest rising with a deep breath.

His seriousness sobered me up all at once, the wine on my brain sizzling up in the heat that seemed to roll off Nico. I said softly, "You never know. There's a gryphon in your house, after all."

I surprised a chuckle out of him. The baritone notes made the hairs on my arms stand on end. I became certain I needed to go on hearing Nico De Falco laugh for a *very* long time.

Silent for a few moments, Nico let out a soft sigh before he lowered his legs and dropped his head. He swirled a pattern on his thigh with his thumb. "I just want to be with people I love. Have a quaint little routine. I just want to be *safe.*"

I swallowed. Sucked in a breath for courage. "I want you to have those things... with me."

His lashes fluttered as he picked up his head to gaze at me in disbelief, as if I was a dream or a wish come to life. Unflinching, earnest, I smiled at him.

Pain and yearning and *relief* flooded Nico's face, relaxing his posture, crinkling his brow. He leaned in, hand lifting to rest on the nape of my neck. My skin tingled as he drew me in as delicately as if I were an effervescent bubble.

Nico pressed his lips to mine; he was warm as sunshine and soft as a cloud. I melted against his chest, wrapping my arms around his shoulders and letting him lift me into his lap as if I weighed nothing more than a kitten. Under the streetlamps and safe in the shelter of a promising future, he held me tightly by the hips and let out the deepest sigh of rapture. Sweet, wine-laced breath entered my lungs and sent my heart spiraling into the cosmos.

CAPSTONE IN CRIMINAL PROCEEDINGS

18 January 1965

The events that transpired this week are deeply painful to reflect upon. Yet they are of the utmost importance both to my life and legacy, as well as to that of the whole of Ravensbourne University. So I must pen them, and face my own vulnerabilities.

While I was preparing to leave Laurier, everyone urged me to add my testimony to the heaps of evidence against Ravensbourne's former president, Stephen Brandon. With the help of a prominent lawyer friend of Mathilda and Claire, the case included statements from nearly fifty Ravensbourne students who were unfairly disciplined throughout Brandon's reign. They brought forth charges of collusion with political extremists and abuse of a public office. It was obvious he wanted to further Technocratic goals using his post at Ravensbourne.

But he had also used his post at Ravensbourne to blackmail me. To sexually intimidate me. To strangle my efforts to publish essays that would educate and inspire people living in the cities to honor the neglected ésprit in the bedrock of our country. If someone even more neutral, such as Doctor Bennett, had run the university when I was hired, where would I be now? Perhaps less jumpy and less angry, but also... without Lunix. Still in Laurier, unchanged. Without Nico.

I don't know. It was a lot to think about and blame on one man when, unfortunately, his final attack against me had sent my life spiraling toward my destiny. It was so complex that I truly would have preferred to look forward, rather than dragging myself through some of the worst memories of my adulthood. For the first five days I was asked, I vehemently refused to participate in the court case against Brandon.

It wasn't that bad, was it? How he preyed on me. People have been treated worse and never gotten justice. But as I tried to avoid taking action, I became jumpier. Tossed and turned all night. Paced the halls at the Bennetts' Laurier estate until Stella yelled at me for keeping her awake.

I had to do it. I had to face him one final time. The tables had been turned, after all. Now he was unemployed, shamed into hiding, friendless, and frightened of me. Not even Laurier's political scene wanted anything to do with him. Deposed from Ravensbourne, he had no prospects.

Just like me.

Brandon's hearing passed like a dream that's so surreal it teeters every now and then into a nightmare. On the witness stand, I said words... I know I spoke. But for the life of me, I don't remember what spilled from my mouth unless I read the court records. And I can't do that without feeling nauseous.

I do, however, remember Stephen Brandon's seething hatred. The sneer fixed on his lips. The shade of deep and livid red that his skin turned. The sight returns to me often, like a curse. So does the sound of his large fist crashing onto the tabletop as the speaker declared him Guilty. Guilty of not only his crimes against Ravensbourne and its students, but also two charges that named me as the victim: sexual harassment and assault. I grow numb merely by writing that sentence.

In that momentous victory against a vile and abusive man, I felt some relief, true, but my body was mostly just... numb. This dismal chapter of my life was now well and truly over.

Applause, cheers, and jeers thundered from the large crowd of students overflowing from the several rows of seating. Laurier's courthouse was old and noble, made of sculpted marble and a copper ceiling. It smelled like mildew and oak and, because of today's heat, very strongly like sweat.

"I can't believe he's getting off without jail time," Claire muttered to my left, gripping both mine and Mathilda's hand.

"I heard his lawyer tell him outside that they would be delighted to help him humiliate 'all those magiq-loving fools,'" Mathilda replied as Claire groaned. The couple stood up, and I thought I followed suit, but when Nico nudged my elbow I realized I hadn't moved.

His frown was deep and his eyes smoldered with fury. The whiteness of his knuckles told me he was fighting the urge to tap at his scar. He and I got to our feet together. Stella and her grandparents stood up as well. The girl looked awkward in such a crowded room, sticking close to Nico's elbow and allowing Doctor Bennett to hold onto her shoulder.

I heard my name from several different sources. People were... congratulating me.

But if people were congratulating me for Brandon's fall from power, that meant they... they knew what he'd done to me, and the petrifying grip he'd had me in for the last three and a half years.

I felt exposed, naked. The most I could force my face to do was smile faintly before I resumed clenching my jaw.

I reminded myself I'd be gone from this city in a matter of days and I could put this all behind me, but that wasn't what it was about, was it? I was considering all that Brandon had kept from me. How different my experience at Ravensbourne could have been if he hadn't marked me as his prey, and set to ruin me whether by forcing me to give him my body or by strangling my academic career.

That feeling of wanting to raze everything to the ground returned with a vengeance. I could practically feel flames licking at my ribs, desperate to burn their way out of my heart.

Startled by the intensity, I clamped onto Nico's hand and swiftly made for the exit. He fell into stride at my side, with Stella on our heels.

"Your hand is scorching," Nico whispered. I must have let some of my magíq loose after all. Mortified, I tried to snatch my hand away, but he held me tight. "It's okay. Just breathe." He caught the double doors before they shut and shouldered them back open.

As I hurried through the doorway, I nearly crashed headlong into Stephen Brandon's back. I wasn't fast enough to smother a gasp. He turned around slowly, like a grizzly bear so confident in his brute strength that he feared no foe.

"Excuse me," I said stiffly, trying to go around him.

Brandon smirked and growled, "Did it feel good, admitting in front of everyone how pitiful you are, Sebring?"

Before he'd even uttered the final syllable of my name, Nico let go of my hand and lunged. His fist flew into Brandon's face and connected with the unsuspecting man's nose in a vicious and exacting punch. The wet crunch was followed immediately by a gushing stream of bright blood, which quickly coated Brandon's mouth and chin.

"What the hell?" Brandon roared, more nasally than usual, as blood dappled his pristine white dress shirt.

Narrow-eyed and teeth bared, Nico shook out his hand and growled, "*Never* look at him again."

A wave of warm dizziness rushed through me. I snorted and covered my mouth, happily looking away as the sound made Brandon's gaze snap onto me.

I looked up at Nico instead, whose glossy curls were pulled back from his face into a little bun. He had two days of stubble darkening his slender jaw. He barely fit into the checkered button-down he was wearing and had rolled the sleeves up to his elbows. The veins were bulging in his right forearm from the sudden exertion caused by breaking the nose of my convicted abuser.

Excitement coiled inside me at the thought. I threaded my fingers through Nico's. "Come on, my dear, let me ice your hand." I tugged him forward, giving Brandon a wide berth, but a glance through my lashes found him glowering at us, head tipped back, eyes watering.

For the first time in three years, I held the man's gaze. Finally I had nothing to fear. I said to Nico, "It won't do for you to be in pain because of such an ugly beast." Casually, using the moisture from my clammy palm, I brushed a sheen of frost over Nico's knuckles.

Distantly behind me, Stella whooped, "Take that, *enfour!*"

Stephen Brandon's lip curled in disgust, and I smiled sweetly.

The tension in Nico's jaw relaxed immediately as he glanced down at me, eyes warm as a jar of sun tea glowing in a windowsill. "Thank you kindly, Doctor Sebring." He slipped his arm around my shoulders and we walked in step with each other away from the little courthouse.

I looked over my shoulder as Brandon emphatically gestured to Doctor Bennett, whose arm was linked through Stella's as they moved past him. Doctor Bennett gave a dismissive shrug, and I think I saw her lips form the word *Nepotism* as she left him behind.

The final thread of unease in my chest frayed and came loose. Around the cab of Nico's truck, my ramshackle family gathered. Doctor and Mister Bennett on either side of Stella, Claire and Mathilda, Billie and Cam, and Craig Dowell soon swarmed us. Nico apologized to his grandmother, who laughed and waved him off. Cam reached out and shook Nico's hand approvingly.

"Can we get ice cream?" Stella asked, childlike hope in her rainstorm eyes.

I grinned, leaning into Nico, meeting Claire's eyes as she tearfully smiled back at me. A laugh bubbled out of my chest. It felt as if the fire in my blood had transformed, and become something new and beautiful.

SEMINAR IN THE HAZEL MOUNTAINS

Morning light bathed our naked flesh with a misty white glow. The breath of the gods came to me in the flawless form of Doctor Ackerleigh Sebring, who tasted heavenly as I traced the column of his throat with the tip of my tongue. His delicious purr vibrated my mouth.

Being buried inside Ackerleigh felt like home even when I held perfectly still like this, our hearts drumming against each other's. Ackerleigh curled his fingers around my shoulders, tugging me down to kiss his slick, rose-red lips. I resumed our languid rocking rhythm as our tongues twirled. A faint static shock zapped my fingers when I combed through Ackerleigh's hair; I leaned back so I could behold the crown of lilac sparks among his ashen locks.

Flushing, Ackerleigh groaned. "Again? I'm—"

I caught his apology in my mouth before it emerged, more insistent as I bucked against him until he squirmed beneath me and gasped with delight.

"Professor!"

We froze, sealed together by our sweat.

Ackerleigh opened one eye to glare like a grumpy owl at the round curtained window beside our bed.

"Pro-fes-*sor!*"

I shifted my hips back, knowing our time was done. Ackerleigh whined, forlorn, and wrapped his knees around me to hold me in place.

"Sweetheart," I laughed against his jaw, "they'll bust the door down."

"I'm implementing strict office hours after this," Ackerleigh said breathlessly as he dropped his legs to the bed and let me go.

After laying a path of kisses over his brow, I climbed to my knees and peeked through the lace curtains Claire had sent us. Bundled against the predawn chill, all three of Ackerleigh's students stood in the meadow outside.

Stella caught me peeking. She thrust her hands out from beneath her black wool poncho and raised her palms toward the window, blasting it with a gust of glittering wind that made that glass rattle.

Ackerleigh joined me with labored movements and more than a few groans, glaring through the curtains. Spots of bright pink all over his flesh marked him as mine. A thrill of pride rose in me. Grinning, I forgot Stella's insistent demand for attention and nuzzled Ackerleigh's neck before wrapping myself around his small form. His fingers carded gently through my curls.

After a few peaceful moments, Dove woke up and yawn-meowed from her pile of blankets by the couch, arching her smoky-gray back as she stretched.

Ackerleigh gently untangled himself from me, leaving a trail of butterfly-soft kisses down my arm as he stood up from the bed and copied Dove with a languid stretch.

He dipped his chin onto his shoulder as he twisted and looked back at me. Ackerleigh's milky-white form was touched with pale gold on his extremities; I could finally see how the sunlight had tanned him. He was perfectly made from sharp angles and soft curves. I could see the dotted red outline of my teeth marking his inner thigh beneath his deliciously plump rear.

My body tingled with excitement the longer I stared at him. I bit my lip, imagining snatching him up by the waist and pulling him back onto the bed to finish what we'd started.

"Nico?" Ackerleigh's voice was a quiet whisper of wind, startling me out of my enjoyable daydreaming.

I dropped my feet over the edge of the bed. "Yes, Darlin'?" The chilly flagstones bit into the soles of my feet, making me hastily grab my discarded wool socks and pull them over my toes.

"Is this what you wanted?" Ackerleigh held my gaze until he slipped into a chenille sweater that moved like water over his arms and chest. "Is this the life you hoped for?" He stepped between my knees, lifting my hands in his and touching his lips to each peak of my knuckles. Then his wonderful gray eyes returned to my face, waiting.

Cupping his cheek in my palm, I gazed up at him and considered how to answer. How could I whittle down into words the way my heart soared? Since we'd moved into the Sebring Farmstead two months ago, it felt like I was constantly flying on Lunix's wings. Weightless, elated, free.

How could I even compare this to my life before I'd met Ackerleigh, when Lunix was still imprisoned and I had no home? That life felt like it belonged to a stranger, some shadow of my true self. Ackerleigh brought with him the orderly swiftness of city life, but he had nestled into this life in the mountains like it, too, was made for him. I was inspired. For the first time in my life, the city and the country were no longer at odds. If he could be both, then so could I.

"Nico?" Ackerleigh prompted, perching on my knee.

I smiled at him, sure and bright. "It's better. I had..." My voice warbled, but I let it, because Ackerleigh never minded when I cried. "I had no idea life could be this marvelous."

Ackerleigh's shoulders relaxed. He slipped his arms around my neck, leaning down and bumping our foreheads together, grinning.

Another powerful gust of wind pummeled our window, knocking over a vase of red rata flowers and sending Dove sprinting under the bed.

"Absolutely not," snapped Ackerleigh, jumping up from my knee and stalking to the window. I had learned to recognize the way he hunched in on himself when he called upon his magíq, so it didn't startle me when a bolt of blinding violet lightning struck right outside our window, snarling and snapping and rattling the windowpanes.

"*Patience!*" Ackerleigh bellowed, using the wind to amplify his voice so it was loud as an avalanche. His powerful connection to magíq was the funniest thing about him never having laid a hand on Stephen Brandon—Ackerleigh was fully capable of wrecking a man like that. That was why I'd snapped outside the courthouse. That enfour didn't even *know* Ackerleigh, and had spent years tormenting some stereotype that could never have come close to the truth.

I stood up in time to see the three students outside scamper away, bounding through the tall grass toward the farmhouse. Laughing, I bent to pull on a pair of form-fitting orange trousers over my socks.

Ackerleigh scowled as he turned away from the window and went to his wardrobe. The massive oak case had come from my grandparents' seaside manor which was now vacant. Ackerleigh's collection of clothing was so plentiful that he needed the whole wardrobe for himself. I didn't mind; I loved the thoughtful artistry that went into his dress, which always offered even more insight into his personality. He had worked hard to adapt his academic style to make it sturdy enough for working on farmhouse restorations and all of the chores that came with maintaining one.

In Hazberg, we'd found some reinforced leggings with a double layer of fabric in the knee, and he, Stella, and I had all stocked up on them. Ackerleigh pulled on a dark gray pair now before slipping on his brocade duster.

The piece was art itself, in shades that matched the breathtaking sunsets we saw each evening. Ackerleigh fixed his double-breasted collar while he turned and watched me pull on a crocheted sweater that was colored like lavender lemonade. He made no point to disguise his eyes from roaming over my stomach muscles and pouted when they vanished under my shirt.

To complete our colorful ensemble, we both threaded rainbow scarves around our necks. They were a gift from my mother she'd hand-delivered last week. I'd driven over to the De Falco farm to get food and some chickens (to keep alive) two weeks ago, expecting to just come and go like usual. But I'd ended up staying for hours, detailing to my mother everything that had transpired since Ackerleigh had entered my life. By the time I left, I felt lighter, at peace.

It was easier for me to visit now. I no longer had to shun my childhood home or my parents when I could leave Stella somewhere safe knowing Ackerleigh—and Lunix—were more than capable of keeping an eye on her. Doctor Bennett's collaboration with Ackerleigh and Ravensbourne had even helped restore some of the closeness of my and Stella's relationship with our complicated grandmother. There was not a single part of my life that Ackerleigh had not brightened, tidied, or mended.

Ackerleigh sat on the short stool by the front door while he laced up his black, knee-high leather boots. The chunky wooden heel clacked on the flagstones when he put his foot down.

I followed him over there, paused, and then planted my hands on my hips. "Ackerleigh."

"Hm?" He stood up, picking his glasses off the windowsill and slipping them onto his face without looking at me.

"Where are my trainers?"

"I don't know. Where did you leave them?"

"Here." I tapped the empty space in front of the door with my toe.

Ackerleigh shrugged, his fair eyebrows high on his forehead. "Doesn't look that way, Love. Better wear those cute little guys." He nodded to where my lace-up boots sat neglected in the corner.

"You hid my shoes again," I groaned.

Ackerleigh sniffed. "That would be so petty."

Glaring at him, I begrudgingly snatched up my boots and pulled them on. "You can try all you want to dress me up like an uppity light-licker, but you've shown your hand, Darlin'."

"Oh, have I?" Unruffled as ever, Ackerleigh opened the round door to the stable we'd converted into our bedroom. This stable was carved into the mountain, and had once been intended to hold six horses. It was a spacious private abode for the two of us to sleep away from the farmstead and the students. We had put down fur rugs everywhere, and both the large sleigh bed and the plush couch were stacked with fluffy pillows and blankets in a dozen different colors. They served to brighten up the room's dark oak frame and stone walls, along with the stained-glass lamps placed throughout the room.

"You told me you fell for me when I was muddy and sweaty, wearin' cut-off shorts an' flannel," I said, playing up my ocky twang. "I know ya got a thing for my rugged side, too." I pinched Ackerleigh's rear. He yelped and swatted my hand, but the merry flush that darkened his ears gave away his amusement.

We strode hand-in-hand out of the stable and into the misty morning. Soft powder-blue light bathed the predawn countryside. Clusters of white, yellow, and purple wildflowers dotted the fields. My mare, Peach, grazed peacefully in the pasture to our left, alongside a cow named Queenie that I'd brought over from the De Falco farm.

Cheese's single bark of excitement echoed against the steep green earth rising at our backs. She shot between the trio of students lingering by the farmhouse and dashed across the meadow toward us with her tail pinwheeling and her bright pink tongue flapping. Ackerleigh edged behind me so her forceful paws crashed into my thighs instead of his as the dog slathered us with kisses of greeting.

She followed us as we veered off into our magnificent, enormous garden plot—at this point it could almost qualify as a whole field ripe for growing. We followed one of the tidy walking paths between the rows of dark, fertile soil, checking on the transplanted crops that had come with us from the bed and breakfast's garden. Those yields were helping support us while we waited for the bountiful harvest that would come to us here in springtime.

This approaching winter at the Sebring farm felt somewhat intimidating, but for the first time since Stella and I had left home, we weren't alone. We had offers of help from all sides. Warm places we could go if we needed to escape the winter for a few days. In fact, Claire had threatened Ackerleigh in no uncertain terms that if we didn't come to stay with her and Mathilda in Laurier, she would disown us.

And anyway, this farmstead was well-equipped to endure snowy mountain winters. Ackerleigh said it was virtually unchanged from how he remembered it. The single-storey farmhouse had good bones. Huge and rambling, it was outfitted with three fireplaces, a wood-burning stove and a gas stove, and four bedrooms which still had sturdy handmade bed frames that we'd filled with brand-new feather mattresses. The place had water pipes and a water heater (Grandmother insisted on putting in a new one), and a well that was easily refilled by two magíqon and a gryphon.

With the work divided up between me, Ackerleigh, and Stella, we'd easily gotten this place up and running in less than two months.

When Billie and Cam had come out to join us, the whole place felt lively and invigorating. Lunix had adopted the two of them easily, adding them to their brood along with Stella.

The pair of students were quite out of place away from Laurier, and they had a lot to learn. Quite by accident, I began giving them naturalist lessons out of worry that one or both of Ackerleigh's students could get themselves hurt if they didn't learn more about the mountain's armpit. Within a week, Ackerleigh had my lessons on the daily schedule, and attentively listened along with Cam and Billie. He even called me Mister De Falco in front of them, which perpetually made me blush.

And gods, speaking of blushing—Billie and Stella were always together, giggling and whispering and staying up late playing cards or grooming Lunix together. Ackerleigh and I both knew without a doubt that there was something sweet and special blossoming between the two of them, but only Cam teased them for it.

Cam was a decent kid, with a biting sense of humor applied equally to everyone except Ackerleigh, whom he treated with soft-spoken reverence. Despite being the only one here who wasn't seemingly paired off, he was quite content that way. He described himself as "wildly uninterested in any physical or romantic connections" and his actions stood by that, but it also made him quite safe and comfortable around Billie and Stella.

Breaking off from the middle of the trio, Stella flipped down the lined hood of her poncho, which was all black except for the embroidery Ackerleigh was helping her add. "Something is wrong with Lunix," she said, panic making lines of worry crease her brow beneath her knit purple hat.

Ackerleigh exclaimed, "*What?*" His gaze darted to the farmhouse roof, where our gryphon had built their enormous eyrie around the central chimney. From the ground, large branches, strips of fuzzy fabric, and piles of dried leaves draped over the gutters. The cacophony of birdsong was louder here, as all of our avian neighbors had moved their nests to the closest treetops to be around Lunix. There was never a moment when there wasn't a wren, fantail, waxwing, or bellbird trilling nearby. I was still training myself to tune them all out, and often found their incessant noise overwhelming.

Ackerleigh looked back at Stella. "What's wrong with them?"

Stella looked stricken. "They *hissed at me.*"

"Oh, that's unprecedented," I said, putting my hands on my hips.

Cam said through chattering teeth, "I n-n-noticed they don't want to leave their nest. Maybe they're sick?" Cam was bundled in a thick red pea coat—which worried me, as it was hardly winter-cold yet—and wearing a gray hat that matched Stella's purple one.

Ackerleigh's expression turned serious as he took several large paces away from the farmhouse. He leaned back, cupped his hands around his mouth, and called, "Lunix, my chaton! May we talk?"

Lunix's wedge-shaped head appeared over the edge of the house at once, ear tufts erect and moon-eyes round. "Allie," they croaked, bobbing their head in assent.

Stella's mouth fell open. "No, they'll talk to you! No fair!" she whined.

Billie put a reassuring arm around Stella's shoulders. They looked much more comfortable than Cam, wearing a short plaid skirt, thigh-high stockings, and an oversized canvas jacket over a chunky sweater. They even had snatches of bare skin on their thighs showing, but they'd been vocal about how the mountain air suited them *much* better than the sea. Ackerleigh was fairly confident they were just trying to impress Stella.

Cam and I moved the ten-foot ladder over to the edge of the house and leaned it against the gutter. Almost as soon as I had it stable, Ackerleigh had both feet on the rungs and swiftly ascended. He had no fear of heights, that one, even though he'd so recently plummeted into the sea.

A moment later, Ackerleigh squeaked, "Oh, my gods! Nico, come quick!"

I shot into action. Cam gasped and quickly stabilized the ladder under my hands as I flew up the rungs. The chilly breeze chased me merrily as I clambered onto the clay tiles and stood up. Up here on the roof, the darkly forested ridges of the Hazel Mountains were gilded by the golden sunrise behind them, with wispy white clouds obscuring the peaks where the gryphon pods lived. Hills rolled away and dipped into crystalline lakes in every direction. It was an eden.

I'd never admit it to Ackerleigh, but these boots were better than my trainers for hopping over the sloping rooftop. I scrambled over toward the pinnacle of the roof, where Ackerleigh had climbed halfway into Lunix's eyrie. He twisted to grin at me over his shoulder, excitedly shoving his calico glasses up on his nose.

"Hey, Lunix, can I come over there?" I called before coming near the eyrie. It was common courtesy to ask before barging into someone's home.

Lunix's head popped into view. Their full-moon eyes were bright and eager. "Nico," they croaked, bobbing their head.

Stepping up onto a large beech branch at the base of Lunix's nest, I braced myself around Ackerleigh's body so I could lean into his back. I planted a quick kiss on his brow before turning my attention to Lunix.

Our gryphon blinked happily at me, purring so powerfully that it vibrated my teeth. They curled around the center of their nest, feathery mane puffing up. Then, they pulled back the veil of their elegant wings.

Nestled into the contours of their powerful body was an egg. Gleaming silver, it was the size of a small child, with a spray of inky black flecks across the rounded top. A halo of down feathers and fuzzy blankets were built up around it.

I slapped my hand over my mouth. "Holy, beautiful heavens! Lunix! Look at that!" Tears sprang into my eyes as I threw my arms around Ackerleigh and squeezed him tightly. He was already weeping, cheeks soaked and shining.

Ackerleigh rambled wetly, "Whatever you need, my precious little chaton, consider it done. Shall we go to the butcher shop? Shall we hire you your own hunter? W-W-We need more food for you, of course. You must remain here around the clock, must you not?"

I rubbed Ackerleigh's shoulders. "Breathe, Darlin'. I suspect Lunix is doing exactly what they need to do, aren't you? We're so proud of you."

Ackerleigh nodded rapidly, grasping my hand.

"Hello?" Stella hollered. "What's wrong?"

Wriggling out from under me, Ackerleigh dropped to the tiles and scampered toward the edge of the roof.

Visions of Ackerleigh falling right over the edge of the roof had me scrambling after him with a yelp. "Hey, careful!"

Ackerleigh threw his arms over his head and exclaimed over my fussing, "We're having a *baby!*"

Cam and Billie exchanged a confused glance.

Stella's expression briefly contorted with bewilderment before her eyes bulged. "Don't tell me! Are you serious?" Her voice rose to a piercing shriek and with it came an eruption of magíq. Sparks exploded on a burst of frigid wind that shot into the heavens and had Ackerleigh rocking back on his heels.

"What's happening?" Cam demanded, bouncing and grabbing Stella's shoulder. "What's he mean—what do you mean, Prof?"

"Lunix laid an egg," I laughed. "There's an egg!"

Ackerleigh whooped, "An egg! An egg!" He flapped his arms and joined Stella's joyous display with his own golden spurts of fire. The heat over my head was pleasant and cozy; any time he used fire, it was with confidence and total control. All his flapping made him lose his balance and panic leapt into his features, his mouth turning into a dark circle.

Horrified, I gasped and lunged to catch his coat. But then mischief and inspiration sparked in his eyes, and as he let himself fall, he snatched my hand and brought me with him over the edge of the roof.

I barely had time to scream before he clamped his arms and legs around me and wrapped us up in a gale. The powerful wind slapped my cheeks, whipped my curls into my eyes, and carried us gently to the ground. My legs turned to noodles and I fell into Ackerleigh, who giggled and helped me upright.

Stella chattered to Ackerleigh about the anticipated baby gryphon while Billie and Cam applauded.

Over our heads, Lunix rose from their eyrie with wings spread, talons grasping the rim of their nest as they looked down at us and opened their gape into a wide smile.

"Congratulations, Lunix!" Billie called, waving at the gryphon. "My final essay is going to be *so* cool!"

Lightning crackled around Lunix's magnificent wingspan as they trilled a joyous song. Ackerleigh and Stella joined our gryphon, filling the air with magíq. Ribbons of glittering water rose from the dew, wind spiraled in beautiful corkscrews, and fire snapped and flickered like wings on Ackerleigh's shoulders.

Tears tracked down my cheeks as I grinned and laughed in wonder. I was among holy beings, and they had chosen me. With Stella, Lunix, and Ackerleigh—despite and because of all the pain, we had fought and clawed our way forward to reach this paradise together. We had found this home and made a family. Not in spite of magíq, but because of it and *for* it. Here at the foot of the Hazel Mountains, my sister was safe. I could breathe again. And when Ackerleigh turned and grinned at me over his shoulder, reaching back and taking my hand with skin that was warmed by fire and buzzing with electricity, I knew I had found my home.

While the whims of a gryphon may sound simple
enough—freedom and companionship being most important of all—these are attributes which we as humans
struggle to offer unimpeded. For all the magíq in the
world, love is the rarest of them all.

Ackolaigh Sabring, Ph. D., Ed. D.

A Magíqon's Guide to Gryphon Liberation

Acknowledgements

First of all I'd like to thank my husband Ryan for being patient with me when I vanish into my imaginary worlds. As much as I try not to hyperfocus and forget where I am when I've got other things to do, I'd be insane to pretend like that didn't happen. What's more, you encourage me, hype me up, and are happy to let me infodump.

Thanks also to my dad Guy Stewart for enduring my insanity during your attempt to edit this manuscript. I didn't realize I had such a specific vision until we found out I would fight for it not to be changed.

Thanks a million to all of my writer friends and your various roles in helping bring this book to fruition. To Al Davidson, thanks for inspiring me to carry out my projects and for letting me fuss about whether to submit to indie presses or to go ahead with self-pub again. Thanks for bearing with every version and transformation that the cast underwent and being excited about them anyway. To Vic Day, thanks for being such an amazing cheerleader, for not letting me give up, for falling in love with my characters, and for being with me since the beginning. To CJ Aralore, thanks for being such an awesome critique partner and I'm so grateful for your kindness and your tireless review of my books and all of our peers in the queer indie book world.

Thanks to every single member of my Discord server and all my beta readers who tirelessly gave feedback, shared opinions, and worked on my book despite how many times I changed things on you. And obviously thank you specifically to my betas: Al, CJ, Pete, Blue, and Elizabeth.

Thanks to all my local friends and industry connections that keep letting me come back and making me feel welcome in the writing world. Amanda, thanks for being my intel into the readers world and for always wanting to see my newest art. Thanks to Lauren and Caitlyn at Tropes and Trifles of course, Emily at Next Chapter, to the folks at Dream Haven Books, Elizabeth at Comma, Angi at House of Hekate and Taylor at Nine Keys for your willingness to carry my books. Thanks to all my market friends for always being friendly and stopping to chat.

And of course, thanks to you: the reader. You have been a dream come true.

About Z.M. Celestaire

Z.M. (they/them) is a writer, artist, and therapist. Writing and art have been a hobby for some twenty years now since they were a goofy little middle schooler. Z.M. grew up devouring urban fantasy authors like Charles De Lint, Holly Black, and Patricia C. Wrede.

Z.M. lives in Saint Paul with their spouse, human child, and fur children.

You can find them on social media under the handle @artcoffeecats. They are primarily active on Instagram.

If you liked this book, please consider leaving a review on Storygraph and Goodreads!

ALSO BY Z.M. CELESTAIRE

THE HEARTWOOD TRILOGY
Deny Me, The Nightshade Boy
Rend Me, The Wayward Knight
Promise, Me Lord Heartwood
Sate Me, My Trickster Fox (short story)